NEW AMERICAN CAFÉ

NEW AMERICAN CAFÉ

Richard Sanford

Odeon Press

Published in the United States by Odeon Press.

Credits:
Estés, C.P. 1992. *Women Who Run With the Wolves: Myths and Stories of the Wild Woman Archetype.* New York: Ballantine Books.
"Tangled Up in Blue," by Bob Dylan. Copyright © 1974 by Ram's Horn Music. Rights assigned to Universal Music Publishing Group. All rights reserved.
"Buzzin' Fly," by Tim Buckley. Copyright © 1969 by Tim Buckley Music ASCAP. All rights reserved.
"Play That Funky Music (White Boy)," by Robert W. Parissi. Copyright © 1976 by RWP Music. Rights assigned to WC Music Corp. All rights reserved.
"What Game Shall We Play Today," by Chick Corea and Neville Potter. Copyright © 1972 by Litha Music Co. Rights assigned to Universal Music Corp. All rights reserved.
"Road Away," by John Stewart. Copyright © 1972 by January Music Corp., a division of A. Schroeder, International, Ltd. All rights reserved.
"You Can't Always Get What You Want," by Mick Jagger and Keith Richards. Copyright © 1969 by ABKCO Music, Inc. All rights reserved.
"I'm Not Sayin'," by Gordon Lightfoot. Copyright © 1964 by Moose Music. Rights assigned to WC Music Corp. All rights reserved.
"Under My Thumb," by Mick Jagger and Keith Richards. Copyright © 1966 by ABKCO Music, Inc. All rights reserved.

Library of Congress Cataloging-in-Publication Data:
Names: Sanford, Richard (Richard Charles)
Title: New American Café: a novel / Richard Sanford.
Description: First Edition. | Odeon Press, ["2024"]
Identifiers: Library of Congress Control Number: 2024919487
ISBN 978-0-9857445-6-4 (Paperback) | ISBN 978-0-9857445-8-8 (Ebook)) | ISBN 978-0-9857445-7-1 (Ebook)

Printed in the United States of America.
Odeonpress.com

For the ghosts in the banyan tree

"Once there was, and once there was not..."
This paradoxical phrase is meant to alert the listener
that the story takes place in the world between worlds
where nothing is as it first seems.

Clarissa Pinkola Estés
Women Who Run With the Wolves

All the people we used to know
Are an illusion to me now

Bob Dylan
Tangled Up in Blue

Prologue

ALWAYS in buildings like this, when I'm past the doorman and across the boundless lobby floor and the elevator doors slide open, I'm home free. It's a story I tell myself because it's protection, like coloration or a force field. I tell it to get in the zone for as long as I need to be, and with present company, I need to be.

My fellow passenger is jockey-height, a dowager dyed blond, coiffed like cotton candy, crisply attired in blue. A vintage gold bar pin graces the pocket of her Bergdorf jacket. It is tastefully restated by gold strips on her black patent cap-toe pumps. She clutches her mail like a raptor. If any rightful building occupant could nail me, it would be this one.

But she could also be a mother, or grandmother, and I fix on that. But whose? One of the Astors. She's a scioness who let a crucial someone slip away and tumbled down to settle in a lesser tower. Was that a sideways glance? She could calcify me with a breath. She pretends to read an envelope. Keep a respectable air, beyond challenge, boost the doubled grocery bag higher. At least no yippee dogs that smell fear. If not she to scupper me, then another like her, or others, so many.

A ding sounds and her disc lights, floor eight. The matron of the Astors exits and I fight the urge to punch the close button. I'm bound for the top.

Alone in the capsule, I take an easy breath. Home free. There's time to take more as the floors count up through the thirties. Tall ones like this, close to the lake, can oscillate in the wind. I roll my shoulders, get loose. You could check my pulse. Mellow as an astronaut's.

My ding calls, floor forty. I step out and I'm in my element. The carpeted hall lies before me, a palette of beiges and tans, ceiling lined with muted light, a fluted sconce beside each door. On this floor of condos, I count ten doors, each frame padded to muffle concussion. At the end of the hall just past the exit, my reflection surprises in a window, a panel of floor-to-ceiling smoked glass. I refocus. I'm sure as a bat in the dark, tuned to my surroundings, the corridors of twenty-eight hundred Lake Shore Drive.

I grab a fistful of the payload, shift the bag to my left arm, and go to work. First door, the fit is perfect—a superior feature of the building: the press fit of the fold between the weather stripping and the door. And handles, not knobs: solid seating for scored and folded twenty-four-pound stock.

I tread silently on the carpet, working both sides of the hall, all facing doors. At the end, the overlook stops me. The tall window frames a wedge of park lawn and the lake. A boat like a toy. An airplane I might ride creeps across the sky. Come on, it says, out into the vastness. And I could, step out and keep going over Lake Michigan. It's a thin skin between us and oblivion. What do I mean, *us*? How can I expect anybody to be like me?

At the exit door I check the knob from the inside. No auto-lock. Then down the steps into the cool concrete smell of the stairwell.

On the landing I stop to listen. Any scuffle of shoes or footfall on the stairs would be audible the height of the long shaft.

On the next floor I push the door handle to mute the click, then rotate and pull. Check the hall. Empty.

Now it's about efficiency. Speed. Doing nothing stupid, nothing false. I'm a gray ghost, a slipstream of silence in my wake. I descend the shaft. I'm winding down the helix, threading the needle.

Next floor. I do all the doors, hit the exit at the end.

I'm an artisan, a freelancer, an agent of possibilities. At the bottom is freedom. Keep it smooth and steady.

Just like a buzzin' fly, I come into your life.

Hit the notes but make it your own. Don't rip off Buckley.

One more practice at John's before Orphans. His Russian squeeze will be at the gig, no doubt. At least not at the practice. Nothing against Sasha, just not what I need.

I work toward the window on a new floor and toward my reflection. "I like you lanky," she had said, and she was right, I am. But maybe lanky works on stage and that's what matters now.

You're the one I think about

Melanie and I are crossing campus in Chapel Hill, fog like a roll of cotton between the poplars.

Everywhere I go

Now she's on the sidewalk heading for her studio on Belden. Who's doing the seeing one more time, the reimaging? Who has the power to expunge? I target her one more time, replace her with a black box.

Will I have enough? The bag is tiring my arm, but probably not. Lower floors will have more units. If I have menus left by the eighth floor, I could skip it. Lady Astor is not a great bet to order.

A TV sounds behind one door, a daytime soap. Then it's back to silence, the hush of privilege.

Opposite end, stairwell.

Four floors done, partway through the fifth, the elevator dings behind me. I keep going, mincing steps.

"Hey." The voice of ignorance, of authority. Doom. Don't turn, don't need to see him. Striding hard. Stash the menus. Where?

"Hey!"

Blood sparkles in my veins. I hit the exit door.

Lady Astor called down. Or one of the others.

I don't need to see the huffing super in khaki with slicked hair, ex-security-fireman-cop. His buddies from the station could be on the way. Trespassing, littering, soliciting.

Down. Firing down the concrete stairs. Missing one, grabbing the rail before pitching to the landing.

I should lose the bag, but it would be waste. Cost per menu? Two and a half cents, burned in the brain. Less than ten bucks. Delivery menus or jail?

A door pulls above me and I hear the super on the stairs. The concrete slabs boom as his shoes land.

I'm guessing forties. Would they hire anyone my age to do his job? I have him by twenty years.

Which end of the building is my stairwell on? An exit in the front would be fatal, across from the desk and the doorman. I need a rear exit. Which end?

He isn't shouting now but I hear him well enough. Which end? I have him by what, two floors? Can he see me?

I guess the other end. On the next floor I pull the door, catch it on the hallway side, and lose the seconds to close it softly.

I'm running full stride, sprinting in the hall. Another Lake Shore building appears in the window of smoke and I hit the exit door.

Heart stopper for both of us. Six feet in front of me, his face blanks. Bug-eyed, gray twist sideburns like Mailer's, wattles. A fund manager in Bermudas and socks and Birkenstocks is stuffing his garbage into the shoot.

"Sorry." For nearly dropping him with an infarction. Sorry, and keep going. Pistoning down. Above, the chute door thungs shut. Who pulls the stairwell door, Mailer or the super? Down.

Firing down, gulping air, rabbit heart. How had I let it happen? Not just this pitfall to possible arrest but the whole fate-tempting curse of unlikeliness? I run out of stairs.

I'm in the final concrete vault, gray steel door with push bar, EXIT above the frame. A stripe of light lines the threshold and I try to decode it, lobby light or daylight? Doorman or alarm? I clench my gut and hit the bar.

A blast of heat and love at first sight: the shocking beauty of dumpsters. Side-by-side, green twin sisters, never found in building lobbies. Into their roofless concrete corral, August light pours down.

Around the baffle, onto the rear access road, I'm flanked by grass, in the open but not the clear.

A step at a time, outward bound from twenty-eight hundred. Waves of shock coursing through, hammering heart that needs to run. Hold it together, steady pace, don't look back.

I reach the sidewalk, a rush of glinting traffic beside me and the smell of exhaust. Halfway to the light and the crosswalk, I allow a backward glance.

A blue-and-white is lurking in the entrance drive. The sight of a Chicago squad car courses through, head to ground, chilling. It wasn't there when I followed the couple in, but it is now, because of me.

Target the end of the block, the newspaper boxes at the bus stop, red kiosk boxes for *Sun-Times*, blue for *Tribune*, city of reds, city of blues. Visualize stowing the evidence in the trunk of the Mustang a block off Lake Shore Drive. Make it real. Steady pace. Keep blending, merging. Breathe back into the ordinary world.

Mine was ordinary plus, a year ago. Extraordinary, because Melanie was in it. Now I operate in an underland—a basement movie set of stairwell vaults, service doors, night streets, and alleyways. In a business with an insatiable appetite for advertising.

I am not who I presumed to be. But there may be power in that, of energy redirected, of all of us together in collision, splitting and melding into other selves. At times our story seems to make itself up, as much in spite of as because.

And so, in humble recognition of all we may not have done by will, once there was, and once there was not . . .

New Year's Eve, 1977

Chapter 1

ONCE there was, in the story of America, a chapter in all caps, a megathrust event, more an era than a decade, known as the nineteen-sixties. Although I was a child of the era, as a son of the South, the slumbering otherland, I came late to the party. Seven years into the seventies, I was still burning the fuel of the decade's dreams and visions, lofty to lunatic.

It may not have been the true reason. But it was the nearest excuse I had for arriving at these coordinates in space and time, in a city too cold for human habitation, on the lip of a frozen lake. A predisposition maybe, but not the true reason. That was the bitter recognition as I put the Mustang in park and rotated the key to off.

I grabbed the hot box and rolled out and the wind bit again. You could burn your lungs inhaling. A leather bomber jacket made a flimsy defense, no matter how high you zipped it. Melville may have had drizzly November in his soul, but he never felt December in Chicago. I punched the door lock and checked the handle.

The recognition took a human form. And it was the human form, mortal muse, lethal pixie, that I had in mind, in gut, in incessant thoughts like an El train running in the brain. The form of Melanie.

"Bitch," I said to no one there, focusing down my long tunnel of jealousy and grief. I crunched in the snow dune before the sidewalk and almost blundered into them. One look and there was no doubt. They had heard me.

The dude, a six-six slab, hulked in the background. Closer to me on the street side of the walk, his girlfriend hijacked the streetlight. It was impossible not to look.

A Latina tottering on platforms, her leopard tights showed below a glossy faux patent coat. Glitter clung to her up-do and spangled her cheeks. They were fresh from a club, it came to me, reality brain cutting through my fog of self-pity and plots of vengeance. Like the others I had been dimly aware of, they were doing their New Year's prowl on Wells Street. Distant thunk-a-booty music pulsed in the frigid air.

They halted and he stepped around her. Huge jacket, black leather. Gold chain. I saw him pumping iron in Elgin State. Benching an engine block. Big. An atmosphere collected around him.

"Hey man, no . . . sorry, just . . . talking to myself."

He shot me a look. Bullet eyes, stone pills. Nose ominously off-center. A chip had been struck from his face.

I pointed to my temple and screwed the finger around then flipped it up and away. Checked out, I mimed. *Mea culpa.* Capeesh?

Expressionless, skeptical. Maybe I could use the hot box for a shield.

At the top of his jacket, a swatch of party shirt popped out, silky purple, collars like fins. He wouldn't want blood stains. I tried to focus on that and the steadying presence of the random public, revelers between watering holes on Wells who would do nothing to intervene in a mauling but who nevertheless could inhibit as eyewitnesses. Two blocks from Second City.

Hands up, open palms, hot box hanging from thumb. Making universal gesture, no mistake possible.

"No offense," I winced. Wind came scything along the block.

She tugged his jacket sleeve south and he responded, her poodle. I saw his back.

Survived. I was in the clear, like the others on Wells, in transit between islands of warmth in clubs or cars. A trio of ladies, coeds from the northern burbs, buzzed and glowing, passed arm-in-arm in their coats and scarves. We checked each other and they frothed with giggles. Behind them a happy couple were coming my way, and another. Some passed under the anointing light of the tomato-sauce-red backlit plastic sign of Gonzo Pizza Pie. It was home. I pulled the door and went back in.

The heat felt like a wraparound drug. The clench in my neck and shoulders began to ease. A bank of three double-table black ovens like megawatt amps lined the left wall. The pizza factory was built for volume, and volume they did. No boxes on top of the ovens meant no pizza orders up, which probably meant no orders of any kind, especially since Sonny was cleaning his pizza paddle with a scraper. The aromas made a mouthwatering blend—baked crust and corn meal on the oven beds, peppery sausage, oregano and garlic.

Play that funky music white boy

Joe's boombox was blasting another volume than before I had left on the last delivery, a sign of the end of the night. No one was authorized to touch it besides Joe, and he was nowhere in sight.

I thought Dewayne was gone too, released back to the halfway house, but then I spotted him behind his table, face down on the rubber mat. He popped up, stiff as a plank, fulcrum at his toes. Push-ups with the right arm only, the left folded behind his back.

"Ten," he spat at the floor.

Iranian Sonny, all five-four of him, was half-cleaning, half-watching.

"Eleven." Dewayne paused for a second, then dropped and pumped. "Twelve."

He was back on his feet, black face gleaming with sweat and victory.

"Still young!" he declared, showing his gold tooth. "Still young." He was bricks on top, pecs and delts inflated under his yellow Gonzo T-shirt. The flying machine logo was stretched, distorted across his chest.

Play that funky music right

"My man," he announced to Sonny, who looked deflated. He slapped his paddle on the table and fished around his apron into his jeans. He stuffed a bill into Dewayne's hand. It looked like a five-spot.

"You so young," Sonny said. "You baby."

Dewayne was shiny and grinning, showing gold. He slipped the bill into his wallet, puffing heavily.

"Mitchie, Mitchie," he said suddenly to me. It was simply because I was standing in front of him, I told myself, the width of the pizza table between us. "What's that stand for?"

"Mitchell."

"Mitchell," he said, like *'nough said.*

"Wash up." Joe reappeared from the back, aiming it at Dewayne, which was a relief. "Use bleach." He had witnessed his feat, at least the end of it.

Joe was a heartthrob, a tall, brooding Detroiter with a black mop that always looked freshly blow-dried. He had Dewayne by almost a foot. The fact that Dewayne could probably bring down Walter Payton counted for nothing in Gonzo Pizza Pie where he was in a work program and Joe was a partner. Dewayne went straight to the sink. Joe and Ozzie, the money partner, complemented each other. Unlike in most ways, they shared a knack for intimidation. Joe popped the register and pulled out a wad of bills. As I thought, it had been a monster night.

Play that funky music till you die

That song may not have been the source of all slack-faced moronism in the country, but it explained a lot. At least it was no "Auld Lang Syne." I had always hated that song. Not a pissed-off, proto-suicidal ditty to dead love, which would have been right. No, a song freighted with enough nostalgia to sink a cruise ship. The thought of it sucked like a vortex, screwing down. And screwed, I was indeed. In thought, word, and deed. And memory.

As in one year ago to the night, the get-together in our humble one bedroom on Elizabeth Street in Chapel Hill. "Our" as in mine and Melanie's. Melanie Barr, poetess laureate of the English department, formerly my so-called beloved.

Whatever we were dancing to, Stevie or "Gonna Take a Miracle," it was not "Auld Lang Syne." Although it might as well have been, because the memory was just as maudlin, down to the bottle of retsina we split camped under our well-worn sleeping bag open flat, a space heater at the foot of the bed.

I was an immigrant. It was her town, not mine. If I were to look for reasons that I followed Melanie to her home turf, that memory must have been one. And others too many to repress—why I reincarnated, an honors graduate, as a driver for Gonzo Pizza Pie, against expectations, a white boy victim of Joe's funky music boombox, still obsessed, haunted, in this grand, merciless city.

It was twelve-thirty and I was past ready to book it, but Joe showed no sign of releasing drivers. I stacked my hot box on top of one other at the end of the table. One box missing meant a driver was still out.

The third driver occupied a stool at the front window. I couldn't say that I felt like talking, but the front was our usual bullpen between deliveries. I pulled off my stocking cap, idiotic-looking concession to the cold, and took a seat a few stools away. At least the view was lively, a ringside seat overlooking Wells Street, which would be dead as an

Edward Hopper at this point on an ordinary night but on this one was still flowing with a ceaseless passage of brake lights and sidewalk refugees. A horn blared and another answered.

The driver sat hunched forward in a pea coat, head in a book. I had seen him before, maybe once, on one of my nights a week that we could have had in common. He glanced up, as though he sensed me checking him.

"Big night," I said.

"Yeah," he half-chuckled. A trace of a grin lingered as he studied me through glasses. He looked lightly distracted, as though a silent broadcast was nibbling at his attention. Curly hair topped a bulbous head, oversized forehead. He would have made a convincing alien.

"Mitch," I said and extended my hand.

"Corey," he said. Tight grip.

"Do you usually work weekends?"

"Unusually," he said. "I'm on alternate status, by choice. Joe calls when he's short a driver, could be any night. I was a full-time driver for a while so I'm a known quantity. You?"

"Four nights, no weekends. I play music with another guy, so I leave those nights free." Like it mattered. We weren't exactly tearing up Chicago. Yet. *We* meaning Wray and me.

"Ah, we know musicians. My wife's a soprano, coloratura. Do you sing? She gives voice lessons, in case you're ever interested. Most singers leave the tone in their throats. They blow out their voices. You should place the tone in the head, especially the high notes. The chest too, but mainly the head. Maybe you know that. You can set the body resonating like an instrument, chest and head. It's much more powerful." Corey clenched his fist like he was hoisting a stein. He looked animated, a man of enthusiasms. "Beth emphasizes placing the tone. It's priority one. Anyway, if you want to talk to her . . ."

He rolled off his hip and extracted his wallet. I took his business card, one end slightly curled.

Corey McGowan

Financial Consultant

Novelist

"It's our home phone," he added.

"You write," I said, aware that I was probably in the presence of a crackpot.

"Novels," he confirmed. "Story collections are impossible to sell. Poetry is worse, with a few exceptions, mostly academics. It's all about novels." His hand cupped air emphatically, cradling a vaporous entity, substantial and full of promise.

The door swung open with a wave of cold and Lenny, the other driver, ducked in. I checked Joe in the back, wondering which of us he would cut loose and when. The phone rang—another order at twelve-forty. Sonny took it.

"You want to split first? He won't need three to close." I had a spooky sense that my mind had been read. Corey's eyebrows lifted behind his glasses. He looked pleased with himself. "How many orders do you have?"

"Sixteen." I didn't need to recount.

"Average a dozen tickets per driver, four drivers a night. Average ticket, ten bucks, round number. Plus pickups. Two hundred K a year, at least." Corey rattled off the calculations, dispassionate. "Fifteen percent cost of sales, minus overhead. Joe and Ozzie take out maybe one-fifty a year." He pushed up his glasses with one finger. I had seen Ozzie a few times. The money partner was in and out, to make his presence known or write checks for suppliers. His honky 'fro looked ludicrous, but not, I imagined, to his tribe of high rollers and trophy babes who dwelt in the condos above Rush Street and partook of his quality coke.

Corey rested his case. His look was saying, think about it. My ambition was not to calculate, it was to go home.

"*Human Action*," I read the title of his book on the counter. "It doesn't sound like a novel."

"Ludwig von Mises," he explained. "The Austrian school of economics. The fundamental tenet is that people act intentionally in their own best interest."

"Uh-huh."

He seemed to come from all directions at once. A polymath or a windy psycho? There must have been a reason he was driving pizzas, a premise that applied equally to me.

Two explosions outside the window made us jump. Firecrackers, or torpedoes. Two girls froze at a parking meter. A punk in a heavy coat slugged another in the shoulder then chased him down the sidewalk.

"Morons," Corey observed.

At least he had the capacity to make me laugh, which was a feat given my bereaved state.

"Who wants to check out? I only need one." Joe the merciful had come to life. We were being released. Wiry Lenny was eager to score the last deliveries of the night, freeing Corey and me to cash in our tickets. As we punched the door into the frigid air, I checked my watch: ten to one under a canopy of cold.

"You drive again on . . ." His breath steamed in the air.

"Day after tomorrow."

"Joe says he wants late-week coverage from me until Mad Dog comes back." The mythical Mad Dog, Armando the Cuban, had driven for Gonzo from the start. His Camaro had blown a head and was being tended to on blocks in the yard of Ozzie's moonlighting mechanic. "So I'll see you Thursday."

More pops, four, but not fireworks—distant but close enough to tell the pock sound of guns.

"Shooting in the air," Corey explained. He could tell I was clueless. "Tradition. Forty-five seconds," he added. "That's how long a bullet fired straight up takes to come down." He flipped his scarf around his neck. "Morons." He laughed, mouth wide open, delighting in the absurdity. I saw a lead filling. "Happy New Year. See ya."

He turned and put his head down. His short, compact body like a wrestler's bulled into the wind. I watched him unlock his door at the end of the block—a gray whale of a Pontiac that no sane delivery driver would want.

I didn't even have time to forget him. Gonzo was closed on New Year's, Monday, but I was back driving on Tuesday. I picked him up through the front window half a block away. Corey pulled the front door and entered, popping off his stocking cap. He gave a perfunctory two-finger salute to Sonny in the back like assurance that all was well, carry on. Then he made a beeline for me.

"You're early," I said.

"Just you and Lenny tonight?" he countered. "I always liked Mondays—good tips, usually better than weekends." It was Monday in a way, close enough. "How many deliveries?" He had removed his fogged glasses and was staring around the top of my head, not making eye contact.

"An even dozen." It was after nine. There would be a few more, especially if Lenny checked out first. "Did you come in to see Joe? He took off early, the usual Monday. Tuesday in this case."

"Nope. You." He parked on the stool beside me and fished in his pea coat pocket, giving off the cold air scent of night. From having talked to him for fifteen minutes, I had learned to expect that whatever I expected would be wrong. He unfolded a sheet of green-lined ledger paper on the counter and flattened it with a slap.

"I worked up some numbers," he started, "a three-year P&L." He checked me. "Profit and loss statement, a projection. Taking off from the guesstimate the other night."

Three columns of the paper were filled with numbers in a tight hand. His finger tracked down the left side, pointing

to each row and explaining where he deemed necessary:
gross sales, cost of sales, rent, utilities, advertising, account-
ing, taxes.

"Size of store, a factor, sure—bigger nut—but . . . break-
even is here, start of year two. This assumes a loan less
than thirty, debt service at current rates plus one point over
three years for conservatism. Turn it over to managers by
year two, each take out ten the first year, subsistence. But
then look at year two: seventy-five each, same as Ozzie and
Joe, and it's running itself. Double that plus by year three."
He pointed to the bottom right corner of the data, year three
net: three hundred twenty thousand.

"The assumptions are conservative. Average three
drivers per night, sixteen deliveries each. Look at your
tickets tonight, right?" Corey's eyebrows went up. "By year
two it's performing like Gonzo now, which is a realistic
assumption, but this place has no walk-in, or almost none.
Imagine a place with a counter, tables, a high-traffic
location.

"You've seen Ozzie with his bank bag, right?" I had
indeed, counting stacks of bills at night's end then stuffing
them into the deposit bag he would leave with tucked in his
coat. "I know they do three thousand in sales Saturdays, a
lot of Sundays."

I was getting uneasy. Where was he going? He was like
the geometry teacher posing the question without asking,
pacing at the front of the room, waiting for our lights to go
on. The acute angles had all been accounted for. What
conclusion was implied? Inevitable?

"Whoa, whoa. Are you saying we try to do this?"

He sat regarding me like a grinning Buddha.

"As in, you and I?"

"It's about freedom, right?" he confirmed, not asked.
"Options. For me it's about writing—novels, book development, concept development. That's another story, another
business. For you, think what it could mean for your music.

You could jump-start it by renting spaces—four-walling your own shows. What about a studio? Have you ever thought about that?"

What group hadn't? "What planet are we on here? I've talked to you for . . . twenty minutes?"

He was grinning again, this time at my reaction, which had to have been predictable.

"First impression is around three quarters of a second. It's about consciousness, really. Have you heard of Eckankar?"

"Like Buddhism?"

"There's meditation, but that isn't the point. It's consciousness. The founder was an enlightened being, like the Buddha. When he translated, his body was like wood, like earth. He had become pure consciousness.

"Eckists believe everybody has emanations—we're like balls of light." No doubt he could see how sympathetic I was, but he went on. "It's an additional way of perceiving, like another sense—reading people's emanations."

"Auras?"

"Sometimes people call them auras. Babies see them. You know how when they look at us they tend to focus above our heads? We surrender the ability as we age. Use it or lose it."

Right. Of course. Get me out of here.

He laughed suddenly, as though he had heard my thought. "Beth's is gold," he added. "From the way she sings." He pointed to his forehead. "Placing the tone in the head. Third eye position."

"This is why you're pitching to me, the color of my aura . . ."

"How do you make decisions? You look at all the factors, not just one, right? I think we weren't driving the same night at the end of the year by accident. And I think you're ready for something."

He was oddly compelling, this esoteric in a wrestler's body. He set off funny echoes. I knew he was using an old mentalist's trick: broad suggestions containing kernels of truth for anyone. But he had a genuine quality too, a naïve enthusiasm.

"So what color is mine?"

"Ha! Green and black, like money. You don't have to decide now." He refolded the ledger sheet.

I was ready to tell him then but didn't have the heart to puncture his balloon after three years of projections. Plus, I had to consider the effect on my aura.

I thanked him for thinking of me, trying to project sincerity. Sonny called from the back; an order was up. I went one way and Corey the other, out the door, back into whatever fantasy factory he came from.

In no conceivable way would I be an Ozzie or a Joe. But that was before the practice gig, and the nightmare.

Chapter 2

"MOGUL." John Wray snapped off a smile and flipped his James Taylor hair back from his eyes. "You brought the Pignose. Excellent."

He preferred to use his boxy portable amplifier for the punchy tone of the mahogany Gibson. The only other choice for the gig would be Janis's Fender amp, and it was already maxed with the mike and the twelve-string. The junior-sized Pignose had wound up at my place after the last practice. He had driven down from his parents' house in Winnetka and I had come up from the city.

He probably wouldn't need the Mossman for this kind of gig, but he had brought it anyway. The Gibson case was open, but John had stored the case of the treasured Mossman under the bay windows, as far from human contact as possible.

"Is this okay, you guys? Need anything else?" Doubt pinched a wrinkle between Janis's eyebrows, eager Bette Davis eyes. In her floor-length gown of burgundy velvet with hoop earrings, she was in her element, the natural hostess, salon diva. She had assembled the two stools, the Fender amp, and a mike with stand, a green Carter-Mondale button on the cord. The threadbare oriental over old hardwood defined the performing space. We would play with the windows at our backs. John gave Janis a hug.

"What could be finer?" he said. "Seriously."

"Oh, good. The booze is . . . you know where the fridge is . . ." She nodded toward the far end of the room then waved to some guest and shimmered away in velvet.

I did know, as we had practiced there before, on the capacious top floor of her parents' house in Evanston. Janis had known John since high school. A graphic artist, theater groupie, and Renaissance aficionada, nee Bernadette, she had adopted "Janis" after Joplin. I liked her from the start. Back from the main room, a couple of bedrooms were tucked off the hall, seraglio-style, the old refrigerator at the end by the down staircase.

A white parachute hung above our heads in the front room. Janis's posters adorned the walls: two Rossettis of demoiselles with alabaster necks, flowing but still as orchids; De Niro in the driver's seat in *Taxi Driver*; a portrait of a Medici; a classic Fillmore of Janis and the Holding Company; prints of Venice and Florence, the Ponte Vecchio.

Taking the cue from John, I settled my case by the window. He was occupied with a quick-talking miss, frizzy nimbus of hair and greedy eyes. The pattern was not unusual for Johnny Wray, who tended to inspire starry looks. I headed for the fridge.

As salon diva, Janis had outperformed. The floor teemed with bodies, almost none of whom I recognized, around the walls in singles and pairs or clumps, and sunken in the old stuffed chairs and swaybacked sofa. On cushions in a corner, a Richie Havens double entertained a blond sprite nodding earnestly behind tented knees. Most looked to be students, Northwestern or Loyola, maybe a smattering of Steppenwolf Theatre hopefuls.

I nodded to Maya standing across the room, cup in hand, sporting a tiara of Christmas bells. Janis had introduced us in a practice weeks before. The most senior of the bunch, Maya owned a gallery on Lincoln Avenue. Divorced. If Janis had an agenda, I appreciated that. Sensuous? Yes. Older? Yes, by maybe a dozen years. And maybe at a future time I would have no problem. But now a sick feeling dwelt in the core, the cause of which had not yet shown. From the front door of Janis's house to the third floor that floated above the world, I hadn't spotted her. I hadn't seen her in weeks, three or four. The adorned Miz Maya brought it all back, recrudescence, shot to the solar plexus. Hump-torrid she may be, but I was numbed by the queen of memories.

"Sorry," I said, bumping my way through couples. A bloom of perfume like patchouli transitioned to an atmosphere of grass and a lingering scent like myrrh. The refrigerator was in sight.

I caught snatches of conversations, among familiars or intimates, or nervous and new. Floating among them from speakers around the floor: *Return to Forever*, Chick Corea and Flora, lyrics inane, music transcendent.

Life is paradise, all together

I pulled the handle of the Kelvinator: two six-packs of Miller, a Colt 45, a crockery bottle of Lancers Rosé, and sparkling wine survivors of New Year's—two Cooks and a Cold Duck.

"Hey." I felt a poke in the ribs. "You gonna play tonight?" Pat whatshername had sneaked in behind me, floater that she was, papillon.

I had met her only once, and the details were foggy, wrapped in some unpleasantness. She looked happy to see me, though, a blue-eyed blonde with curls, lips like Janis's Rossetti, or a Burne-Jones, a little pursed as I remembered them.

"Hey hey. That's the plan, I guess. Janis's, that is— Duello live, practice with an audience. Why not? First gig of the year."

She nodded with the purse-lipped half-smile, not tall but seeming tall, or long, in her stretchy knee-length dress and boots.

"The gigs will come," she said. "You never know. There are a lot of clubs. Dale thought you were really good."

That loosed the memory. Dale was the manic fiddle player. The party was at Melanie's in-law apartment above the garage on Belden, and Wray and I had just started playing together. Melanie had introduced us, naturally. She and I were living apart already, I on Southport in the Cavern as I thought of it because it was, a basement apartment with little sunlight and ancient black hardwood but rooms that sprawled, half of the downstairs of the building. Pat and Dale had been at Melanie's together, and Wray and I had played while Dale jammed along.

No doubt Dale's fiddle was the trigger, the reason I worked an old-timey tune into the jam, likely "Wreck of the Old 97," because it linked back. A chain of jams wound behind me like a trail into the woods, and following it back could take me to resting places, pockets of normalcy. If I followed far enough, I could even come across clarity of purpose, and an explanation for Chicago. Both of those and, I could make the case, all that had propelled me into whoever I believed I was and spun up the dream I dreamed for myself linked back to Jim Dewey's jams.

Melanie always said, probably lying sweetly, that hearing me play won her over. By senior year when she applied to the graduate writing program in Chicago, she had already trolled enticing bait, a lively music scene more open than Boston or New York, in clubs with names like the Earl of Old Town, Somebody Else's Troubles, and the Bulls. I had my rationale: I wasn't merely tagging after my girlfriend to her hometown—I was answering to a higher calling.

But now I was faking it all, as though we were still in our old life, a couple in some way but pursuing our own aspirations in separate places. Such was my delusion, and the association with Melanie's get-together on Belden that I had to unwrap before I could see Pat clearly again. Tremaine, that was her last name. Someone had called her PT, probably Melanie. I pulled a Miller and popped the top.

"Thanks for the plus vibes," I said. "Happy New Year." We tapped, my Miller can to her paper cup of something golden, I guessed Cold Duck.

What game shall we play today

Over Pat's shoulder I spotted Dale in one of the bedrooms. She nodded in his direction and I followed. A couple sunken in a chair traded a roach clip in slow motion. A short table lamp with a red bulb gave the little bedroom a cozy hemp-den ambience. Dale seemed as wired as I remembered him, grinning, sleeves rolled halfway up his biceps, looking ready to rumble, pointy face, pointy goatee. As we traded greetings, Pat slipped her arm around his waist. He was working kitchen prep and backup cook at Lou Mitchell's downtown on Jackson. We commiserated about our jobs, sharing the conviction that they were dues only, and temporary. Dale wanted to start a band too. And who didn't?

He bounced as he talked, shifting his weight to one foot then the other. I could see him as a fighter, bobbing and weaving in a past life. At one point Pat slipped away into the next bedroom. I noticed she was barefoot, which enhanced her glide, and I wondered when she had lost her boots.

It occurred to me suddenly that Wray and I had committed to play for these people, or at least in front of them or in proximity. All of them. I took a swig of Miller and then another and tried to inhale as much second-hand high as possible.

The music had changed.

"Weather Report?" I guessed to Dale, testing his hipness.

"The first, *I Sing the Body Electric*." He nodded, glowing, rabbit teeth.

I glanced around the room for his fiddle case and felt some relief when I didn't see it. Dale was a likable live wire, but I wasn't in the mood for a jam. A dude with a music dream, dude with a dead-end job—he tweaked me like a snatch of reflection—myself caught sideways in a merciless mirror. Playing parties would get Wray and me nowhere. And I needed to get somewhere.

"Where's the music?"

Dale nodded to the second bedroom and I followed. Pat was dancing with a jack-booted young lady in a biker jacket. Janis was holding forth to a straight-looking couple, happily incongruous. The female reminded me of Tricia Nixon. I imagined they could be another gallery connection, or even theater money, FOJs, friends of Janis. I spotted the turntable and tuner on a low coffee table beside a Chianti bottle encrusted with candle drippings. Album covers, a couple dog-chewed, surrounded the table and lined the wall to the corner. Dale was fingering through the stack.

"Oh shit, check this." He held up a vintage Frank Zappa I recognized, but my attention had turned to motion in the hall. Bodies were reshuffling, clearing a space. I held my breath. Just outside the door, only a glimpse but unmistakable, and behind her, he was clear enough. I edged next to the door for a clear view of the main room.

Melanie was wearing the red cloth coat, smartly cut, the one she had kept at the end of the closet in Chapel Hill, a college gift from her parents, a festive choice. She pulled off her stocking cap and her hair bounced free over her collar, chestnut with lights. It was her most beguiling feature, or among the most.

He stood beside her, just as I expected: Adam Champion, curly haired, beard precisely trimmed, burgundy scarf tossed over his shoulder—the Shelley of University of Illinois, Circle Campus. The lord and lady of Circle poetry, marriage made in *collegium artium*. How long she had had her eye on him, I didn't know. I had met him at one of the

Sunday brunches of her friends and their friends in the
Oxford Pub during our first month in Chicago. I had sat
across from him in the days when she was on my side of the
table. He seemed decent enough, "sensitive" in a way I
would only come to disdain later, in my spurned nights
infused with jug wine, waking with abrasions of unknown
origin on my fist or forehead like the wolfman, nights of
howling at the moon.

Yes, they had arrived together, but that was inconclusive. We did not arrive together, that much was known.
Whether they were truly together, conjoined soulmates as
we once were, or whether Adam played the harmless
cicisbeo, was TBD.

I spied on her around the door frame. Her eyes searched
the room, brows raised, a lightness in her gaze, but I saw
feigned delight. It was her social flashcard. I knew the
others beneath, all the layers of Melanie.

Petite, demure-looking, nevertheless she had her trade-
mark glow, a signature emanation, radiance born of her
intelligence. It was a daunting package for the unsuspecting
consort. Was young Shelley up to the task? She was
probably looking for Janis. Or could it be for me?

She laughed at something he said, covering her mouth
with one hand, an affectation I knew well. Her other touched
his arm, a lingering touch, only seconds but seconds in a
skid, attenuated. Then the hand slid an inch up toward his
shoulder. His arm slipped comfortably around hers. That
was all. It was undeniable then. I was collapsing into some
chakra in the gut.

I was folding, on my knees at the end of the record
stack.

"Hey, man." Dale was looking at me, wrong end of the
telescope. Was I okay?

I was not okay in my body or in my mind. The red light
was my blues, bitch Melanie was my mind. Dale got up,
perhaps to get the nurse. I started working through the

stack of albums. Over halfway to the wall, I found one that should work. Perverse? Admittedly. *Nina Simone and Piano.* I checked the back of the cover, scanned the tracks.

Dale was back, proffering the prescription. I caught PT behind him looking toked, her blue-eyed focus a bit off-center. He was offering a smoking joint on the monstrous side, rolled by a cyclops.

"Thanks," I said, meaning he was right, they both were, perfectly right as a dead-struck cymbal in a Wagnerian heartbeat.

I took the burning weed and sucked it, bitter medicine, and held it down. I let it do its work permeating membranes, fogging warrens of the skull. I passed it back and slipped Nina out of her paper sleeve. Then I emptied the Miller can to steady my hands and went to work.

First was the tuner volume. I dropped Weather Report, faded them out. Battling my fevered brain, concentration pure, resolute, I switched the platters. The joint came around again. I took it from Dale for a final hit. Eyes level with the playing surface, I positioned the stylus and eased the arm down. The target was the first track. I hit the sweet hiss of the lead-in groove and boosted the volume.

Clambering up one leg at a time, lightheaded, heart booming, then rocking on my feet. Dale and PT, fellow conspirators, looked sympathetic, encouraging. We checked one another's eyes. It was time.

Chapter 3

CROSSING the front room I had to remember, there was only the music now. Melanie and Adam were standing, backs toward me and drinks in hand, with John Wray who knew the whole story and more of Melanie and me. He was smiling the frozen smile. Except for John who spotted me, I had the element of surprise.

"The only emperor..." Shelley was saying.

"Is the emperor of ice cream!" Melanie finished. The jolly couple were laughing. I racked my brain. To name the poet would be a triumph. Not Williams.

"What does it all mean?" I said instead.

The two young wordsmiths appeared suitably stunned. Smiles lingered, decaying into half-smiles.

Despite the complicated threat I posed, Melanie had the open look in her eyes, the one she was hard-put to repress, wide brows, moonchild. Adam, rosy-cheeked and ringleted, looked caught in the act, leftover grin, humorous interruptus.

"How many kinds of ambiguity?" I went on, dropping the most esoteric allusion that hit the brainpan, lips numb, cotton tongue. I was amping the confusion, and it felt fine. "Time's up. Seven."

"Very good," she said. "Empson."

"A classic in its day," Adam added.

"Out of favor? Who would have thunk? I'm out of touch. Speaking of . . . how are things at Circle, the beating heart of the living prosody?" I knew I was rolling on with brain unzipped—automatic speaking, trancelike state?

"Good," he coughed up. "Good." The most he could manage.

"Oh God," she said. Her expression changed, falling apart just enough. It was the desired effect.

Seems I'm never tired . . . Nina threaded the line out into the dark night . . . *lovin' you.*

As the long, pure tone reached us, Melanie's reaction betrayed her. Summer evenings on the floor, sitting backs against the sofa, eyes closed, reverent until the last note. It was a top tune of our old soundtrack. I was hoping for a response like nostalgia, a word that derived from both "love" and "pain."

"Janis had it," I said, as though that explained it. It occurred to me that Melanie's expression might be about me only, maybe horror, or pity. She blinked and smiled a smile she couldn't quite arrange. It was enough.

But not enough. I had reached the point of no return, of started and cannot stop, the fate of the wolfman. I was about to spatter the innocents with blood.

Maybe John could sense it because he turned away and knelt before his guitar case and lifted out the Gibson. Pitiable? No doubt I was, but how many chances would I have?

"And what of that professor . . . is he head of the department . . ." I directed it at Adam. Beneath his tidy beard, his jaw clenched.

"Michael Andonati."

"Ah yes, the kingmaker. What was his book, *Dead Head*?"

A detectable wince. "*Dead Red.*"

"Right. A slim volume. A paean to lost youth, isn't it? What would he say to 'as I was green and easy in the mercy of his means, time held me green and dying though I sang in my chains like the sea'? Out, no doubt. Excessive!"

"I don't think he discussed 'Fern Hill'." Adam checked Melanie for help.

"Just as well," I preempted her. My temples pulsed. The couple against the opposite wall looked farther away. "Better than well. Because it still sings, and what is it, three decades old. Let's see who remembers *Red Head* in thirty years. Let's meet again on the spot—New Year's two thousand eight—and compare longevities. Not necessarily here, as in the third floor of Janis Rosen's house. The sidewalk would work, weather permitting." I maintained a cordial smile, I knew I did, but young Shelley's lips were stiff and pale pink. I hoped he would make a miserable attempt to have a go at me. He was almost there. I ran through evasive moves and a takedown. The couple behind him were fated to go down too, innocent bystanders, wrong place, wrong time. "We could invite the great man himself."

Melanie was searching me.

"No, huh?"

In the silent wake, I heard clapping. I could be hallucinating. But then I saw the couple in the back, clapping far away. They were not alone, and ponderous abiding jealousy was shot through with panic. Even Maya was clapping, ensconced in her corner, a pair of glass rings twinkling. In the front bedroom, Janis was smiling expectantly.

"Duty calls," I said and half-bowed absurdly. Melanie and Adam were not clapping. I had done all the damage possible. Had it been worth it? Would it be tomorrow? The wolfman had no use for scales of justice.

John was tuning on his stool. I popped open the Martin's case and joined him. Soon I was sliding the chords of "Corrina, Corrina," which we never played. The reason I was doing it escaped me. My heart was galloping and I was revisiting the nightmares when I couldn't remember chords or words. John fell in, getting loose. A blue plastic tumbler was half empty beside his stool.

Janis had found Melanie and Adam in the front. She was standing on young Shelley's other side, close enough to hear me.

"My dear," I asked, "could you score me a beer?"

I picked up the reek of pot, with perspiration and incense. I could detect the scent of my twelve steel strings. I listened for Nina, but she had been silenced.

"What do you think?" I put to John. He knew what I meant: first number.

"Voilà," Janis said, presenting a golden can, already popped.

I thanked her and chugged, hoping for decision-making power, open to inspiration. We usually started slow and easy, "Reason to Believe" or early Lightfoot. Beside Janis, Melanie and Adam still lingered. Hadn't I done enough? Apparently not. I chugged another and centered the can on a stool with a spare pick.

"Road Away?"

Wray stared at me, acknowledging the challenge. Then he grinned and fingered through scales in the key. While he was noodling unplugged, conversation bubbled on. When he flipped on the Pignose and played a riff, it dropped. I blew into the mike and heard my breath.

"One," I said and our eyes locked, partners in crime, "two."

Wray hit the first three notes, the signature triplet.

I laid chords over the next three, then the decrescendo together, and we were into it.

Well he left his home in San Jose
He was just a boy of nine

It was less music than a tantrum, childish, flat-out. Each verse had a long tandem descent into the chorus. "Road Away" was a breakneck run, and it suited us. We kept biking to the end of the tightwire and were met with applause. It took that much to settle me down.

I had probably been singing with my eyes shut when Melanie and Adam worked their way back from the stage. Pat and Dale had materialized between our rug and the bedroom door. Dale was gripping his fiddle case for the first time, as though he had come to audition.

"Yes-no?" I asked John, who had noticed him too.

"Hey," he said, high as I was on our opening salvo, "tune him up!" He hoisted the blue tumbler and swigged.

"Jam?" I said in Dale's direction, and he was already kneeling, eagerly popping his case.

Wray and I started again lightly, a progression we used in C. Dale took his place beside John, feet planted, knees bent on the verge of a leap, and worked his way in. His tone, a gypsy bite, quivered with anticipation. PT was bobbing, grooving like a slow-motion runner in place.

I tried to resist, but soon I was scanning the room, and I picked them out again on the right side, just past Maya, who was entertaining Richie Havens. They were talking with a guy I didn't know, Adam's back toward me, she in profile.

I started changing the progression. I was bending the jam in a direction I knew. Adolescent? Absolutely. Shameful? No doubt. So what? I didn't tell her to check out with all her dues unpaid.

The tune was my own little black love ditty. John picked up on the chords, leaned on them, and edged his way into the intro. Dale joined, stepping gingerly. I sang toward PT, and the imaginary audience in the bedroom and beyond.

I was like your very lover, I was the cool hand in your hair

I came to you and I was gone again like your footstep on the stair

I stayed inside the words, tight as chains, exactly as I wrote them. When we hit the break, Wray punched the lead, rapidfire and restless, bullets from the Pignose. When his space opened, Dale attacked the strings, violin slicing, carving up the air. A kindred spirit, the kid was reading my soul. He punched us higher. We were caustic, working it, building it. I was aware of people moving around the floor in Janis's murky salon.

When the dogs came after us, they never did find me
They found you by your skin
But I was on the outside, you were in

By the last verse I was almost too dazed and wasted to hear the applause. John Wray was never uncool, but his forehead was shiny with sweat. Dale was a wiry imp amped with delight, rodentine grin.

I checked the room again, quickly at first and then to confirm. Melanie and Adam were gone, retreated into a bedroom or faded back into their otherness. Either way, they were out of range. Wallace Stevens. A lot of good that did me now.

PT delivered a six-pack to our empty stool and we refueled and tried to pick up on the vibe in the room, which was clearly a need to move. "Silver Threads and Golden Needles" fit the bill, showcasing Dale's fiddle. Soon Janis's third floor was jumping. PT was bopping with Janis. Even the Nixons were moving.

We backed off into a break, a Dead-style, rambling jam. After that Dale picked one, "Allison," and we stumbled through an attempt at harmony. By the end I had sweated out most of three Miller's but not all. When I made it back from the john, even Dale was looking winded, perched on my stool.

Wray had switched to his beloved Mossman, with fingerpicks. He worked his way softly into his own version of "The Saints of God," stately and precise, tones like smoke rings. As people recognized it, they fell silent. I was amazed at his ability to do that, to put us in a space we still cherished, regardless of our break-away paths.

Our part was done, Dale's and mine. I was more than ready to fold. I had done what I could to exorcise all fantasies of the perfect pair, wherever they were. As I closed the twelve-string into its case, another joint came around, and I reminded myself that there was an art to forgetting. Practice could make perfect, and we were there to practice.

At some point John left, being less blasted than I. Several of us remained, at Janis's invitation. Her parents were not expected home from Naperville until morning. We distributed ourselves, couples or more, to the collapsed sofa and stuffed chairs and the beds. Suspended on the third floor, on Janis's magic carpet with Christmas lights lining the windows, we had escaped the ghosts of our grounded lives.

Maya had a difficult headdress but an easy smile. No doubt that was why I wound up thigh-to-thigh with her on the sofa. Practice could make perfect. As muse of the art of forgetting, Maya Andropoulos was not bad at all.

Chapter 4

I was beating Janis's parents home. That was the goal on the Monday morning after, I reminded myself as I descended the red front steps, Frye boots wary of ice on concrete. The morning air was frozen mist, air in suspension. North Side air, atmosphere of privilege, air of Northwestern, far from the trapped exhalations of Chicago. A trace of exhaust reached me as one truck rolled down Sherman Avenue, and then the cold that blocked all smell.

Martin case in hand, I touched down on the sidewalk and tried to gauge the overnight snow and freeze by the crunch, a clue to the scraping that awaited on the car. Moderate dusting lay on the walk over compacted snow, beaten ruts, and an occasional track of bike tread. Parked cars hunched down the block against berms of dirty snow plowed to curbside.

Puffing smoke, a man bustled around me in a black topcoat and fur hat with ear muffs. His rubber shoe skins must have had traction soles.

I spotted the Mustang toward the end of the block, black top and cream body paled under powder and frost. The case would go inside, not in the trunk. The back seat would be cold enough.

It was a delivery night again, too soon. After our gig, such as it was, not exactly the Earl of Old Town. Our pay: unlimited Miller High Life, one powdered doughnut from the box in Janis's kitchen, and a slug of coffee. Fun? It must have been. Why else would we do it? Humiliating? I tried to recall dispassionately. By adult standards, it should have been. But how much of my heckling even registered with Shelley and the queen?

I was starting to spiral. Could one thought of them trigger it? Or was it the breath-stopping cold air at an unnatural hour? Or a half-night of sofa crashing instead of sleep? No doubt all three. The combination of punches had softened my defenses as I crunched along, taking stock.

First deficit: a dead-end, placeholder, subsistence job, a ringing disappointment to anyone with knowledge of me and hopes for my future. Start with Dr. Knox, the only professor who cared enough to argue seriously for grad school. Then Dr. Muller, because she was closest to us both, when we were "both." And always, and most to be feared, if Mom had been watching since I was twelve through some heavenly Episcopalian peephole on the loved ones left behind. Dad now too, although Hank was less of a threat to lead an afterlife, at least a watchful one. Valerie would get it. With two years between us, she always had ways of letting me know she had faith in little brother, although long ago she had taken a safe seat in the lifeboat beside Chuck and did not rock it or share great affinity with any who did.

In summary, the job bespoke radical underachievement. In the service of what? An addiction acquired in Jim Dewey's living room in Chapel Hill.

Professor James Dewey left his mark in freshman year, predating Melanie, predating awakening. To be precise, Jim was an associate professor, and I never attended his biology seminars. But like most in my incoming class, I came to know "Country Dick" Ogden, who showed up on the first day in a ten-gallon hat toting guitar and banjo cases, while I came dressed as a GQ preppy. Dick heard that I played, and after a couple of months invited me to one of the hootenannies that Jim hosted in his house not far from campus. Two styles were permitted: bluegrass and country. Dick traded off between banjo and guitar, and I and a couple of others brought our six-strings. Jim added the critical fiddle.

His repertoire spanned a catalog of old good-time tunes, Carter family classics like "Wabash Cannonball" and "Keep on the Sunny Side" and a long list of favorites and obscurities by Jim and Jesse, Hank Williams, Jimmie Rodgers, and others. As a kid I had heard more than a few, especially on WSM from Nashville as I lay in bed at night with my transistor. But Jim's PhD was from Smith, and the closest "country" to his hometown of Worcester was the rolling hills and fields of the Pioneer Valley, Deerfield to Springfield. In his own student days, he had been bitten by the music in Boston coffeehouses.

Red-haired and freckled, Jim was not imposing in stature, but he brought a ball of energy to the jams, and to the experiment of life. In one of our breaks early on—it could have been the first night I sat in—I found myself talking with him one-on-one. Bluegrass wasn't the only music he heard in the coffeehouses of Boston in the late sixties. Rooms like the Phoenix and the Sword in the Stone hosted a crop of New England folkies, Tom Rush and Chris Smither and Eric Von Schmidt. And others rotated through, Tom Paxton and Odetta and Phil Ochs. I knew most of the names but missed them by a few years and a wide world, coming of age in the metropolis of High Point, North Carolina. Jim loaned me albums, and his tales of hearing the acts live set them aglow in me, so when I listened to the songs I could project myself into the dark rooms with the stage at the end under the spotlight.

I hoarded all the folk songbooks and sheet music I could find in Chapel Hill. Jim introduced me to others he hadn't seen but knew from their records. Buffalo Springfield,

Lightfoot, and Laura Nyro struck sparks and flared. By the time I was through the Fariñas and Dylan, the crown of my head had been lifted and I had been transported. I knew what I wanted and expected of myself, with no evidence, only arrogance and blind faith. My obsession had been loosed, and I had Jim Dewey to thank and to blame.

Even Dick Ogden caught the bug, and because he was similarly naïve and starry-eyed, we started learning the songs together. A trip to the Cellar Door in D.C. to see the Dillards dosed us with envy and stoked our resolve. Inevitably, we screwed up the courage to face an open mike night at the Tar Pit campus coffeehouse. Due mainly to the kooky charisma of Country Dick, we made enough of a hit to be invited back. Our open mikes led to spots on a few weekend nights, and by the summer of sophomore year, we had graduated to gigs at the Loft in Chapel Hill, our first earnings of thirty-five dollars a night, split two ways. The real payoff was the jolt of confidence and the fire in the belly, the irresistible lure that there could be space in the crowded field for one more sound, if it could be fresh and new.

Whether a grand dream or a pipedream, time would tell. But for now Wray and I were stalled in the queue of the many called but as yet unchosen.

And of course last, and best, beyond any job or music blues, I could not hear the shortest strain of a bubblegum love song without gagging on pure vitriol.

Such was my state, regurgitated in an odd moment when I lacked the resources to stuff it down as usual because it implied the tedious question: what to do about it?

Striding over the berm of snow and soot to the driver's side, hand in my pocket, I fingered the cold keys. The skin of snow on the windows looked translucent, pristine.

A screech pierced the air. I fumbled the keys and caught them. It came from above the roofs of the cars, at the end of the block. The fur hat, that was his destination.

On the El platform above the street, the train was pulling out. In the low light of Sunday evening, I hadn't realized I had parked so close. I could read the sign above the track: the Noyes Street stop.

The green cars were packed. It was the work-week Monday prison train, principal destination: the Loop. Riders jammed the aisles, stuffed coat-to-coat, rocking, hanging by one hand from the straps and bars. How many of the willingly incarcerated times how many days? Years?

Tons were rattling and rolling on the elevated track, the lead cars screeching over the next block, leaning into a turn. I watched the last car rumble out of sight.

Regardless of my miserable current state, murky expectations, and indeterminate dues to pay, I swore that was one place—in a way yet to be revealed—I would never be.

By eleven-thirty my night was over: thirteen deliveries, close enough to Corey's estimate, which proved nothing. I took Lincoln Avenue north toward the apartment. Three revelers were leaving Wise Fools, and I caught a snatch of the Koko Taylor show before the door swung shut. Across the street a glow emanated from John Barleycorn Memorial Pub, which was high on our wish list for bookings. Past the Biograph the street was empty. Massifs of snow hunched on the corners of blocks. Cold fog haloed the streetlights.

Where was I going? In whose eyes? Melanie's? Valerie's? Mom's? Anybody's.

Duello might have a shot, but who's telling us that but friends and lovers? Past lovers. There was nothing special about self-delusion.

And what about the Buddha wrestler pizza guy? Was he nuts or crazy like a fox? Doubly deluded did not equal sane.

On the green sheet he was assuming a loan, against what, I had no idea. Maybe his house, but that seemed unlikely. He would have no way of knowing about my inheritance, or its intended use, grad school. It was no great fortune but maybe enough to open the door of a modest restaurant. I resisted touching it, although the music could find uses for it; a studio, for example. Being able to cut demos on our own time, under our control—he was spot on about that. That we wanted one we knew, but how to finance it on our own, we didn't. What else was he right about?

On Fletcher heading for Southport, only my headlights were left, opening up a block of packed snow and blacktop. The streetlights thinned out, old and yellow-eyed.

Was Corey a lucky accident or a train wreck in the making? I had been in Chicago less than half a year, a naïf, and I was probably being hustled by a lunatic. Add to that, I was alone in a frigid city with a couple of guitars. I had been softened up, an easy target.

A vision of Ozzie with his money sack brought a sour taste. I deflected to Melanie. What of the poetess doyenne? She had always been a cheerleader for the music, a champion of the arts. What if she secretly craved a stable hunter-gatherer, an alpha one? I pictured her and Ozzie happily ensconced in a brownstone on Dearborn. And where was I heading? To a basement apartment with a bread pan of water on the radiator. What was my case to her to pick an underperformer over Ozzie? I was a dream merchant with a bias against what was once quaintly known as selling out. Ozzie was not a sellout. He was what he was.

An underperformer in whose eyes? Hers, of course—a habit of heart and mind.

Pat Tremaine is wearing her hair up. Her lipstick is an eye-catcher, and her gown, attire appropriate to a prom, shimmers subtly. We're above ground level, on a hotel mezzanine like a pool of marble, outside a conference room or ballroom.

She takes a sip from her glass, a red plastic tumbler, then lifts it to my mouth. The taste is sweet-tart, like apple wine.

She's standing close, looking bemused in that way she has, as though she knows what I know, and what I'm thinking. I'm feeling the pull of her lips. I lean in.

She takes a step back, and then another. I wonder if I've misread her, but it's about something else, completely different. She's focused past my shoulder, behind me.

Down a long track a train is coming out of pewter light. The floor beneath us is not a mezzanine but a platform, elevated, two sides bisected by tracks. I detect a rumble, and a vibration is beginning under our feet. The El train, green-headed, is closing fast.

The rush and rattle of coupled cars is split by the shriek of steel on steel. It is starting to slow. I don't want to see this train, don't want it to stop for me.

I turn to grab Pat's hand, but she's gone. She has found the stairway down from the platform, the stairway I need.

The train is braking, grinding and screeching. The lead car passes, and I have my first view through the windows. Riders pack the cars from side to side, a number gripping the overhead hooks and rails. They peer through the windows, sullen, leaden-eyed. Palms press against the glass.

And then, like a premonition, the first twists of smoke escape above the window tops. As the cars slow, sending a shudder underfoot, blurred faces come into focus. One makes eye contact—a man in a fur hat, pressed against a window.

In the next car, tongues of orange flame lick out above the glass. Screaming starts. People are jostling, surging to the windows, trapped, pounding on the glass panes of the sliding doors. Orange embers whip into the air above the car tops.

As far as I can see to the end of the train, cars are venting smoke, the riders trapped, windows throbbing with pulses of orange light. The train is groaning, nearly stopped, stopping for me.

I flipped onto my back, gulping air, a drowning man breaking the surface. Light around the blinds had tinted the ceiling pearl gray, a hue of familiarity, life on Earth. My chest was racing, wet, and I threw the blankets off. I rolled out, elbows on knees and head down, and let the race play out. The sight of the empty tall boy can beside my alarm clock that reported eight-ten filled me with thanks. I tilted back on the mattress, grateful, spared, and watched the ceiling brighten.

Before making breakfast I fished Corey McGowan's card out of my wallet. I dialed the number, and he picked up before the second ring. I was both surprised and not.

"It's Mitch," I said. "Let's find a location."

Chapter 5

"THIS not New York, boys, know what I'm sayin'?" Sammy A delivered his cautionary truism from the corner of the booth. Under a red Phillies cap, his black brow was wrinkled and nicked. He peered out at us as though we should know better. Corey had speculated that with the foot traffic we could expect, we might be able to thrive like a New York sandwich shop with no deliveries. We took slugs from our coffees, as though it would help us digest a lump of truth.

"We can do sandwiches, all kinds." Corey rebutted. "All drinks—pop, fruit smoothies."

Sammy winced.

"Old-time shakes if we have ice cream." He was on a roll. "And slices, we could do slice pies."

"You said there's an oven in there," Sammy confirmed.

"Right, two tables," I added, a rare fact of our pending acquisition I was sure of. I wanted to offset Corey's fervor. We had requested the meeting with our grizzled oracle to get his advice, not sell him.

"It's in New Town, so no parking, not a destination spot. You might do the volume, but your gross will be too low." Sammy sat back, resting his prophecy. "Do deliveries."

Sammy was gray around the edges, but he had the cred. In the sixties he had managed a string of full-service restaurants on the West Side. His diner on Halsted had been open only half a year, a few weeks longer than I had been in Chicago. It was the kind of place where the waitress poured the coffee without asking. Already it was full at eleven with a cross-section of the North Side: Com Ed workers, a sales team in suits, a Rocky Horror trio who converged in the pursuit of breakfast served all day. Before his restaurant career, Sammy A had been a welterweight boxer, his ticket from Cuba and the source of his moniker. If anyone knew his last name, I hadn't heard it. Corey had been chatting him up since the diner opened, and now he was perfectly positioned to be our mentor.

My mentee partner was taking in the delivery advice, appearing open to enlightenment. I didn't crave the complication of deliveries either, but I could see the wisdom. If Gonzo was our competition, we would need more than sandwiches.

"What about ice cream?" he went on. "With soft serve, the cost of sales is under twenty percent. We could do cones and shakes—"

"Good, for three or four months. Have you got a machine?" Sammy tilted forward, thick knuckles and a fat ring on the table. "I'll call my boy in Miami. He has stores down there, one in Biscayne, another up in Hollywood. He closed one in Coconut Grove—the nut's a motherfucker now, utterly—sixty cents a foot. He had two machines in there, double-barrel Taylors. I might could persuade him to part with one. I'll get you a price, all right?"

Of course it was all right, knowing what we knew, which was nearly nothing. Sammy slid out and stood.

"You signed yet?" His eyes tightened like he was ready to duck.

"Next," Corey said.

"You know what the trainer would tell you before you get in the ring?" A silent beat. "Pox wo-biscum." Our *éminence grise* made the sign of the cross at us, knuckles and ring, and grinned. "*Con dios,*" he added. "I'll talk to Buddy, let you know." He disappeared into the kitchen.

Corey was grinning, having received not only wisdom, but Sammy's blessing. To me, Sammy had the air of a prophet who favored the essentials. He wouldn't have bestowed a blessing if we weren't going to need it.

"Ready to see Sydney?" Corey said.

We downed our coffees and headed for Corey's boat of a Pontiac, bound for downtown.

Sydney Malowitz, attorney, existed in the zone above LaSalle Street, on a plane rarely visited by mortals of our station. Access was gained across a marble floor of a soaring lobby through elaborately wrought brass elevator doors, craftwork of a style gilded and grand. A microslice of humanity passed there routinely.

"Louis Sullivan, you think?" Corey quizzed at the elevator. "Daniel Burnham, has to be. 'Make no little plans.' I love that. Apropos, right? Maybe we'll get T-shirts."

I wanted to match his mania, but I wasn't there yet.

Malowitz's office on the eighteenth floor was the highest and most expensive real estate I had set foot in. It smelled of brass polish and oiled leather.

"You're satisfied with your financing?" Malowitz's eyes through wire-rimmed glasses were base metal, but his expression was charitable. His three-piece suit, gray pinstripe, looked Hart Schaffner & Marx. Or did the partner in estate law have a bespoke clothier? His broad silk tie was gold with cobalt pastilles like Christmas ornaments, an expression both Jewish and Christian. Leaving Sammy A's, I realized I should have come up with a tie, even one as preppy as Corey's. At least I had worn a decent blue button-down, and my leather bomber jacket would more or less blend into the wing chair. Like Sammy, Sydney was Corey's connection, a classmate of his father-in-law at Brandeis.

Corey described the loan against my assets. That I was the silent "money" partner struck me as absurd, but no more than the entire path I had set myself on. As Malowitz took it in, he extracted a cigar from a cylindrical, leather-bound humidor.

"You should be fine," he said. "Rates are high but reasonable, historically speaking, and look to remain stable." A device the size of a pocket knife appeared from a drawer and he unfolded a gold-plated blade. "Of course, if any of us could call interest rates, we'd never go to the office again."

Corey laughed heartily, which I took as my cue to laugh. We were financial traders bonding in the ether above LaSalle. Malowitz leaned forward and trimmed the top of the cigar into an amber glass ashtray the size of a Frisbee.

"Let's take a look at this." He was referring to the subject of our meeting.

Corey turned over our copy of the lease and Sydney began to scan. We maintained silence as he turned the pages. He made a check on one with a stout ballpoint, Mount Blanc, no doubt.

"The term is two years," he said, looking up at us as though he had spotted a fly. "You want longer."

"Absolutely," Corey agreed. "Tie it up as long as possible."

"The subletting clause is standard."

I probably looked alarmed because Corey whispered a translation: "We could get out if we needed to, no penalty."

"They might kick it back if we ask for five," Malowitz continued, "but they'll go for three. I'm crossing it out now. You're going over there next? I'll call and give them a heads-up."

He asked if Midway Management had given us a card, which I produced. He punched the number and swiveled in his leather chair to face the gray expanse.

"Sydney Malowitz, of Danzig, Malowitz and Paine. I'm representing . . . Corey McGowan and Mitch Lanier regarding the lease on your Broadway property." He declared the strikeout, did not ask. We were modifying the term. Period. It was over in a minute.

"If there's any problem," he said, adding his card to the marked-up lease, "call me."

We could think of no more to ask. We thanked Sydney then stood and shook hands. He would mail the invoice to the café. I sensed he was eager to light his cigar.

"Isn't he great?" Corey enthused in the elevator. I understood I should be uplifted, but I only felt my insides drifting up until we reached the lobby.

By the time we made it back to the North Side—the twenty-nine hundred block of Broadway just north of Diversey—it was close to four and the mid-February sun was low. Only one other location had been in the running, an established pizza, ribs, and chicken spot on Cornelia next to a corner pub with an Old Style sign. The vibe on Broadway was much closer to Gonzo's on Wells, where I was still stringing my job along until we took possession. We were scheduled to meet the building manager at the top of the hour. Corey parked around the corner on Oakdale.

In the middle of the block on the east side of Broadway, we stopped and peered in through the front window of the narrow but deep store we had inspected only once. Even in the dark, the black end of the grand oven was visible against the right wall. The wind off the lake wrapping around both corners of the block had us turning up our coat collars.

"You gentlemen remember the premises, and a super little place it is. Welcome to your new home, twenty-nine thirteen Broadway." Manny, our original showing agent, unlocked and flipped on the lights. It matched my memory reasonably—about sixty feet deep, a counter in the front across from the oven, narrow but with mirrors on opposite walls to give the illusion of more width. The three faux Greek chandeliers were clear candidates for replacement. The previous tenant had taken his gyro cone but left eight wooden booths in the dining room, four on each wall, honey-colored and substantial.

"Nice, right?" Manny added and pushed the door closed behind us. A bell mounted on the inside made a quaint ding.

"Our attorney made a mod—"

"Yeah yeah, I talked to him. You're in, that's the thing. May you have many more years." Manny was quick, with rodent-like movements that triggered a fleeting thought about mice in the basement.

We slid into the first booth to execute the paperwork. I initialed the pages and signed with Corey at the bottom of the lease, but my other signature brought everything into focus, on the deposit check that it was my solemn duty to make out to Midway Management. A rush of power squared my shoulders. I was sitting taller. We were bona fide high-rollers, clients of Malowitz. Rush of power, followed by dread. Capitalists we were, on the teeter-totter of power and doom.

Manny put two keys on the table, folded the check into his pocket, shook our hands, two quick shakes, and weaseled his way out the door.

"Well, all right," Corey declared. We gazed around at the premises where we had cast our lots together, our stucco-walled tunnel not unlike a cave. I thought of the Beatles in Hamburg. He ducked under the table across from us and pinched something off the floor.

"Ha! Seed money. American buffalo." He held up the nickel, grinning as though he had discovered a doubloon. Our bell dinged and his expression flattened.

A derelict stood unsteadily in the entryway beside the counter, furtive eyes, ragged Viking beard, ratty cloth coat to his ankles.

"No," Corey said, "we're not open. Sorry." He took a couple of steps toward the visitor who immediately backed out sheepishly, pulling the door behind him. Instead of closing, the door inched its way open, then swung back against the wall.

I went to the front, pushed the door halfway and watched it swing back. "Bad closer," I said.

"Evil," Corey confirmed. "We call Manny in the morning. I'll see if there's anything else." He headed for the bathroom in the rear.

I pushed it closed. Ding. I expected the derelict to move along, but instead he was planted in the middle of the sidewalk, staring back at me like a Bolshevik at the czar's palace. Wind lifted his coat collar. His look, bewildered, accusatory, seemed to be saying, "What have you done?"

A salient question, the one I was avoiding. Was mine a case of right intuition or temporary insanity? The guy in front of me might have had a right intuition once. I stared back just as dumbly, ruefully raised my hand. I sent him the blessing of Saint Sammy.

Pax vobiscum.

Chapter 6

JOHN Wray's apartment on Arlington was technically a studio, but a good-sized one, and the bay windows on the second floor gave it an expansive view over the street. It was an ideal practice space. A chessboard was set on a table in the corner, and a forlorn-looking spider plant clung to life on the window ledge. Furnishings were as spare as mine in the Cavern. None of us had much unrelated to our passions.

We were in our traditional positions: John on the side of his bed in front of the windows and I opposite on a folding chair. Viewed one way, it was an admission of failure on a Friday night in a city of eligible women, even in February with sloppy rain. We were social disasters. In another way, the music was improving, and that was our highest goal.

I knew the timing would be critical, the way John could pick up on hints of changes in a jam—he tuned instinctively to moods, anticipating, staying ahead. It let him play as he did, which was more than occasionally breath-stopping. He could be a reed in the wind. To him, it was all about timing and flow. The vibe was everything.

These were the reasons I had waited through the first set. Some nights outshone others, and maybe owing to the inclemency, a feeling that we could have been playing in a remote cabin on the borderline, this had been among the better ones. When the last chord and last note of the last song in the set rang out and faded, we burst into laughter like fools. The spasm erupted whenever we had nailed a practice.

I waited until the levity died down and we had accepted our greatness. Then I waited through the first swigs of Leinenkugel's until we had recharged. I didn't wait long enough.

A little at a time, starting with meeting Corey, I broke the news of the venture. It was only a job, I explained, like his at Kinko Copy. I had a partner, we would split the time. It would be manageable. I was also pep-talking myself.

John regarded me intently through his wireframes as I laid it all out. When I was finished he took a swig, hung his head, and shook it once. Since the end of the set, the Gibson had been resting against the bed. He retrieved it and picked his way into a soft blues, bending a few notes like punctuation. It was his way of talking to himself, mulling it over. I laid one chord in the background, then another. He broke it off.

"Makes no sense," he said into the silence, shaking his head, no longer looking me in the eye. He put his glasses on the table. "You can't serve two masters."

I didn't expect him to be excited about it, regardless of timing. I thought I was ready, but what I was feeling surprised me, a ripple like panic. There was a chill in the way he said it.

I had met John a week after my move to Chicago, and when we began to jam, which was no doubt the next day, we clicked from the start. High in his pantheon of guitar gods was Mike Bloomfield, another kid from Chicago who attended John's own New Trier High for a couple of years. Also Clapton, back to Yardbirds days. And the acoustic spaceman, John Fahey. Wray's mix of styles blended with my folk and country influences, and we were testing common ground with Buckley, Hardin, and others who were pushing acoustic into improv. We told ourselves we had an original sound, knowing that the many called were doing the same.

He had graduated from Kenyon in the spring, and so we shared that too. As holders of new degrees, freed at last, we were hot to break out and leave garden city suburbs behind. We were cracking the city at the same time, dateless on weekends, bucking each other up. Coinciding were my split and descent into dark days, suddenly alone in city and world, untethered. Music was my lifeline. It meant survival, and John Wray was key to it.

"Not at all. It'll be a haul at first, no doubt, but we've discussed it. I get any gig nights off. And we'll work out practice times, I'm sure."

"You're dreaming, man. A restaurant is a life sentence—"

"No way. My partner's done a whole work-up—"

"Has he run one?"

"He's been around, knows a lot—he has financial experience, believe me."

"But not a restaurant."

"We've both seen it at Gonzo, the whole operation. It's not magic. The two dudes who run it aren't geniuses. And they're almost all delivery. They don't have anything like the foot traffic we'll have."

"But not a restaurant."

"No, did I say that? Look, we'll pay our dues at first, yes, but a very realistic projection shows us being able to work our way out in a year, turn it over to managers."

"Realistic projection. Do you like hear yourself?"

"It's a plan, all right? As in view of the future, not based on nothing." He was observing remotely. "When we work our way out, turn it over to employees, that's when the huge plus for the music kicks in. My time will be wide open. The store will be a cash machine. And we'll be able to stand up a studio. Think about it—we could do it at the Cavern, make our own demos. It would be a huge plus for clubs, radio stations. And an agent. It's about the music, that's all it is—much more freedom for me, much stronger position for us long-term."

John's eyes tilted from me to the floor. He studied it like a chessboard and he was facing Capablanca. Then he took his glasses from the side table, picked up the Gibson, and sighted down the neck, as though he had sensed warpage. Put it down. He retrieved the beer, took a swig, and stood up.

"You've seen my parent's place," he said. Indeed I had, an upscale rambler, pristinely landscaped, in the near-north suburb of Winnetka, coveted schools, country club. "They want me to apply to grad school. This is my year off in their minds. I don't have like forever to make this work."

He padded in socks to the spider plant by the window and gave it the rest of the beer.

"I don't either," I said. "I want to keep this going as much as you do." He studied me. "I think we've got something here. I know it."

John crumpled the can thoughtfully.

"We have the Tin Cup in two weeks," I said, which we both knew anyway. "They love us there."

"They do," he said and grinned. "Okay, Mogul. Let's see how it goes. I'm going to crash. Got those workin' man blues."

"Drink a little beer in the evenin'," I intoned as I snapped the Martin into its case.

"Cry a little bit of these working man blues," we both crooned, butchering the end of Merle's classic.

I pulled John's back door. Descending the stairs I had my first transcendent experience: identifying with a spider plant. Still hanging in. Still in the game.

Chapter 7

COREY took the short step backwards onto the raised floor behind the counter. The six inches of elevation would keep us above the eye level of walk-in customers, which was a fortuitous feature unless you were moving a floor-model commercial dough mixer. He slid one foot backwards then the other. He had the U-shaped steel base, and I had the heavier motor end. Delivery from Giant Restaurant Supply on Western would have been twenty bucks. Fortunately, Corey's father-in-law, the source of Malowitz, lent us a van, and we had made it this far. The base had to be in position first.

"That's good," I said before he pinned himself between the butcher block pizza table and the cooler. "Let's walk it back."

He set the base down and we rocked it side-to-side backwards.

"Fuck!" A couple of rocks from the wall, a vinyl floor tile tore loose, pinned under one end of the U. That meant tile adhesive, which we didn't have, and no way to match the ancient tile. We tilted the steel monster with care and Corey fished out the vinyl square, still in one piece.

"You have a trowel?" I said, hoping for one less one-use expense. He was staring at the back of the square with amber streaks of ossified glue. The phone rang. He was closer.

When he heard the voice he brightened. He assured the caller that this was a good time, we would be around.

"Sammy says Buddy made it from Miami with the machine," he reported. "He's at the restaurant now, will be over in fifteen."

I swept the empty patch of floor at the opposite end of the table where the soft serve ice cream machine would go. This gizmo would be three hundred cash, which would be a relief. I was tired of writing checks from the business checkbook, three to a sheet. For our outlay, how had our state improved? A cheese block grinder, industrial strength. Three glass globes for the ceiling lights, replacing the Greek stalactites. A two-pot Bunn coffee machine. Two dozen unbreakable Victor coffee mugs. Tongs, pizza paddles, silverware, pans, mixed utensils. Dish detergent, bleach, and floor soap. A push vacuum. Plastic bins and pots. Napkin holders. Cases of pop, Pepsi brand, so we could keep the one glass-door cooler, a loaner from Pepsi. A griddle for "walking crêpes," one of Corey's enthusiasms which I tried unsuccessfully to talk him out of, based on his memory of a hole-in-the-wall vendor in Paris. Menu boards, hand-painted to look warm and homey but which, we realized after hanging them, could only be changed by hand painting again, to raise prices, for example, if we survived long enough to try. And our prize acquisition: a manual chrome-plated cash register mounted on the glass-top black tile counter that ran the length of the entryway.

I could check those off the to-do list, but the list kept growing. How many pieces to go? I wasn't confident that we knew half of them. Supplies would be first, then inventory. I repaired to a table in the back where I was keeping the list on one of Corey's green sheets.

"What about the jukebox?" I asked.

"The one on Maxwell Street." He slid into the opposite booth. "The Wurlitzer." We agreed on that one, but it didn't make it easier to record the price in its column.

"They'll bargain," he added, picking up on my discomfort. We were hemorrhaging money and would be until we could get the door open. How long? I scanned down the list.

Paper: napkins, cups, salad bowls, pizza boxes. Canned sauce. Coffee. The perishable inventory, for which we already had salesmen calling with price lists but no decision—meats, produce, cheese, milk. When and if Buddy arrives, soft serve ice cream mix.

But there was a higher priority than all others. Before the hanging sign, which was required for visibility on the block, and the paper menus, which were the *sine qua non* of Chicago pizza, came the hardest part.

"Where are we with the name?" I said.

He groaned. I knew very well where we were. We had been around this block before. I kicked it off this time.

"Good Earth Café."

"Sounds like bread and vitamins. Magic Pie," he countered.

"Pizza in Wonderland."

"People's Pizza. Right?" Corey knew when he was close. I wrote it down.

"It's not just pizza, though."

"What's on the list from last time?" he asked.

"Only a couple." I read from the right side of the green sheet. "Broadway Café and New Town Natural."

"I'd take People's over those."

"Too *communista*, comrade. This is capitalist *Weltanschauung*."

"For capitalist morons," he clarified. "Shrink the brain to the size of an insect. Monosyllables only. Eat Good!"

It never took us long to degenerate.

"Outta Bite."

"Man Bites Dog."

"Bake It Easy."

"Sit and Fart."

The pinnacle of wit. I slapped the table top, blond maple, Varathaned, one of the eight we had taken possession of with no way to make use of any. Corey was in spasm, red in the face. My sides ached. Eventually we could breathe again.

Corey went to the cooler, pulled a Pepsi, and chugged, reducing our inventory by one. I remembered the repairs and appended to the list: door closer, floor tile adhesive.

"Do you have a trowel?" I tried again.

"What?"

"Trowel, as in floor adhesive. Here he is." I had been facing the front and saw the rig halt outside the door, a pickup towing a trailer with an aluminum-looking box the size of an ice cream machine. Flashers came on, blinking red in the front window.

"Buddy." Corey greeted him as we crossed the sidewalk. He was dropping the tailgate. As we made our intros, I tried to see Buddy as Sammy A's offspring. A wide load with a buzz cut and bull neck, he was more wrestler than welterweight, and lighter skinned than Sammy. His cap said "Hang Ten" in gold over a cartoon curl of a wave.

Behind him on the bed of the trailer, two boxes sat next to a freestanding metal frame with the Taylor logo. He hopped up and dragged the boxes back to us. We traded looks, each waiting for the other to say it first. Since I would be paying, the negotiation fell to me.

"We thought it would be ready to use . . . like, assembled."

"Oh no," he said, shaking his head, a Little Havana accent. Our ignorance appeared to make him sad. "We break them down like this to move. You would bust it up getting inside otherwise. Guaranteed." In one box I saw two cylindrical steel frames with helix blades—the mixers, I guessed. There were also a pair of steel cylinders, the barrels that held the mixers, two chrome heads with lifter handles, half a dozen chrome knobs, and plastic bags of bolts and nuts. In the other box under a coil of electric cord was an assortment of belts and wires, two hamburger-sized wheels with belt grooves, and an electric motor that must have been the reason for the plywood insert on the bottom of the box. What I did not see was a parts list or instructions.

"Assembly *facil*, a piece of cake." He rocked the aluminum casing and rotated it to show the back. "You mount the barrels here." He pointed to crossmembers toward the top. "And the motor here." The platform was halfway to the bottom. "*Facil*, very straightforward. Utterly." I wondered where he had copped the machine, and how many parts might be missing. He checked our reaction. His neck was noticeably wider than his head. "Hey señor, you don't feel comfortable, fine. This is doing you a favor." He started to rotate the frame back. No deal would mean time, money, grief.

"No," I said. "We're not saying . . . this is the thing. With two of us, it will take what, an hour at least. Maybe two."

"Okay, I'll knock twenty off," he said. "But that's like super favor. Will take you twenty minutes. I'll put it in place. Where it goes?"

In the front of the trailer he stood up an orange hand truck, which we lacked. It was a masterful move, capping a deal impossible to refuse.

Corey grabbed the closer box. I hefted the box with the motor, swearing to myself I would make it to the store over the patches of sidewalk ice. Buddy strapped the frame onto his hand truck and plowed through the snow on the curb and through the door. With all of us inside, Corey and I steadied the front, and he pulled it up the short step onto the platform and rolled it into place by the front window, the back exposed for assembly. As I paid up, I thought about letting him keep the twenty, but another glance at the boxes persuaded me otherwise. When he exited, he did pull the door, but it swung back open in seconds.

Corey went to close it, and I dragged the boxes of parts down the floor to the job site. The future lay at my feet: a tangle of junk in two jumbo moving boxes. What did any of this have to do with the music? I stood accused of serving two masters, neither of which was in a recognizable state. Did Elvis do anything like this? Costello, that is. Presley drove a truck. Tom Waits for sure. They were all nothings at one time, serving the lords of day jobs. So what if they loved us at the Tin Cup in Rogers Park? We needed to do more, a lot more. And the boxes of machine guts demanded more. The door dinged shut.

It could have been our bell, perky but dumb as a parrot, calling me to attention. Or the heaps of parts like absurdity colliding with despair that caused the words to converge, to present themselves like a flash card. Corey had joined me and was staring down into the boxes, rubbing his oversized forehead. I turned to him until he was looking me in the eye.

"New American Café," I said and nodded.

Behind his glasses, surprise morphed into recognition, a satori moment.

"New American Café." He repeated the name with reverence, just above a whisper.

Chapter 8

THE Tin Cup was the only room John Wray and I played that did the white light intro, and the only one in my humble career, back to Tar Pit Coffeehouse days. Tin Cup weekend crowds maxed at around thirty a night, but the owners saw their club as the Earl or the Cellar Door. Truth be told, they weren't even the No Exit. But we had no objection.

We took our stools center stage, in the dark. The absence of curtains probably diluted the impact. We could see the pale faces at the tables in the candlelight, and they could watch ghostly us, setting up our second guitars in their stands, and capos and picks on the stool between us.

Perched next to John in the dark, I wanted nothing more than to go to sleep. The joint wasn't to blame. My half-comatose condition was not the result of three tokes in John's dad's car before lugging in our instruments. One joint of moderate dimensions had been shared by the three of us. It was a surprise threesome. John had told me about Sasha, but meeting her in the flesh was wholly different, and a confirmation of worst case, staggeringly depressing. We had agreed Wray would pick me up on Fletcher. He may have mentioned that Sasha wanted to hear us play, but I didn't know I would meet her for the first time that night coming from his place.

John and Sasha Kravitz of Glencoe were new, less than two weeks, but already we were scheduling practices, no more dropping in unannounced. Like a bunny, he reported, wearing him out. Not the most original, but clear enough, and being in her presence sharpened the picture to vivid.

"So fine," he had summed her up, but his praise was inadequate: striking eyes, both dark and bright, glossy black hair, full ponytail, a showstopper smile, and legs that carried on, undeniably thoroughbred. Sasha was a junior at Northwestern. It wasn't jealousy I felt exactly, more like one more turn of the knife that the post-Melanie universe administered whenever the mood struck.

"Some nerves are good," she had said in the car. We were parked a block from the club, out of the streetlights. The joint was Wray's idea. The topic was best performing state of mind, from stage fright to high to nearly wiped. Sasha played piano, no doubt compulsory for a Glencoe daughter, the highest solution to the "learn an instrument" requirement.

"Which ones?" I asked, buzzed, hoping to trigger her smile. She passed the joint to me, fresh from her lips, pianist's fingers.

I could see her clearly at the front-row table, high-contrast features, black and light in the dark and candlelight. We could start the set in seconds. Eyes closed, I took a last breath.

The joint wasn't putting me under a few heartbeats from our first set. It was having to open the door of the café at the ungodly Sunday hour of eight for another of Corey's connections, Carl Varnadore. Carl knew refrigeration, and he had the tools to help assemble our boxes of Miami junk into a double-barreled Taylor soft-serve machine. Corey was sidelined at home until ten, so the duty of meeting Carl fell to me. In a little under three hours, roughly ten times

Buddy's estimate, we had the machine up and running, but it took us the rest of the day to charge and test it. By five, the Taylor was cold and we were cranking twists of strawberry into Styro cups. Leaving Corey to pay Varnadore and close up, I hauled home in time to shower and inhale a day-old gyro with Heineken before Wray arrived. If I toppled off my stool unconscious, my lead player would not know the real reason. Two masters, he had said, and he was not going to be right.

"Ladies and gentlemen." The voice in the dark meant showtime. "Please welcome to the Tin Cup . . . Duello."

The ritual of white light hit us, a fleck of the big time. Automatic applause.

Wray began his intro: a triplet repeated, three spaced notes, a cat walking a ledge. The spoken part was mine.

The nerveless men
are abiding like sentries
through nights of near ice
and withering days,
heads full of desert wind
that whirs without ceasing
for whom time has no meaning
whom no promise binds.

Intense? Yes, but our name was Duello, the call of no quarter. To give them what they had not imagined, that was our mission. You're like Patti Smith, they said. You're like the Moody Blues. What we were like was Duello.

Wray's lead-in trailed to silence. My first chords from the twelve-string boomed in the sound system, clear and full. John's lead joined me and we were into it.

No bridge off the island, men here let it fall

I was wide awake now, adrenaline junkie.

Sea birds on the pilings till they hear the ocean call

My eyes had adjusted enough to make out Sasha in candlelight, her expression between surprise and delight. It was the desired effect. I couldn't see the others clearly, but Sasha's look was pure inspiration.

I took small liberties, leaned into the lyrics, and Wray responded. Sometimes songs or entire sets happened like that. Call it jazz or jam or mojo, from the smallest riff, or from some glint of reaction in front of us, the here and there collapse together. The magic was working and it was well and good, but by the end of the first song I was lightheaded.

Wray flowed into his transition. It was the Duello way in set one, our signature set—no breaks between the pieces, movements of a piece, spoken, vocal, instrumental. Gravitas early, good-timey later.

I was seeing Corey in the café with the first perfect twist of strawberry soft-serve curled in the cup, an artful twirl on top. His belly laugh of victory, his shiny pate under the track lights.

Refocus. Tune two would be "Highway Heroes." Wray was over halfway through his interlude. No net, it was clear now. I had driven my last for Gonzo. No going back, only forward into the café. When I told the partners about our venture, Joe was characteristically mum as a mobster, but Ozzie wished us luck.

John's last chord fanned out and faded. My cue.

High people on the road tonight

No way. Wrong. What was it? We traded looks.

Summer burning, turning the wheel

Wrong key. Should be A, not G. I capo the second fret during Wray's interlude. Always. Except this time. Keep going.

John curled over the Gibson, peering into the fretboard. He could have been looking for a place to hide. He tried a few notes then started transposing on the fly. In another bar, his lead was back, faking it, like a lifeline I could grab and hold on to until the end. I wound up growling the lyrics a full step lower, but overall, it felt like a salvage.

Wray took the next break. How did I do that? Rhetorical question, obvious answer. My butt had been on the stool, but my brain had been on Broadway. The sad undeniability of it haunted the rest of the set. I needed to focus, stay on task, full automaton.

I switched to the six-string for one number, then back to the twelve for the closer, "Peace on the Sea." I was over-compensating, singing too loud and pushing too hard. Somewhere in the refrain, trying to flog the rhythm, I felt the pick break. It snaggled in half like a fingernail, leaving just enough to fake it. Grab the spare on the stool between us? No, keep going. We staggered through to the end.

Our last notes boomed heroically in the sound system, decayed, and vanished. Silence. Seconds without end. I had blown it and they knew it. I was naked in a dream.

Then applause, a portion of it spirited. One hoot, and I convinced myself it wasn't Sasha.

We thanked them, and thanked again, and John per-formed the duty that fell to us as the warm-up act, an-nouncing that the headliner, Mike Dunbar, would be on shortly.

We retreated in the direction we had come. I headed for the crescent of shadow on the floor where the spotlight ended. There was one step down in the rear corner of the stage.

"Great! You were so great, really." Sasha was there to greet us, beaming. If I detected forced enthusiasm, it was only a trace. She hugged John first and then me. A scent like evergreens.

"Did you break your pick?" she said.

We caught Mike Dunbar's set from Sasha's table in the front. With the two of them perched like lovebirds in candlelight, I was left to ignore them and try to deny my envy of Mike, how he worked the room and how the room responded. Yes, he was a superior guitarist with licks I wouldn't attempt, but I told myself the lyrics of his own songs were trite or derivative, sometimes both. Small solace.

I would have traded my half of our pay for one cold beer, but since the Tin Cup served no booze, I had to settle for a hot cider on the house. That started me wondering about a liquor license for the café, what it would mean on Broadway on weekend nights in the summer. Maybe more than we were ready for. Or maybe a question for Sammy A.

"Here's one y'all know," Dunbar confirmed. "By my buddy Steve Goodman."

I could contain my enthusiasm. Covering "City of New Orleans" in front of a hometown crowd was shameless pandering, but it brought home fundamentals: Lighten up. Do what's been done before, just change it a little bit. When in doubt, spin off.

Sasha was singing along like a lovely North Side pianist who knew a little folk. The hootenanny ended in a burst of applause, and Wray and I looked at each other. He leaned over.

"I'm thinking set three instead?"

He meant our good-time bunch of singles, over half covers, instead of our "set two" material, which was more like set one, a medley too demanding, Duelloesque.

"Agreed."

And so, after Dunbar's set and a break of taped background, which included none other than Steve Goodman doing his signature original, we launched into our last set. We kept it conservative and marched through incident-free. I finished our version of "Memphis" on fumes. Before Dunbar's last set, John collected our pay.

"Nolan asked if we had auditioned at the No Exit," he said, handing over my barely countable half.

"That's good, right?" I said.

"I guess."

"Anything else?"

"'Thanks, good work.' That was about it."

'We'll be in touch' was not part of the report. After our third gig at the Tin Cup, maybe Nolan's question was inviting us to move on. No way to tell yet but yes, we did need to audition at the No Exit, and at least a dozen other rooms. But not tonight.

We made our escape before Mike's finale, and Sasha was all smiles and positivity. As we headed for the car, the night air was wake-up cold and still.

I had been preparing for what was coming and knew what I was going to say. It wasn't my preferred option, but I had had enough of being a third wheel. Third wheel on fire, this wheel shall explode. The kids were dying to be alone, no witnesses.

"We need to pop up north to take Sash home," John said when she was in his dad's Winnetka Buick and he was loading his cases into the trunk. "It shouldn't take long."

"You go. It's a decent night, I'm going to El back."

"No way. It's twenty minutes round-trip, max."

"I want to get some air and crash. The Morse stop is what, maybe two blocks."

"We can drop you."

"No problem. You just take the six-string." I added my case on top of the Mossman. "Next practice at your place." I would get the guitar then, although the prospect of playing any more ever was supremely enervating.

"Okay Mogul, good gig."

Sasha cracked her window as I passed and congratulated me again on our night. I thanked her for coming and blew her an exaggerated kiss which she returned in kind. The window rose, sealing her inside with her fingerpicking beau, who would soon be kissing her for real. Ah yes, young love. Don't think twice. Don't think, period. I hoofed it toward the Morse Avenue station, and soon I could see the white lights on the platform.

I rolled my token down and hoisted the Martin case over the turnstile. At the top of the stairs I saw only four waiting—two couples, naturally. They stood tucked together, nested. The heart of Sunday night on the El. I took up a position behind a column and turned my coat collar up to wait. I was starting to replay the set of the missing capo and the broken pick when I heard the train. *Gonna ride a blue train. Gonna ride a blue train.*

Avoiding the couples, I boarded a car that looked nearly empty. The heat was a reminder of basic needs, survival in Chicago. Soon muscles began to unclench, and feeling started to return to the fingers. With nothing else to focus on and a need to remain conscious, I found myself checking the woman across the aisle a few seats away. In a plain cloth coat and practical shoes, she rested her hand on a small purse in her lap. She was twenty-something and attractive, but her arresting feature was her presence, an elegance in her expression, chin high as though sitting for a portrait instead of watching her own thoughts in the opposite window of the car. A waitress, or a bartender, maybe on her way home to Pilsen. Her other hand was in her coat pocket—I couldn't see a ring.

She glanced at me, caught me off guard. I looked away. Maybe she was checking the guitar case that rode between my knees. It could be my entrée, conversation starter. Which, I was beat enough to understand, would go nowhere. Maybe on another night when I encounter her *par hasard* in the Chicagoland game of chance. I ventured another glance. Her gaze was back on the window, but she must have sensed me watching and looked away toward the end of the aisle.

I closed my eyes and rocked with the car, following her home, down the hall of her first floor flat, into the bedroom. Unmade bed, her jewelry and lamp, brocade shade from a fiesta day bazaar, her hairbrush on the dresser. In the closet, her clothes only. Hanging her coat, turning into my arms. Her steady look, eyes on mine, nothing coy. The feel of her back, the hook under her hair, and the zipper. And for the first time in months, desire not mixed with the hollow-heart numbness of loss.

The train screeching, leaning into a curve. Eyes open only enough to orient. Then trying to sink back to the bedroom in Pilsen. The train returning to rock and rattle, the warmth of the car. Replaying with no capo, singing in G, faking it. Milky faces in the floating room.

It must have been Friday. Overpaying Swanson, the meat and dairy supplier on Argyle by half, for three gallons of soft-serve mix. Varnadore tensioning the belt in the back of the Taylor.

The warm, rocking car heading for Pilsen. Rocking with Dulcinea in her floating bed. *Rockin', reelin', rollin' ride.* Going under.

A screech, merciless, and a lurching halt. Across from me her seat was empty. Switched cars? People were waiting on the platform, and I caught only a corner of the white sign. The door slid open and they crowded on, spirited, joking. I stood and scrambled to read the letters: Diversey. The first time I had missed my stop. Bulling straight ahead through them would have been fastest, but because of the case, I had to work my way around. The doors were rattling shut as I bolted out into the bitter air. Diversey to Southport—too far to walk on a night at the end of February.

I lugged the case down the steel steps and up to the opposite platform. My jellied knees were climbing mountains, my penance for stupidity. At first I joined three waiting, then a couple, then half a dozen more. We cowered, elevated victims, our backs to the Hawk blowing off the lake, the night no longer still but pedantic, impressing on us that no Chicago winter night, regardless of first impression, was our element. The train, belaboring the point, was long in coming. The wind penetrated my jeans and I tried to stay centered in the shelter of the upright Martin case. At last the white light was coming down the track.

Taking no chances, I stood for the two stops to Belmont. On street level the Hawk died down, making the long blocks to the apartment tolerable. I plodded along, staying aware of my surroundings with an instrument case on streets of anonymous buildings and mostly dark windows. Except for an occasional car, Fletcher was quiet. I welcomed the patches of old and shoveled snow. Crunching through them was the sound of progress. Soon I picked out the traffic light at Southport, and finally, the streetlights on my block.

I had been switching hands, the handle of the case in one, the other in my jacket pocket, but even through gloves my fingers were numb. The Martin had put on a slug of weight over the long evening. Half a dozen strides from my walkway, I envisioned the goal line. In the end zone were a warm shower and my unmade bed.

"Mitch."

Hearing my name in the voice of a woman, I fantasized for a ghost of a second that it was Sasha's, or Dulcinea's. Then it chilled like the slap of a summons.

She was out of a car parked at the curb, closing the door, heading my way with a shiver. When I saw her face trembling with trouble yet to be named, I appreciated fully for the first time the persistence of Job, the acceptance of Shantideva, the steady temper of the martyrs.

"Janis," I said, and hugged her with the arm that had been free.

Chapter 9

"GOD, I'm sorry. I totally surprised you, didn't I?"

I heard her, but I was focused on the locks. With gloves off and paralyzed fingers, I had opened the deadbolt and was trying to center the key in the doorknob.

"I talked to John this afternoon," she continued. "I thought he would tell you."

Finally we were in my front hall, in the embrace of radiator heat, and I could set the case down. I recalled John at the table, enthralled with Sasha.

"No," I said, "but not a surprise. That he didn't tell me, that is. Can I get you something? I've got Heineken's but that's not warm. Some jug wine, and Muscatel—don't blame me, it was a gift." The bottle came from Gonzo, Ozzie giving away wines at the end of a big night. His brother had a liquor store in Tinley Park. Instead of the bright overhead light in the kitchen, I clicked on the short table lamp. The yellow bulb threw enough light to see.

"Muscatel is fine. Thanks."

"What would he have told me?" I took two glasses and we headed for my sofa, a mattress and box spring with Indian spread and pillows.

"I was just like hoping I could . . ." Her face was heavy and I saw for the first time she was close to tears. "I needed

to get out of my parents' place. John said you were playing
tonight—that's how I knew you'd be here later—"

"How long have you—"

"Not long, way less than an hour, I wanted to ask—and
you can totally say no—"

The tears she had been battling took over. I wrapped an
arm around her and was surprised by how small she felt, as
though she had been reduced by humiliation over having to
ask a favor.

"You need a place to crash?" The situation was both
obvious and unlikely. I was surprised she had remembered
where I lived. As far as I knew, she had been to the
apartment only once before, when John helped me move in.
She and a friend were grabbing a ride north with him and
carried in a few boxes.

"Just for tonight. I could sleep anywhere, on a sofa . . ."

"Sure, sure," I said, wondering why she had chosen me
out of her well-seeded circle. "What's going on?"

I released her, buzzed from the warm contact, and
focused on pouring the two glasses. Sniffling, she took off
her long coat.

In my last memory of Janis, on the ethereal third floor,
she was attired as the kitsch hostess in a loose velveteen
shift, a la Renaissance fair costume shop. Now under the
coat she was wearing a close-fitting zipper dress, dark
denim, with a ring pull at mid-sternum. It stopped an
encouraging distance above her boots. We sat on my
mattress sofa and tapped our glasses and braved the taste
of the wine for the alcohol and the warmth.

"I had to get out of the house," she repeated. "Except for
my first two years at Loyola, I've been living there my whole
life, even since graduating. I'm sick of it. It's about
expectations, really." She took another healthy drink and I
refilled her glass.

"Your parents?" I imagined typical ones, marriage,
maybe career, or both.

"No, they're all right. I mean my own. You know what I do? Of course no way would you." Her voice was stronger, and she seemed more animated, looser. "I tutor two elementary school kids in Niles in reading and math and we do a little art—two times a week, that's it. You, John, Melanie, the others—you all have real jobs or grad school. I'm doing shit. Nothing with my art. I'm nowhere."

That was it? I could tell her she was being too severe, but I was enjoying her confession to me. It was flattering and more. I was aware she was leaning forward. Her hem was halfway up her thigh, and our knees were inches apart. I was trying to keep my eyes on hers. I emptied my glass.

"I have enough for a deposit on an apartment down here, out of the burbs. The Steppenwolf guys want a logo, so maybe that could be a start. I have old portfolio stuff from school. And I'll get a job, I don't care what for a while, it doesn't have to be design."

"This is breakout time, then. I totally get it, but why did you think of me? You have—"

"I know, 'friends of Janis'. They all either live with somebody or they see me as who I've been. You know?"

She was conjuring High Point, the knothole view from my hometown, the many small towns.

"Or maybe it's just me stressing about what they would think, how they expect me to be." A shadow crossed her face in what light there was. "And . . . I have to say, you made an impression." Her dark hair fell straight, veiling one eye. She focused, checking my reaction, her face inches from mine.

First was the warm scent of patchouli and the bouquet of cheap wine from Ozzie's brother on her breath, and then her lips. We started tentatively, but soon we could have been spliced into a scene in my dreams. We were struggling with each other, in a race, breathing hard. I cupped the swells at the top of her dress that had been praying on my mind since her coat came off. Her hand was on my thigh and then all the way up and I slipped one hand under her hem. I licked her lips and laughed and she responded in kind, and whatever reticence was left between us fell away.

I gave a quick tug at the zipper ring on her chest and she popped up to give me clear access. I unzipped her in one pull and worked the denim dress off her shoulders. She shrugged out of it and stood before me, a teeny-bopper fantasy in a short white slip and boots.

Exaggerating impatience, she yanked my shirt and undershirt out of my pants and tugged my belt open. We finished pulling off our own clothes and admired each other by touch and sight, standing naked in the low yellow light. Her body, a petite Primavera, was wondrously new to me, not a foldout but a female animal, a real festival of delights.

We clenched together like crazed dance partners. I eased her onto the Indian spread, and we were possessed, tangled up and struggling, tussling cats. I was exhausted from the day and night, nearly hallucinating, primed by long-legged Sasha and Dulcinea, the siren of Pilsen.

Time protracted then collapsed. She clutched me from behind, holding me in. The raw eloquence of it annihilated control. I blew across borders, crossing deserts of anguish and desire at light speed, crashing into Janis of the floating house. The joyous wreck of me lay in pieces, sweating and grateful, in my whirling room.

When we could stand, we picked our way through the patches of clothes to my bedroom. I brought the Muscatel and we rehydrated. I was a beggar no longer. Did I owe it all to Ozzie's brother? I was willing to credit him. But it was Janis who had stepped in and punched a chunk of universe, and my bad luck had crumbled. As we stood naked as Adam and Eve toasting life in my dark garden, she offered again to sleep on the mattress couch, but what could have been sane half an hour earlier had become absurd.

We settled onto my broader bed. The radiator thunked twice and went back to sleep. I was exhausted to a point of wonder. Nevertheless, sharing a mattress with less than a foot between us soon led to an inexorable repeat. At some point I shut down and slept the sleep of the dead.

John and Sasha, Janis and I had brought our suitcases. Inside were the costumes we would change into to perform, Indian tunics and saris. Jasmine incense sweetened the air. We had left our bags in the tiny closet backstage. I pulled them all out, confirming my fear. Mine was missing. If it wasn't there, I must have left it on the El. I would never retrieve it in time.

There was an explosion.

My eyes popped open, heart firing. A milky rectangle hung on the wall, a frame of light around the blinds.

Another blast, from the living room. It was the hotline.

Janis propped up looking groggy, hair straight on her breast, a Gauguin princess.

"Jesus fuck!" I cursed myself for failing to unplug it, which I routinely did when I had a need for privacy. The red phone, my hotline, which seemed amusing at one time, sat under the yellow bulb, still burning. Not enough blood in the head. The little red demon went off again. I bent over, hand on one knee, and answered.

"Hey, it's Corey."

"Are you in the store?"

"Yeah. We've got a problem with Queen." Monday was assembling itself, emerging from the fog. Corey was in to meet an inspector. "Sammy says he'll talk with us. How fast can you make it to the diner?"

"Give me forty minutes." I heard an affirmative grunt and a hang-up.

The yellow bulb lingered like bourbon and cigarette smoke, anything but normal for a Monday morning. I killed the lamp. Our clothes littered the floor and I collected mine, including my watch, which I had no memory of taking off. Nine-twenty.

"Sorry about that," I told Janis. "Some highly critical emergency, my partner thinks, anyway."

"Can I make breakfast, or coffee?" Somehow she looked bright-eyed and eager to please, unconscious of her Tahitian persona.

"Just for yourself. I have to meet him at a restaurant—I'll get something there. Why don't you hang here as long as you want. I'll be back probably late afternoon."

A ten-minute shower was followed by a ten-minute shave between toothpaste specks on the mirror. With Janis around I would have to clean up my act. Later. As I cranked the cold Mustang, I tried to shake the song that had been cycling in my head since the call, the merciless mantra by that other Elvis: "Welcome to the Working Week."

Chapter 10

"IT'S the ventilation inspector," Corey told Sammy A. I was hearing the story for the first time too. "This huge dude."

"Queenie!" Sammy said before Corey passed him the card.

"*Mister* Queen to us. Pompous meathead."

"Utterly." Sammy grinned. "*Mister* Queen, the main man." He tilted forward in the booth. "What did he tell you?"

"He said we can't open. He started out checking the hood over the oven. He had to turn sideways to get behind the counter." Sammy let out a wheeze, big-tooth smile. "Then he walks the length of the ductwork out the back of the building to the exhaust. Comes back in and says we've got twenty-two gauge aluminum and it's too light. I told him it was a restaurant before us, same oven, same hood. He rattles off some city code number, total *non sequitur*. He's saying we can't open the door until we replace the whole ventilation, hood to exhaust. It's insane," Corey summarized. "Can he do this? He said to call his beeper if we wanted to talk. I don't know if he meant today or what."

Sammy was grinning into the table, shaking his head.

"Oh, he'll be around. You boys been to college, right? You're college boys. Well, this is Chicago U. Here's what you do."

Corey called Queen's beeper from the phone in the café then joined me at the car.

"He says he'll meet you there at twelve-thirty. Thanks for taking this one."

"I'll call you," I said. I had an hour and a half.

The honor defaulted to me because Corey was off at noon to care for Arlo, his two-year-old, while Beth was teaching her twice-a-week voice class at a girl's school in Schaumburg. Neither of us had to say any more about it; my meeting with Queen would be critical.

I made a stop at our LaSalle Bank on Belmont and arrived at the café early. It took me ten minutes to open the back door, rehearse, and rehearse again. I had been running through versions of my lines since I left Sammy's, and fifteen more minutes of sitting behind the counter while my stomach knotted failed to improve on them. As twelve-thirty came and went, I realized I should have gotten Queen's card from Corey. I was ready to call him when the main man arrived. He didn't have to knock; his bulk blocked the light through the front door.

Queen resembled Orson Welles in a tent-sized khaki Sears jacket and a mud-colored fedora. I introduced myself as Corey's partner and he bumped his head once and waddled inside, giving off cigarette smoke from a closed car mixed with drugstore cologne. We faced off in the middle of the room. He maintained a commanding silence.

"It sounds like we have an issue with the hood," I said.

"You got a problem with all your ductwork, hood to tail pipe." Queen traced the length of the room with an imperious finger, underlining the scope of the offense.

"That's twenty-two gauge aluminum. You need twenty. City code."

Queen was doing what he was born to do, a fascist wielding the sway of empire. Saggy-faced, he was the fat loser in high school who had scrambled to the top of a scrapheap, trampling junior inspectors less motivated by stores of adolescent rage. He humphed a breath as though he had finished a tough climb and punctuated with a stare, dull-eyed, contemptuous.

"This was a gyros place for years, right? How did they—"

"Gyros isn't cooked on premises. Pizza is totally different. And code gets revised. When ownership changes, it's the responsibility of the new owner."

To do what, he didn't need to say. Be informed. Know and comply. Or do what he needed to do.

"Can you show me?" I started toward the back where the exhaust ductwork was exposed behind the building. I was meaning more, wanting Queen to pick up on it. He checked me for a moment then followed.

"That's twenty-two gauge?" We gazed up at the unpainted aluminum stack. I was adding a few beats, seconds I needed to get situated.

"Correct." Queen's head lolled in my direction. He was looking pained, constipated.

It was a moment so unlikely, so asynchronous, that it seemed to be tumbling in space, untethered, but it was within the compass of my life, and it had to be claimed. It mattered not that less than a year earlier I had occupied a seat in a classroom in Chapel Hill, clean-nosed and naïve, discussing Heidegger and Norman Brown. I was now in the Chicago crawlspace, bellying around with the reptiles.

"Look," I said, and I could hear the waver in my voice on the word I had been rehearsing in my head for an hour, and I was sure Queen could too, "can we talk about this?"

I had assumed the pragmatic stance, the posture demonstrated by Sammy A, hands in jeans pockets, right hip closer to the chief inspector of ventilation. From the right pocket I slipped my hand out far enough to expose the fold of bills under the thumb—a wrap of ten new twenties. I felt like KKK flashing their sign: three fingers like a K outside the pocket.

What if Sammy was wrong? What if times had changed? What was the penalty for bribing a city official?

Queen's eyes homed on the cash like radar. His head made a barely perceptible bump, the brim of his Fedora up and back half an inch. The bills were out of my pocket and into his hand, which ducked into the pocket of his X-large khaki jacket. He didn't count them to confirm Sammy's recommended sum. I could hear him, impresario, inquisitor, old pro: *You do a few, you can tell by touch.*

Who was I now? KKK passing backsheesh in a back room, and holding my breath for the verdict.

"You've got thirty-two seats in there," the big man said. "Anything over thirty requires twenty gauge. Take out one booth, you'll have twenty-eight seats. Good to go."

That was it. Over in seconds like a merciful shot of opiate, an exigency of doing business. Breath was returning, heart downshifting. I blubbered thanks to his back as he lumbered in through the door.

At the counter he extracted a pad of forms from his other pocket, scrawled his name across the bottom of one, and left a copy. I thought he was checking the hood again, but he was scanning our menu board.

"You going to have deep dish? You know Giordano's? Lou Malnati's in Lincolnwood? They're the best. You got to have deep dish, that's all. You add it, you'll do all right."

Then Queenie was gone, into the history of extortion, maybe knocking off early, back to Lincolnwood or Elk Grove Village. I sat at the end of the counter feeling dazed, staring into our copy of compliance. Queenie's capital letters were huge, consistent with heightened spirituality. H and Q, the H in Howard. The high priest of HVAC.

I called Corey at home and recounted the details of our bribe and the outcome, all as Sammy had predicted. I heard Arlo call his dad in the background.

"Eh, you did good," Corey grunted, imitating Queen and the legions of other inspectors, Chicago-bred, low-browed. I took it to heart, like the other rare pronouncements that stick for whatever reason to certain people and occasions. The associations were keen, fragments that resurfaced unsummoned and reconstituted the whole. I took it to heart because neither of us knew if I, the business rookie, could pull it off. I had survived my hazing, beaten up and peed on only figuratively.

What it meant first was that we could continue to receive deliveries, including the one I had to wait for and finally let in a few minutes before five. The driver unloaded two cases of pizza sauce cans, a box of coffee bags, and the last of the paper: napkins, cups, pizza boxes, salad bowls. I asked him to leave the invoice because my partner had the checkbook. I was emboldened in my role now, seasoned, full partner: volunteer nothing, respond only if forced to. I would see the supplier again in two days anyway, for the perishables.

The reality of that fact sank in over the drive home. The final order would arrive on Wednesday. On Thursday we would put on new red body aprons, unlock the door at noon, and await our fate behind the counter. We would have a day to work out the kinks before Friday and the weekend.

Peoples Republic of China conducts nuclear test at Lop Nor. U.S. conducts nuclear test in Nevada. The radio news switched to weather. High clouds and colder later in the week with a chance of flurries.

Had any two restaurateurs been less prepared to launch? Of course. Restaurants open every day, the easiest business to start. We had seen it up close, closer than many, from front row seats in delivery cars. We also had Sammy A in our corner.

I punched FM. "Lay Down Sally" lasted to Fletcher. It wasn't altogether unexpected, but I sank a little inside when I saw that Janis's car was gone. Over the day I had been thinking about the night before, but the thoughts weren't simple. A lot had happened fast, and the waters could get suddenly deep. Maybe she had felt it too and had beaten a retreat to Evanston. I envisioned a note on the floor in the front hall. An odd sense of relief came over me as I pulled into a parking space. I was back in the simple life of the solitary man with the rambling apartment to myself, back to double-edged freedom. It wasn't until I got out that I spotted her car on the opposite side of the street a little farther down the block. The reversal was a light jolt, but in a few moments I was rolling with it, open to all options.

"Hey there," I called, heading for the kitchen. "That smells . . . terrific."

Janis turned off the water in the sink and greeted me brightly in a Loyola sweatshirt and jeans. For a second I didn't know what to do with her. The aroma of domesticity, though mouthwatering, felt a bit unnerving. I gave her a squeeze, which triggered a pleasant rush, and a kiss on the cheek, and she kissed back.

"What are you making?"

"It's ziti. I hope it turns out okay. I've made it a couple of times, so I don't think it will be too bad, but I don't know if maybe your oven runs hot . . . I used some oregano and basil, I hope that's all right."

"Of course. How did you get the rest—"

"I made a run out to Nottoli on Harlem and Foster. It's this great old Italian grocery. I needed to go by the house anyway," she added. "Are you hungry?"

I wasn't but predicted I would be in an hour. In the shower, I ran through it again: she had gone home and come back. Was I glad about that? Overall, yes, but how one night was becoming two felt slippery. Well into baked ziti and salad and following a glass of jug wine, the pieces flew together on fast-forward. I asked if she had started the apartment hunt.

"I found some places in the *Reader*, like three or four. I have appointments to see two tomorrow. I have to think about a job too, though. I don't want to live too far away. You were lovely to let me crash here last night. Is there any way I could pay you—"

"No way, of course not."

"I mean . . . is there a way I could pay you to stay for a week or two? It would be so convenient to have a base of operations . . ."

My first micro-slice of a thought was wondering how I hadn't seen it coming. That was followed by the undeniable recognition of room in the Cavern—the second bedroom, dark but spacious, ample closet—and then micro-slices of the trade-offs—physical, emotional, musical, practical. The second was dragging itself out, and Janis was watching me like a child.

"Sure, you can stay here until—you can have a whole bedroom to yourself. There's a mattress in there already, and an old dresser I inherited when I moved in."

"God, that would be so perfect. Let me pay you."

"No, please. If you want to pick up some food now and then—"

"Of course, and I'll make the dinners. That will give you more time for your music, and the café when it opens." She had clearly given the arrangement some thought.

For the rest of the dinner I turned my decision, ill-considered as it was, over in mind, coming to the conclusion, however forgone, that it should work fine. No reason it shouldn't.

After dinner I gave her the tour of bedroom two. An old dome ceiling fixture dropped light the color of dust. The focus of the room was a vintage dresser with curved drawer faces and a mirror. A few wire hangers hung in the closet above boxes I hadn't unpacked, school papers and various artifacts from home. The mattress and box spring were covered in pale blue stripes like prison issue. Still, the room was a commodious old box, like all rooms in the Cavern, and Janis was happy as a kid on a camping trip. I lent her my spares for the bed and bath, which consisted of a sheet and pillow, a sleeping bag to use as a blanket, and a bath towel.

While I did dishes, she went outside to her car. I knew she must have been planning how and when to ask me, but seeing her return with her suitcase and head to the bedroom raised a question. The lady was a planner. Had she played me? If so, at this point maybe I was ready to be played, all twelve strings.

When I left the kitchen, I could hear her in the shower. Practicing was one option. Queenie said do deep dish. I crossed to last night's scene of the crime and took the hotline off the hook. If Corey needed to call me, there was tomorrow. Practicing was a question of vibe. It wasn't that I had to be alone, but I would wind up playing to an audience, and the idea of performing made me tired. Queenie was stashing his cash in a lock box in Berwyn.

The TV in my bedroom sat on one-by-sixes on cinder blocks. I pulled the On button. *Happy Days.* I rotated the dial three clicks to the last of the news.

"The rock festival known as Cal Jam II began today in Ontario, California. The original California Jam Festival took place in 1974 on the grounds of the same motor speedway." An aerial shot showed a tiny stage and a field of pinheads that spread out well beyond the speedway grounds over the desert. "Attendees have been arriving in the area for days, and today the crowd is estimated at two hundred fifty thousand."

The shot cut to a reporter on the ground shouting into his mike, battling the concert speakers. I guessed the act was Dave Mason, but no tune I recognized. "The headliners include Santana, Ted Nugent, and Aerosmith. This crowd is here to rock, and barring an earthquake, the music will not stop anytime soon."

I didn't listen to Ted Nugent. I barely knew who Aerosmith were. They were monster rock, I knew that; they filled stadia. As did the Bee Gees in the disco camp. And Donna Summer. Punk slashers were hacking back. A dumbing down had begun, like the music I knew was being drawn off, bled away. And Duello were playing to thirty in the Tin Cup.

The news was folding its tent. An ad for Arthur Treacher's came on and I punched it off.

Next practice would be at the Cavern, mid-week because I would be behind the counter all weekend, starting Thursday. Two more days before we opened the door. In my stomach butterflies scrambled, lifted off.

Janis was out of the shower, padding to her bedroom. I was staring into a gray-faced TV in an empty room. It came to me, for once in so long it barely seemed possible, that I didn't have to be alone.

"Hi," she said in a tiny voice when I appeared in her door. She was wearing only my bath towel, wrapped from her armpits to the top of her thighs. Her wet hair was combed long and straight, and a bit of moisture like dew glistened on her forehead. Ah, Gauguin.

I should be refocusing, leaving Janis to her new room in peace. Paul Gauguin, I recalled, late Impressionist, or post-Impressionist, contemporary and booster of van Gogh, desperado champion of creative freedom, was a domestic deserter. Anthony Quinn.

She dropped her head slightly, a coy look in her eyes. A come-hither smile.

"You're making an impression," I said, an in-joke we now shared. Behind her along the wall, a sheet was spread on an unchristened mattress.

I closed the distance between us. She smelled like fresh coconut as I undid the towel. Art history was useless.

Chapter 11

THE jukebox arrived on Tuesday. Sammy had told us to expect a huckster offering a free generic box in return for the quarters. His employer would be the Mafia. It could be problematic to refuse but only, he was quick to add, if we were bigger.

We wanted our own box because we had to pick the music. No metalhead schlock rock or disco—the memory of Joe's boombox was too fresh. The supplier on Maxwell Street had aisles of forty-fives culled from the used machines they took in for resale. Choosing the box was quick compared to picking the fifty records: "Revolution," "Born to Run," "Stop! In the Name of Love," Stevie's "Superstition," Glenn Miller's "In the Mood," "Pretty Woman," "That'll be the Day," and forty-some more.

Plugged in, the Wurlitzer transformed the front of the store with a retro color infusion. Roman columns, chromatic wonders of red, yellow, and blue, framed the front. A red and yellow arch glowed above the turntable and the carousel of discs. It was delivered loaded, and I played the first test. "Honky Tonk Women" rocked the empty café like a honky tonk garage.

The same delivery man who had brought the paper, Norm from Great Lakes Supply, arrived on Wednesday with the perishable inventory. I had steeled myself to write one more check, but Norm said that as newbies with no sales, we had a standard two-week grace period.

For Corey and me, the rest of the day was a shakedown run. We made a practice slice pie with Great Lakes ingredients instead of groceries from Jewel. The "walking crêpes" required superior skill. Batter had to be spread on a hot griddle by twirling a wooden crêpe rake, T-shaped. The goal was to spread evenly, but we poked holes and raked every thickness but even. After three or four test runs each, we were sufficiently mediocre. In our day of practice with the lights on, a few passersby stopped at the door and peered in around the Closed sign, which provided crumbs of encouragement. I left an hour early to swing by the bank, and Corey locked up at five. We agreed to meet at eleven and flip the sign in the door at noon.

At six-thirty my apartment buzzer buzzed. Since I knew Janis would be gone, I had dined alone on the last of the ziti. The expected guest had arrived on time.

"Looks messy out there," I said. John was toting a guitar case in each hand, and his hair and coat shoulders were wet. "Thanks for coming here." One case was my six-string, which I had promised to pick up at his place on Arlington. We had moved the practice night up from Friday because I would be in the café.

"Have you got a rag?"

First priority, we wiped down the cases. John had had no time to eat after Kinko's, so I told him to take whatever looked good. He settled for cheese and crackers with a Bass ale. We took our practice places in the dining room, in facing chairs beside the table, which was dark and stout and like Janis's dresser, more than the previous tenant had wanted to move. He munched and swigged while I tuned the Favilla.

"I called the No Exit," he said.

"Wow." It was unexpected because we hadn't discussed it. There was also more to it.

"Just to see what they want." He had assumed I didn't have the time, and wouldn't. "It wasn't the owner, some flunky. He was on automatic, like he got the question every day. They want a demo tape, or an agent, just to try out."

"Did you get the owner's name?"

"Flunky hung up. He could've been the bartender."

"Let me follow up. I'll do that."

"Uh-huh."

"Should be next week . . . Monday." After another round of cracker dinner and beer, Wray produced the Gibson and we tuned to each other. We were sadly out. I played a cornball Nashville intro and dropped into one of our warm-ups, Cash's "Home of the Blues." Wray came in boom-chicking, Luther Perkins style. By the time we hit the break, he was channeling Carl Perkins.

The front door was opening. John heard it a second before me and looked up. Janis had used her copy of the key.

"Hey hey," he said.

She was as wet as John had been, but she made a beeline for him and they hugged. I was next, and my hug came with a cheek-side kiss. She was glowing, happy to see us both. I could see John was guessing.

"Jan's crashing here for a while," I told him. "She's looking for her own place." I had considered telling him in advance but hadn't brought myself to do it. No friends at practice, ladies or other—we had the agreement from the start. Janis's third floor was an exception, more a gig than a practice. It was like "Home of the Blues," a tune we never played in public. It wasn't meant to be performed, by us. It was internal to practice. A Duello practice, our one-on-one, had to be free to screw up and redo, invent and scrap, and mumble out loud. Although I only pretended to understand when I first encountered it, I fundamentally appreciated the notion of Heisenberg's principle, that by observing things we change them. I was learning that the proof was in the practice.

"How's it going?" he said, sitting back from his guitar.

Janis's purse landed on the table and she took the chair beside mine. She had seen two apartments, a one-bedroom in the morning on the North Side too close to home, and had just finished the other, a studio in New Town in the same general neighborhood as the café. My mixed feelings resolved as she launched into a critique of the four-plus-one building with paper walls and the smell of insect spray in the apartment and two roach carcasses in the shower. John nodded along. When she started on the story of her job search, the lights went out in his eyes. He tilted the last drops from the bottle. Janis was rolling. I wasn't going to check my watch in front of her, but I knew we had about an hour to practice.

I strummed my way softly into a progression, wondering if she would take the hint. She did stop talking but sat back politely, expectantly, eyes wide, as though the movie was about to start. John, who had made the No Exit call and steamed over to my place after work in the middle of the week, lugging my guitar case in the rain, was not playing along.

"Hey," I said before I knew what the sentence would be, "we . . . have a couple of ideas we need to work out."

"We do?" Her expression flipped to surprise.

"No, I mean—"

"Oh, you and John. Sure, sorry—"

"No, that's fine." She looked off balance, still unsure. "So if you'd excuse—"

"Ack! Of course, don't let me stop you. Although I just did." Janis dropped into her hostess mode, bustling out the way she came in. "Carry-on, guys. Toodle-loo."

Seconds later Wray's guitar went on the table. He was on his feet too, leaving the room, and I was sitting suddenly, dumbly alone.

Nothing was simple. I knew John and Janis went back years, to high school at least. Had they ever? Any reason to address it? This was their turf, and as always, I was the outsider. I heard the refrigerator door and then the pop of a bottle cap.

He was swigging as he came back to the table. I owed more than another beer at that point. Given that he wasn't meeting my eye, I knew a discussion was not the way to go. John was in simmering mode.

Without a word he retrieved the Gibson and traded his bottle for the empty one. With the guitar face up across his knees and using the glass neck as a slide, he angled his way into a blues. After a few bars, I guessed it was Bloomfield-inspired, from the Butterfield Band days. It could be any of several. I sang what I knew of the lyrics to one.

I was born in Chicago, nineteen and forty-one

Whatever was unspoken about Janis was working out. After the blues I kept chording the obvious intro until Wray couldn't resist—our acoustic "Good Lovin'." I probably picked it because he had to sing backup on the chorus, which always lightened us up.

At the end, a one-person burst of applause came from the living room. I had assumed Janis was in a bedroom. I hadn't heard her navigating back to the space opposite ours, on the other side of the wall. It was easy to imagine her hovering, hanging on each note. John's expression rewound to a place before the Butterfield blues. He took a long swig, laid the Gibson to rest in its case, and snapped it shut.

"Workin' Man Blues," he said, shrugging into his coat.

"I'll follow up with the No Exit."

"Right," he said and headed for the door. In the hall he stopped as Janis reappeared, in a dashiki this time. He put on his Winnetka social smile. They clenched and exchanged pleasantries and he was out the door. He wasn't expecting me to follow.

"Hey," I said. On the walkway beside my building, he had gone halfway to the street. He turned. The rain had become cold mist that thickened the air. "That won't happen again. She's just staying a few days." He gave a skeptical-looking nod. "And your place next time."

"Good luck," he said, his glasses starting to mist over. He paced on to his car, and I wondered which he meant. With the No Exit? Janis?

I had done what I could. I had Day One to think about, or better, to avoid thinking about. When I returned, Janis was where I expected her to be, waiting just inside the door.

"Was it a good practice? You sounded really good, the part I heard."

She was being glowingly, unabashedly positive. How could I have a smoldering desire to deck her and be done with it? First, I owed her the courtesy of an explanation. Practices were sacrosanct. Her Johnny Wray was also half of Duello, and my soulmate and confidant since my stranding on the unlikely shoals of Chicago. Moreover, he was skeptical about the café, a two-man sailboat in which I was about to cast off and strap myself to the mast. I was not inclined to be magnanimous. I was not capable of offsetting perspectives. These were points I could voice in the face of her annoying positivism, if I had the will to deal with how much to say and not say and the likely aftermath of hurt. She could easily be gone by the next practice anyway. I tried to put on Wray's grinning Winnetka expression, which no doubt looked crazed.

"It was okay," I said, satisfied that I sounded even-tempered. "A little shorter than usual because it's mid-week and John has to work in the morning. We moved it from Friday because I'll have the café this weekend."

"And you open tomorrow, right?"

"You remembered."

"I'll come by. Only problem . . . I don't like pizza very much. You can tell me what else you have. I'll buy something, I promise."

"We do have something." I was thinking of flubbing a walking crêpe. "It's on Broadway—"

"Between Surf and Oakdale."

When did I tell her? The night she made dinner, which was two nights ago but now seemed like no specific time, as unreal as the rest of life at the moment, including her toothbrush on the bathroom sink and shampoo in the shower rack.

"I have an interview tomorrow at ten in a wine and cheese place at Clark and Fullerton, so if I'm up and out before you, have a great start." My pique over the practice was gone, and I was ashamed to have felt it at all. I gave her a squeeze. The hotline went off.

"Hey." It was Corey, sounding upbeat like a coach before the game.

"Hey yourself," I said. Janis waved out of the room, leaving me with the call.

"I was wondering if you got the change."

"Yep, on the way home. Two hundred, including the coin rolls."

"Great. I picked up the closer. I'll install it tomorrow. It should be slow early." The broken door closer had been the subject of phone messages to Manny over the last two weeks. Surprisingly, our building manager had become unresponsive.

"We must be ready," I said, stuffed to the gills with doubt.

He didn't answer. There was silence, a tacet, and I tried to hear through it into his apartment. I imagined a distraction, maybe Arlo, or Beth signaling him to get off the call. No background sound, no breathing. Too long. Disconnected?

"We're always ready," he responded out of nowhere. "We just don't know it. *Semper paratus.*"

"Is that like Marines or Boy Scouts?"

"Freaking Coast Guard. Ha!" Corey was back from whatever plane he had checked out to. "Hey, break a leg."

"You too. See you at eleven."

By the time I was off the call, Janis had retired, and I could hear the radio behind her bedroom door. For company, I turned on the TV with no sound and resumed my paperback, *Humboldt's Gift.* I was trying to keep my mind off Corey's call. Even Cantabile's hectoring of Charlie Citrine couldn't do it, and eventually I killed the light.

It was his silence, which had started as a moment then refused to resolve, stretching out between us as I strained to hear it give itself away. What do we hear in the silence of others? Fears, fantasies, doubts—our own fill-ins. Silence inclines forward. It implies a question: the what's next of it. Even Corey must have had a question. The same question had caught up with us both, and only we could answer it, whether we knew it or not.

Chapter 12

"WE need a frame." Corey was holding up the first dollar to the side of the cooler. He had been considering tape.

"Just so it's cheap," I said. I wanted to block any suggestion of a frame crafter and a velvet background. To make one dollar and spend two on a frame was not my goal. And instead of two, it was edging up to twenty thousand for the glowing promise of our high-foot-traffic location. Not to say that Dollar One wasn't deserving. From early on Day One, it promised to be a high point.

I arrived at the store at ten to eleven, with Corey right behind me. The day was drizzling cool. As wound up as I was, he launched into prep, loading the Taylor, firing up the crêpe griddle, and rolling out a large slice pie. We combined efforts on replacing the door closer and declared victory five minutes before opening. At noon we reversed the front door sign for the first time and flipped on the front lights. They lit up whirls of white. The first flurries posed the obvious question: What did you expect?

Over the next hour, the snow steadily increased. Although New Town was a dense neighborhood, young and hip, the source of our coveted foot traffic, lunch hour filled up with car traffic but few feet. What pedestrians there were on Broadway plodded, heads down, in the cold and wet. At first, to keep a hopeful eye on the sidewalk, we busied ourselves close to the front, cleaning counters, rotating the slice pie in the window, adjusting the fire under the griddle,. I recalled the Lord's Prayer, the blessing before meals, key paragraphs of the Episcopalian general confession. Our Bolshevik in the long winter coat passed on the opposite sidewalk, shuffling south. I retreated from the window.

I was arranging pop cans in the cooler and Corey was stuffing napkin holders on the tables. The ding of the front door surprised us.

"Hi," I said. "Welcome to New American Café."

The guy at the counter was staring up at the menu board, reading under his breath. He did not commit to removing his stocking cap, which was flecked with white. He was a weather refugee who happened to wind up in a restaurant, faced with choices he hadn't anticipated. Corey arrived from the back.

"What kind of slices?" the guy asked.

"Right now we have pepperoni and vegetable, and plain cheese," Corey answered, as though the slice pie was the latest of many.

Our potential customer commanded the silence. Our fate was in his hands. He surveyed the board again. He could have been another Bolshevik, from the same village as our wandering friend. Shorter, with a black beard, a little walleyed, he had the same bruised demeanor of a survivor of Chicago. The earth stood still.

"I'll have one of each," he said, and pulled off his cap.

Spatula in hand, I closed the distance to the slice pie. I was stoked but shaky. Slices on the pan, not the floor. The first slices of many, many that needed to follow. How many times could I do this?

"And what to drink?" Corey followed up. I slid the slice pan into the oven and heat tumbled out. "We have pop, shakes, coffee—"

"Coffee, please. Black."

Corey poured and set the steaming mug on the counter. "Since you have the distinct good fortune of being the first customer of New American Café," he announced, "your total bill is . . . one dollar." He chuckled, pushing his glasses up. Customer One brightened, rocked his weight side-to-side and produced his wallet.

"I am honored," he said, "indeed." He slapped the bill flat on the glass-top counter and we all laughed. Corey closed Dollar One into our chrome-plated register, shiny with possibility.

"So you just opened," he said.

"A few minutes ago." We introduced ourselves.

Customer One was Bruce. He lived a couple of blocks north on Barry, west of Broadway. He settled into a booth, and as soon as I pulled the slices, Corey hustled them back to his table. As was his custom, he proceeded to chat Bruce up when he brought coffee refills, which were unlimited by policy, our stout green-line Victor mugs holding no more than eight ounces filled to the brim. Watching him, I was learning: give away product, lose money, create a debt, make a friend. Invest.

For the next half hour Bruce seemed comfortable enough reading a sci-fi paperback, fueled by three cups. When he was re-coated and capped and heading for the door, we invited him to come again, make it his place.

"Full price next time or my partner will kill me," Corey barked out a laugh and waved and Bruce laughed and waved back. I waved too, in the role my perceptive partner had typecast for me: bean counter in the green eyeshade. The door dinged. The closer worked and the dollar was in the drawer. We high-fived.

"He's an alcoholic," Corey said. "Recovering. Said he's been dry for over a year. He has a part-time gig at Barbara's Bookstore, walks past here all the time, and this was the first time he noticed the café. We have to get the sign. I've got their number . . ." He pulled out his wallet and unfolded a note paper, heading for the phone. We had approved the design with the sign maker over two weeks ago, five feet tall, red and white. I mumbled agreement, basically speechless over the information he had induced Bruce to spill in less than ten minutes of chat.

Bruce wasn't the only customer. Within the half hour, a squat, burly guy puffing like he had been shoveling snow surveyed the menu board, asked if we had cheeseburgers, and left. Number three was Janis, bless her. I introduced Corey and to my relief, she ordered an avocado and cream cheese sandwich instead of putting me to the test with a crêpe. She had nailed down the job at the Chalet, starting at twenty hours a week, with training on Sunday. Flush with success, she glistened under melting snowflakes. I made her a strawberry shake to celebrate and following Corey's lead, her tab was on the house. She wished us the best of luck, but after her departure, we were in for a wait.

It ended with a couple, he with a 'fro flocked with white and sporting rings on both hands, funk-band-looking, and she, a platinum-haired waif with raccoon eyeshadow. They were the source of our first full-price sale, six-fifty plus tax, a large sausage and onion to go.

Then came a serious wait. Past the lunch hour, mid-afternoon, I was feeling the drilling boredom and creeping fatigue of my new occupation. The angle of the sun was low, and by late afternoon the snow had thickened the light.

By five, we had exhausted all cleaning and prep options. For the homebound commute, Broadway traffic swelled, but pedestrians remained few, mostly with collars up and attention down, intent on their destinations. I rolled a pair of quarters into the jukebox, partly to wake myself up but mainly to catch the attention of any stragglers who might drift close enough to hear through the door. "Stop! In The Name of Love." But they kept going. Our boat was becalmed, dead in the water. Over the next two hours we sold one Italian Stallion, our meatball sandwich, and a Pepsi.

At seven we agreed to kill the crêpe griddle. No need to scrape it clean. The sidewalk was empty.

"You hungry?" I said, an admission of defeat.

"Sure," he said.

I threw in four slices and he carried two coffees to the back. We took the first booth past the jukebox, Corey facing the door to spot any action.

"How's the music?" He was avoiding the obvious subject of Day One.

"We need to get around more. And make a demo tape. And get an agent." Hearing myself state the reality was dispiriting, but I was starving and the slice tasted fantastic. We both only ate for a minute.

"Music is hard," he went on between bites. "Art's hard, dance, any of it. A lot of crap gets recorded. Like I need to tell you. And published. Because something has two covers, people think it's a book. Beth struggles with the same. She studied for years, has this perfectly pure tone, like Montserrat Caballé. But she didn't matriculate, you know? Doesn't have the connections. So she gives lessons at a prep school, sings weddings, church gigs, things like that." Corey focused past my shoulder at the front and I turned. A curious head peered in through the window then ducked away.

"How did you two meet?"

"I was living in New York, Hell's Kitchen it was called then, before it was Clinton—the forties west of Eighth Avenue. Six years ago. Beth was working downtown, at an art school in Chelsea."

I flashed on Jim Dewey in Boston. "A killer time to be in New York. Did you hear any music?"

"The Gaslight, Village Vanguard, Bitter End." Corey threw out the names of the sacred sites. "The Fugs. Elvin Bishop at the Vanguard. Tom Paxton. Dylan was gone by then. A lot of comics—David Steinberg." I hung on while he chewed. "The heaviest was Jimi Hendrix at Café Wha. A mind blower. Ha!"

I could only nod and wow at the perfect intersection of the time and the place and the music. Corey must have been older than I thought, maybe seven or eight years older than I, and a man of many lifetimes.

"Anyway, you'll meet her, Beth. You have to come over sometime. I'll put on *La Bohème*, the Mimi aria, and get her to sing along. She can't resist. Maybe '*Donde lieta*'. I bet you're a big opera fan." His eyebrows popped up, promising incredulity at any response but yes.

"Huge."

He smirked. "I told you I wanted to do this place to finance my writing habit. Which it will do. But it's about Beth too. She hates Chicago, the vibe and the gangs. She grew up in upstate New York, Ithaca. Her dad taught econ at Cornell, a freaking Keynesian. We agree to disagree. Ha!"

A siren cut in, an on-cue reminder of the city. Lights flashed by in the front window, heading north.

"She wants us to get out, move to a town, not too small, maybe close to a college. Carbondale or someplace like that."

I thought of High Point, trying to imagine Corey in the provinces. I told him I came from such a place, minus the college. I left out the provincial mindsets and politics and old-line expectations.

"My sis Caroline and her husband, similar thing. They have a house on an acre in western Pennsylvania, Mill Run. A Wright house is there, the one with the waterfall. I visited last summer. There are lots of waterfalls and glens, like upstate New York. It's a good place to raise a kid, better than here. They have one, a boy. Caroline's two years younger."

We were both runners-up to our sisters in the categories of stability and achievement. At least Val was older.

"I told Beth the goal is three years . . . to buy a place outside the city. So by that time we need to turn this place into a cash machine. Which we can do. We'll be in Carbondale or Lake Forest Park, and you'll be in Abbey Road."

"Just a humble studio, please, with two Tandberg decks, a mixer, and a few Marshall amps. Thank you." My fantasy was simple in comparison. Corey's was a postcard idyll as green as a salad, a jigsaw puzzle photo. I finished off the slices and coffee.

"Take your time," I said and migrated back to the front. On the way I rolled my own quarter down and punched up "Going to a Go-Go."

From behind the counter I looked out the front window, down on any customers within range. To the wondering world of the auto travelers, I was framed in the window, a fool on display. A white swarm of snow tumbled through our floodlights.

How many times would I preside over that patch of sidewalk? Hundreds? Thousands? If we stayed open. Do not look desperate. Time to lean, time to clean. At the long pizza table, I took the scraper to micro-bumps of flour.

I rolled out one more slice pie and slid it in to bake, assuming it would be the last of the night. Rescraped the table. Scraped the paddle. Smokey had gone to a go-go.

Corey had joined me on deck. "Break down the Taylor?" he said.

"Sure."

He started by lifting the silver handle, looping ropes of strawberry into a plastic pot. He had the barrel drained and the parts in the sink, ingloriously washing, and I was stowing the pot in the cooler when the door opened. The vision arrested both of us.

Two females, complements, one dark, one light, materialized under the track lights. Their coat hoods fell back, and as they checked both of us then looked up to scan the menu board, we enjoyed the full effect. The black woman's eyes caught the lights, and her lips parted slightly, on the edge of a smile. Her blond counterpart appeared resolute, firmer lips and jaw, defenses conditioned by the years of guys magnetized by her Janet Leigh eyes.

"Welcome," Corey ventured.

"It smells great," the black woman said, bright teeth.

"We'll have fresh slices in a minute. My name's Mitch; this young man is my partner Corey."

"Thalía," the black woman said, long *a*. "Denise," said her friend, loosening a bit.

Was I wrong to think of Thalia as black? It was inadequate. Mocha? Caramel? Stunning. And Thalía—short *a*—was the perfect name for her. One of the muses, I remembered dimly from classical lit. Thalía was the muse of light poetry and comedy. The two of them had come to our rescue, the muses of dark and light.

"Did you just open?" Denise sounded almost friendly.

"First day," Corey said.

"We pass by here pretty often."

"You live close?"

"Around the corner, on Surf." Naturally, she trusted Corey, nodding, no threat.

Thalía was scanning the board. She could probably pick up on me watching her, feigning nonchalance.

"Let's see," she said. "You have crêpes . . ."

I felt the elevator drop.

"Actually," I started, "usually we do but . . . I guess we shut the griddle down too early."

"What idiot made that call?" Corey was indignant. We pointed at each other, which brought the sought-after grins.

"Hey, you got to have hope. Anybody could come in, right?" There it was, from Thalía's own lips. I couldn't agree more.

"Let this be a lesson to us," Corey declared.

"Can I interest you in slices instead?"

"What kind?" Denise was no pushover.

"This one has . . ." I dropped the Blodgett door to peer in, as though I didn't remember. I considered it salesmanship. "Pepperoni, veg, and plain cheese. Time to come out."

I slipped the aluminum paddle under it with one professional thrust and slipped it, steaming, onto a platter on the pizza table, showcased under bright light. The aroma worked its magic. They deliberated for seconds and Denise ordered.

"We'll have two pepperoni, one veg, and one cheese."

"To go, or . . ." Corey lightened his tone to his most charming and swept his arm to the back, "for here? At the moment you have your choice of table. And anything to drink, pop, juice—"

"That'll be to go," Thalía said. "We have wine at home."

Ah yes, wine at home with Thalía and Denise. Holding that vision, I hit the big pie with the round cutter—four cuts, eight slices. While Corey collected, I slipped the wedges into a medium box and covered with a sheet of foil. Corey's going-in position was no deliveries. We needed to discuss immediately. I could be delivering to Surf at that moment, Thalía and Denise in their bathrobes. Instead I stapled a menu to their box.

"Keep it flat," I advised in the soft, ingratiating voice of experience.

Corey thanked them, I thanked them, and we solicited their return. The hoods came up over the muses of dark and light and we watched them exit and pass into the now snowless night, heading south toward Surf Street. We sang their praises and celebrated their charms. The diversion lasted about a minute. It was past nine-thirty and the street was dead.

I wasn't going to be the one to say it. I could stick it out as long as he could, but that didn't mean I was going to play the jukebox again to make the end of Night One less oppressively obvious. I arranged the slices in the window then brushed the butcher block table. Corey opened the register and counted. Closed the drawer.

"Well," he said, "another day, another fifty cents. Want to bag it?"

"I'll mop," I said, heading for the back, "you pack up."

We split the last four slices to take home and cleaned up in ten minutes.

"Hey, we got the door open," I said as we exited into the cold night. He locked up, the only sound on the sidewalk.

"I'll pick up the frame on the way in," I said. He checked me for a second.

"Ah, Bruce's dollar. See you at eleven-thirty?"

"Why not," I said and gave a thumbs up, which Corey returned and then headed for his car on Oakdale. I had the good fortune to have parked on Surf, but west of Broadway. Denise had nodded toward the lake side when she volunteered their location. As I started the Mustang I was spinning on black women of dreams—Diane Carol, Nina Simone, Tina Turner. Lieutenant Uhuru. I was tempted to cross Broadway and keep going down their possible blocks, follow the siren song to the end of reason. What would I do with Thalia? Invite her home to my overcrowded basement apartment? I let the only other car go and turned left onto Broadway.

A block ahead another car turned, and I recognized the wide rear of Corey's Pontiac. I replayed the stories of his sister in the country, and Beth and Arlo. He had more to lose. The thought was reassuring, even if perversely. I was motivated, but he had to be more so. I welcomed all pieces of the puzzle of my business partner and how he had gotten me into this. He had business smarts and a few connections, but the biggest piece was an intuition I had about him, even as he had claimed the same about me. And if we're talking intuition, maybe that came straight from Johnny Wray bent over his Mossman stretching out on some Fahey mainline. If the café crashed in pieces, I could blame it on John. Corey turned left at Belmont and I kept going north.

Whatever I had been expecting from Day One, I had gotten something else. Zero encouragement in sales, but at least glimmers of possibilities. Or if I had to be honest, a glimmer of one kind. If Thalía was impossible, a door had been opened. The female half of the city was on the move out there, and the door closer was working.

Janis would be home, no doubt. Did I resent it or welcome it? Yes, and yes. I was sick of being alone but I needed space—for the music and the muses, and if not Thalía, then for whatever muse could be. Left on Southport.

Was I obsessed, supercharged, with Thalía? Rhetorical question. Should I express it with Janis? How fair was that? Not exactly the first time it had ever been done. And what did fair have to do with anything? Janis was lovable in a way, and I loved her in a way. And I had to get her out of there. I would be early, if she was expecting me at all.

I stepped into the cone of light at my door and turned the key. In the outflow of warmth, I heard her voice. It sounded charming and coy in the recesses of the apartment. Whoever she had in there, I had given no okay. Did it matter? Did she have to ask my permission to entertain a friend, some guy? Hell, yes. It was my Cavern. It was basic. The reason to invite her out was squatting somewhere in my space.

As I rounded the hall, Janis was standing in the living room, one finger twirling her long hair, the other hand holding the red hotline handset to her ear. When she saw me, she separated from the phone, bright-eyed, delighted.

"It's Adam," she said. "We've all been invited."

Chapter 13

"APPRECIATE you guys being on time." Our hostess, short black-cat hair and a quick smile, held open the heavy front door. Janis had already introduced us to Sandy, and we knew where to go.

"Our pleasure," I said, and it was. A week after opening, the order for eight large pizzas exceeded our take on an ordinary night. On this one it allowed us to close early.

The old brick building on Barry Street was all peaks and gables, a former church revived as a performing space, mainly for dance. The sign by the door said "MoMing." I hauled one hot box of four pies inside, and Corey followed with the other.

Across the hardwood floor, rows of folding chairs faced a stage. About half of the crowd of several dozen were seated, the rest chatting in the back. They were an eclectic-looking lot, some graying academic types but easily half around my age—scarves and bangles to grubby, Chicago hip. We navigated around them to the kitchen where we left the hot boxes, and Sandy set two stacks of paper plates on a folding table in the hall. I saw Janis talking with two women seated in the middle. When she spotted us, she waved and bustled over.

"So glad you could do this, guys," hugging both of us. "Thank you." She was in her hostess persona, although this time she was a guest like us.

"It looks like a nice turnout," Corey said.

I had no idea what the goal was for the two little magazines, *La Raza* and *Another Chicago Magazine*, but I imagined the attendees, at least the senior ones, were chipping in more than the ten-dollar price of a ticket. As the chief caterers, we were attending gratis, but we had agreed to kick back ten percent of our take to the benefit. Corey didn't miss the chance to stack our menus beside the plates.

"Adam said *Another Chicago Mag* would be happy with fifty, so . . ." Janis scanned the room, nodding. I estimated the crowd at close to seventy, and more were drifting in. I was glad we had decided to cut the pizzas into squares, appetizer-size for the multitudes. A few had paper cups of wine. I spied a couple of jugs on a sideboard, BYO only, no liquor license—a thought I would not have had before inspectors and supplier bills and rent. In another fifteen minutes the lights dropped, and we took chairs toward the back with Janis.

On the stage five chairs faced the audience. In a moment the readers we had come to hear entered from stage left to enthusiastic applause. As I expected when I first heard the details of the invitation from Janis a week earlier, I was feeling too much to make sense of. Melanie was first in line, smiling and looking composed, crossing confidently to the chair on the far end. She wore a slate gray dress and boots, and in a generous loop around her neck, a navy blue scarf with twists of scarlet. She looked new, reinterpreted, like an actress playing herself.

The others filed in and took their seats, Adam Champion beside her, then two other men. The senior one I guessed to be the Don of Circle poetics, Michael Andonati. The last in line, a slender blonde woman, stepped to the podium.

She introduced herself, looking as surprised as we were by the sudden clarity of the microphone, then thanked all for coming out to support the two journals. Toni was her name, or Dawn. I couldn't concentrate. Melanie was listening politely, her Shelley on her right.

Toni-Dawn was an editor of *Another Chicago Magazine*, I caught that much. She began to read one of her own poems, which featured a performing monkey and a panther. The next was an elegy for Kansas City, whether Kansas or Missouri, unspecified. Did Melanie disdain or admire? I couldn't tell. Once I would have known. Her third was a sardonic fantasy of one day, nearing thirty, marrying, shedding her defects and heaviness of heart, her body lightening then levitating. Suddenly people were clapping and I understood the format, a few works each, a sampler, live magazine. She acknowledged the applause and introduced the next reader, the editor of *La Raza*.

Carlos Calderon made an arresting figure at the mike, slender with a shock of black hair and high cheekbones that suggested a long bloodline, Incan or Aztec. He started with images of oranges shining in creates and a broken skyway against an orange horizon.

We sat attentively in the lights from the stage. We were in a sacred space, flanked by windows of stained glass. My fellow attendees would be the perfect Duello audience, but there was no reason to imagine us on that stage, none. In our four gigs, we had played to an audience of that size once, at an open mike in a temple rec hall in Skokie.

And the Corn King washes Fritos down
with a wine called Thunderbird
on the corner where the streetlight crowns
the Phoenix head of Pilsen.

Carlos finished with thanks for supporting *La Raza* and passed the baton. As I guessed, next was the Don.

Michael Andonati rose from his chair into his presence, robustly forty-something, black hair and dark eyes, charcoal sport coat, red sweater, *rouge et noir*. Under a shower of applause, he shook Carlos's hand as they passed, *compadres*. He tilted the microphone up and cleared a bang from his forehead with a tilt of his head and one finger.

"This is outstanding," he began, nodding. "You are the juice! You are the lifeblood of poetry in Chicago!" Cheers. Bubbles of laughter. We were looser, a family united in the cause. "Thank you much. I'd like to read to you tonight from . . ."

Ah yes, *Dead Red*, the volume I had ridiculed in my green-eyed adolescence on Janis's third floor. He opened by linking *lucidity* and *the sky's intent*. I found myself focusing on his tone, measured and confident. Only Adam was left after Andonati and then . . . was she nervous? She still looked cool. Did she have no nerves or only the right ones?

The Don went on about the *plane tree's inclination* and the *angle of incidence* and distance. Cautious, properly elusive, unassailable by colleagues. I admired his poise, and his use of silence. I could learn something about delivery. I hung in through poem three.

Like listening to a John Cage concert, for several beats we weren't sure when it was over. At a point we reached consensus and offered our applause. Andonati accepted humbly, pressing his palms together like a *bodhisattva*, but not too long.

"And now it's my distinct pleasure to introduce to you," a look to the end of the row, "two of my students."

They were a set! Two for one. How fun! The Don acknowledged his good fortune to have them both in his class. A happy accident. Students this gifted were rare, et cetera.

"Few of us who apply this craft for very long are so arrogant as to believe that we teach real poets. We can only try to expose facets, potentials, that may have gone unnoticed. I don't teach these students—we nourish one another."

Together in the nest. In the cradle of matriculation I eschewed. For what? For life in the university of experience. Like slicing slice pies and reporting to beef-headed man that we didn't serve cheeseburgers.

The Don turned to young Shelley. "You're on, Adam. Ladies and gentlemen, Adam Champion."

As they crossed, Andonati shook his hand, two manly shakes, outbulking him and towering over him by most of a foot.

Adam tilted the mike back down and acknowledged the last of the applause, a soft *thank you*. A black turtleneck showcased his bearded countenance. The stage lights anointed his curls. The first poem was entitled "Caveat to Covet."

Your poolside presence euthanizes care

Adam's reading pace matched his mentor's. Melanie was listening, but more intently than any of us? I checked the two on my right. Corey was sitting straight-backed, head slightly cocked, as though one ear was better. Beside me, Janis was barely breathing, lips parted.

. . . the camber of your shoulders,
Your pelvic revolvers.
In the pools of your sunglasses
I am wee but happy.
In a pagan ceremony, your leg
Uncrosses in the sun, warning that
Love inclines to avarice
And avarice to love.

We the audience laughed. Melanie laughed, a toss of her hair, teeth visible, the picture of delight. "Poetry sings," Professor Knox once told me, hoping to save me from the morass of pop, "all by itself." I had no use for literary bromides. But the eighty-something sharing the sacred space were engaged, many delighted, and Duello was— somewhere.

Adam began again. There was a chamber like a cenacle, and it was *foreign yet familiar.* His noble brow and narrow shoulders were features in balance, patrician, a study in equipoise.

. . . the words we bound to courses
of intention now
fall apart . . .

Was ever a candidate so syntonic with the qualities of Master of Fine Arts? This was Adam's night, but there would be others.

They were applauding. I applauded. How enthusiastic were they? Enthusiastic. Adam was nodding and thanking, the image of humility.

"And now, it's my pleasure, and privilege, to introduce my classmate and colleague, for whom I have the deepest admiration . . ."

I wanted to bolt for the men's room. Melanie was standing into the applause, my stomach knotting. Would they hug, cheek-side kisses? No, she was past him, courteous smiles only. Then she was glowing in the light that Adam had vacated, tilting the mike lower. With the silk scarf at her throat, a wraparound dash of color, she began the King Kong poem, the one to Fay Wray.

Enough's enough, she nearly said
of the hominid from Hollywood
when anthropoidal furs emerged
from the tunnels of his trousers.

I was in her parents' house in Hyde Park late in the summer, after we had moved and before we were living apart. We were on the sofa with her kid brother across from the White Sox on the cabinet TV. Her folks lingered at the picnic table in the backyard where the cookout had been. The daylight was endless.

We clapped at the end of the witty lead-off one, smiling, satisfied. And then she had us holding our breath.

From where I lie, directionless

in a rushing room, above a twining slick
of traffic, my feet lose their way
with the world, my hands curling homeward
to rest, night crossing and recrossing
the soul's map.

Her fellow poets on the stage, and we her flock, gazed up at her. What did I know of this Madonna in her chapel of words? She was reading another.

Nothing was more fatal than that night,
not the spell of bobcat or the sudden ghost of copperhead

What would it be like to touch her again, under her prim gray and her silky slip? Would my fingers know her? Or would she feel unfamiliar, as remote from me as her spot on the stage from her parents' sofa?

Sleep that night was a white crane's stroke
above the lake's brown shadow

She may have morphed away. Our molecules decay like fireworks. They retire and reorganize.

I know we had stolen out that morning
from the hotel as we had passed from
all the other rooms, spaces
that had come to hold both more
and less. I feared we had gone
too far when I heard it . . .

She bestowed the words, clear and interlocked as stained glass. She was in her zone, and we were bearing witness.

. . . and far back,
as in memory, we will hear the night begin,
the tapping of rain on the stones of the city,
the glutted gutters whirling past all doors,
a healing festival. The rain finding us
where we lie, our shoulders surrendering to sand,
relinquishing our bodies to our body.

Silence held the last lines then closed around them. There was applause, and my hands were moving, miming.

Melanie was nodding, smiling graciously. Her colleagues were on their feet, applauding too. Then she was gliding back in the direction of her chair. All of the bards faced the audience and bowed.

A few stood in the front, and the wave swept back until we were all standing. As I rose, my leg nearly buckled. The muscles had clenched into a cramp, and I stretched it out as the editor who had led off was joined at the mike by Carlos. They thanked everyone again. Magazines were available for purchase on a table by the door. The readers began to descend the stage to mingle with the mortals.

In the wake of her reading, it came to me suddenly that what had happened to us was not her fault. Melanie was making it. A land of enchantment had simply been waiting for her, and not for me.

"Wasn't that . . ." Janis grabbed my arm, then Corey's. "My God, they were great, weren't they?" She was babbling, eyes wide. "Back in a sec." She was off, picking a path to the stage. Corey gave me an eyebrows-up look and we followed.

I had already spotted Melanie with Carlos in front of the stage, and of course Corey headed straight for them. He began talking to Carlos and Melanie was smiling. Her attention swung to me.

"That was beautiful," I said. She looked warm, relieved, inviting.

"Thanks for coming."

"Did you change those lines . . . the crane and the shadow . . ."

"*A white crane's stroke above the lake's brown shadow.* That's right."

". . . reminded me of Neruda," Corey was saying and Carlos was thanking him. A fuzzy-haired restaurateur in Doc Martens might have known Neruda in Lima, but in Chicago pizza land, I was willing to bet it was unusual.

"Have you met my biz partner?" I said. "This is Corey McGowan. Corey, Melanie Barr."

"That was great. I'm a big fan of Fay Wray! And the title of your last poem—'She Doesn't Swim in English.' Super." He was nodding seriously, then, "I hear Conrad dreamed in Polish. Ha!"

They hit it off immediately. He moved on to lucid dreaming, followed by admiration for Nicanor Parra, which pulled Carlos in.

"Where do I get a magazine?" Corey asked, ensuring most favored status. Carlos enthusiastically led him off, and I was alone with Melanie.

"So," I quipped.

"So, I hear you catered. I can't wait to taste New American pizza."

It could be my chance to repair to the table and serve her a square on a paper plate, but whatever I wanted to do, it wasn't that. I had an uneasy feeling and scanned the room for young Adonis. He was on the side with the jug wine, being entertained by Janis. She was touching his arm.

"How's Duello?" She could probably see how her catering comment landed. Or maybe she actually cared.

"We're in a holding pattern. Getting the café off the ground has been a haul. We need to . . . get out more."

"You were sounding very pro the last time I heard you, at Janis's . . ."

"After New Year's. That seems like another . . . I'm sorry about that night—"

"No."

"No, really." I needed to atone. What would it sound like? "Adam's stuff was interesting, too. Not your level in my opinion, but—"

"He's so good, you could kill yourself."

"You don't need to be that generous."

She grinned and I was spinning backward, both of us crossing a green campus.

"Mel." Michael Andonati was by the stage steps, his hand in the air, trying to get her attention. Any remorse I had over trashing his book title vanished. She turned and waved in reply.

"One minute," she began to excuse herself, "I'll catch you—"

"Hey," I said and nodded, "poetry . . . yours . . . it sings all by itself."

She halted for a beat, the way we had all halted for her, breath suspended. Then she broke into the smile I knew well and was off to her master.

I was falling back, trying to assimilate, merge into the chatting congregation, patrons of the art, hip to splendid, some no doubt gifted in their own right. Do not obtrude. Crave anonymity. Do you know the poets? No, I'm the caterer, pizza boy with the blue guitar. I kept my grin, navigating past islands of talk.

"The *Daily News* may fold."

"No way—Royko?"

"Rates are out of sight . . ." A wave of perfume off a lofty blonde from the Miracle Mile. Pizza man Bojangles, ma'am. Happy to make your acquaintance and lick your ear. I drinks a bit.

"*Godfather Two* is better . . ."

The pizza table was ganged and I hoped somebody was taking a menu. A few others hovered at the magazine table with Corey and Carlos. I checked the BYO wines where at least one more jug had arrived. Now I had a goal. Young Shelley had moved on, as had Janis. Then I spotted her alone in mid-room, drifting back toward our empty chairs. I waved her over.

"Where's Adam?" I was half-thinking I should thank him for inviting us. Our official catering invitation had come through Sandy, but he and Melanie had probably proposed us.

"Oh . . ." She trailed off, glancing back at the front of the room.

Andonati and "Mel" had been joined by others, including Adam. Beside Andonati, not quite on his arm, a black-haired woman posed languorously holding a wine cup, arm folded across her waist, elbow propped on her wrist. She wore a black sheath with white trim, formal for the occasion. A goldish necklace fanned out below her collar, an eye-catcher even at a distance.

"Is she Andonati's squeeze?"

"Don't know. Her name's Anita Russo. She's at Circle too. It's a real Circle circle," she said with a note I hadn't heard from her.

"Who's the tall one in the beret?" He was holding forth to the readers, and even Andonati was only listening.

"Paul Carroll, a muckety-muck in the poetry scene here forever."

Janis didn't look good. Her effervescence after the reading was gone, eyes overcast.

"You okay? I was going to get some wine—"

"You go. I'm checking out." She took a few steps toward the door and I caught her arm.

"Hey, like that? What's up?" She turned on me.

"The princess bitch, that's what's up. Everything falls into Melanie's lap, doesn't it? I bet you can relate, right?" Tears were welling. A couple beside us turned to look. Janis was trembling, looking ready to blow. A disconcerting wave ran through me—I didn't know her now.

"Pizza guys—New American pizza?" Sandy hurried in from outside looking tense. Janis and I were a few strides from the door so Sandy spotted me first. I motioned Corey over.

"Either of you guys park in the red? There's a cop car out there—"

"It's mine." Corey popped out the door waving a magazine. I needed to go with him, but nothing was making sense. What had Melanie done? I hadn't even seen her and Janis together.

She turned away, I thought at first hiding tears, but then I realized she was looking back at the stage. She was obsessed with the Circle circle, the in-crowd she had just tried to put behind her. I was ready to leave and let Janis play out her own drama, but the mystery of Melanie stopped me. In the next second, all came clear.

Rewind a week. I had gotten home early on the short night of miserable Day One. Janis was standing in the warm light, on my red phone. He wouldn't have known my number. She had called him.

"Adam?" I said.

She gave me a hot, dark look. She had been sitting beside me, enthralled by his every syllable. After the reading, her hand on his sleeve . . .

"Crazy, right? Of course crazy. I plead insanity." Yes, I could relate. She bit her lip and righted herself. No more tears. "I'll see you later."

I glanced back at the crime scene. Young Shelley was in position at Melanie's side. Janis punched the door handle and I followed her out into the chill. In a whirling beacon of red and white lights, Corey was pleading his case to an officer between the squad car and his guilty Pontiac.

Janis paused on the top step. A week ago, or maybe even yesterday, I might have been ranting about Melanie with her, but now I didn't need to hear it. And the last thing I needed was another female stuck on young Adonis. Good night, sweet prince. Enough adoration. Too much confusion. It was my chance to invite her out of the Cavern.

And then, in the suspended moment, in my chance not taken, she told me what she had done, like a proof of quantum physics. Two micro-particles, or waves not yet particles, are magically entangled over space and time. Just beyond imagining, a linkage exists so that as one particle gyrates, it sets the other spinning. Janis and I had shared a quantum moment. My thought had manifested in her words as smoke in the cold. And then we split and descended the steps, displaced particles, she to the Cavern and I to Corey and the police.

"Here." He handed the officer a stack of menus. "Pass them around. Call in your order or come by. Anytime. We'll take care of you. This is my partner."

I waved. The lights whipped over us. I saw for the first time that the officer was a woman. Her male partner looked warm on the passenger side.

She took the menus, giving both of us a world-weary look. Then she was rounding the front of the squad and opening the door. She waved the menus once and gave up a hint of a grin. The door whomped shut, but they only sat there.

"I need to move it," Corey said.

"Can you drop me at the store?" I should have brought my car, but at the time we only needed one. "I need to split—Janis is . . . or I could walk it, not that far."

The suggestion drew a disgusted look. "Come on."

The squad car followed, lashing us with lights for half a block. Then we turned south on Clark and the white Dodge Monaco, blue stripe, continued straight.

"Pergolesi!" Corey announced and boosted the radio volume. Waves of strings. "Do you know him? He wrote operas, sacred music. 'Stabat Mater,' Beth sings it. He was a freaking genius, died at twenty-six, same as Otis Redding. There's a café here named after him. We'll go." He dropped the volume. "What about Janis?"

"She's moving out. She found an apartment, just told me." As my moment was opening. As she intercepted my thought wave before I converted it to speech on the top front step of MoMing. "I need to help her get some stuff together." Which was a lie but less a lie than a substitute for the longer, recursive story of why I was done for the night. He didn't pursue it and I was glad. You don't explain quantum.

He did go on about Melanie. I guessed he was probing, but I didn't take the bait, other than to say we moved out together from Chapel Hill. He nodded, suspicion confirmed.

Melanie had arrived. She had caught her star. The Circle circle glittered in their firmament. We were all on the make in some way. I called myself a musician. *By their fruits ye shall know them.* My fruit was pepperoni. We crossed Broadway. The lights of a high-rise burned in my sight.

"Hey look, I need more time." They were my words, unbidden. I had loosed them.

Corey pulled over and cut the radio.

"Time?"

"For the music, it's shot to hell. It's freaking nowhere."

He pushed his glasses up, stared at me like I was suing for divorce. "We've been open for what, eight days?"

"If I miss every weekend for six months, Duello will be history. My partner's going to bail."

"Your partner." He was zoomed out, regarding me from a distance.

"Okay, right, of course—you're my partner too."

"Right now, it's slow enough that we could off-shift, but we need to go the other way—we have to grow sales. If we do that, we can hire employees and cut our hours. We've been over this." He was getting hot. "We don't make a business plan and tear it up in a week."

And who's putting up the cash for this? Is your name on the loan? What do I have but a gentleman's agreement? What's a fair trade for being on the hook for twenty K? These things I did not say. I took a deep breath and watched his flashers blink on a mud-splattered fender. We let our debris settle.

"It's the only way, we have to grow ourselves out."

"Right, it's about the sales. I get it. Sorry, I'm out of it tonight. I'll work it."

Corey stared through the windshield at nothing. After a long moment he nodded and we rolled the last couple of blocks to my car. When he let me out, he said he was heading home too.

It wasn't below freezing, but my lock was stuck. I could see my WD-40 squirt can inside on the passenger floor mat.

"Fine," I said. "Fine, goddammit! Motherfucker!" I was more than ready to pound, and the door was better than victims who shall go unnamed and who would land me in the bucket on West Addison. With a glove on, the edge of my fist didn't hurt until I landed three next to the door handle. The key turned. A knockout.

The numbness then ache in my hand felt right, but it did nothing to clear the bitter taste. Sealed in the Mustang with the doors and windows tight, I yelled like a lunatic. Like the tortured. Like the burned out on love and at war with themselves. I cranked the engine and sat shivering, waiting for the defroster to clear a patch on the windshield.

When I walked in I heard Janis's radio. Fleetwood Mac. The light from her door made a patch in the hall. She was packing, back toward me in a kimono-style robe, suitcase open on her bed.

I flashed on the last time I had seen the suitcase, when she moved in. Had she moved out of her house to bloom in the big city, or was it all about Adam, needing her own place to score him? Maybe I was a station on her way. Did I care? Did she even know?

When she heard me she turned, pulling the robe closed. Her face wet with tears, she looked the way I felt. We had both been flogging ourselves with comparisons to others and we were raw.

"I'm so sorry I said that about Melanie." Her voice quivered. "It's not her, I was a shit to say it . . ."

I closed the distance and hugged her. She sobbed quietly against me while "Don't Stop" played. The bones of her back and shoulder felt delicate under the silk. She looked up at me, eyeliner streaked, eyes of a supplicant. I knew she was about to apologize again.

Forces bind seemingly random particles. I parted her kimono robe.

"Shut up," I said. Her cheek tasted salty.

Chapter 14

WHEN Janis left, my rooms with their low ceilings and factory-floor hardwood reasserted themselves as the Cavern. I practiced again in the vacant spaces, grooving on the acoustics of each room. The bathroom was always the best, with ceramic tile and an iron clawfoot tub.

A week after his adamant stand on time, Corey reversed position. I imagine appeasing me was part of it, but he needed to reclaim part of his own life too, as Beth was decrying his obsession with the café. We started to off-shift on weekdays with one of us in at eleven-thirty and the other at four-thirty. For the music it wasn't ideal, but better. Wray had Sundays and Mondays off, so we practiced early Monday afternoons. I tried to stick to a discipline of solo practice every day that I wasn't opening, and I wrote my first new song in two months. The café and music started to seem they could coexist, although neither was going much of anywhere.

It was a Wednesday after solo practice. As I pulled the café door at four-thirty, I could hear the phone.

"For you," Corey said, holding up the receiver like proof of something unlikely. I half-feared a meltdown call from Janis.

"Mogul." Behind Wray I heard a copier pulling paper. Ramped up, with childish excitement in his voice, he proceeded to tell me what we had stopped hoping for.

It hit with a thrill and a jolt. Wray had tried them, I had tried them and gotten the same story: no tryouts at the No Exit without a demo tape or an agent. "How did—"

"I left my number, like weeks ago. It was Dunbar! Mike Dunbar told them we opened for him at the Tin Cup and we're 'different as hell'. He said we were like—"

"Patti Smith?"

"Buckley and Fahey."

"No shit! Mike Dunbar, always loved that guy. He can stay." I could see Wray folded over his copier, laughing his wheezing, almost silent laugh until he was red in the face.

Our tryout was on Friday afternoon on Wray's extended lunch hour. We played a taste of set one, to prove we were as different as Dunbar had said, and Buckley's "Happy Time." Sue the booking manager with a silver pin in her nostril scheduled us for the following Thursday night. I took Corey's Tuesday, opening to closing, in return for our gig night off.

Wray and I decided to invite no one we knew, not even Sasha. Attendance was not a problem at the No Exit. When we went on at eight, the place was packed and loud, but the volume dropped as Wray's stark lead-in set up my intro. With the total anonymity of the audience and no distractions of well-intended wishes and expectations, we got what we wanted—a free zone. We left space, didn't push the river, allowing the music to come to us and build, and we stayed inside it where the flame was.

We shared the night with a spunky blues chick from Cicero who played left-handed and copped a lot of Albert King and Junior Wells and some Bonnie Raitt. Before our closing set we pitched a scheme to her and let her pick the tune. We had practiced it once at most, but that was all Johnny Wray would need, and I knew enough of the lyrics to fake it. For our last number of the night, we invited Cicero to join us, and we jammed through "Sweet Home Chicago." The crowd stood up and the stars shone down. It was the kind of night we played for and dreamed of. We had finally caught up to it.

When we collected from Sue, she signed us up for a night in May, but I was riding so high that the date escaped me. Wray and I had taken our separate cars, and after a victory beer, he left first. I packed my guitars in the trunk but decided to hit the men's room before leaving. When I came out I was replaying the glories of the second set. Distracted in the dim hallway, I blundered into someone.

"Whoa, sorry," I said, pulling my hand from her shoulder where it had landed instinctively. She was short and compact, startled eyes and huge lashes. We had collided in front of the women's room door. Suddenly she popped a smile.

"You're Duello!" she said. "You were like, so boss."

"Half of it, anyway. Thanks."

"I came with this guy, he thought you were going to be a Latin group." She was coming into clearer focus, black braids coiled on her head, lipstick as subtle as the lashes. "When he asked me I was like, why not. Now is why not." From her accent, I guessed Philippine. "He took off with this dude, said he'd be like twenty minutes. That was over an hour ago. He's a lowlife. At least I got some pizza out of it." She let out a wacky laugh.

In the half-light of the tight bathroom hall, the moment could go either way. Yes, she had said "pizza," like a crazy clang association, but that wasn't it. Whether to seize the moment was riding on what Corey told me one day when I had asked if he had seen Thalía and Denise since the first day. Indeed, they had been in the day before. He broke it to me that our loveliest patrons were lesbian partners. I didn't question the veracity or ask how he possibly found out. I had ceased to doubt that he could make anyone spill their guts in minutes. My fantasy of Thalia didn't implode immediately, but it was punctured. Was she a lesbian absolute or by degree? A toggle switch or a rheostat? Did it matter? No doubt they were committed to each other in some way. The odds of Thalia ever gracing the intimate recesses of the Cavern were near zero.

The bathroom door pulled open and a beefy blonde wanted out. We stepped into the back of the No Exit where only a few stragglers remained, and I saw her in the light. Pretty, with an uncomplicated expression, skin an island shade, a black vinyl coat wrapped tight, in boots with heels to raise her. A pixie package.

The moment was coming together. Thalia had created a void, and rushing in to fill it was the undeniable momentum of the night. I was on a roll and things were worth a try.

"So, do you need a ride?"

"I was starting to call a cab—"

"Well, I was just going to split. I could easily drop you."

She asked if I was sure, and I was as sure as I could be at the moment. Her name was Lucy, and I felt the rush of a jewel thief as I closed her, my first groupie, my prize won by craft and art, into the bucket seat beside me.

While I drove she chatted on about the music, asked how long we had played together, if we lived together. As the heater began to take effect, I became aware of her perfume, nicely overdone like her makeup, encouraging. Her place was less than fifteen minutes west of the club, on Walcott. She directed me into a short driveway and I pulled even with the back of her building, a two-story house. Her apartment was on the first floor, entrance in the rear. The terminus was dark and moonless, dangerous, electric.

"Thank you, thank you," she chirped. "You're a savior, really." Then, "Come in for a drink? It will warm you up." She nodded, the spider to the fly.

"Won't your date come looking for you?"

"We're not like that. He's a lowlife. We're not like anything."

Being persuaded was oddly discomfiting, but a heady rush. With her sitting the span of a hand from my right leg, an aromatic package of lips and lashes, I thought of the guitars in the trunk—less about theft than cold. But the night wasn't bitter, and I could rescue them at any time.

We entered through her back porch room, blinds drawn on all sides. In her living room she clicked a table lamp on low, and we took to her sofa with a jug Burgundy, a salsa station in the background. Under the vinyl coat, Lucy wore a short dress with horizontal stripes like a bee. At some point with the coat off and slipped out of her boots, she started dancing, shaking out her braids, hip stripes rolling, feet padding. Then I was padding with her, the crown of her head in the middle of my chest. On our first kiss, my tongue licked plastic, a retainer behind her top teeth. She was perfecting her smile, which struck me as irresistible. I started her zipper and the bee was licking back.

I had won her with music and sweet synchronicity that I had had the guts and wisdom to accept, carpe diem. With it came the essence of liberation: I could be someone whom no one I knew could identify. It struck like a bolt, like a gift of freedom from the sprawling city where uncountable others were doing what we were, answerable to no one in the city of Chicago where it had all been done.

Her bedroom was warm and cozy, the bed flush in the corner. On the dresser photos of her family flanked a silver crucifix. A certificate of completion of a radiology tech program had been presented to Luz Guillen.

The top of her bee dress was around her waist, and I had pulled off my second boot when a light rolled across her blind. An engine rumbled outside and went silent. She popped the dress back over her shoulders and peeked around the slats.

"Shit, you gotta go, okay?" She darted back to the living room and snagged my jacket off the sofa. Then she had my shirt sleeve, dragging me down the short hall into pitch black.

Her apartment buzzer blatted.

She hit a light and we were in her stunningly bright kitchen. She was pushing me to the back door, flipping the lock.

"Lowlife, right? No problem?" I wasn't going to let her off with nothing. She gave me her doe-eye, doe-lash look, clearly in pain.

"Sorry," she said, hushed, and added, "sometimes he has a gun, like in his car."

"Ah, great."

The buzzer again. The back door was open and she shoved me with emergency strength. Bee lifts car off trapped kid. Jacket in one hand, boots in the other, on her turnaround back landing in stocking feet, I awaited instructions.

"Wait a sec while I let him in, then go. Sorry," she said again and blew an aborted kiss. Then the door shut, the lock clicked, and the kitchen light went out.

Shivering on the bottom step, I pulled on boots and jacket while my eyes adjusted to the dark. I heard what could have been her front door and peeked around the corner of the building. There was an empty space beside the Mustang, but the lowlife had chosen to box me in, a silver Scirocco on my rear bumper. A sometimes gun, in his glove box or console or in his dumb fist as he laid for me on the porch.

Keys in hand I made my break, holding a crouch. Head below the roof of the Scirocco and then the Mustang. Feeling for the lock in the dark, missing with the key, missing again, then pulling the door and the interior still almost warm.

I rotated the key a half turn and the wipers beat off a dusting of frost. No headlights, but ahead of me I could make out a mulched-over brown garden bed, a few training sticks fenced off with a single wire. I was gauging the room to turn around when the bed burst into shocking clarity from the light over Luz's door.

I didn't check the porch. The engine caught and I gunned forward into the mulch, angled enough to pick up the drive, and slammed into reverse.

"Jesuuus!" The rear window was filmed with the same frost and I was backing blind. I popped on the lights and could make out barely enough in the red fog of the tail lights to keep from ditching. Then I was peeling down Walcott, out of the wild.

At the Cavern, unloading the guitars from the trunk, I could laugh about it and my senses returned, most acutely the sweet taste of failure. Lucy was my groupie, undeniably, consummation to be wished but not required. She was the embodiment of the spoils of rock 'n' roll, harbinger of a happy future. On the walkway to my building I drew in the air, still iron cold but charged with opportunity.

My victory hangover, such as it was, lasted through Friday, up to the pull of the café door. Corey had done the turnaround shift, so I was in at four in recognition of his sacrifice. My mistake. He asked how Duello had fared, and after reporting to him on our success, up to the encounter with Lucy Guillen, I still had time to open the mail, the utility bill first. Contrary to instinct, I flipped open the checkbook. In the wake of April rent and the last meat and produce bill, if I were to write a Com Ed check, our balance would dip below three hundred. The other envelope was worse. Our loan rate, the bank informed us, was rising. A fine time to take a loan, rates will stabilize, et cetera. I would share the news with my business partner, informing him that Malowitz, the financial guru of LaSalle Street, was a moron, but now was not the time.

"Welcome back," I croaked.

Corey checked me from the far end of the counter.

"Nothing," I said.

The second Saturday in April brought the first warm rush of spring. By noon the last mounds of snow on the sidewalk were glistening in the sun, and trickles of thaw crept onto the concrete. In the unfrozen air, earth smells returned with hints of green.

"Should we open the door?" I put to Bruce at the end of the counter. I was fairly sure how our first customer of the day, and our only reliable regular, would respond.

"Do and I'm out of here." With his cap off but his jacket still on, he evinced a shiver.

"Cheese crêpe?" Corey confirmed. He was already pouring the coffee.

"Perk seech," Bruce nodded. He was doing it again.

"With strawberries?" I egged him on.

"Seerbwarts thew."

It was like spitting into the wind. Like playing every cut on the White Album backwards.

"You're amazing, my friend." Corey shook his head and poured the batter onto the griddle.

"Dnerf eim gnizama ru. I know. I'm extraordinary, but it doesn't help me." His right eye drifted sideways like evidence.

I might as well have propped open the door. Bruce had just started his crêpe when the door dinged. A fuzzy-haired dude in aviators and his farm girl with barrettes scanned the menu board. Two regular cones: one strawberry, one banana. Corey served and I collected. A David Bowie clone held the door as they left. Corey didn't have to move. David, wearing red warpaint, wanted a strawberry cup with nuts.

Four junior high chicks crowded in and David worked his way around them to stares and giggles. Mohammed, our

Pakistani buddy from the men's boutique next door, nearly blundered into the girls then waited politely behind them. As always, he dressed the part: tan leisure suit and black Travolta shirt with wing collars.

"Mister Snappy," I said, our sobriquet for him. He raised his eyebrows, mugging surprise that we had actual customers. Corey waved him to the end of the counter to pour his usual, a large coffee to go with room for milk.

The sidewalk had come alive. Our fabled foot traffic had materialized at last. Somewhere upstream the ice had shifted and Chicago winter was breaking up. Two faces lingered in the front window, checking the slice pie. Walkers slowed at the door, peering in through the glass.

The young ladies had decided. They were in the mood for crêpes: a cheese, two sugar, and a Grand Marnier, pronounced *mariner*. The designated orderer wore braces. One apple juice, one strawberry shake, and two Diet Pepsis. They gravitated to the jukebox and peered down, searching for any tune they could relate to. Disco was not an option. Eventually they settled on "Rocket Man," about as commercial as we got, non-retro.

"They're swarming out here," Corey reported from the griddle, looking out the front window, his voice tight. I had rung the girls' sales and was starting on their pop and juice when the door dinged again.

My first thought was Sly Stone and the family. A lanky black dude with a 'fro and goggles was in the lead. Four others filed in behind him, two male, one female, and an indeterminate. I finished the girls' drinks and started writing a ticket for Sly: two slices, an avocado sandwich, an Italian Stallion meatball sandwich. Bruce was getting up for a refill. Elton was crooning. Corey whipped around me, taking the crêpe baskets to the back. The indeterminate hadn't decided yet.

Where to start? I threw in the slices, which gave me seconds to think. Sly and company were going to eat in house. They would need drinks.

The door dinged. A bearded disciple this time, probably of Maharaj Ji. Corey was still in the back, only standing, talking to Bruce beside his table.

"A little help here?" I had to project over Elton. I had meant Corey who was hustling back, but Bruce was following with his jacket, stuffing his mouth with the last of his crêpe. Then they were both behind the counter.

"I asked Bruce if he wanted to help us, five bucks an hour. He has rotating Saturdays off at Barbara's."

At that point I would have taken the Maharaj. I pulled a red apron out of the cabinet and Bruce popped the strap over his head.

"I need an avocado sandwich," I told Corey, "and an Italian Stallion." I pulled out the slices seconds before they burned and greeted the disciple who looked wasted and peaceful.

"I'll have an avocado sandwich," said the indeterminate. We tried to collect when an order was placed, but Sly and the rest started toward the back. "Three Pepsis and a Sprite," Sly added over his shoulder. "I'll have a papaya juice," the indeterminate finished off.

Corey had Bruce at the register, unfolding a menu and slapping it flat, giving a crash course on pricing. Then, "Two avocados, one Stallion," he confirmed in my direction, pushing up his glasses. He pivoted to the table and pulled the bread.

"Do you have tea?" the disciple asked.

"We do," I said, and tried to find it on the menu board. "Red Zinger, Orange Spice, and Peppermint. And English Breakfast." Profit margin on one tea? Eighty-five cents? Sorry, no Lapsang Souchong.

Two chicks were up and bopping to Elton. Sly and the family were in two booths, taking it all in.

"That was three Pepsis . . ." Bruce said.

"And a Sprite. I'll get the papaya juice. We'll collect on their way out."

He scribbled the order and hurried to pull the pops from the cooler.

By the next wave, we had settled into our grooves—Bruce writing tickets, collecting, pulling pop, and pouring coffee. I took slices and full pies and sandwiches, and Corey played utility infielder for ice cream and anything else.

The afternoon rolled on, gloriously warm and bright. The citizenry were on parade, the first escapees of spring. New Towners overflowed the sidewalk, and a number routinely deflected into our eddy, staring wide-eyed over the oven at the menu board. Most ordered light and rejoined the flow, but even so, by mid-afternoon our tables were full.

At one point I turned from making a slice pie and was surprised to see a woman standing alone in the center of the counter. She had materialized, a willowy dream date with a platinum do and a leopard jacket. Her partner, in a tight zippered jumpsuit of black leather, reflecto shades and shaved head, held on to their Doberman's leash with both hands. The monster squatted in our vestibule.

Corey looped a twist of strawberry soft-serve into her shake cup, then two half-twists of banana. He set the cup beneath the spindle and whipped and whipped as though the perfect consistency of a strawberry-banana shake was not only achievable, it was routine.

I collected from Ms. Glam, complementing her on her canine which was equally glorious but which, she informed me with cellophaned eyes and a contemptuous affect, was not a Doberman but a Rottweiler. "Honky Tonk Women" started cranking out of the box before I could say easy mistake. Precious, I reminded myself, each customer was precious. I tried to maintain that insight when I saw Glam bent over the curb, presenting the cup with the top half torn off to slurping glorious.

The natural break came around six. The anomalous sun was below the building tops and the chill returned. Broadway was still flowing, but the natives had migrated to their cars.

"You saved us, man. What can we say?" I shook Bruce's hand and Corey put thirty in his other.

"Was it like Barbara's?" Corey's eyebrows elevated.

"Christ," Bruce said and hung out his tongue. We set him up with slices and a salad.

"*Vista la hasta,*" he groaned, affecting a limp, and dragged his broken body through the door. Alone in the café, we high-fived and laughed like fools, celebrating our triumphs. We had survived our trial by fire, the sudden burst of patronage, the ring of the register and the ding of the door, an outpouring of acceptance like the first evidence that we were not insane and doomed. Mostly we celebrated the sidewalk now dead, being dead ourselves, but jubilant.

I retreated to the stool but Corey opened the register. He pulled out the bills and stacked them on the table below the counter, out of sight of the window and the door. He started counting, scribbling subtotals on a ticket slip.

The tables were littered with the spoils of victory: wadded napkins, crushed cans, and plastic boats of wax paper. The public, god bless 'em, failed to spot our four-foot waste can with red lid between the dining room and the Wurlitzer. Mental note to move it to the center of the room. Small saviors they were, the public, saviors of the checkbook, every one. I forced myself to stand. I cleared the tables and wiped them down. When I returned, Corey was closing the register.

"Incredible day, right?"

He didn't answer, but he was rubbing his forehead. He turned to the plastic pot on the pizza table where we kept the tickets. We had sworn to be diligent about writing a ticket for every order, but in the heat of battle and while training Bruce, we had probably missed a quarter. He thumbed through them, dropped them back in the pot.

"Two pizzas," he said, cryptic, complete. He sat on the edge of the steel sink next to pizza pans fanning up out of the water.

"A koan, oh master? *No comprende.*"

"We sold two full pizzas all day."

Okay, I thought, the best of good luck, since the Blodgett had been working constantly on at least one slice pie since Sly and the family. I didn't see how we could have handled more orders. He gazed at me like a sad proctologist.

"We just worked our asses off for six hours—and grossed three hundred thirty-seven dollars. That's twenty-eight bucks an hour for each of us, gross—and crazy busy."

Corey's face was a window. Through it I saw Sammy A in a Phillies cap. His voice filled our heads, echoed from the front door to Queenie's ventilation tailpipe. *You might do the volume, but your gross will be too low.*

Slump-shouldered in his red apron, parked on the side of the sink, Corey was Hector, vanquished. "We have to do deliveries," he said.

Chapter 15

"WHAT do you call this freak?" I asked. Corey and I had already cracked up and settled back to Earth after Janis unveiled her creation.

"You're right, he does need a name." She cocked her head for the right viewing angle and considered a moment. "Weevil Knievel! Think I could be sued?" She was clearly delighted and had every reason to be.

Comparing Janis's ho-daddy surfer to the photos of Evil in the *Sports Illustrated* on her work table, the resemblance came down to the crash helmet. After that, her conception took off. Bug-eyed Weevil balanced a stack of pizza boxes on one hand, leaning into a downhill curve on a skateboard powered by three spewing jets. His grin looked cranked up and crazed, like Joe Cocker in ecstasy.

"I didn't know you had it in you," I said. "It must have felt good to get it out!"

"It's beautiful," Corey confirmed.

"Changes?" Janis was eager for input. She had landed on her feet in her new studio on Deming, only a couple of blocks from Wray's on Arlington. As much as the Cavern was my ideal space, a dark rambling underground for the echoes I was after, Janis's was like Prospero's island, her fantasy incubator. I recognized two posters from her third floor in Evanston, the Medici portrait and the Pre-Raphaelite woman with flowing hair like her own. Beside a mirror with a baroque frame repainted blue, a marionette with a sparkling tiara hung suspended in air. Two plump gnomes huddled on the end of her sofa which was spread with magazine photos of skateboarders. On a sunny window table under a Tiffany lamp, I recognized Janson's *History of Art*, open to the early Renaissance, beside a pile of *Life* and *Popular Photography* and a playbill from the Goodman Theatre. A book of Beardsley line drawings peeked out from under a sketchpad covered with details of Weevil.

We studied the image, trying to come up with suggestions. For a commission of two hundred dollars, half in advance, it was clear we had made out like bandits. Fortunately for both parties, Janis wanted to expand her portfolio. Our main requirement was to be eye-catching, exceptional. We were there, no doubt. But Janis stated the question that had to be topmost in our minds.

"Do you think people will want to buy a pizza from this man?"

This was to be the image of the café, our one and only delivery menu cover. I tried to envision an eight-and-a-half by eleven sheet folded in half then folded again: a four-and-a-quarter by five-and-a-half portrait of our goggle-eyed pizza man, stapled to every box.

"I love it," Corey said, dismissing all objections from the timid and the humorless. While I was weighing my reservations, he cut to the chase like a samurai, blindfolded but second-sighted.

"I want it on everything," I said. "'Make no little plans'. Napkins, aprons," knowing we weren't about to redo any of those.

"No tattoos?" she prodded. "You said a menu cover, I believe. I'll tell my attorney to draw up a license thingy for all these uses."

"Yeah, tell him to send it to my accountant Corey in the café. He has the early shift." One spot on the drawing caught my attention. "You might soften up his mouth a little."

"The teeth," Corey added. "Maybe close up some spaces. Ha! See ya. Great job."

"See you at four-thirty," I said.

Janis hit the area with an eraser and a few pencil strokes, upgrading his smile.

"Like this? You could see it again when I'm done, or I could do the final ink and paste him up."

"We trust you." I was aware of being alone with Janis's new persona, artist in her studio, for the first time since she moved out of the Cavern. "How are you doing? Your place looks like great." I wondered where things stood with Adam.

"I'm getting settled in. Staying busy." She had a practical air, businesswoman, designer, hair pulled back. I waited a few beats for more but that was all.

"*The Fifth of July.*" I read from a work in progress, what appeared to be a poster for a play. The lettering was blocked in and the treatment was nothing like ours—a skeleton tree hung with moss and a rail fence vanishing into sundown colors.

"It's for Steppenwolf. They'll be putting it on at the St. Nicholas this summer."

"Hey, it's what you wanted to do. I'm proud of you."

"It's a start. You two are my only clients so far."

"When Weevil hits the streets . . . give us some cards for the café." I could sense her holding back. "How are things with Adam?"

She went to her window table and started stacking magazines. "I think he's gone. Maybe a late spring break or something. Melanie's out of town too. The way they're going, I wouldn't be surprised if they got hitched." She turned, checked my reaction. "That's just me saying."

We had Melanie in common, from different angles. We had outgrown our adolescent fits, but like a family ghost, she could still unsettle both of us.

"Anyway . . ." Spring clouds had blown in under the late morning sun. Janis switched on her lamp and the Tiffany dome glowed green, copper, and gold. "There's this guy in Stepp—Gary, he's in the repertory cast. He's hot, but who knows. How about you?" She turned to face me, squaring up. Her gaze was level and womanly, no longer the runaway girl from the suburb. She was a free agent like the rest of us, on the make, and I felt a tug.

"Not much," I said, flashing on Luz Guillen in her bumblebee stripes.

"That sounds like more than nothing." She was looking coy in her simple button blouse and jeans. She had no sofa in her studio, only an old stuffed chair, a couple of stools, and two wooden chairs at her breakfast table. Separated from the main room by a little dresser, her bed was spread with a plush coverlet, deep blue like royal velvet.

"How about not like anything?"

She grinned and I was falling toward her by force of nature, field of gravity. One arm around her, under her silky ponytail, I licked her lips before she pushed lightly away.

"I have to go to my day job," she whispered, throaty, keeping the coy grin. I backed off, hands in the air.

"You're staying busy, for sure. You are an all-busyness woman. In keeping with which . . ." I took a card from her holder: Janis Rosen, Graphic Design. "Now I have your office number."

"I can bring Weevil to the café day after tomorrow. He'll be camera-ready."

"We'll have your pathetic second hundred for you. Maybe more for good behavior." I pinched at her and she dodged.

"Get outta here," she said. Then, "Call me."

A few steps into the hall, I glanced back. She had left her door ajar and was sending a toodle-oo wave. Janis was in the realm of possibility. It was a city of possibilities. We were all free agents, all in the game.

As the days warmed, the walk-in business continued to pick up. Soon we were able to afford a minimum run of the delivery menu, five thousand on goldenrod stock, scored and folded. Janis's crazed pizza hustler needed to find his way to every potential customer in our start-up delivery area, which ran from Belden north to Belmont and from the lake west to Halsted.

Corey and I started menuing together an hour before opening, toting a couple of hundred menus in grocery bags, working opposite sides of the street. Single houses were the easiest: one menu on the front door handle or through the mail slot. The only downside was our random nemesis, a barking guard dog hitting the inside of the door, stopping breath like a slug of curare.

Apartment buildings were next. We left a short stack close to the mailboxes, a conservative number in case the building super confiscated them. The four-plus-one buildings with their sunken fishbowl fronts were a hybrid. The four floors of tenants above one of parking meant at least thirty mailboxes in the lobby, tall ones with enough space around the aluminum faces to slip a menu inside, technically an illegal act with no postage. Fortunately, it was Chicago, where technically illegal seldom interfered with what worked. Four-plus-ones illustrated the principle in another way. Occasionally a tenant leaving or entering would let the glass door close at its own rate, so slowly that building code must have spec'ed it. The first time it happened, I recognized the fortuity—right place, right time. Inside, I crossed the little faux lobby to the elevator and rode it, smelly with an unnerving bounce in the floor, to the top.

One menu went on each doorknob, wedged between the door face and the jamb. I could easily do both sides of the hall, facing doors, in a single pass then take the stairway down, floor by floor. Occasionally a high-strung mutt would go off inside an apartment, but overall, the tacky four-plus-ones were made to be menued. I could do a building in under ten minutes.

All of these residences were within our zone, thousands of potential calls for delivery. But I was haunted by a memory of delivering for Gonzo—the calls from the high-rises. When I made those deliveries, occasional menus were still visible in the halls, propped on door handles yet to be turned or slipped under the slabs, corners showing on the transoms. Those buildings were the real challenge, each one a potential mother lode, and a fearless menuer had taken them on.

I hadn't planned on my first. I was working Lincoln Park West alone. After a couple of mornings together, Corey reported that menuing was not his gig. He was happy to trade hours behind the counter for mine on the street, an arrangement that suited me fine. Working the North Side neighborhoods in spring was invigorating. April hail increasingly gave way to racing clouds and sun. The variety in the dense blocks—brownstones and frame houses and bungalows, two-flats and brick apartment buildings like fortresses that anchored the ends of the blocks—gave each trip to a lobby or a mail slot a tinge of adventure. I appreciated the freelancing freedom of it, the micro-trespass with the constant possibility of having to adapt or finesse. If the café failed, I could see postman as my day job, although the fantasy tended not to include winter. John Prine had done it, once. Maybe "Angel From Montgomery" came to him in the six steps between a squeaky iron gate and a metal mailbox beside a door on Wolfram. But I was on Lincoln Park West, outside the range of inspiration, when my first high-rise presented itself.

It was a newer building, about a dozen stories. I was only thinking about the mailboxes when I pulled the outside door, but as I spotted them on the side of the short lobby, a harried-looking woman my age in a trench coat and armed with a black leather portfolio clicked past me. The inner door was still open but closing. The automatic calculation: rate of closure to distance in strides, three maximum. Physics was ineluctable, not a matter of choice. In a moment I was alone in the lobby.

The elevator she had taken opened immediately. A trace of cologne lingered from her rushing self. The panel had two columns of discs, P on the lower left and 10 on the upper right. I pressed 10 and the doors closed.

My pulse rose with the floors. By the time I stepped out at the top, the realization had caught up with me: I was an illegal alien feeling the thrill of trespass. Each floor and connecting stairwell could mean discovery. A door could open in my face. The elevator could ding on my floor. Occupants and transients, we were random scatter in a tower in the sky. Sooner or later we would collide, or nearly miss. This was menuing without a net. It required cool, and a special cunning.

Silent and quick, I worked the carpeted halls, crowning door handles with Weevil, winding down the stairwell. When I reached the bottom and exited through the lobby doors, crossing the line to safety, the air never smelled so fresh. The rush was like the end of a perfect set. It was late morning on a Thursday, prime time for low occupant activity, and low risk. I had done nearly one hundred doors and escaped undetected. One high-rise down.

But there were more, challenges looming like mountains, like a cordillera heaved up against the lake. Painted on the glass front doors: No Soliciting. No Trespassing.

The doorman buildings ranged from worse to impossible, but each one was a potential bonanza. For these, I refined my technique. My one pair of slacks, not jeans. A button-down Oxford, blue. A Goodwill trench coat or my one sports jacket from freshman year, depending on weather. Doubled grocery bags held high enough to conceal the contents: a few hundred menus on goldenrod stock scored and folded. Start by lingering outside, appearing not to linger. Targeting a group to follow in was best, but singles worked too and were much more common. When they saw my arms around the bag, a surprising number would hold the door. Pulling out jingling keys was a good reinforcement, an auditory cue that I belonged and was readying my apartment key.

In the elevator I let any other occupants choose their floors first then punched a higher one. The grand top floor wasn't necessary. It could raise eyebrows.

Once in the hall, I became a stealth aircraft, cruising, missing no doors. If a tenant appeared I would keep going, bag held high, above suspicion, through the exit door at the end of the hall and down the stairs.

The specter of Chicago's finest was never distant. What easier way to protect and serve than to bust a kid for trespassing in a lakeside tower? College kid. Smartass. Welcome to Addison and Halsted. An attorney will be appointed for you.

Menuing the mountains took a cool head, planning and focus, physical agility, and the capacity to adapt. Most, it required a viral ability to penetrate the consciousness of tenants so as to move among them without fear. I modeled myself on the fugitives in *Invasion of the Body Snatchers*, blending seamlessly with the pod people.

Keep your head, execute the plan, and reap the rewards: the ground floor and the air of freedom, together with the sweet knowledge that one building was the equivalent of blocks of mail slots. Those who would arrive home to the ethereal floors that glittered by night had the means, and the irresistible longing, to be served. The object was to make the phone ring.

We were holding our own, but barely. We had paid and we kept paying. Utilities and rent and meat and produce, and monthly on the loan. Paying was our only constant. We had paid to bait our delivery area. The afternoon of the first menuing day came and went. After five I checked to make sure we had a dial tone. At twenty to six with two at the counter and one couple at a table who had chosen a rarely played classic on the jukebox, Morricone's theme to *The Good, the Bad and the Ugly*, we heard a new beast: electronic coyote. We checked each other and then the phone. The white light was blinking. Line one.

Our ring sounded like Gonzo's, but the call was ours alone. Out there an anonymous feeder had taken our bait. Over the next nights there were more, and each one was a high, a well-placed Weevil and a strike. As our calls multiplied, the addresses became familiar, ones I had menued that morning or earlier in the week. Corey and I started off trading deliveries and manning the counter, but since I had menued most of the buildings, more deliveries fell to me by way of efficiency, and Corey specialized in pounding out orders.

Like menuing versus minding the store, the division of labor suited us both. Driving the nighttime city was my gig. I needed a musician's illusion of freedom. Corey was the family man. In my stint of driving for Gonzo, the city's fall descent had begun, and although deliveries rose as the temperature dropped, I drove through a city mostly locked in. Now the unlocking was under way. The denizens were leaving their dens, trying out their limbs.

The moving city was all fascination after dark. Dense parkas were giving way to jackets and coats, female forms emerging out of wraps. Occasional crowds spilled onto sidewalks in pools of light from a movie marquee or nightclub neon on Belmont or Lincoln. Chicago was reimagining itself, a city of light rising again like an invitation, drawing hopefuls from the plains and up the river, schemers and writers and musicians on the make.

The buildings I had menued were transformed by night. The lighted windows of high-rises looked orderly and magical stacked and set back into stories of sky. Doors I had visited in stealth became doorbells I could press legally or numbers I could give to doormen I had passed earlier that day or on another day, incognito.

The traffic was my element. I rolled with the groan and sigh of buses and complaining horns. There was a jamming, shambling rhythm to it. All the needed notes were there, blended with overtones and undertones. Snatches of tunes and lyrics, motifs and themes, conjoined in instants then dissolved, fleeting but not impossible to capture. Tuning in was all I needed to find the pulse in the shimmering veins of traffic, and that Wray needed to match the rocking, rolling hum to chords and runs on steel strings. Alone in the Mustang with the windows up, I had the time and space for the hidden music to reveal itself, and if it didn't, I could punch my presets, boost the volume, and elevate closer to inspiration. Such were the pluses of driving.

Delivery was working, and our nightly gross began to climb. After two weeks we expanded our area north to Irving Park and west to Racine. The Saturday after I menued the high-rises north of Belmont, we got too much of a good thing.

Chapter 16

"I'M telling them over an hour," Corey said as soon as I pulled the door. He looked shiny-faced and frazzled. Four boxes sat on top of the oven, probably already late. The pizza table was chaos, two prep pots empty. Three tables were uncleared in the back. Bruce was handling a customer at the counter.

"What did they say?"

"Thanks but no thanks. An hour is their cutoff. It's fifty-six nineteen. Pay when you get back." He stacked the boxes on the counter and retired to the cooler for the bag of pop.

Not only were we losing orders, we were wasting the menus and the menuing time and no doubt alienating customers for good. It was Saturday night but there would be other nights. Sunday finished earlier, but it could be just as fast.

We had offered Bruce fifty cents an hour more than Barbara's, cash, and signed him up for Friday through Sunday nights. With two behind the counter on the weekends and one of us driving, we found we could match the flow. But the flow wasn't smooth. Rushes happened for no clear reason, only dumb synchronicity. Undocumented it may have been, but it was clearly a law of human behavior. On whatever circadian alarm, they all sat up at once and lit up both our phone lines long enough for deliveries to back up and turn into cancellations. That was the fundamental issue. The other, although neither of us admitted it outright, was that since we had started delivering, both Corey and I had been stuck in the café every weekend, and we were ragged. It was time to hire a driver.

We started by propping a Wanted sign in the front window, and it didn't take long to generate action. After a panhandler we recognized who asked if it was a salaried position and a young woman with a bike but no car, we hired a stubble-faced guy in his forties who claimed he was an ex cab driver and knew all the streets from Howard to the Loop. He started on a Friday, handled the night well, and vanished without a trace before his Sunday shift. We learned to get phone numbers.

Next we decided to try a two-line classified in the *Reader*. The paper hit the street on Thursday, and I had just unlocked the door at noon when it opened behind me and a young man followed me in.

"I saw your ad," he said. Short and clean-cut, he wore a lemon-colored jacket, as though he had come straight from the golf course.

"You're quick," Corey said.

"That's good, right? I saw you open at twelve." His accent reminded me of Sonny at Gonzo, Iranian or Iraqi.

"Have you driven before?" I asked.

"Oh yes, every day. All over. My brother and I have business machine repair shop. On Addison. I pick up, deliver all over, North Side, West Side. We fix typewriters, calculators, registers. We fix that for you when it goes out." He nodded toward our chrome beauty and flashed a smile, crooked teeth. His lips popped back over them.

We introduced ourselves.

"Kip," he said. "Hegazy."

"A Saudi name?" Corey asked.

"Egyptian. My family came from Egypt." He glanced between us anxiously. "My father is citizen," he added.

While Corey wrote down his name and phone, I checked the curb for his car and guessed at one parked a couple of spaces down the block.

"Your Pinto?"

"Yes, is in tune-up, everything. Compact, park anywhere." It was a seventy-two or three, copper-colored, with a back bumper dent. But he was right, it was a scatmobile built for delivery.

Corey was chatting with him, trying to guess the city. I heard Cairo. Kip said Luxor.

"What do you think?" Corey asked in front of our applicant, his eyebrows up, which meant Kip had hit a bull's-eye, no reason to mess around.

"Sure," I said, "Let's start at five." We had agreed on a driver for the weekend, but I wanted a tryout night first. Plus, I didn't want to lose a good driver on only three nights a week, which I guessed had failed to inspire our taxi driver.

Kip reappeared exactly at five. He had only a ten-dollar bill for change so we banked him thirty in small bills, to be repaid at the end of the night. Between deliveries, he sat quietly at the farthest table in the back working a tile game on a palm-sized tablet. He still wore his natty yellow jacket, but his shoes, black Converse high-tops, had worn-through spots around the toe caps. He passed tryout night with flying colors. Nights of freedom were within our reach, and we both knew Corey's first would be the next night, on Friday.

"You think this will work?" he said. It was a couple of minutes before five, and we had spotted Kip's car pull up outside. Bruce had started his Friday shift and had built a slice pie, start to finish. Our team was at full strength.

"Absolutely. We've got it," I said. "You want a pie to take?" Corey had a meeting of the Eckists. I tried to picture meditation with a potluck. Maybe they fasted.

"No, can't stand it." We both consumed more than enough on premises. He untied his apron and the phone rang. Bruce took it and Corey watched him write the ticket.

"It's Racine," he said. "I could take it on the way."

"Get outta here," I said. "Our driver needs to pay for his gas."

Corey did, and then I was the sole boss, dependent on my staff of two, an employee and a contractor. By five-thirty the phone started to ring and customers began drifting in. I recognized one couple as repeaters, which was encouraging. I switched to the phone and counter, giving Bruce practice as chief cook.

By seven I was starting to admit to myself that we were handling it. Bruce was slinging pizzas and I was boxing orders and ringing sales. Kip was our Hermes in a Pinto. I allowed myself to fantasize we were a well-oiled machine, even if we were anything but. One day, maybe.

I was slicing peppers for Bruce but revisiting Lucy, compact package, dancing bee. She could have been a lucky accident on a perfect night, or a preview of the delights to be found in gig-land. And then I was on to Janis on the first night, denim dress, the glory of exhaustion. Free agents, we were. There were songs in that wonderment. The bell woke me.

"Good evening," I said. The disciple was back, in the company of a drag queen with major eye makeup. Two Red Zinger teas and two crêpes, a cheese and a Grand Marnier. The in-house traffic alternated, rushes and lows. I invited one panhandler to leave, nothing special. Deliveries held steady. Kip had a dozen by nine, and with no orders up, he retreated to his back table with a Pepsi and a slice.

In another five minutes, based on the principle of all at once for no known reason, the phone exploded. I wrote six tickets in a row without leaving the stool.

"I'm going to need . . ." Bruce started when he saw the orders.

"Everything," I said. "I'm on it." I prepped Bruce when I could and started bagging the pop and side orders. Queen was at the box and then the chorus of sopranos filled the café like Saint James Cathedral.

I saw her today at the reception

Queen was bopping in slo-mo and Keith was playing unplugged.

"I can take one," I told Bruce and took the ticket for one of the twelve-inchers, which would fit on the front table.

You can't always get what you want

I would have to be done on the table by the time the others needed to come out of the oven. I was willing the door to stay closed for another three minutes when it dinged open. Had they been waiting for their theme song?

"Well, hey there. Corey said you've been in but I've always been out. How are you doing?" I was spinning. Keep wheels on rails.

"We're good. We brought you a new customer. This is Toni."

I was greeting solid-looking Toni with a pompadour but my focus was gone. I was under the spell of her friend who had introduced her, no-nonsense Denise with the Janet Leigh eyes. And on Denise's other side, white-toothed and dreamy-eyed and deep-skinned like a princess of Bahia Carnival, the muse Thalia.

"What can we . . ." I started as they scanned the board. Denise glanced toward the window and so did I, knowing already what I would see: one slice. I should have been on top of it.

"We'll have another slice pie out in just a few."

"Good," Denise said, checking the others. "That's what we want—samplers."

A little bit me glanced off the brainpan. *A little bit you.*

"Great. What can I get you to drink while you're waiting? On the house . . . because you shouldn't have to wait." Although muses are perfectly welcome to wait in the café, especially after closing with the dinging door locked.

I set them up with a Diet Pepsi and two Mountain Dew. On the way to a table Thalia swung a few steps to the Stones, and Queen, who was still standing, joined her. They bopped impromptu in the middle of the floor as Mick and Keith were grinding gears of the spheres and Denise and Toni nodded along. The disciple was impassive, most likely stoned.

"Let's get a slice pie in next," I told Bruce before he started the last order. The other pies were starting to brown. I pulled and boxed the two darkest ones in the window, threw mine together, and slid it in.

Thalia was undulating, but mercifully I had no time to watch. I stapled the tickets to the boxes and considered Kip's route. Thirty-three hundred Clifton was the farthest. He could hit Seminary and Wellington on the way. Then working east and south, the eighteen hundred block of Buckingham. That customer was a repeater, a guaranteed five-buck tip. Finally Melrose west of Broadway. The other two were close and wouldn't be ready for a while. I could take them in a pinch.

"I'm giving you four," I told Kip. "This order makes sense to me, top to bottom, but you're the driver. Pay me when you get back. I'll have more for you." With his side orders, it took him two trips to the car. A few minutes after he left, I pulled the last two.

"How you doing?" I asked Bruce.

"Ni gnignah. That's 'hanging in' to you."

"Pepsi?"

"Can't stand the stuff. Except with rum, which I no longer drink. I could use a pineapple-coconut juice, though." He ambled toward the cooler. "I'll pretend it's a piña colada." Then he added, "slices."

Panicked, I dropped the oven door. Burning Thalía's slice pie would be humiliating beyond ruin. I pulled it onto a clean platter. Only a couple of pepperoni edges had turned.

"Slices are up," I called to the back. As I started to roll the cutter, two more drifted in, a tough-looking buzz cut with inked arms and his sallow waif. As they stood at the counter, I knew the fresh slices were working on them. We could run out again.

"Hi, folks, I'll be right with you." The tough stared back, dull-eyed. Fortunately, everyone from the back made it to the front, including the disciple and Queen, so I was able to load them up first. One cheese slice was left.

"Can I start you off with this one? We'll have another slice pie up in a minute." The buzz cut glowered at me. "On the house. It will only be five minutes," I lied.

I split the one slice in half on the paper plate and they took it back to a table. Peace for the moment. Bruce, yet to get his pineapple-coconut, had started another slice pie when the couple arrived, and he slid it in.

Denise's trio were at the box and another tune started. Thalia and Toni were laughing, playing a pinching game. "Really Got a Hold on Me," the Laura Nyro version.

Then Queen and Toni were sway-dancing while they ate. The tough frowned at them and the disciple continued impassive. Thalía was facing away at her table. Just as well.

The last two orders were waiting on top of the oven. I checked my watch and Bruce must have seen me because he said what I was thinking.

"He's been gone a while."

"Thirty-five minutes. I should take these two. One's on Briar and Orchard, the other is right there on the lake. Twenty minutes max. Will you be okay?"

"I've got it," he said and left to get his juice. "Go."

The night air was cool and fresh. I was back in the saddle, the freelance driver in a Mustang. I hit the two-flat on Briar first and then the condo in thirty-three hundred Lake Shore Drive where I rode the same elevator I had taken to menu the building two days earlier. On the way back I took Belmont to Broadway, which was always slow and which I never would have done if I hadn't been distracted. I needed to see our other driver.

I pulled the door and checked the back table. There was no music and only the three tables were occupied.

"Hear from Kip?"

Bruce shook his head.

Over an hour. I joined him behind the counter.

"Maybe car trouble?" He scraped the oven. New orders were up.

I couldn't convince myself. "He should have the sense to call in."

Pay when you get back, I had said, to save time. Thalía was laughing and the trio were animated. Queen and disciple were in heavy discussion, and the tough was slouched in the corner of his booth looking like he would have to be dragged out. I was seeing them and not seeing. *If you get back.* What had I set up?

Ten-forty. Corey could be home; he probably was. No, no call. It was my night.

In the pot of ticket copies I pulled the four he had taken and totaled them. Sixty-eight bucks. And we had banked him thirty at the start of the night. Take a breath. I was fantasizing this. What were the odds? Minimal. Car trouble was much more likely.

I was refusing to face it. I was being played. Kip, our clean-cut hustler from Luxor, was betting I'd do nothing. He was an import all right, but god knows from where, or where he was now.

The phone rang and light one was blinking. My breath stopped. The kid could be at a pay phone—a flat on the way back. Or Corey checking in. We were both staring at the light. Another ring.

"New American Café."

A voice from the world we solicited, the normal one, the alien one now.

"Sorry, we're not delivering for the rest of the night. But we'll resume tomorrow. Please try us again. Thanks."

Another one we had paid and scrambled for was lost, for sure. I pulled the cabinet drawer below the counter. Corey had written Kip's phone number on a ticket, and I found it where I had stuffed it.

What good would it do? If he was on the road, pointless. If he was home with our money, was he going to pick up? But he could have a roommate who might know something. I read the numbers, read them again. The disciple and Queen were gathering their paper plates and cups. Bruce was watching me.

"I'm going to call him." I spoke it like an oath. I punched the numbers.

Silence. "The number . . . out of service at this time . . . If you think—"

I slammed the receiver down and Bruce flinched. My heart was hammering like a fist. He said his brother's shop was on Addison. Where? I could find the listing. He could live around there. He could be anywhere.

Out a hundred bucks and flushing customers. On my night. I had left the door wide open. It was theft. Betting I would do nothing.

I lifted the receiver and punched the numbers, evenly, in succession: 9-1-1.

The operator's voice was female but tough, horrored-out.

"I want to report a burglary in progress." My voice was shaking with rage. "Twenty-nine thirteen Broadway." Bruce turned away. " New American Café."

Queen and the disciple were up, preparing to leave. The others went on at their tables. Thalia was only a customer now.

"Maybe I should tell them," I wondered aloud to Bruce. Or maybe no need—I'll meet the cops outside." He was giving me a wrong-end-of-the-shot-glass look. "What, you don't think I should have called them?"

"I don't know," he said, "if the burglary thing was exactly right."

What, then? A realization was dawning, one I didn't want to admit: Bruce was older, maybe Corey's age, and he had many more years of navigating Chicago. I turned to the back room to announce that we were expecting visitors.

Lights burst in and rolled around the walls and around the walls.

Queen and the disciple froze mid-floor, dropping white paper. The tough was out of his booth, scrambling to the back door. Denise's face was blank.

A crash behind me and a bell, the door slammed back against the wall. Red and white lights, red and white—two squad cars in the street. Two hulks in blue inside, jamming the aisle along the counter. Bruce stumbled back into the table.

"Chicago police—where is it?" the one in front blurted, no hat, jaw clenched, meaty forearms together like a prow, black pistol pointed at the ceiling. Somebody screamed. A muse. "Where!"

Chapter 17

"DRIVER," I stammered, numb tongue. Hulking black cop in the lead, eyes nailing me. Red-white. A third in the doorway and another on the sidewalk. Red-white. "Delivery driver ripped us . . ."

The leader pivoted to face the others, hand up, palm out. "Stand down! It's bullshit!"

The second officer, younger and white, lowered his gun. Shoulders dropped, chest rising, falling. The third in the doorway resnapped his holster guard. Stand down.

Queen trashed her paper plate and edged her way past the first two cops, the disciple close behind. The third cop followed them out. The waif took the tough by the hand and hauled him from the back door matter-of-factly through the front.

"Ladies." I tried to dissuade, but there was no stopping them. "So sorry about this. It doesn't happen every night." Denise was in the lead, stone-faced. Thalia picked her way gingerly around the hulking presence of police. Toni was trying a half-grin appropriate to the fiasco. "Come see us again, please." I was abandoning that hope, on all levels. They exited into the red-and-white beacons announcing to the neighborhood that New American Café was the scene of crime. We four were left inside.

"You want to break down the Taylor?" I directed at Bruce.

"Sure." He headed toward the machine with a wobble.

"You call it in?" The black officer's tone had modulated. The younger one flipped open a notepad. I nodded.

"You're Mitch?" The young one read off the pad.

"Are you the manager?" the other asked.

"Worse. I'm one of the owners."

His eyes said it all—disdainful, weary of ignorance. *Owner? This kid? Where's he from, college? Pity the kid.* The senior officer was at least forty. He would bench two hundred. He turned to junior and they changed places. He was ceding the interview, too dispirited to go on.

The younger started by asking how much was taken, then, "The driver, do you have ID?"

"He said his name was Hegazy. H-E-G . . ." He printed on the pad. I dug in the drawer for the ticket with his name and number. "He gave us a phone but it's dead."

He looked up, stared, waiting. I steadied the ticket with both hands and read the number.

"And the vehicle, make and model? Plate number?"

"It's a Ford Pinto, a copper color." And no license, abysmally stupid. I tried to recall what I saw through the window—ding on the right bumper, the colors of the plate. "Illinois plate. I don't have the full number, but there's a two-five."

He printed, curls of contempt at the corners of his mouth. Officer, what class? Lieutenant or grunt? His name tag said A. Hecker. He looked up.

"Is that it?"

How did I know? Sure. "I guess so."

"Give us a minute," senior ordered, name tag, L. Duchamp. They went out to their squad car under the lights that whipped on, unabated. At least the other car was gone. And the lights would discourage any walk-ins, which I was in no shape to deal with. I retired to the back to clean up the litter left in haste. Part of Thalia's slice lay on her plate, her teeth marks visible. The waif had folded her napkin crisply into a bird in flight.

Ninety-eight bucks. Customers lost. The Muses alienated. Crime scene and lights. I had plenty of time to think before they came back in.

"Shakir Hegazy." Duchamp read off Hecker's pad. "Seventy-two Pinto. He's in the neighborhood, thirty-five fifty Pine Grove. You want to get your money back?" He grinned, avuncular. "Let's take a ride."

"Chicago police!" Duchamp pounded the door with the side of his fist, and it reverberated in the hallway of hollow doors and drumskin walls. The building was not a four-plus-one, but the quality was the same for as many floors as could be crammed into the height limit.

No response. But I had spotted his car in the same block and Hecker confirmed the plate.

Duchamp pounded twice more. "Chicago police!" He let a few beats pass then nodded to his partner.

Hecker was holding a metal wedge the shape of a staple gun. The front tapered into a proboscis, a three-inch pick as thin as a hacksaw blade. He inserted the pick into the deadbolt lock and squeezed the trigger twice. Then he traded the pick gun for a short rod like an Allen wrench and twisted. The lock turned.

Incomprehensibly, I was in a hallway in a building I had gained access to by Chicago police pressing half a dozen buzzers. We were going to break into the apartment of the driver I had hired in the sane light of day.

Hecker had switched to a flat metal strip thin enough to work in beside the doorknob.

I pictured Kip in the café, yellow jacket, threadbare high-tops. What were the odds he had a gun?

Hecker checked Duchamp who nodded, and Hecker nodded. A turn of the knob and we were in.

"Police!" Duchamp called again into the dark. Hecker's flashlight came on.

A flashback of light from a mirror. A low table with floor pillows: two crushed Coke cans, soiled paper plates with burned stick matches, and a bong. By the front window, a padded swivel chair heaped with clothes. Between the table and the window, a sofa bed pulled out with rumpled covers and a pair of jeans. Lingering dark scents of incense or spices.

"Hegazy," Duchamp called. "Shakir."

The silence brought a perverse sense of relief. Gone, a good try. Did all we could do. But I was denying his undeniable car. A stirring sound on the other side of the wall.

Around the corner Hecker's light hit a closed door. Duchamp double-knocked and gripped the knob. I was seeing Kip, concealed carry, pocket pistol. Knob turned, unlocked. Door opened inches, caught. Behind Duchamp, Hecker angled the beam into the crack. Duchamp yanked the door shut then shoved it. Again. His gun was out. He shouldered the hollow slab once. In a loud rap and crack of wood the door flew open.

"I no, no—please no," from the darkness. Duchamp hit the wall switch. On a bed in the corner of a white room bare as a cell, Kip cowered under a blanket, knees drawn up, face a mask of terror.

"Hands up. Show me your hands!"

"Please no." Kip's hands surfaced, skinny arms, white T-shirt.

"Let's have the money. Come on."

"No, no, please."

"What you mean, no? Who sleeps in the other room? Is that your roommate? Your boyfriend? Has he got it?" Duchamp holstered his pistol but moved closer to the bed, towering over Kip, tilting forward, looking set to heave him up and into the wall.

"No no, I was coming back, bring money when I work tomorrow. No. Allah, I swear."

"No Alibaba, Shakir!" Duchamp whipped the cover off him. White briefs, skinny legs, body folded in, birdlike. "Don't dis me, man. You are freaking dissing me. You're in deep shit, Shakir. You know what deported means? Let's have it, all of it."

Kip edged off the bed, crouching, servile. He kept his hands in the air then mimed a move with one, saucer eyes checking for permission. He slipped the hand under the mattress and extracted a fold of bills in a chrome clip, handed them over.

Hecker stepped forward and Kip cringed, but the cop lifted the light mattress onto its side, checking the box spring for more. Let it drop.

Duchamp pulled off the clip and dropped it on the bed then passed the bills to me. They felt strange, like contraband. I counted.

"You want to press charges?" Duchamp dominated the room, huge as a linebacker. I wasn't sure he meant it as a question. Hecker flipped open his pad.

Dwarfed by his captors, Shakir appeared to fold into himself. We were the machinery of justice. He had tried to screw me, and there were consequences, according to the laws of nature and physics. And to society, there was a debt to pay.

I had separated ninety from the bills, and I dropped the rest, the cash he had brought to start, on the bed. As I did, I noticed for the first time the wooden folding chair he had wedged under the doorknob. It lay busted on the floor, halfway between the door and the closet. In the closet hung two shirts, and between them, a lemon yellow jacket.

Chicago's finest were waiting for closure.

"I got what we came for. It could've been a misunder-standing." Everyone in the room knew what it was and wasn't. I held up the bills like proof of victory, a token of appreciation. "Plus, I left an employee. He can't close by himself." That fact seemed persuasive. Hecker gave a nod.

Duchamp appeared to uncoil. "You are one lucky Aliba-ba, Shakir," he pronounced deliberately, nodding to drive it home. He resnapped his holster guard, pulled the door that had rebounded halfway closed, and left the room. Hecker folded his pad and followed.

I was alone with the prisoner I had spared. But I had also loosed the jackals on him. He could shower me with gratitude or curse me to the pits of hell. We avoided each other's eyes. Shakir was shock-waved, frozen in place. The room swelled with exhaustion. We had been through an evil episode together, but nothing we would ever talk about. I followed Hecker out the door.

"You saved my partner a shitload of paperwork at the station," Duchamp said on the way back to the cafe. "Now we'll be off in ten. A win-win, right?" He glanced in the rearview, testing out his jargon on the college boy.

A few minutes before midnight, the lights were still on and Bruce was hanging in behind the counter. I would let him go and finish closing myself, get a start on my penance.

"Thanks again. You guys come by the café anytime. We'll take care of you." I thought that was the way Corey had said it, although I didn't have menus to pass around at the station.

"Hey," Duchamp said, "next time, no 'burglary in pro-gress', all right?"

"Yeah, it wasn't the thing to say." Corey was massaging his forehead. Suddenly he laughed, as though he had banished the pain. After waking and replaying the scenes every couple of hours through the night, I called in the morning to let him know. He insisted I come over for breakfast and meet Beth and Arlo. They lived in Logan Square, fifteen minutes west of the café, on the top floor of a two-flat, less than modest.

"What, then? Dear sirs, our driver may or may not have forgotten to come back. That would get us high priority on a Friday night, right?" I was trying to keep my voice down in the dining nook as Beth warmed up around the corner in the living room. She played chords on the upright then cycled up and down the octaves. Arlo imitated her soprano, improvising in his own key.

"Well, next time we get the plate number."

"Insurance," I agreed.

"There is no insurance." Corey, still in his morning T-shirt, scratched his belly.

Great, thanks much. Easy for him to wax existential. I assumed he was in the afterglow of his meeting, on a higher level of Eckist consciousness. I downed the last of my coffee.

"If not insurance, then leverage. I don't want to go through that again. I'm standing with these two cops in his totally bare bedroom in this sleazeball building the thugs have basically broken into, at my request. And I'm like the capitalist pig with a boot over the kid's head. The law was on my side. I was the freaking Bad Man. Screw that. I'm glad he didn't piss his Jockeys."

Corey retrieved the coffee pot and Beth started humming. I stopped him at half a cup.

"She's placing the tone in her head," he said. "The forehead then the top, the final chakra." Then, after a sip, "What could you do, right? The situation was out of balance. Kip unbalanced it."

I nodded. Corey was having a satori hangover. I wasn't there yet, but I was zooming out, seeing the city differently, stratified, all of us in our own bands, affluent to desperate. Following my Friday from hell, I didn't anticipate admitting, as I did now, our good fortune.

"We're all struggling," Corey said, as though I had been thinking aloud. "An opportunity for insight, and spiritual advancement." He pointed to his temple with thumb cocked like a pistol. Clearly bemused, his eyebrows rose, a demented Buddha in glasses. "Hey, I want to show you something. I'll open a little later."

We took our coffees through the living room where Beth smiled with her eyes and went on powerfully humming. Outside another door, Arlo intercepted me, presenting his ring toy. I thanked him, gave it a shake, and handed it back, to which he responded with a total smile and more shakes.

"This is the one room he knows not to go in. I think this could be huge." Corey closed the door behind us.

Undersized for a bedroom, it was ideal as a study. He pulled his chair up to a desk bordered with stacks of paper and paperbacks. In the bookcase against the back of his desk: *The Intelligent Investor, Working, Flash Gordon: The Fall of Ming, Ragtime* in hardcover. On the floor, a stack of *Barron's* beside an open box, red and black, from Radio-Shack.

Centered on the desk, what appeared to be a miniature black-and-white TV sat on an aluminum box. In front of the box, attached by a wire, was a keyboard, smaller and flatter than a typewriter. The only familiar component was a cassette tape recorder wired to the side of the box. I had seen pictures, but not the real thing.

"Very sci-fi," I said. "Is it your birthday?"

"An Eckist left it to me last night. He just finished electronics school and he's moving to Denver with his girlfriend. They didn't have room in their Datsun. He said he had done all he wanted with it. Lars is an electronics genius."

And Varnadore had been a "mechanical genius." And Malowitz, financial. Corey was batting five hundred.

"This is the RadioShack one," I said. "There are others, right? Atari?"

"Right. Commodore, others. This is a TRS-80. Lars said the cognoscenti call it 'Trash-80'. But check this . . ."

He clicked a switch on the box and the screen came to life. A few white letters appeared in the upper left corner. He started to type and the keys made hollow clacking sounds.

`The quick brown fox jumped`

The white letters displayed one by one. He slapped a final key like punctuation and the Trash-80 talked back:

`Program not found`

"That's because it's just text, not a computer command with proper syntax."

"What a bitch."

"But now . . ."

He typed a few white letters, DIR, and slapped the final key and a list of single words rolled up the screen. Not English. He checked my reaction for amazement.

"This is like an inventory, or a catalog, of what's stored on here." His eyes glowed. "Now, this is the deal." In the other room, Beth had ended her warm-up and Arlo was crying. I tried not to take it as an omen.

"All kinds of programs run on this. The programming language is included. It's called BASIC. There are a couple of programs on these cassettes, and Lars wrote one, it's a filer, like a file to keep notes, or like a card catalog in a library. For example, I could make a card for this book—title, author, subject—and store it on this cassette. Later, I could type a command to find that card in the catalog and it would pop up. I could change it, print it, whatever.

"Now imagine if customers were books." He was beaming, delighted with his cliffhanger. "What do we know about all our delivery customers?"

"Name, usually last name. Address, phone."

"And most critically . . ." He allowed one beat. "What they ordered. We know what they want, what they pay for. It's right there on every ticket. And . . ." He was possessed by insight. "It's all about getting them to repeat. Repeat customers make a business. They're no-cost. Getting a new customer is expensive, menus, menuing time—you know it well, right? We can *cause* them to repeat. We use the computer to create customer cards, like book cards in a catalog. We can use the cards to print coupons—we can attach a printer to this. Make them offers they can't refuse. Staple the coupon to the box or mail it with a menu. If they ordered a medium last time, give them incentive to go for a large. Add sides." He was rolling faster. "We *manage the customers*. Nobody's doing this with deliveries."

"Who do we get to do this program, IBM? How about Kip's brother? He's in the biz machine biz, right? Maybe not."

"Ah! So glad you asked. We could start with Lars's program and modify it. There's a manual here." He pulled a spiral-bound paperback from under a thesaurus—*BASIC User's Manual for Level 1.* "That should be all you'll need." His deadpan implied he wasn't completely serious, but maybe hopeful.

"Oh right. Why not you?"

"Not exactly my thing. Plus, too many balls in the air—besides the café, financial counseling, the novel. You could have a career in programming as a fallback. But more likely, we could start a franchise of delivery places. Or sell the program to every delivery place in the country, and not just restaurants—any business with delivery. Think of it."

I thumbed through the manual. I didn't expect the cartoons. Make it fun! Science kid humor. Maybe it could be a market for Janis, I could show her. No doubt Corey sensed my level of enthusiasm.

"Or—what about your music partner?"

"John?"

"He's a lead player, right? And you said he plays chess. He's probably good in math. This could be the perfect hobby for him. It's the way a lot of programmers start out. And they read *Popular Science*."

I wasn't about to admit I once read *Popular Science.*

"I bet he'd go nuts with it." Corey concluded his argument, letting it percolate while I flipped through the BASIC manual, wondering if atonement might not always take a conventional form. In the wake of my screw-up, maybe more was required to restore balance in the cosmos, although I couldn't prove Corey was thinking that.

"Okay, I'll talk to him."

In another fifteen minutes we had loaded two boxes of electronics, the manual, and cassettes into the trunk of the Mustang.

"So we start over for a driver," I said.

"Bruce will be in tonight so we can trade off the deliveries. Which means mostly you."

"I'll place another *Reader* ad but it won't run until Thursday."

"I'll put the sign back in the window," Corey said. "We could get lucky. And we'll make sure the phone works this time, and get the plate number. Maybe we should make a copy of the driver's license. We could pick up a cheap used copier."

Right, and cram it into the back room with the mop bucket and cans of tomato sauce. And a printer. John could code back there too.

"I'll check into it," Corey finished.

"Thanks for breakfast," and a weak wave, was the most I could manage. "See you at four-thirty."

On the way home, the brilliance of Corey's scheme sank in. How many hot dog stands manage their customers by computer? But by the time I got to the Cavern, the genius was revealing its dark side. Someday, on some computer, together with my name, address, and phone on my customer card, an anonymous pair of eyes could peruse my purchases—what albums, what underwear, what booze—

and set out to manage me. Ingestion, then manipulation. Act now, trade up. Be first, last chance. Be new, ground floor. Be all you can be. How long would we have to keep anything to ourselves?

Dark visions didn't deter me from checking out the Trash-80. I set it up on the dining table, and within the half hour I had cabled the pieces together and plugged it in and was typing a few commands from the manual. In addition to Lars's cassette, we had a game cassette and one for storing recipes. Finally, one program claimed to do what the manual called word processing, with one-page examples: a letter, a contract, a page of *Twenty Thousand Leagues Under the Sea*.

I had my Smith Corona from college, which I used to make my lyrics appear published and copyrighted whenever I got around to transcribing them from yellow pads and scratch paper. But the Trash-80 called out to me in a different way. The electric lockbox could hold the primordium, shield the embryonic from the withering light. Inchoate inspirations and scraps of ideas could be tried out and stored, invisibly. Snatches of lyrics, messages from semiconscious states. Vestiges, mementoes. A state of notes before notes. Maybe a diary, or a form of diary, a miscellany.

The label on the cassette read *The Electric Pencil*. I slipped it into the Realistic tape recorder, typed the load/read command in the manual and pressed the white key marked ENTER. The title screen was followed by a blinking block. It was awaiting creation. I began to create.

May 27, 1978

Today is the first day of the rest, etc.
All god's children want a shot at redemption.

A year has gone round, days getting longer
Kids in the street here all through the night

```
Nobody knows if you're wakin' or sleepin'
My lady and I know that's all right
Lady and I know that's all right.

Now if I can store this . . .
```

In the manual I found a section that looked promising. First a mode key, K, then a "tape writer" key, W. Give the file a name, eight characters or fewer. The tape was spinning and my pulse was thumping. "WRITTEN" displayed.

"Yes!"

Celebrating by myself in the dining room of the Cavern, I could see how Eckist Lars became addicted. The "tape reader" command was next. An R, a space, and the name of the file: NOJOKE. The cassette cranked for a second and there was NOJOKE, in white on black. I read all the lines and sat back in a new dining room.

I would deflect Corey's enthusiasm for customer management until it went the way of his other visions, including frozen yogurt. I had found what I wanted. As for Johnny Wray and programming, we would soon have enough to do. It came in the form of Dale, who was waiting for me in the café at four-thirty.

Chapter 18

"CURTIS makes the tape," Dale said. "He contracts these out on request."

On the round, white label was a decal, three lines of bold type on gold:

Day In and Night Out

Andrew Calhoun

Not for Resale

Printed below the decal on the white: Recorded at Groove Town, Chicago, IL. At a table in the back of the café I slipped the product out of its white sleeve. Black radians shimmered on the fine tracks. Dale was excited, and he had a reason to be. He wasn't the only one. After he left, I waited to call Wray until Bruce came on at five.

"Hey, Dale the fiddler was in the café."

"Yeah?" I could hear the end of the week in his voice.

"A buddy of his has a recording studio on Argyle. He's just starting out."

"Okay. There were movie studios out there once. Chaplain had one in Uptown."

"Good sign. Listen to this . . ."

Corey was standing close, giving me a look. Fortunately, no delivery calls were coming in, but a couple were at the counter. Bruce took them, but I had spent the first half hour with Dale instead of prepping and now I had to call Wray because it couldn't wait. I covered the mouthpiece.

"It's John," I said. "I'll be off in a minute." From his nod, I could tell he thought I was pitching the computer project.

"I need to make this quick. The guy, Dale's buddy, will give us a startup rate. He's in shakeout mode, but I saw a demo forty-five and it looks super. For a hundred bucks he'll do a tape, up to thirty minutes, four-track. That includes two copies, he keeps the master. To get demos pressed, it's only ten per. Right? Like nothing! Dale says he could meet with us tomorrow afternoon. I could pick you up at twelve-thirty. Yes?" Since the studio was north and west, it would have made more sense for Wray to pick me up, if he had a Winnetka car for the weekend, but Dale was my connection, going back to the gig at Janis's where I told him we needed to cut a demo. I also wanted to demo to John that the music was still job one.

"Damn straight."

That was the right tone, which was fortunate because the ringer was ringing and line two was blinking. I cut over and wrote up the order as another couple came in and the night was under way. The order was fortunate too because I would take it to three hundred north State at the bottom of our delivery range, allowing me to duck questions about Wray and programming, at least for the time being.

Groove Town studio was on Argyle, but past Pulaski, almost five miles west of Uptown. The address was a brick ranch-style house from the fifties, in a West Side neighborhood with suburban pretensions. I had a strong hunch the black Barracuda parked in front, rear fender bottom rust-eaten by rock salt, was Dale's.

It was a warm Sunday. The inner door was open and we could see through the screen into the old dark rooms, no lights before the back window. I rang the bell and in a minute both of their silhouettes appeared.

Dale was his usual cranked-up self, avid, marginally earthbound. Curtis was his counterweight, dumpy, with a mop of dark hair that fanned over his shoulders. His handshake was soft, and he moved with a kind of languid bop, shirt tail out, cruising to his own Paul Desmond. They had met as inmates in Senn High School, and it was clear that misfits had found each other. Dale told me Curtis owned the house, which he could have bought furnished from an elderly couple and declined to change a thing. The studio was in the basement, and we followed him through a door off the kitchen with "Groove Town" on a jigsaw sign and down the stairs with worn carpet into musty air.

The first hit was subterranean limbo world, cool and dank. Three red lights peered out of the dark, wolflike. Curtis hit a switch and a pair of floor lamps came on—New Orleans decadent, antique brass with bordello shades, one tasseled. The yellow bulbs sustained the mood but threw enough light to read music. The red eyes were the power LEDs on three amps: a Marshall and two Gibsons, a ten-inch and a twelve. On a threadbare oriental rug, three microphones faced three stools, a spare setup but serviceable. The walls and ceiling were muted with acoustical tile, ivory colored—no empty garage reverb, but the tone would be pure. Posters broke up the walls: Tina Turner, Dylan from *Highway 61*, Jefferson Starship, Bonnie Koloc at the Earl, and the Ronettes, likely a nod to the Wall of Sound. The fridge door was reserved for a classic Fillmore of Santana. We were drawn to the table and chair that sat front and center opposite the microphones.

"Tanberg," John said, nodding approval. We stared into the tape deck and mixer.

"I use a lavalier mike too," Curtis said. "We can move it where we need to. It's all four-track." He flipped on the tape deck and sound boomed out of speakers behind us in the corners of the ceiling. One male vocal and folk guitar, and a tasteful touch of background bass filled the basement. I guessed Andrew Calhoun. Curtis was letting his tape do the selling.

"Hear the bass?" He picked up the headphones and held one cup to his ear. "That's Dale." He snort–giggled and passed the headphones to Dale who listened, delighted, snuffling back, head bobbing. Curtis cleared a bang from his forehead with one finger, nail polish a jellybean color, and waited.

"It's perfect," I said.

On the way back to John's place, I picked up the Martin at the Cavern, and in the hour we had left before I reported for duty, we practiced furiously. With no driver, I would need to go in every night again, but since Wray had Saturdays and Mondays off, our recording session came down to Monday afternoon. Our signature set one was a must, and we picked two singles to complement—our "Wrong Is Right" and John Stewart's "Lost Her in the Sun" because Wray had a rare vocal on the chorus.

When we arrived at one, I had regained consciousness from closing Sunday at midnight, the earliest of the weekend nights. As before, Dale was there before us, but this time he had brought PT. His line cook job started at six, and Pat's bartending gig was part time, Mondays off.

Curtis had configured our stations in advance, but with Wray on my left, which wouldn't work because he needed to see my hands. After we switched places, he had us play snatches at different volumes as he moved the lavalier mike from my shirt to John's mike cord, checking through his headphones. It wound up on a music stand between us a few feet in front.

He asked us to start the first set. Half a minute into the vocal, he cut then replayed, and our sound, shockingly intimate, flooded the basement. He had us repeat, and then again, as he made micro adjustments to the mix. Wray and I traded looks. We would be stale before we started.

"Good enough for jazz," Curtis said. Whether he had picked up on our vibe, I couldn't tell.

Before he started to tape, he signaled a break and ceremoniously tapped out a line of coke on a blue glass plate on his table. Dale added a joint. Curtis offered the straw to us first, but we settled for brief tokes, just enough to take the edge off. PT, Dale, and Curtis split the line. PT the bartender padded barefoot to the refrig, liberated a Stroh's can, and set it on the stool between us with two plastic cups.

We took our stools and readied ourselves. PT floated around us, deftly avoiding cords, patting our shoulders to settle us and bestow blessings. Her fragrance took me back to Janis's third floor. It was a tantalizing blend of lavender or lilac, the essence of an elementary school teacher, and a trace of sweat.

"Are we ready?" Curtis pinched the start lever of the Tanberg. "Quiet, and wait for the light." The reels started to turn, adding a leader to the tape, and we stared at the ceramic socket base on the table. The red bulb popped on and Wray was into his intro.

As we played alone with the tape mercilessly capturing everything, PT was a rapt audience, her expressions keyed to the songs, rocking and swaying. She loosened us and sharpened us at the same time. Set one wound up, pushing too hard but with no obvious disasters, and applause from Dale and PT. Curtis immediately kicked off a replay. We sat back with tepid beers and endured every measure that slipped out of sync and every patch of rocky dynamics.

"It's a rough. I'll mix those out," Curtis said at the end. "Another take?"

"'Peace on the Sea'," I directed mainly at Dale. "What did you think?"

He tried to check a wince.

"That's what I thought. Flat."

"You want just that one again?" Curtis offered.

"We have a couple of singles too," John said. "Will we run over?"

"No problem, it's sounding good. If you redo that one and like it better, I'll cut it in. Seamless." Curtis made air quotes.

Wray flexed his left hand and shook out his fingers. We took breaths and settled in and waited for the red light.

We took it lighter the second time, and it came to us, à la the No Exit. Knowing we had two versions took the pressure off and we caught a second wind. Wray switched to the Gibson with a pickup for the singles. He had brought the Pignose, but Curtis offered his amps, and after John tried the twelve-inch, he was sold.

Pat replaced our beer. We were loose now, in the zone, playing off each other. We nailed "Lost Her in the Sun," and we had what we needed after two takes of "Wrong Is Right."

We were well into our second hour, but Dale had a way of materializing for last calls and encores. Curtis responded by rolling off more leader. I had the impression he wanted to give his buddy as much tape time as possible. Dale could easily have his sights set on studio sideman gigs. Wray riffed a two-bar hint of "Gotta Go," and it was an inspired choice.

Dale strapped on Curtis's studio bass, an Hohner, and plugged into the ten-inch amp. I capo'ed the Favilla on the fifth fret and set the up-tempo four-four. John repeated his hint licks, and Dale anticipated the vocal perfectly in two bars.

Annie hit the highway
Leaving me behind
I had one short night in her loving arms
And I can't get her off my mind
Gotta go gotta go
Like a wind gotta blow

Got to ride that highway
South to Mexico

PT was grooving, swimming in air. Dale switched to his fiddle for the break and maintained a tasteful presence to the end.

Besides our two tape copies, we ordered three forty-fives with a few minutes of set one on the A side and the singles on the B. On the way to drop off John on Arlington, I hit a steaming traffic jam from a Monday makeup game at Wrigley Field. By the time I arrived at the café, I was over half an hour late. One look from Corey was enough.

"Sorry, I had to wait for John to get home from work. I wanted to give him the computer for a while, let him play with it, get hooked."

He nodded once, sour-faced.

"What have we got?" I tried to sound eager.

"One on Buckingham. It just went in." His mood was about more than my tardiness. Maybe a fight with Beth— not a first, usually over raising a kid in Logan Square tagged with gang graffiti. Plus, he had opened four days in a row.

"Hey, you want to get out of here? Let's shake it up. I'll take the counter tonight, you get the big money." I popped the apron over my head and took over the pizza table before he could object. We had a walk-in at the same time, which Corey probably saw as synchronicity.

That was how we finished the Monday night which felt endless, with Corey behind the wheel and me behind the counter on automatic, replaying the fantastic session in Groove Town. The break appeared to lighten Corey, but by the time we locked up, I was dragging a ponderous chain. Back in the cool of the Cavern, I shed shoes and jeans but skipped the rest. My first vision in the morning was of a flat half-bottle of Leinie on the nightstand.

"What kind of freaking life?" I croaked. Hearing no answer, I flailed around in memory. The tape was in the can, finally. We would get two copies, for which we had no player, but agents would. We would have the forty-fives in a week. This was a giant step. To where? With no driver, it was back to square one—both of us in the café nightly. No auditions in the evenings, no gigs possible.

Over the next days, the drought continued. Our window sign, besides cheapening the view of the storefront, had predictable results. By Wednesday Corey took it down. We pinned all our hopes on our *Reader* ad, but Thursday came and went with one crank call. Friday brought an eager-sounding query from a kid on summer break who made an appointment, then no-showed. By Saturday I was feeling a shift, a rift of expectations. I was a slave on a pizza pyramid, being my own boss. That night after closing, I dreamed of delivering to a high-rise on an island in Lake Michigan, leaving to find my car gone, stolen or towed—no pay phones, no way back to the café, or anywhere. The room was lighter than it should have been when the hotline woke me.

"Mogul," Wray said. What was it? An edge in his voice. Nothing good. "What's with you, man?"

I was spinning, rewinding through possible offenses, misdemeanors. It was Sunday.

"Oh shit, I spaced. What time—" I could see the kitchen clock. We were due at Groove Town in five minutes. "I'll call Curtis. I can be at your place in twenty."

"Yeah, right." Then I was listening to an empty earpiece.

How I could have slept through the appointment to pick up our tapes and forty-fives, I had no idea. That was my first thought. But if I had to be honest, I knew very well. I hadn't set the alarm because at one-something when I got home from the café, I was in a zomboid state. Instead of telling Wray that when I picked him up, I was ready with a story about a power failure and a blinking clock radio, but I couldn't tell if he bought it.

The ride started in stony silence, and after a couple of minutes he turned on the radio, which precluded conversation. When we met Curtis, we heard enough of the tape and discs to approve them, but that was all. Ordinarily we would have indulged over beers at John's apartment, playing both sides of the forty-fives at least once and scheming over where to send them, but that would have to wait. I insisted he keep them at his place, an empty gesture but the only one I could come up with.

Another driver wasn't a plus, it was critical. The *Reader* ad was free but would not run again for five days. That evening I was ready to push hard for a classified in the *Tribune*. Bruce was in early. Looking upbeat and proud as a cat with a sparrow, Corey nodded to the back.

"Donny," he called. "This is my partner."

A lean dude slid out of the booth. He was average height but seemed taller in stovepipe jeans and Harley T-shirt, orange logo on black. He met me halfway, smooth strides. His arms were sinewy like a swimmer's but his shake was surprisingly soft, deferential.

"Donny saw the ad. He used to drive for Gonzo." Corey was poker-faced but his eyes betrayed him. Not only had a warm body responded, he could be a Gonzo defector.

"Recently?"

"A few months." He inspected me, wide-set eyes dark and striking. His straight black hair was parted in the middle, thrown back. "Off and on over the years. Me and Ozzie, we go back."

"Why did you leave?"

"Too many drivers there now. I want to make more bread, man. You left too, right?" He flashed a knockout smile, like a toothpaste ad. So Corey had already told him we shared a history at Gonzo. "I need like five nights. Plus, you have a badass menu."

He was leaving no doubt who was in charge of the situation. We would have said yes to Weevil on roller skates, and he could easily be picking up on it. I told myself that regardless of who had the upper hand at the moment, we had symbiotic interests, and that drove business. Also politics, the global balance of power, and quite possibly the whole extemporaneous dance. I checked Corey although no need to.

"That should work," I said. "I need to get your license plate. Are you in front?" I headed toward the door, reclaiming a flake of authority.

"We got screwed," Corey felt obliged to explain and laughed and Donny grinned.

"Sure man, no prob-lem," Donny intoned behind me, sing-song, not quite mocking.

"Is it a Duster," I asked behind his red machine, trying to sound impressed.

"Road Runner. A three-eighteen, dual carbs. Beep-beep. And A-body, compact so it parks easy."

"You could drive the next five straight if you want, or take Monday and Tuesday off. They're slower, but you'd be the only driver. We definitely need you on weekends."

"Let's do tonight, see how she goes." He snapped all the fingers on his right hand and slapped the heel into his left palm. He flashed the smile again.

I committed his plate to memory. A pair of feathers, eagle-sized, and a loop of beads dangled from his mirror, confirming my impression. I wondered which tribe, but that would wait, if Donny the road runner somehow worked out.

Before we were back inside, I heard the phone ringing through the open door. Bruce took the order, and I wrote the plate number on the note Corey had started: Donny George. Beside his phone number was a one-word note.

"Pager?" I asked so only Corey would hear.

He looked pained, shrugged. I had to agree. Donny may have had no phone or refused to give it out, but here he was, looking for symbiosis. Another plus was no bank necessary. He came with enough cash to buy the orders. Next was proof that he walked his talk, returning consistently faster than expected. By eight we could have let Bruce go for the night, but since Corey had been living in the store for days, I kicked him out instead. Luckily, orders kept Donny on the road with no break until after ten. While he was having a slice, I tried to ingratiate myself with the only local native fact I knew.

"Wasn't this Potawatomi land?"

"*Is*, you might say, present tense, since Potawatomi live here now. I'm Dakota, Sioux to you. All the way from Minnesota to our big city. And you? Which of deez coloneez?"

"North Carolina, the Piedmont."

"Tuscarora." He was seeing the country through an overlay. Then, "The winners write the story, right? His-story, her-story, so they say."

At the end of the night he seemed happy, at least happy enough to commit to driving through the week. Corey and I were holding our breath on Monday, but he arrived on time. On Tuesday the junior high teenyboppers were back, and between his deliveries, their eyes were all over our new driver with the ponytail. They swooned and giggled whenever he left.

Three nights did not guarantee Donny would stick, but I had to wait at least that long before calling Wray. To restart the music and then be sucked back into the café was not the goal. Alone in the store on Tuesday night and with Donny on a run, I called John's apartment. After six rings I hung up.

Late the next morning I called Kinko's. A young lady, sounding harried, told me John wasn't in. I asked when he had worked last, and she confessed she didn't know who he was, having started her job two days earlier. She said she would leave a note to call me, the odds of which I put close to death by comet.

The final option was to show up at his place unannounced. While it had the best odds of pinning him down, it also had the highest risk of a lethal backfire. Since he had begun the romance of the century, I knew I needed to call first. If I had the café, he had Sasha. It was hard to tell which was more consuming.

With the driver issue settled, at least temporarily, Corey and I had snatches of liberty to be whoever we thought we still were. Which in my case had been reduced to pizza papa, progenitor of Weevil, employer of beep-beep, the heartthrob. I was being my own boss, and I had no lead player.

Chapter 19

June 21, 1978
    The solstice it was, but what I remember is
the shortest night. The sound of John's intro
triplets inside the Buick came to us like a
message from space. The broadcast wasn't studio
quality but it didn't matter. It was authentic.
We had joined the great emanation, changed state,
purified by the alembic of the FM band.

Wray and Sasha picked me up in his dad's car and told
me nothing about our destination. John gave me one day's
notice, enough to trade shifts with Corey.

We took Sheridan Road north, and the sun had set by
the time we were passing Evanston. Then we were in
Winnetka, and I wondered if I had been volunteered for
some painful event at John's parents' place. No. New Trier
Township High, John's alma mater.

We cruised in and parked in the empty lot. John and
Sasha sat grinning like cats while he checked his watch.
Then he clicked on the radio and tuned to a clear signal.
The Eddie Clearwater Band was playing and I was
wondering why we had come, and then Sasha boosted the

volume and all I remembered of the DJ's lead-in was that he could pronounce Duello.

Wray cranked up the pimp sedan and rolled in a slow circle in the lot, doing his wheezing laugh. Beside him Sasha threw her head back laughing, flashes of dark and light.

The Duello sound boomed around us, our tape filling the speakers, enveloping. The windows were down and we were on air, in radio nirvana with the immortals, blasting Duello music into the night. We laughed insanely, circling on top of the world, the blue-black sky salted with stars.

So despite his vanishing act after my sleeping through our Groove Town appointment, John was neither dead nor terminally aggrieved as I had feared. He had three vacation days I had heard nothing about, I assumed not coincidentally, and he and Sasha had absconded to Lake Geneva. Maybe to atone for blowing opportunities for practice, with the demo copies in his possession, he had stepped up. Before they left, he met a buddy from his New Trier days. The buddy's sister was the girlfriend of a WNTH DJ.

Saturday Night Live it wasn't, but the high of hearing ourselves on air was matchless. Our wobbly marketing machine was off the ground. The next level would require another piece, and New Trier radio stoked us enough to put out for it.

"Jesus!" The edge gave way under my foot like scree sliding on granite. Wray grabbed my shirt collar with his free hand.

"Oh my God!" Janis was the most shocked of all of us.

I caught John's arm and righted myself, hugging the Martin case, trying to blank the vision of it end-over-ending onto the asphalt.

"Hey, break a leg, not your neck." Wray was highly amused.

"Thanks for that. Freaking original."

"You okay up there?" Janis was standing, one hand still in the air after lunging to break my fall, which could only have ended in absurdity. I was glad she didn't drop her camera.

"Maybe we should both be falling off this heap. How fast is your shutter speed?" I resettled my footing. "You heard about this place at Loyola?"

"There's a photo locations file. I thought you'd like it. No appreciation." She feigned hurt, although I was the one who had done the driving, to her direction, half an hour south into the sprawling latticework of the Chicago train yards.

"We should gig here at night," Wray said. "Invite the whole South Side."

"Dang, we should have done the shoot at night." Janis was sighting up at us through her lens. "With lights the shadows would pop, like on the moon. Let's come back." She could have been only half-joking.

I could see Wray's idea perfectly. It could be the anti-Ravinia or Tanglewood. We were perched on the front rampart of what looked like a double-thick, two-level wall. Each thickness consisted of paper, compacted and baled into blocks, six feet long and four feet on the sides. A train would haul them south, I guessed, to the pulp mills of Gary. Every form of flattened box, sheet, stuffing, and lining made up the conglomerate. Ripped remnants hung out of the blocks like flags. Corrugated cardboard strata mixed with layers of blue and red. The wall behind us ascended another double-height of eight feet. We were posing on a fortress in the apocalypse, which was syntonic with Duello. We approved of Janis's choice without reservation.

"John, that's good. Now raise your chin a little and look down at me." Wray was leaning one arm on the Mossman case standing on its base beside him like an upright shovel, a tool of his trade. Janis was going for an imperious look. "Now, Mitch, can you crouch a bit? I need a height contrast."

I perched against an outcropping of flattened boxes, one wrist on knee, the other on the Martin case.

"I love it. Now look here, over my shoulder." She pointed with her left hand while sighting me with her right. I guessed I was supposed to be gazing toward a brightening horizon of Duello sunrises. I could play the part, but behind my faraway look, I was replaying what Janis had said on the long drive south.

"Melanie was asking about you." WLS was on low and the windows were down on Lake Shore Drive, but I heard her clearly enough.

"Is that good? When?"

"This week, in the Chalet. She comes in fairly often. It's only a couple of blocks from her apartment." As well I knew, on Belden. "I told her you were fine, she should drop by the café and buy something. Has she ever?"

"Not when I've been in. Maybe Corey's shift . . ." If she had, he would have told me.

"She's working in Evanston, as an assistant editor at *TriQuarterly*. It's an internship, but it could go to a staff position in the fall.

"And her other big news—*Poetry* has accepted one of her poems. And two of Mr. Champion's. I don't know if he recommended her or what. As in capital *What*. Or if Andonati pulled some strings. It's all very incestuous, you know."

"*Who* you know," I agreed, trying to sound unfazed.

"I imagine two by Adam because he's the older man, by a year. She'll have another year in the program, right?"

I nodded. I knew that one, and she may have thought I knew about Adam, but I didn't. Shelley as her senior seemed absurd, also depressing, although I couldn't say exactly why. That he may have had the clout to recommend her, like an Andonati, like a Knox or a Muller, irked me. Worse was the fact of my habitual response to the two of them. As I squatted against a protrusion of paper, play-casting my gaze onto Duello and the dream unfolding, in my reality I was contemplating the ascent of the matriculating duo, hand-in-hand.

Janis was snapping in front of us, then angling to the side.

"Mitch, keep looking right there. John, you follow me with your eyes. That's right, chin up. Make a fist on top of the guitar case. Perfect."

But, now we had a demo, which had landed us New Trier radio, which, although asymptotically close to nothing, was not nothing. And soon we would have a flyer because we had to have one to pitch to clubs and agents, and especially whenever we had gigs, for as many lamp posts as we could visit with tape. Janis had argued for gratis, but we insisted on paying a hundred.

"You've got time for a beer," Wray said, not asked, when we were back in Lincoln Park. He was right. It was a little after two and I wasn't due in the café for hours. It had also been a long, hot drive from the train yards on a Sunday afternoon with a concert at the pier and construction on a lane of Lake Shore Drive. John took his case and I locked mine in the trunk. Janis was clearly included in "you," which I appreciated, especially because Sasha had been waiting in his apartment.

"How was the shoot?" She met us at the back door, which was my usual portal for practices, looking as she invariably did, which was difficult to ignore. This time she wore a purple V-neck T, comfortably faded, and cutoffs that did nothing to diminish her forever legs, which could have powered her to a letter in swimming or track at Glencoe High. She was asking all of us but giving John the squeeze. I looked to Janis.

"They performed nobly," she reported. "Mitch almost wound up in the ER, but—"

"I did not wind up in the ER. We were on this paper mountain that was sliding away under our feet. High on a mountain of pulp."

"Janis took us to a paper dump down in the train yards. Surreal," John said grinning, inches from Sasha's kissable face. He was in gazing mode again, into her eyes, which was understandable. Janis and Sasha drifted to the front room and John snapped out of the spell and distributed Bass ales.

The wide bay windows were raised and a fan was moving the lazy air of Sunday afternoon. Sasha curled up next to John on the sofa bed, and Janis chatted along in her easy way about photography, saying she loved doing it but noting that Susan Sontag said it was a "fatally easy" art form. When she was taken with her subject, she had a charming way of talking with her hands, which were tiny but expressive. A dewy glow shown pleasantly on her lip and forehead and the fan stirred her hair.

"I'll have comps for you by Wednesday—a proof sheet of all the photos and a layout of 'Duello' in a few fonts. If you like one of the photos, I could have your copies by next weekend, or John—"

"I can run the copies—it's my only perq."

"Okay, I'll give you a couple of layouts instead. Should I bring them here, or the café?"

"How about neither?" I said. "John's home after five and we could come by your studio, no problem. Just give us a time when you know."

My beer was mostly gone when John pulled the drawer of the end table we had rescued, like the sofa at the end of my dining room, from an alley. He extracted a joint and lit it and offered it to Janis and me.

Janis passed with a swig instead.

"One hit," I said. I could easily imagine falling asleep on my first delivery. I held it down then washed it down. Sasha and John went next, then he passed the joint back to me and I took it, but only to tempt Janis. My motives may have been complex, but I was disinclined to examine them.

"One hit," I told her. "You saw my example. It's fatally easy."

"You set a splendid example, and you are a silver-tongued devil." She took a drag and held it down, exhaled smiling. I had known what she was wearing all afternoon, but I saw it for the first time—a light Indian shift with tiny blue flowers, the top gathered by a drawstring in a bow on her sternum, hem above her knees, and sandals.

"I have a request, and you can't ask me why," Sasha said as Janis passed her the remains of the joint. We were suitably spellbound.

"Can we ask you what?" I said, which struck Janis as hilarious.

"I want two of your flyers when they're done, one of the demo tapes, and one of the records, the fun one with the fiddle." Delight crinkled around her eyes.

We stared, then John rolled his hand in the air, prompting her to go on. Sasha zipped her lips and grinned. He responded, in hick persona: "Can't trust that wo-man with a little bit o' weed."

She smacked him, catching us all off guard, especially her boyfriend. It was an audible slap, maybe a little harder than intended, or clapping too much cheek, and I felt a twinge, a fantasy tweak of our North Side suburban madonna as dominatrix. Wray tumbled back on the bed, clearly making light of it. Sasha proceeded to tickle his ribs, wheezing laugh.

"No argument here," I said, a light case of marbles in the mouth. "The lady means biz."

I downed the rest of the beer and soon Janis and I exchanged a time-to-split glance. Wray and I agreed to convene at Janis's when she set the time, and as I wound down the back stairs, I tried to imagine what Sasha was scheming. Then Janis and I were on the sidewalk, back in the high heat, moving in the general direction of my car and her apartment.

"What I said on the way back about Melanie and Adam—I'm sorry if that bothered you."

"Was I that obvious? I mean no, not really. If you saw something, it was just habit . . ."

"Second nature, right? We're both second, aren't we? I guess most people are at some point. Not Melanie or Adam, though—they live charmed lives. But that doesn't bother me so much anymore." She didn't sound finished.

"What, then?"

"What if we're second, period? Second regardless of anybody else."

"You mean eternally second, as in never make it?"

"The fate of most, right?"

"Many are called," I agreed but cut it. I wasn't in the mood for routine fatalism, aphorisms, or -isms in general. "But us? Hell, no. You've got it and I've got it. We keep the faith and keep going, we'll thread the needle." I spoke it with bravado, like an incantation to banish the demons. Janis wasn't arguing, right away, anyway.

"What are you up to now?" I said.

"Probably checking a few fonts for your name, maybe left margin under the photo. I have some ideas."

"It's a couple of hours before work. Maybe I could have a look?" I held a breath.

"Sure, sounds good," she said evenly, in professional mode. Her building on Deming, a venerable-looking brick monolith, came up before my car. We praised the cool of her elevator. Inside her apartment she went straight to the fan and then the windows.

"Dammit, this one always—"

"Here, let me." I bumped the sides of the frame a couple of times and heaved and the window jittered up, not quite painted shut.

"Thank you, superman." She patted my arm.

This time, her work table was spread with sketch paper and two volumes open to color plates of Renaissance figures. She appeared to be designing costumes. Beside them was a box of light cardboard, about a foot from front to back and a little less wide, the top adorned with bright fruit: oranges and strawberries, lemons and banana. The front opened like a stage, inviting a view inside. Four stick crosses stood in the space, barely visible strips hanging from the crossmembers, nearly transparent, like tiny banners of clear plastic. As I crouched to inspect the crosses, I saw through to the back. It appeared to be a thin skin of plastic also, translucent, a dark orange sunset color. On it in pen and ink were squiggle figures, thin as stick men, hunters on a cave wall.

"What's this?"

"Just a thing I'm working on," she confessed shyly. "The series is called Little Boxes." She clicked on a light no larger than a nightlight behind the back. The inside was lit by a fiery sky. In the bottom, jagged lines of red and black radiated from the bottoms of the crosses. The sides were hillocks, humps of shadow. In the middle of the stage, the black stick men projected onto the hanging strips, suspended from the crossbars. Other black projections flared upward like naked limbs. "This one is 'Strange Fruit'."

It glowed before me, dreadful and original, drawing me in, a burnt sundown vision of Lady Day's South. "It's terrible," I said, "and fantastic."

"Yes! Thank you." She clicked off the light.

"And this?" Another pattern lay beside the box, trim lines inscribed on flat cardboard and a strip of cutouts like a stencil—a band of horses. She picked it up and pressed the ends together, making a loop. Carousel.

"I'm thinking 'Circle Game'. This will be kind of a subseries, a musical theme."

"Music Boxes."

"Perfect! Can I steal it?"

"Be my guest." I loved seeing her vibrant with vision, her own work. "You should have a show. I'll be your agent."

"Maybe someday." She looked down, appearing a bit cowed by the idea, and flattened the horses. "I thought maybe I could try the Waggoner Gallery on Lincoln. Maya suggested it. She would show me, but it's not really her thing—nothing freaky-deaky."

"The lady wears bells in her hair."

"I know, but she has to sell stuff. She has a son in high school."

On the side of the table, papers were weighted with a half-stone encrusted with tan sediment, sliced to expose an iridescent core of blues and reds.

"A geode? I don't remember it."

"Gary gave it to me. Otherworldly, isn't it?" I recalled Gary and Steppenwolf and the poster for the St. Nicholas, which I guessed was at the printer by now. She opened a font catalog on the table and started flipping pages. We were a foot apart, and I caught the scent of her perfume, spicy, raised by the heat.

She fanned her face a couple of times. "I could use an ice tea. Can I get you one? What do you think about these for 'Duello'?"

I declined the tea, my lowest priority at the moment, and pretended to focus on the fonts, ITC Ronda and Gill Sans. She was back, tumbler with ice cubes in hand. Gary wasn't here now.

"I like all on this page. Speaking for Duello, we trust your judgment explicitly."

"I'll work up a comp with three, maybe a couple lower-case, but bold or outline."

Indian shift, patchouli emanation. She raised the tumbler and the cubes clacked forward to meet her lips. Put it down.

"Can I get you another beer?"

"I'd fall asleep before work."

"You can't do that." She was regarding me straight-on, noncommittal, tough to read.

Scanning her apartment when we entered, I had taken in her bed again beyond the low dresser, unmade this time, a tumbled sheet and one light blanket. On the far end of the dresser her stereo sat open, an album on the turntable. The cover lay on top of a stack of others, the colors and astral imagery dimly recognizable, the band in white against a night sky.

"Pentangle?" I was compelled to confirm it. I flipped the familiar cover over to the liner notes, and it took me back to Chapel Hill, maybe Jim Dewey's archive. Janis joined me, lured by the notes, or by something. "I haven't heard Renbourn in forever. May I?"

"May you what?" She let a grin escape. She was looking up at me now with her Bette eyes, the ones in *Now Voyager*, when she was as luminous as Marilyn. It was a wondrous question, resonant as a koan, encapsulating as it did the full view of what I had been up to, back to my time to kill and font review proposal and likely back to partaking of the pot at John's. It forced me to glimpse my inchoate motives in the electric moment between the descent of the needle onto Pentangle and the pull of the ends of Janis's drawstring bow—to quench the embers of rumination over Shelley and the queen, to counter visions of the erotic escapades of Johnny Wray and his sultry Russian domina, to give a little and take a little and in so doing, make all others go away.

True, I had motives and an irrefutable, if half-baked, agenda. But simply sliding from half-conscious to conscious admission of that in the Pentangle moment was not the reason I left Janis with only a squeeze and thanks for taking our case. There was a new presence, an equilibrium of forces, in her apartment, her studio, in her miniature backlit boxes. Her vision was asserting its weight, striking a balance against the odds of eternal second place, and it filled me with happiness. I had a hunch, an illogical but undeniable sense, that the balance was as fragile as it was new and careless intrusion could upset it. The intruder would not be me.

With over an hour to kill before the café, I started by walking off the remains of intoxicants, the beer and the joint and the buzz of Janis. I didn't need to slice a finger, especially on my chording hand.

July 14, 1978

I'm looking at two stacks of Duello flyers, one for each of the photos John and I chose. Janis knocked it out of the park. Two bizarros on a proscenium, setbacks of nothing that looks like paper, more like a landing port for UFOs. Nice textured tan stock, a little folk-feeling but not too much. 'Duello' in lowercase font, strong, tubular. Space at the bottom to add a gig location and a date. That detail Janis couldn't provide for us.

Sasha is trying, though. Wray told me at practice why she wanted the flyers and our demo copies. She was a high school flame of Rich Warren, a DJ with the Midnight Special show on WFMT. She met with him and pitched us, and no doubt Rich was powerless to refuse. No guaran-tees, but she thinks we'll be on tomorrow night's show. Sweet Sasha, irresistible force. Maybe she could be our agent.

Only problem: I'm working. It's my Saturday and we're starting a new driver with Donny. Corey is off, to preserve domestic tranquility. Maybe I can steal some time in the car to tune in, but we don't know when, or if, we'll be on. Saturday night is no problem for John, other than to keep his silky minx entertained, so he says he'll try to tape us.

July 16, 1978

Best laid plans--Saturday in the café was a mess. The new guy, Lorenzo, forgot a side and drove all the way back from Irving Park, which resulted in a cancellation of his other order. Then, around nine it became clear that our doughball prep from the day side wasn't going to last the night. (Mental note to assassinate partner.) I had to make dough while working the counter, red apron flour-bombed with white, a professional look.

Consequently, I didn't make it to the car to listen to the show, but I did hear that it happened. An hour before closing, Pat Tremaine fluttered in asking if I had heard us and bubbling about how great we sounded, etc. She was with a tall brother she introduced as Coleman, a conga player. They had listened in his car. I didn't see Dale and didn't ask. Her enthusiasm made my night, admittedly a low bar.

Wray said he had called but the hotline was off the hook, which I do more now to block sales calls in the morning, so he only got me after eleven. He said he taped it, and allowing for cassette quality, it wasn't bad. I'll hear it at practice tomorrow. I told him to thank his lady fair.

We have tapes and flyers out to Orphans, a possibility, and Holsteins, a long shot. Maybe a manager caught a few minutes of the show, but on a Saturday night, how likely?

"Everybody's going higher—Chicken and Ribs on Addison, Ozzie . . ."

"Fifty cents a ticket? Gas is up what, a cent?" The last time I put in ten bucks, it was sixty-six nine. I remembered because delivering had sharpened my focus.

"No, man, two cents in the last month. And it isn't just gas, we all know that. Inflation nation—need a vacation." Donny was sing-songing and Lorenzo was nodding.

Bruce had the counter, and Corey and I were with them in a back booth for the negotiation. Strategically, they had picked the perfect time, a Friday. Rather, Donny had. Lorenzo was along for moral support, mainly his own.

I ran the quick calculation, as I knew Corey already had. He was gazing impassively behind his glasses, but I could hear his gears turning. Raising by fifty cents a delivery would be seventy to eighty bucks a week. We owed the printer a hundred fifty for menus. We always owed Great Lakes.

"Fifty is huge." I shook my head. Lorenzo's shoulders dropped a bit, but enough. He looked ready to fold. A high school grad who lived not far from Corey in Logan Square, Lorenzo impressed us both as smart and eager. After his first-night screw-up, he found his groove. He was driving on Fridays and Saturdays and as a backup for Donny, as required. We saw a counter job in his future if all worked out, which included raising our net, which raising his pay per delivery would do nothing to accomplish.

"You bump your delivery charge," Donny explained, "tick it up a little bit. They'll never see it."

"We can't do that—some places deliver free." As usual, in areas related to cost, I was the bad cop; Corey, the silent cop.

"No, man, nobody's free now. Maybe Gino's, but that's Rush Street only." Donny was in battle regalia—a headband à la Santana and a little silver chain around his neck, the kind you would buy for your high school sweetheart at a county fair. A gift from a lady, no doubt.

We sat in silence. Lorenzo was folding a napkin into strips. Corey gave a little priestly nod I had seen before, as though the glitter of recognition had settled on his open cranium. He was going to speak.

The phone rang. We were facing the front, and I saw Bruce pick up. A driver would have to take the delivery and we all knew it. Donny gazed at us like a mathematician waiting for his proof to settle in.

Corey nodded at me. "He's thinking about how many napkins this would cost us."

The drivers cracked grins and lightened up and Corey belly-laughed, at my expense. Whatever worked.

"We're almost into August," he went on. "What if we do twenty-five cents now and the rest in September?" His glance included me for objections. "Deliveries pick up in the fall so you'll have a multiplier effect." Lorenzo checked Donny. Donny was watching Corey. "Interesting that you brought this up tonight. Mitch and I were just talking about a new benefit. For drivers who've been here three months, a paid night of vacation based on average deliveries, plus tips. Then again every three months." He nodded again, letting the fiction of our agreement register. "What we're trying to do here is build a real team, the way we're building a customer base. You could call it a benefit, but it's appreciation—for everybody on the team doing their best. That's what works."

I had been ready to cut him off after his raise proposal. By the time he was into the vacation day, I couldn't tell if he was jamming, and by the end I only knew I was in the presence of a pro.

Donny studied us both, poker-faced, then checked Lorenzo who was clearly ready to roll with it.

"Mr. Corey, you are *wičháša*," Donny said, "the *man*."

"Eh, I the man," Corey confirmed, thumb up. They exchanged a soul shake.

"See you." Donny started to get up. "I got a vacation day coming. Lorenzo will take this one."

The kid blanked, looking ready to believe him.

"We'll let you know the vacation days," I said. "The clock starts tonight."

"Hey man, like the *wičháša* gives credit for time served."

"We'll see," I said, bad cop. The phone was ringing and relief for Bruce was in order. I popped an apron over my head as Corey stuffed his into the laundry bag and tied it to take home. I waited for him to bring it up.

"Sorry to drop the vacation day thing on you. Great, though, isn't it? Nobody else does it."

"There's a reason for that. I can show you the checkbook."

"But this is a huge advantage. Turnover means insanity for us. It will cost us fifty bucks a quarter and we'll have these guys ready to die here. Plus, I'd like to see flexibility, and redundancy. Drivers who can take a phone order then swing behind the counter and make an order in a crunch. It'll save orders and customers."

"Who's up?" Bruce called to the back.

Lorenzo slid out to take the first delivery.

"And something else." Corey powered on. "We should think about expanding. It's early now but we need to keep it on our radar. Let's see what Mohammed does." Corey nodded to the front and I followed him out with his leaf bag bulging with aprons. We stopped in the vestibule. "The fall is hot for retail, but right after Christmas his traffic will drop by ninety percent. And no delivery, right?" He stepped onto the sidewalk and looked back at Mohammed's Consort Boutique. "He might want to bail on his lease. We could assume it and knock out the wall. Move the kitchen to the back and go full-service. We could even keep the delivery. I'm working up some numbers. We should talk about it soon. See ya."

I watched him retreat down the sidewalk with the black plastic hump on his back. We were making our payments, but if we had to double the loan to expand, we wouldn't even be close. I would be on the hook, twisting in the wind. Make no little plans. Not going to happen.

Bleach-blond Venus in cutoffs weaved by on rollerblades with her message, pure and simple, *give it up*. The gift of the sidewalk was flowing before me on a sultry evening, end of July Friday in Chicago.

Boombox street king strutted by on the wrong side of the walk. Young prince Dos Equis leaving Consort, coat bag on his arm, nearly collided with professional Sonya on her way home from the Loop, classy in her business suit. She kept going without a wobble and prince checked her backside.

The flow mesmerized. Females of high summer on the *paseo*, the promenade. From where I stood in the vestibule, they clicked, padded, and floated by, tropicals behind aquarium glass. Unattainable.

The music was feeling similar. *Midnight Special* had come and gone, a day short of two weeks with no replies from either Orphans or Holsteins. The phone was ringing inside. I wound around two ladies at the counter through a bloom of scent like suntan cream. Bruce was taking the order and I dropped the oven door and pulled and boxed the fourteen.

"Order up."

Donny cruised to the counter and the two females who had been perusing the menu board checked him out.

"Ten twenty-four," I said. The track lights glinted on his black hair, tight and cinched in the headband. The silver chain circled his throat above his Bob Marley T.

As I made change, who Donny truly was struck me. He was simply who we wanted to be, Johnny Wray and me. And all stagestruck and aspiring players. He possessed X factor. The light played on his hair and his neck chain and on the little bold letters and star shape in the middle of it that I noticed for the first time. Then he was through the door.

"Can I help you?" I asked the ladies, trying to focus off of who I was. Pizza guy. Unfactored.

I slid in their slices. Bruce had started the phone ticket.

"Did you catch his neck chain?" I said. "The three letters in the middle?"

"CTX?"

"What do you think that's about? Cindy Teresa . . . XOXO . . . ?"

Bruce stared into the back wall above the tickets. Considered.

"XTC," he said, employing his special gift. He was waiting for me to appreciate it. Then he gave up. "Ecstasy. Street name, XTC. One of them, anyway."

"Bruce, you can stay," I said, acknowledging his inestimable value. Strangely, I recognized it. It made sense to me in some way I already knew. I tried to get back to it, and might have, but the phone was ringing again.

"New American Café," I said.

"Mogul!"

"Well, hell. What can I do you for?"

"No pizza, no way."

"Figures."

"Sash just called me. Are you ready for this?"

"Only one way to know."

"Rich Warren called her, said Riley-Strauss had called *him*." He was leaving a space for reaction. "As in Riley-Strauss Agency. As in Willie Dixon's agent. As in Mavis Staples' freaking agent."

"No way."

"Way! Warren said they heard the show and thought we had something."

"Whoa!"

"Know what he asked? Have we talked to anybody else yet!" Then it was Johnny Wray's wheezing laugh I was hearing and I was laughing and slapping the counter, doubled over, and Bruce was tracking me with at least one eye, probably wondering what service to call for me if I ever hung up the phone.

Chapter 20

Aug. 19, 1978

We grind for most of a year and then two gigs in three weeks. And it feels like it's only the beginning. Overnight success, as the old pros say, after 20 years. That's the difference Riley-Strauss has made--night and day.

When we signed, they asked first where we had tapes out. Orphans booked two days later. We hacked it but the room was loud and we were pushing. Last night at the Bulls was as tight as we get. The room was perfect, low-ceilinged and intimate, and it was a good-mood crowd on a Friday night. Mark Riley knew the owner from a college job, bartending at O'Rourke's.

R-S wanted five more tape copies and a dozen forty-fives, on our dime, but it's an investment. Janis added their logo to the bottom of our flyers and John made 100 copies on a slow afternoon. They know reviewers and they say the Reader is only a matter of time and the right venue.

Christ, is it happening? It doesn't feel real.

Also unreal--it's been a year. However she put it, space to ourselves, or together just living apart, I've blocked what she said exactly. Melanie took the studio over the garage on Belden and I went to the Cavern. My new lease is here, a 10-buck increase. I'll sign and mail back on Monday.

                                        Aug. 23

Look at me honey, bringing you money
Last man in the line that leads to your door.
I'll be your king, I'll be your lead singer
Ring for your finger, you know what that's for.

You know there's a reason--
But goodbye is the hardest word--

Who is your mother standing there
Stranded in the light?
Tell her stories through the day,
Fold her hands by night.
You are leaving now
She is empty now
She is lost in her childhood.
Who can show you how?
Who can free you now?
One eye on the window pane
And one eye on the woods,
Round and round the wheel keeps turning,
In and out of her arms.

                                        Sept. 3

The Last Blast was Corey's idea, hatched a couple of weeks ago--he picked up on Wray and me getting in gear. Finish off summer by throwing open the doors of the café, front and back. Knock together a two-foot-high stage in the back on the asphalt across from the dumpsters and host music and any other variety of performance we can recruit. Why not. Maybe we can get Bruce to reverse sentences but probably not, since we'll need him behind the counter while Wray and I anchor the stage and Corey plays boss man, utility man, THE man, WICHASA.

Last Blast is Labor Day, tomorrow. We've invited everyone we know, and they're asked to do the same. We also doubled our inventory for the weekend.

Lorenzo has worked out fine behind the counter, and we've hired another driver to join Donny, a woman named Kat, no nonsense and quick, with a silver change machine on her hip. Odds are good Donny won't hit on her, or vice versa.

It was a mistake to start with the poets. They were looking impossible to follow.

Let's devise criminal strategies
like flinging dung for the unsung

"Yeah-yuh!" Adam burst like a groupie in front of the stage. He and Melanie and Carlos had already done their slam reading and finished with a rendition of "Goin' to a Go-Go." Adam's adrenaline must have been cresting and he was feeling the love.

because we're a SORRY generation

Jerome Lala in a striped pullover that minimized his skinny torso and magnified his outsized head belted into the mike. Behind him his female counterpart, Lurlene, fire-breathing Lurlene in tiger tights, pointed her ray-gun fingers, queuing the front of the crowd.

"Sorry generation!" the poets chorused back and Jerry lit up, a criminal child.

if I took a perk to circle-jerk you around

SORRY ME
but shit—
Lurlene reached out to the chorus.
"Shit!"
We didn't make this world, fuck—
we didn't even make breakfast
"Yeah-yuh!"
"Woo woo woo!" The poets gave it up, and the couple of dozen who had assembled behind the café fell in with hoots and applause. Jerry and Lurlene bowed and curtsied and hopped off the stage. The poets high-fived and hoisted cans and cups. The ones who performed had clearly made a pact to wear eye makeup and make fashion statements. Adam stood out in his Hawaiian hibiscus shirt, and Carlos wore a black and gold La Raza T and beaded headband. Melanie laughed with tigress Lurlene, throwing her head back, looking partly hippie and partly punk in short brown corduroy cutoffs and Doc Marten boots.

Since Last Blast was Corey's idea, I had coaxed him into emceeing. It didn't take much. My job was to fill dead air, so after the poets, on the back of the stage I fired up the boombox lent to us by Lorenzo. "Beast of Burden" cranked out in the space enclosed by the back walls of the apartment buildings. The steel dumpsters probably provided resonance too, although a couple of café customers had taken up a perch on top of ours. Since our start time around four, walk-ins had drifted out the open back door to check the goings-on. We weren't selling the beer, but we did have a couple of Styrofoam chests as a defense against the warm Labor Day afternoon and the heat of the asphalt. Invitees had BYO privileges, so a jug of Chablis also nested in the ice. Our patch of back alley was shared by other stores on the block, and a couple of employees of Barbara's Bookstore had been enticed out their back door.

"Happy Labor Day." The voice surprised from behind.

"Mohammed! Glad you could make it." We did a clumsy soul shake. He was in his vest and open collar shirt this time, no jacket. "It's late for your coffee. How about a beer?"

As he was declining, citing responsibility to reopen the store soon, someone I recognized materialized behind him.

"*Another Chicago Magazine,*" I said.

She checked me through wire rims, guarded, willowy as I remembered. "Right. Sorry? . . ."

"I saw you read at the benefit. You're an editor. Is it Toni?"

"Dawn. Thanks for coming, to the reading. And remembering." She was examining me, birdlike.

"What did you think of Jerry?"

"He's . . . epicentric."

"Ha! So true." I preferred her critique to her poetry, as I remembered it. No doubt Dawn was a player, but outside the Circle circle.

"Mohammed, this is Dawn. She's a poet and a magazine editor. Mohammed is one of our local merchants. He owns Consort next door."

They stared at me, and then each other. My initiative was indefensible, I realized, springing from intuition, possibly perverse. But as the oddest couple dropped into chit-chat about their incongruent worlds, I imagined lightness overtook them, a testament to the rightness of my vision. Last Blast would tolerate no wallflowers.

"Hey, I heard Duello was playing here." Janis had slipped up on me with two guys in tow.

"Hey sunshine, thanks for coming." I gave her a squeeze. "If the lead player shows up."

"Mitch, this is Gary. Mitch is the boss man."

"And you are Steppenwolf Theatre."

"Only part of it." Gary was naturally arresting, black hair with blue eyes and wavy brows like tildes. He introduced his accomplices, Terry and Jeff, actors and cofounders.

"I'm glad we didn't miss you," Janis said.

"No, but you did miss the poets, although they might be back by popular acclaim. Right now I'm waiting for Dale and company."

"They're right inside." I pictured them waylaid by Corey, but then they were out the back door.

"Speak of the devil."

Dale was in the lead, cigarette in one hand and violin case in the other. Coleman came next hauling two tall congas strapped together over his shoulder and carrying a pair of hand drums. PT had a brown bag in the shape of a six-pack.

"What happened to you?" Dale had an obvious shiner covered with makeup.

"A little scuffle, nothing. A slimer at O'Banion's after our gig. Wasn't even about us. Curtis said break a leg. He probably won't come all the way down." Dale took a puff, looking at least as wound up as usual.

"No problem. He's been Santa already. We'd be renting the mike and amp without him."

I popped three of their Heineken bottles and they made their way toward the stage. The Stones were on to "Shattered." As I stowed their other three in ice, I saw Donny a few feet away, taking it all in. He was sharing the night with Kat, so I was glad to see he wasn't drinking.

"I hear you have a band, *kemosabe*. Am I going to hear you play?"

"It could happen. You can tell your grandkids you heard us in a parking lot."

"Do you take requests, like Pink Floyd? But no disco, all right? I don't feel like dancing." A smile flashed between his reflecto shades and the Ecstasy necklace.

"You're safe."

I joined Dale and Coleman on stage and fetched them a stool to use as their beer table. "Plugged or unplugged?" I asked Dale.

"You tell me."

"You won't need it. It's like playing in the bathroom."

From my vantage point I saw Donny talking to PT, or vice versa. Janis and the Stepps had hooked up with the Circle circle. Melanie was talking to Janis, back to the stage. For the first time I noticed someone else from the reading at MoMing. Slender, with dark hair and eyes, she had worn the gold necklace, arrayed like Nefertiti, in the company of the Don of Circle poetry. No such formality today, but she caught my attention nonetheless.

"Order up." Corey emerged from the rear door, directing the announcement at Donny who headed inside. I waved Corey down.

"How's tricks back here?" He was in costume, wearing an impresario's black top hat.

"Great. Don't go anywhere." I led him to the stage and introduced Coleman and Dale. The Stones cassette ended and Corey took over as emcee, announcing the duo. Dale's fiddle drew a long line over an open plain and Coleman's rhythm edged in dancing over it. I went inside to take Corey's place.

A party of four were leaving their table with slices and drinks, heading toward the music. Bruce had two at the counter and another couple were drifting in. Last Blast was boosting business with no more than two open doors. I slid behind the counter with Bruce, and each of us took a couple while Lorenzo practiced making slice pies. Soon Kat returned to handle the next delivery. Bruce confirmed all was under control.

When I made my way back outside, Mohammed was closest to the door, this time with a beer, still engaged with Dawn. Coleman was on a conga solo, and Dale was laying in riffs and notes like stepping stones.

"*Flash* would be incredible on stage!" Corey was next on my left in the spot vacated by Donny. He had cornered Terry the Stepp and was regaling him. I had missed which of them had floated the idea of adapting Corey's novel in progress.

"Your designer could go nuts with Ming's costume." He made a peak over his top hat with both hands, and his eyes popped wide. "Also Princess Aura's—Ming's daughter. And there's a whole subplot with period references. There's a part for FDR! His dog Fala is one of the narrators in the book—from his point of view. Have you read *Ragtime*? It's a 'comp' they call it in the publishing industry, a comparable title."

"That's great," Terry confirmed. By turns, he had been smiling fiercely, nodding along, and deeply serious, a gamut of expressions from the actor's toolbox. He might have been my age, but less experienced at deflecting pitches.

Standing with them, looking bemused at Corey's latest enthusiasm, was Melanie. And beside her was the slender mystery woman from the magazine benefit.

"Congrats on the agent. Janis told me." Melanie's voice, the familiarity of it, felt reassuring. She was otherly otherwise, in her kabuki eye makeup that feathered out to her temples, looking parrotlike, one more persona.

"Thanks, you too, on cracking *Poetry*, I mean. That's a high bar." I asked if I knew the poem, but it was new, a composition from life after us. I couldn't remember whether *Poetry* was monthly or quarterly.

"Probably the December issue," she said. Corey was rattling on, and the fiddle and drums were a constant. These were distractions, but mostly I was finding it impossible not to look at the taller woman beside her, and I realized it was the third time. Melanie picked up on it.

"This is my friend, Anita Russo."

I took in her face for the first time. Her eyes were the most striking, dark, Italian, I assumed from her name, emphatic brows. She was finely featured but with a delightfully imperfect smile—a slight overlap of her front teeth. The flamboyant necklace I remembered had been replaced by a simple gold chain with a tiny charm in the center, I imagined a saint. Hoop earrings matched the gold.

As we shook I noticed an ornate ring on her little finger, vintage, with a fat brown stone. She held a cup of the white jug wine in her left, no wedding band.

"How did you two meet? Are you in the Circle program?"

"I'm a poetry department groupie. I write a bit, but I so admire these guys, Melanie especially. I'm at Circle, but in Comms. I met Melanie in the cafeteria. Since she was reading Margaret Drabble, I knew she had good taste."

I recalled that particular enthusiasm. Melanie went on. "Besides the Comms Masters, Anita works for PBS. WTTW."

What was she doing? Setting me up? Trying to atone?

"Melanie." Corey got her attention. "Terry says Steppenwolf might do *Flash* as a musical. How would you like to write the libretto? Iambic pentameter. Beth could do the music. Like Gilbert and Sullivan: 'modern major general' for Ming the Merciless!" Both Melanie and Terry were laughing. I was alone with Anita.

"TV, that's crazy," I said. "People would pay to do that. I'd pay to do that."

"Don't worry, I am. It's an internship, not paid at all, yet."

She glanced toward the stage. Jet hair, straight, in a no-nonsense, professional trim that showcased her face and graceful neck. A black leotard top, scoop neck below her gold chain. Soft-looking jeans washed to a summer blue, no belt, rolled at the ankles. She wore sandals with cork soles that raised her, and I tried to envision her height without them. She had to know I was looking.

"What do you do there?" I recovered. "At the station, I mean."

"Production assistant. I'm in the tiny credits at the end that you miss when you blink." At least she was looking at me.

"I never blink during credits."

"I see, you're one of those." Amusement in her lips.

"It sounds like a dream job."

"Right now I'm like an apprentice, but it's fine. There's a lot to learn about producing, and it's what I want to do. Producers own the stories. But now it's about paying dues, you know?"

"I do." Her smile was girlish, but Anita seemed a bit older than Melanie and me. Maybe late to be paying dues, maybe starting over.

"I couldn't do what you do," she continued. "Restaurants are harder than they seem to most people." Melanie had told her at least that.

"Sounds like you're experienced."

"I've waitressed like a lot of girls, but my aunt and uncle owned a place for twenty years, on South Halsted. He died of a heart attack in his fifties." Her ring hand rose for a moment, index finger brushing her lips as though it held a rosary. "Don't let me freak you out." She smiled apologetically and touched my arm, sweet electrode. "Did Melanie say you're a musician too?"

Must have. As an afterthought? Or selectively, in whatever backstory of us she chose to reveal?

"I play a little, with a friend. When we both get time—an avocation, as it were."

"I see. What did she mean about an agent?" She was toying with me, she had to know. But her expression was innocent.

"She meant an agency—ad agency for the café. They gave us a marketing rep, pro bono, a friend-of-a-friend thing."

She gave an up-nod, seemingly buying it. Then I lost her to the stage again where PT was looking limber in the front row, half-dancing with Janis and Gary and Jeff, the other Stepp.

"I've seen you before," I said. "At the magazine benefit. It looked like you were with Andonati."

"Michael's a friend, that's all. We grew up in the same neighborhood not far from Circle . . . in Little Italy, the Chicago version. He has two kids."

That she added the last note was encouraging. What I was going to ask required encouragement.

"Thank you. Thanks for coming." Dale cut in, amplified more than he needed, putting the capper on the set. Applause fluttered up in front and we joined in, and I knew I would have to restart the boombox soon.

"Do you have a number? I mean a phone number, that I could have, that is?"

Amusement in her lips again. How many times had she been here, a dork inviting her to the prom?

"That you could have? Where's your black book?" The deflection came first, Novocain to forestall the pain.

"I'll remember. You have to try me."

A glimmer of her teeth, then she was laughing, the girlish smile and a crinkle in her nose.

Laughter broke out behind us. Everyone had heard me. They were laughing at the fool. No. It was Corey.

Melanie and Terry were red-faced, joined by Janis and the other Stepps. Corey was doing a slow pirouette with hands out, helicoptering in his top hat like a demented W.C. Fields, probably demonstrating choreography for a character in *Flash*, maybe Princess Aura. We had bunched in front of him, and Jeff the Stepp came between Anita and me.

Janis turned and waved to someone behind me. Sasha was in the lead as she and John emerged from the back of the store.

"Are we late?" He looked like he had lugged the guitar case and amp across the Mojave. "Sash's parents were having a barbecue and we were trapped. It was like they weren't going to let her go. Then I had to park down by the lake. I thought people split on Labor Day."

"You're fine, Dale just finished. He had a hand drummer. Hang on, I've got dead air here. Beer and wine in the cooler."

By the time I fired up Otis at the Café a Go-Go on the boombox, the audience had redistributed itself. From my spot behind the stage, I saw Corey had disappeared, I assumed to check the café. Anita was left, framed by Terry and Jeff, and Janis and Gary were paired with Sasha and John.

I was trying to think of a way to insert myself into whatever Anita and the Stepps were talking about, but I needed her one-on-one. I was starting to imagine how that could happen when I caught an odd sight of Melanie. She was temporarily between worlds, I guessed from having followed Corey partway in, glancing over the crowd, her eyes betraying if not panic, at least unease. She must have been looking for Adam who had vanished, probably into the café or around the corner into Barbara's. Or maybe it was an illusion, an association with her eye makeup, sad clown. Then tiger-legged Lurlene had her arm, confiding something, and the moment passed. As I left the rear of the stage, Wray found me, still toting his guitar and amp and looking nervous.

"I need to tune," he said. Anyone who knew John knew he had a low tolerance for the possibility that a guitar of his could be out of tune. It was early, but I could come up with no way to circle back to Anita in a winsome fashion. Tuning would give me time to work on it. I nodded to the back door and he followed me in. Two tables were occupied, and Corey was loading up Donny with an order. I unlocked the store room, which was the size of a generous walk-in closet. Shelves lined both side walls, stocked with cans and boxes of backup inventory. In front of us the Martin case sat on its bottom beside the mop bucket.

"Quaint." John knelt on the concrete and liberated the Gibson. As I popped the Martin case, the idea floated up to me like a genie.

"One small change," I started. "Let's lead off with 'You Would Know'." I picked the top E string.

"I thought this was going to be all set three—singles, no heavies." John was a bit flat.

"Right, and we'll do those next, but this one will fit, trust me." I went on to A.

"The 'Stalking' piece too?" He meant the spoken intro.

"Of course."

He shook his head once but didn't argue. We worked through B and high E and he fine-tuned, tapping harmonics. At the end I rolled off G and C chords against the supersized cans of tomato sauce, and Wray fired off scales. The sound resonated, larger than life.

"We cut the first album in here," he said.

"Title, Mop Bucket."

We took the stage close to six-thirty. About half of the crowd had turned over, but our contingent was intact, including the poets. Adam had reappeared and was engaged with Janis and Gary. Finally I spotted Anita laughing with Lurlene at Jerry doing pantomime. More slices had appeared, and more beer, and the group was raucous. John plugged into the Pignose and tested the volume with riffs. PT and company, and then the poets, started yelling and clapping even before Corey introduced us. When he had to restart his intro to get the attention of the rest of the audience, my switch of the first number was not looking like a great idea. I was getting tight, out of proportion to the venue—our patch of back alley, not the Earl, not Comiskey. But then he was done and waving his impresarial arm at us and our people gave up hoots and applause and there was no turning back.

I heard it under the beards of the trees
like a brushing of bodies

in the corridors of sleep

It was only my voice in the mike, and I hoped no one else could hear the quaver. The chatter broke off and pockets of laughter fell silent.

I rose and followed, heel to toe,
stalking the voice of a reticent animal,
so rare as to be beautiful

I caught the sudden stares, a captive audience interrupted by what they were hearing, by whatever it was that I was doing. I spotted the eyes I was looking for.

I would have been the first
to find it beyond the cloaks of the trees
but at the edge of the clearing
you were there before me

Then I was chording the intro and John came in with me and ratcheted up, overlaying the same chords, and the sound caromed off the brick walls and dumpster steel, and I took a breath.

Something in an outlaw knows an outlaw in disguise
Heat settled on the city and the darkness hid your eyes

I was targeting her, tuning her in, trying to connect.

You could say that we did not hear voices call our names
down where the waters flow
but only you would know

Wray was off and rolling and no one could stand still. Anita was drawing closer, little by little, wine cup gone, looking surprised, maybe even charmed.

You always wore your white lace to go living on the lam
Now you wear your traveling dress in the port of Amster-
dam

John was high on the back-court resonance, mixing licks with my fat seventh chords.

I could say that you made me as free as I will be
Free enough to let you go
And only you would know.

We finished to polite applause and hoots from our people, half of the other drop-ins not sure what we had put them through. Anita was standing away from the poets in the middle of the crowd, twenty feet in front of me. She applauded with the others but then only regarded me straight-on, half smiling, as though she was seeing me for the first time. I was pizza boy no longer, and that was all I wanted.

"We're going to lighten it up now." John took over the mike, clearly to keep me from doing any more damage. "Here's a little ditty from Brooklyn. The Monkees did okay with it." He stole my rhythm and first line then dropped back to playing lead until rejoining me on the chorus.

Now I'm a believer

In front of the stage it was white kids imitating *Soul Train*. The sun had settled below most of the building tops and the heat had started to lift. Anita was dancing with electroconvulsive Jerome who was half a foot shorter.

"You gotta believe!" I added at the end, wondering if Anita caught it. A few, led by Janis and Gary in unison, started pitching requests, mostly for tunes we didn't know, but we did try to substitute. For "Proud Mary," we did "Bad Moon Rising." I had no chance with the words to "Stoned Soul Picnic," but Janis who requested it teamed up with PT and Wray, and I camped in the background. Coleman was adding congas from the back wall, so we waved him and Dale up for the last two numbers—"Mandolin Wind" with Dale's fiddle swapped for guitar and "Silver Threads" with Dale and Coleman and Johnny Wray stretching out a break while I sat back catching a drift of maryjane. All present, on and off stage, howled the chorus.

By the time we finished I was stoked, and blasted. The rest of our crowd who weren't already on stage closed in with applause and high-fives and a groupie glow. PT hugged Dale and Coleman. Janis produced a stack of flyers and began passing them out. Carlos told us he first heard "Silver Threads" done live by Bal Huerta, a.k.a. Freddy Fender.

The lights had come on outside the back door and the audience was starting to break up. Last Blast was to be a daylight affair, before deliveries took over. Melanie, with Adam and Lurlene, waved her congratulations from the opposite wall then took off down the alley behind Barbara's.

Corey appeared from the store to take in the ice chest and trash the empty bottles and other evidence of intoxicants. As Wray and I secured Curtis's sound system, I searched the dwindling crowd.

"Hang on to these a sec." I left Wray with the mike and the Martin case and worked my way through the rear door around couples shuffling back through the restaurant. Lorenzo was taking a phone order. I caught up with Bruce behind the counter.

"Did you see a woman leave through here—black top . . . leotard, dark hair and eyes, hot, maybe a little older—"

"She went with Donny."

"What?" The worst case. Who the hell was she? Did I want to know?

"He had one going to Webster, offered to give her a lift to her place, she said Lincoln Park around Fullerton."

It couldn't have been long. I was out the front door on the sidewalk of strangers, checking Broadway in both directions. I started south to the light at Diversey.

"Hey! Mitch!" Bruce was in front of the store waving a paper scrap. Then he held it up like a stop sign, a delivery ticket.

"She left this for you."

He turned and ambled back to his position, leaving me to steady the shaking three-by-five rectangle and pore over its two lines on a diagonal—the digits of a phone number, clear but with a dash of flair, and the letter strokes of her name above, confident and open, the two generous A's, all inclined forward.

Chapter 21

IT was too early, before ten. I was lying prone, pillow bunched under my chin, in position to watch her returning from the bathroom. Buck naked and unselfconscious, she was padding on my rutted hardwood across the bedroom threshold, terminus of the Cavern.

"It drove me nuts that you left with him, you know."

"Who?" Anita was the kid looking surprised, but not quite innocent. She stopped at the bedside, standing tall, those long legs that made our pubic heights nearly match when we had stood clenched together in the same room in the night. I had made that calibration first when we talked front-to-front behind the café, our eyes on the same level when she wore the raised sandals and summer-soft jeans.

"Donny, the driver. You know who."

"That was a week ago!"

"Five days."

"A lot's happened since then." From the advantage position, she raised the sheet and slapped my bare cheek then rolled back in beside me. "Hey boy, I know what you're thinkin', but he only dropped me off. Is this the way it's going to be?"

She was feigning annoyance, head propped on hand, lying inches away, undulating line of her torso and hip. I smothered her mouth with mine. I thought I could taste a cigarette, but it was probably only my memory of the night before when she had one at the table, an occasional habit, she said after asking my permission. I had only been with one woman who smoked, Norma Sue Rowe, senior year in high school.

I was possessed, infused, obsessed with the closed-eye snapshot and the flow of her body, its contours and slopes of light and shade. And the current of her voice, the ripple and rush of microtones from her mouth and throat and heart, her every syllable.

She rolled on top. I was stuck on her "thinkin'." She was hamming it up a little, but I could hear Chicago South Side in her voice, Little Italy, neighborhood of Anita and Andonati. And of her dad, who had been a Chicago cop, which she told me the evening before at Julia's. Those hours could have been days ago, time both compressed and exploded, our big bang. I had called her the day after Last Blast, but between her classes and the café, Friday was our first opportunity. Having broken the ice on Labor Day, we rolled along easily, although in real-life ways and rhythms we were different, which only served to charge the electromagnet.

"I'm not saying he isn't cute." She gave me a teasing grin, inches away, eyes a little crossed.

"Indigenous—that's the heartthrob thing, right? What if he's really from Little Bighorn outside Little Italy?" She tickled me, highly offended. "Calumet City! Cicero!" I tickled back mercilessly. We eventually caught our breath.

I rolled on top and fell into her eyes, dramatic with liner and lashes with liberal mascara, unapologetic, which worked for me without reservation. I nipped her lip and met her tongue and I was back to where I had been for half the night. I was tired but not that tired.

"I was so hot for you," I whispered into her ear, modest pearl earring made for action, nothing to catch. Had she thought of that? No, I was the only one who thought that way. Maybe.

"It feels like the wrong tense," she whispered back. Was tumescence the natural state? "Since when?"

"Since the reading. You glowed."

"Why didn't you say something then?"

"You were there with the Godfather of Poesie. And there was a lot going on."

"Like Melanie. She told me you two had a history."

It was killing the moment, but masochism was real. I needed to hear it.

"Let me guess—that's not all."

"I can tell you she's very fond of you."

Fond, milksop modifier infested with past tense. "And my fatal flaw was—" Maybe I was asking too much, but she had brought up Melanie, I hadn't. I rolled off her to let her talk. She considered a moment.

"Melanie is a poet. She sees things differently, like Adam and the others, and I love that they do that." It landed like a gut punch but I tried not to show it. "But maybe they need people to be other than who they are. Fascinating. Mysterious." Nonboring. I knew it well. "Or with blank spaces they can bring their own pieces to until the puzzle is filled out. Not realistic." Anita rested her case assuredly, putting space between herself and Melanie's world, and I had no objections.

"Anyway, what she didn't tell me about was your music. If I were Melanie I wouldn't tell me either. But I wouldn't let me hear you play. Look what that did. It was like 'Killing Me Softly'—I love that song. I went into total meltdown. That's what I mean, not realistic. Thankgod." She licked my lips, tugging me out of Melanie's puzzle and back to her in a millisecond.

"Now I get to ask you one." She rolled on her side to face me, front-to-front. "I told you, I'm older than you by years, not saying how many. What about that?" Her eyes widened.

"Mmmm. Hello, Mrs. Robinson."

"Not that old!"

I flattened against her, slipped one hand behind.

"I gotta go," she whispered, throaty.

"No way. It's Saturday."

"I need to be in the studio at noon. There's a briefing on a series we're going to do. Don't know what it is yet, but it's three-part, a big deal."

"You're the practical one, aren't you? I bet it's optional for you." I was thinking student intern, realizing too late it probably sounded condescending.

"You have to work too, don't you, since you had yesterday off?" A realistic assessment, and by ignoring my question, no doubt an adroit way of admitting that yes, for her the meeting was optional. So she was not only realistic, but ambitious.

"I'll get in when I do. I'll take you. Do I get to see your place?"

"Not now but someday, if you're good. That place is special to me, Henry." She sounded abruptly defensive. Why she was inflating the importance of an apartment, I had no idea. Her teasing "Henry" softened it a little. We had exchanged middle names, and she took delight in using mine partly as diminutive, partly as mock reproach. Hers was Marie, not much teasing material there.

"Okay, but this isn't over."

"Okay!"

Just as quickly, she recovered from whatever needed defending, probably because she saw the effect on me, and pulled me on top of her. "But I have time for one more," she said, a gleam in her eye. I felt her legs wrap around my waist, and once more into the whirl of Anita Marie, I was gone.

It was two days before the end of September. The killer cold had not bitten down on the city yet, but the season had passed for sleeping in the park. I had opened and was watching for Corey. I would need to tell him because he would be closing.

I thought I was lucky when he steamed in early, ahead of both Bruce and Donny, which gave us space, but that notion vaporized. He said nothing, focused straight ahead, strode the length of the counter through the empty dining room, and stowed the bag of clean aprons in the storage room. I had seen him ignore people and things before when he was in Corey scheming space, but this was different. He was back, refocused. He thumped his folded apron on the counter.

"Where the fuck were you?" He was behind the counter now, gray-faced and cold-eyed. He looked like the stocky wrestler I had first imagined in Gonzo and I braced myself.

"What are you talking about?"

"I couldn't get through to you at all last night, busy signal for hours. Phone off the hook, right?"

"I was off last night."

"Right, you and Miss Italy. I'm in here with Lorenzo, get a call around eight—it's Kat at a pay phone. She's broken down at thirty-nine hundred north with an order for Schulte in the car—the two large pies, salads, great customer, right? I call him and apologize, tell him the order will be a little late. Then I try you, the first time. I have to leave Lorenzo alone, haul ass up there. By the time I get it to Schulte on Irving Park, it's over an hour. I apologize, give the order away, but I can tell he's pissed. That'll be the last of Schulte. Then I haul back to Kat in case I have to drop her somewhere, but she had a tow en route. By the time I get back, it's after nine-thirty and Lorenzo can't stay any later." I knew he was off at nine on Thursdays, his only week night. "I call you again. Try Donny's fucking pager." Donny had only started taking two week nights off. "And of course the phone's ringing. I had to tell them no deliveries—I don't know how many we lost." He slumped down on the stool.

"Kat called in later. Her tow driver thought it was a blown head. Kat's screwed. We're screwed."

"Shit," I said. "Sorry." I imagined reversing it, calling him at home where the phone would never be off the hook because there was no reason. Yes, the night had been a disaster, but we had both battled through those before, and Kat left a void, but we had Lorenzo and some unsolicited names and numbers in the drawer. There was more to Corey's punctured aura, and from his assessment early on of Anita—stone fox—I guessed it had much to do with simple envy. Regardless of that and as non sequitur as it would seem, I still had to let him know while we had the break.

"I told the baker and the pixie they could sleep here for two nights."

He stared back, out of steam or incredulous.

They were two of our favorite customers. Sebastian, tall and rangy with a George Harrison beard and ponytail, looked the part of a commune escapee, which he was. There he had learned his trade as a baker, which he practiced at Roeser's on North Avenue. He towered over his wood nymph Claire by at least a foot, a blue-eyed sprite who wore diaphanous summer dresses and a beaded leather anklet and usually traveled barefoot. Together, they bore Woodstock Nation on their shoulders. They were also the only customers we would treat to free slices or cheese crêpes when cash was thin. Sebastian always insisted that we add to their tab, a running total kept by no one.

For most of the summer they had lived in Lincoln Park, moving their tent every few days to evade detection. In mid-August the police caught up and encouraged them to avoid a charge of vagrancy. They were able to crash with a friend who rented a room in a house until he left for Madison in mid-September. They bounced back to Lincoln, the south end of the park, which was closer to Sebastian's job but popular with winos and junkies. They were ready to snowbird to Florida with a friend of Claire's brother, sharing driving and gas, but he wasn't leaving until Monday and a cold storm was moving in for the weekend. Corey and I both followed the forecast, since dips in the weather correlated with calls for deliveries.

"They said they could sleep in their bags on the floor. I told them they could pull a couple of booths together."

"Did they ask?"

"No, Sebastian just told me the story. Their packs were stuffed with everything they had. They said they would help with cleaning and prep, whatever we wanted." They lived like nomads, but they were energetic and fastidious. I imagined any tasks we would give them would be done. "You can lock them in. I'll let them out in the morning."

I intended the last offer as the clincher. Corey grunted acquiescence and slipped the apron loop over his head. Then, I caught only a glimpse but I couldn't have been more unprepared. A dark presence was settling over him. His eyes filled and glistened. The door dinged and Bruce saluted as he loped in to start the night. Five before five.

"I need to be able to get you," Corey said past me as he went to check the prep, which I had overdone.

"I'll hang around for a while," I said to his back. I collected the envelopes of bills and headed to a rear table with the checkbook.

I would cover for Kat through the rush, until about nine. Donny arrived before the first order. Whatever was nagging Corey, I had plenty of time to try to puzzle it out. It wasn't only Anita, not as simple as what I suddenly had and he didn't. Odds were good there had been a fight at home. I had heard about a few of those, but I, and sometimes Bruce and Donny, caught only the fallout. Deep in Corey was a nuclear pile, a cauldron of needs and conflicts. He embraced Eck to subdue his devils, and the two mixed it up in his oversized cranial dome. I pictured this battle centered around Beth and Arlo and the ticking clock to make it and break out of Chicago—as simple as that must have seemed to him, somehow, when we started. As unrealistic as it was turning out to be anytime soon. For me, I was paying rent and that was enough, but it wouldn't be for Corey. If the topic was big dreams and small odds, what about the music? And what about all of us? Who wasn't on the make, playing a long shot? Was I watching the crackup when the dreams hit the wall? It seemed premature to be admitting defeat, but Corey was always steps ahead.

After writing the checks, I made a show of collecting the names of potential drivers in the drawer, although it wasn't the time for interviews. I was trying to give him space to open up, but soon the phone was ringing and Friday night rolled on.

When it came to Anita versus the phone on the hook and the risk of a call to duty, I was a repeat offender. I was gone on her in every way, and the rare times we had free between school and WTTW and the café and the music, we spent together. My address was Cloud Nine.

I even blew off a practice in early October. Riley-Strauss had booked a gig a week later, at Barbarossa, and before we had an agent, we probably would have crammed in two practices and taken the stage tight as kids playing recitals. Instead, we went in with an attitude. It was one more date on the road, on our cross-country tour. The venue fit the fantasy—the loudest place we had played, on the edge of the Rush Street district. We were on our game that night and more, probably from not being overly practiced. Plus, it was the first time Anita had heard us play a club. Now there were two lovely women at the table in front of the stage, not just Sasha, and that gave me a heady shot. I had achieved parity with Wray, and as we rebalanced, for the first time in months it felt more like the days when we started.

The rest of October held crisp and fine as the maples turned and their crowns blazed in the sun. Anita smiled her kid-woman smile and I throbbed with intoxicants. The month ended at the movies.

"The ending was horrible!" she complained as her chilly hand squeezed mine on the way to the car. "He's still out there! How can you stand movies like that?" She screwed up her face, appalled and delighted, radiant in the streetlight. Around and behind us, the crowd was chattering, discharging from the Biograph onto Lincoln. A five-foot Darth Vader towed a four-foot wicked witch past us in the opposite direction.

"It *was* the boogie man," I whimpered and then, with a whiff of Pleasance, "As a matter of fact, it was." I tickled her midriff through her trench coat and she slugged mine. We were both shaking with chills by the time we reached the car. The bucket seat was cool but the engine caught right away.

We sat for a moment and let the heat flow. I was replaying the theme, hypnotic, ominous bass, lead line skipping and looping, electronic. Could that be in Duello's future, adding a synth? Why not? I glanced at her and caught the smallest glisten.

"Hey, you all right?" Anita was staring straight ahead, eyes brimming.

"It's stupid." She was blinking back the tears, wiping with her fingers. "In the movie, the sheriff who's the father, he reminded me of my dad. That's all—crazy."

I gathered her to me, squeezing, her cool cheek against mine. I had heard enough about her father to know how close they had been. A cop on the South Side, he died in his fifties, like his brother the restaurateur. He was still on the force, but he didn't die in the line of duty. It was Lou Gehrig's disease, diagnosed while Anita was an undergrad downstate in UI Urbana. She had spent the rest of the year at home. I held her and we breathed together until the windows fogged.

The ride back to the Cavern lifted our spirits. Although most of Halloween night had already passed while we were inside fearing for Laurie in jeopardy, enough ghoulish stragglers, especially adult ones crowding the pubs, were still out to make things interesting. On Southport, a pair of vampires on skates rolled past us at a light. Across from my building in the front yard, a plastic jack-o'-lantern the size of Charlie Brown's pumpkin lit up a scarecrow like footlights.

I was hoping any trick-or-treaters would ring the obvious two bells on the front of the building and not mine on the side. How much might have been our closeness in those moments in the car, my need to enfold her, make us inseparable, and how much was the carnal sensation of sudden warmth in the hall, I couldn't tell. They blended, joining forces, rolling over me as one compulsion, and I couldn't let her go.

She was going nowhere. Her back against the wall, my mouth on hers, we were breathing the same breath again. I was opening the belt that cinched her coat, and the buttons, and then her blouse. She started on me, and by the time both our shirts were open, she drew back, deep eyes, lips parted and breathing hard in the pearl gray half-light from my downstairs window. She unzipped her boots and I pulled off mine. As she started toward the bedroom, I caught her wrist and pulled her back. With my accomplice in hand, I took the hotline off the hook.

I sat in the middle of my mattress-and-box-spring sofa and held her hips, positioning her in front of me. She picked up on it and did what I wished without being asked. She unzipped the black pleated skirt and stepped out. Then the last button on her blouse and all was off. Her necklace of leaves, gold plated, and hoop earrings caught what light there was. She was a Klimt of gold and dark and light, Judith to my willing Holofernes. Judith of the South Side and her dad the cop, no doubt on one floor of a two-flat before the Russos could afford a clapboard house in Little Italy. That modesty explained the gold, arrayed as Anita often was like a lady of higher station. Now the Russo's daughter stood before me, slender, naked goddess-creature in our secret grotto, hidden from all but an eyeless beam of streetlight or moonlight. I raised my right arm in pantomime and she responded, her left elbow bent and hand behind her hair, raising her breast in the filmy light of gray and white. No moment, I knew then, could be repeated. I locked the snapshot in memory, vowing it would be the last I would return to on this earth.

Beeping attacked us, sharp, insistent. I recoiled and Anita covered up. And then we were laughing at the open phone and its robotic alert, and I pulled her down with me. Her crinkled-nose laugh, her open smile.

This was new—desire compounded by an otherly connection, a need to shelter her, celebrate her, obliterate our boundaries. It had powered us out of her sadness and the clutches of memory. I had felt nothing like it, and only in comparison to what I had known, which was mainly Melanie. We weren't kids in high school then, but we were still naïve and stumbling. Not this. I was sure, in the taste of her mouth and in her breath and scent, and in the warm press of our bodies, I would know only one Anita. The beeping hotline gave up and left us to each other.

I didn't find it surprising that however the fates might penalize the café for my inattention and however I might derail the music that had just begun to roll, being with her was worth it. I didn't care how at a point you suspend everything, drop all defenses based on what you know in that moment, heedless of what you do not know, or want to learn.

Chapter 22

So it's Vet's Day one more time. Carter lays the wreath and we beat the drum one more time. With Loc Ninh and An Loc and Saigon in the bag, let's have a round of When Johnny Comes Marching Home, the real version.

You have no arms, you have no legs,
huroo, huroo
You have no arms and you have no legs—
You're a spineless, boneless, chickenless egg
And you'll have to be put in a bowl to beg
Oh Johnny, I hardly knew you.

They're rolling out the guns again,
huroo, huroo
They're rolling out the guns again,
But they'll never take my sons again.
They'll never take my sons again,
Johnny, I'm swearing to you.

Sebastian and Claire are long gone, down to the peninsula. Totally free. I've chosen no

escape, from the café or this town. I had two
good reasons to stay, now one. Andy Strauss is
talking Flying Fish Records. We're not there yet,
but he said it "could happen," and in this game,
any hint is golden. Now I can refocus on the
music.

The radiator bangs and Old Chicago is darkening down. The label says Burgundy, but it could
be anything, fortified. Jet fuel. But you only
taste the first one. What have I been doing here
but freaking deja vu? One thing I know for sure:
it was not my fault.

"Why didn't you tell me? It's nuts."

"You can't figure it out?" Anita flashed a look at me and I
was chilled to see how her eyes could turn. I was on my feet,
propelled out of the dining room chair. I had made Saturday
breakfast in another lifetime. Our dishes, mostly empty,
looked like wreckage. She dumped one last half slice of toast
onto her napkin and carried the side plate past me into the
living room.

"You thought I would just check out?" I said to her back.
"Really?"

She parked on the sofa and rummaged in her bucket
purse. Her hair was back and up and off her neck and she
looked younger. I felt sadness settling over anger and
confusion.

It was another Saturday and I could drive her back, she
said, but as always, not see her apartment. She had stalled
for weeks. Now I had given her a key to my place but had
never set foot in hers. It was her space, she claimed, and I
had no idea what test I would have to pass to be granted
access. I had finally forced the question, without a thought
that I couldn't handle the answer.

She had a cigarette out of the purse, and her own
matches, and was going to use the former toast plate as an

ashtray. On the rare times she had smoked when we were together, she had taken it outside. I made a show of cracking the window, although the air spilling in was too cool.

"The number you gave me, when I called you—"

"It's on Lincoln Park West." I flashed on Donny dropping her off after Last Blast, maybe at the building with RJ Grunts on the street level. I wondered if I had menued her door, the door of the married lady. "We've been separated. He got his own place in July."

"You told me you were on Wrightwood."

"Since October. The lease on Lincoln Park West is up December one. I haven't moved everything yet. There are things to take care of." Statement of fact, things I wasn't privy to. She drew and exhaled, looking out the window, her thoughts traveling.

How many places did they have? Aspen? Cabo? I wondered what she may have moved: a vase, an ashtray. Then pictured him coming and going, the couple splitting their things, clinging and crying together and revisiting the whole decision.

"And you filed in August." I parroted what she had told me. I expected her to defend the time it was taking to sign papers, but she inhaled, avoiding my eyes. A compact was being negotiated between them. Their divorce could as easily fall apart as ever be final. At least we were even in recent failures. Comrades. There should be a positive in that.

"It doesn't have to be this huge thing." I needed to simplify, make the truth that spun like a mirror ball clear and simple. "It doesn't have to be anything between us." What was required: put the menace back in the box. Seal off contagion, contain the spread.

I sat down beside her and felt the chill. She stared into the plate and I saw her eyes widen for a moment in that alarming way she had, as though she was seeing too much. She ground out the butt and dropped the pack of Virginia

Slims back in her bag. I stood up again and closed the window, and when I came back we sat for a while without talking. I took her hand, and both our hands were cold.

"You don't get it," she went on, less defended now. "For me, I mean. There's no reason you should." Her eyes glistened and she blinked. I steeled myself for a rhapsody. I was going to hear about how long they had been together and a poignant event or two they had shared and whatever else she had seen in the plate. But no.

"The church doesn't recognize divorce."

I heard the words but they failed to process. I stared at her, stupefied. I was holding the hand of a stranger.

"For a Catholic it's breaking a sacrament between us and God."

Music was one thing. Her idea of it peaked with Dino Martin and Paul Anka, but she was open and learning. We could get beyond that. This was something else. It was obvious that she was, but incredulity demanded the question: "Are you serious?"

She took her hand back. "Are you trivializing my faith?"

"Trivializing? Hardly. Sorry, no, farthest thing from it."

"What, then?"

"What? Throwing in a little reality, just pitching it out there."

"Reality. Yours."

My reality, my apostasy. "Yes, mine. This isn't part of any faith I can use. What's the good of whipping yourself over a decision you've made, and I assume he has too, although I don't want to hear about it." I was on my feet again but I didn't want to be. Containment. "You don't deserve it."

I saw her trying to take it in, and in retrospect maybe that was the point of return to solid ground. I should have stopped there but I couldn't because crazy fingers had loosened my harness and I was dropping.

"Religion is an accident of birth, like eye color. Do you think you'd be caring about the judgment of the Catholic Church right now if you'd been born in . . . Luxor?" Kip the driver was listening in, having the last laugh.

She flashed a look that froze.

"I mean people grow apart, they split. This is reality. Making a sin out of it—"

"Do they?" She zipped a pocket closed inside her purse and I thought I saw her shake her head.

I tried to remember wherever else her things might be, bathroom or bedroom. I positioned myself between her and the front door. How to make her stay? Keep her talking. What to say? The viper circling in my gut, gnawing, I needed to purge it.

"Is your name Russo, or is that his?"

"We kept our own names when we married." The verb was a punch, regardless of the tense.

"And his is?"

"You don't need to know."

I didn't need to know any of this but here it was. Contain it. Choke it all down until you blow.

"Okay, then just tell me what he does." Partly simple masochism, partly an attempt to tame the fantasy, get him in focus. I wanted to see a red-haired guy with freckles in a tweed jacket. She had no reason to tell me that either, but I imagine she did to throw it in my face.

"He's an attorney."

Too perfect. And I was her slumming diversion until a real opportunity came along.

She was glancing around, looking for things she could be leaving. I would pin her to the sofa if I had to.

"And what's his club? The Atlantic on Michigan, right? Or the Ralph Lauren club in Northbrook, little polo player on his shorts?"

"He's a public defender."

The first and only time I had been clocked on the chin was by a punk on a playground when I was nine or ten. Then I was on my butt in the dirt, and it didn't hurt much but it stunned, totally. Anita's cool statement of fact felt like the second.

"He knew how to treat a beautiful woman," she added. Caught flat-footed. Staggered. Speechless. "He would make love to me in the mornings." Cold-cocked.

What guy could take that? Or would, more to the point. I was going down, trying to remember how you fall, how you protect whatever you have left.

Who was she? Anita whatever her name was for whom I had fallen. Where had we been?

My detonation could take out the room, the ground floor, the foundation. I could fall on my own grenade. Instead I fled, blurred away. I was in the bedroom behind the door that had slammed too loud, folded over my gut, retching into a silent howl.

I dropped onto the bed that had been our bed, hands clamped over my ears, but I couldn't un-hear what she had said. Even worse was the taste of bitter truth: she had not volunteered it—I had pushed her.

Half an hour ago we were normal. We could rewind, minutes at a time. It could take days. What if it did? I had lost minutes and I was losing more. I was on my feet, not enough blood in the head. I steadied myself against the door and turned the knob.

Deserted living room, traces of cigarette smoke. I started with the dining room, plates cold as we had left them. She had returned the toast plate, dumped the cigarette. I checked the other rooms, couldn't call her name. Then I was out the door, empty sidewalk in both directions. In thirty seconds I had my wallet and keys and in another minute I was in the Mustang, circling the block. Two were waiting at the Southport bus stop, no Anita.

Vanishing suited her, back to her multiple places, or no place. Maybe back to Mr. Right, defender of lost souls, mister not-quite-gone, and obviously not forgotten. I could have missed her by seconds. She could have lucked into a cab, or stuck out her thumb—that wouldn't have taken long.

I called the one number I had over the day and again from the café, a little before midnight. No pickup. I checked the phone book in the café, the same one I had checked long ago. No Russo in Lincoln Park. Even as I arrived home, on the walkway to the door, I was close to praying, call it envisioning, that she had used her key. But the Cavern was dark, and never so huge.

Wray and I had scheduled a practice at his place on Sunday, and playing got me through until sundown. On Monday I called her TV station, but they didn't track interns. By Tuesday I was losing it. It didn't help that I had the day off, and I could have menued and should have, but not while there was a ghost of a chance. For breakfast I took two donuts and coffee in the car and headed south.

Far from rolling hills and ivy, UI at Chicago Circle was a Soviet-looking cluster of medium- and high-rises on brick and concrete flats, functional, institutional, built to deter vandals. Chicago maples occurred randomly, stripped and stunted. I crossed courtyards with students only a few years younger, in a separate world. Some looked older by the time I reached the grad school buildings, having been pointed there by an assistant professor type. He might have challenged my status as a visitor if he had not been regaling a likely student, a colleen bursting with fresh youth and chestnut locks tumbling from her stocking cap.

In the Department of Communications building I wandered the halls, adopting my high-rise menuing mindset, blending in, looking purposeful. A few classes were in session and I slowed as I passed them, trying to scan as many faces as possible through the narrow embrasures in the steel doors. One room labeled "sound studio" was locked and dark. Her class would probably meet twice a week at most. The chance was no chance.

Back in the parking lot, I extracted a campus parking ticket from under my wiper. They could sue me. I retreated north under a gunmetal November sky. I thought of calling Melanie for Anita's address, but I wouldn't go that far. If I waited, maybe my madness would decay, if madness had a half-life.

Looking back on the weekend, I'm sure the dread of Saturday coming again had everything to do with the way Friday night played out. I had stopped calling. She had unplugged her phone, or the apartment on Lincoln Park West was vacant. Almost a week had passed and I was facing the specter of the weekend alone.

Synchronicity? Providence? A sixth sense for heartache? It was my Friday to close. After eleven-thirty the three of them entered in a burst of cold air and giggles: the poet Lurlene, a guy with blond spiked hair and a fur coat who wasn't Jerry Lala, and Pat Tremaine. They had a severe case of the munchies and the cause was clear from the size of their pupils. I threw slices into the oven and they rolled quarters into the box. I had let Donny go and Lorenzo would be gone on deliveries for a while. After they had chowed for a few minutes, everyone started dancing, including me with PT, her coat off, her tube dress and boots, her so admirable form. Smokey and "The Tracks of My Tears."

By the time Lorenzo returned, flurries were starting and the sidewalk had been dead for hours. I paid him and flipped the sign around at midnight. Then there was chatter about a cab that Lurlene and Spike could take south and PT could take back north, but I intervened and insisted on driving her, since I was heading north anyway. I'd be lying if I said that dancing with her had nothing to do with it.

"From way across the room, Lady Love." There was a world in which repeating the lyrics purred by a velvety Caribbean crooner was absurd, but I wasn't in it. Targeting them precisely for the lady's ear, six inches above my mouth, was appropriate in all ways. We were rolling in the words and music, conjoining our malleable selves.

Her place was in Germantown where Lincoln, Damen, and Irving Park converged. By the time we arrived, a couple of inches had whitened the blocks, and few cars were moving on Lincoln. I was welcome to crash, the lady said, and I welcomed crashing with the week of phone calls behind me and the sword of a Saturday over my head. Her apartment was dark and enveloping with high-ceilings and heavy built-in bookcases and drawers. We left our boots at the door and dropped our coats on a dun-colored cloth sofa, clearly inherited and probably unmovable. I sized it up as my likely bed. In PT's room of shadows, her hair, gold ringlets, made a breath-stopping contrast, points of snow melting like falling stars.

"Hey, Captain Serious," she said because she had already diagnosed me, in the car or dancing to the Miracles, and she didn't ask, only prescribed. She lit her hash pipe, short and stout. I puffed and the bowl gleamed. Soon I was rolling on about Anita. She gave me the space, and her blue eyes were like an open door.

"Can anybody who's into God the Daddy and the whole dumpster load of sins not be a total fool?"

"I guess if she lives in a certain way."

"What do you think of her?"

Her lips pursed a moment. "The lady has places to go."

"*We* have places to go," I said, a reaction, tongue loosened. I meant Wray and I.

"You could get lucky." Fine-tuned, she had picked up on it.

I realized she was skipping her turn, retaining the pipe for a time then passing it back. She took in my tale of woe then unfolded from the sofa and slipped away. I focused for the first time on the low table in front of the sofa, the property of my physician: *To The Lighthouse*, *Nightwood*, a ceramic bowl and candle, a brass incense burner, a Herbie Hancock album, Gilberto Gil, *A Love Supreme*. Music started, African, Caribbean, rum-warmed. Then she was back, and with the same calm self-assurance that she had produced the pipe, she stroked my cheek once.

She was waiting and I was gaining my feet, rising to a dizzying height. Then she had my hand, Eurydice leading the way down a short hall to a darker room. Island rhythm rolling like waves, a voice like wings, dropping down, banking away.

At first only her hair caught what light there was, and then I could make out the forms of her dresser and bed. Her scent was next, the hint of lilac, and before I was sure that we were, we were dancing in the shadows and I asked what the music was.

"John Lucien," she said. "Do you like it?"

"Sure," I said. We were on a ballroom floor, on an El platform. Almost nothing between us, I was thinking, when her fingers touched my chest and undid one button. Then she pulled the tube dress over her head and there was enough light for the gift of the sight of her. And there was nothing between us then.

Even as we came together, straining sweetly against each other and resting, our conversation went on, and the dance continued to the music that coursed through us like warm waters.

"Lady love," I echoed in her ear, and our lips met. Under the lilac was the delicious, exotic, lightly perspired scent she had. She could have been grooving with Lurlene and Spike, how did I know? My physician was not from our planet. We rolled to our sides and my fingers were in her hair.

"I thought she was divorced," she said. The simple statement, utterly unselfish, caring, rushed through me.

"Glad I wasn't alone," I said. Glad in every way. I was in one moment only with my sexual healer. This lover. This friend.

At some point the music had stopped and we were in each other's arms. The snow was outside and we were in with a sighing radiator in the old Germantown building like a fortress against the cold.

"You're not," she whispered, "alone."

In the morning, standing in her bathroom above Lincoln Avenue and Irving Park, it came to me, however fleetingly, that I could be with PT for eternity, or at least for breakfast. I was unaccustomed to smoking hash, and although I trusted myself to get us to Sammy A's, it took two coffees and a dose of scrambled eggs and grits to bring me around.

PT was her usual self, having prescribed the treatment and shared little of it. Since we had more than covered my story the night before, we focused on hers. She had enrolled in Northern but left at the end of her second year to get space and weigh other options. She admitted, a bit timidly, that she had taken an interest in herbals, macrobiotics, and supplements, to counter the toxins in our habitat, et cetera, which suited her perfectly, although her vision of self-support in that direction was as blurry as any of ours. A trip to Mexico was in the dream stage, whether with Dale I didn't ask. PT could be our exemplar, the apotheosis of all our malformed agendas but Corey's. We were all in collision, in a grand game of pinball, seeking someone to indulge our dreams with. We could go on forever, fit to be tethered, but only blithely.

"Do you work tonight?" she asked.

"I would be off but I'm driving. After three months our drivers get a day off, paid. Tonight it's our main driver, Donny. I think you met him at Last Blast. He's deferred it for a month. He can always make more than the average, which is what we pay for the vacation day." She looked pensive and I wondered if she might be considering a repeat. "I'll probably check out after nine," I added. Instead, she took an entirely different tack.

"I guess he wants to make as much as he can. For the kid," she added, checking me, no doubt seeing that it was news. "He has a lady and a daughter—she's three or four. The mom is Latina, I think, a home care person, an aide. There's a grandmother too. They live in Uptown."

"Does Donny live with them? We never got his address." I was testing now, more curious about her than him.

"No. Larrabee, under Clybourn."

South of North Avenue, closer to Gonzo. I felt a twinge and found myself trying to deny she had been there with him. To be jealous after a night with PT would be *contra naturam*, and fundamentally uncool. I might as well try to bottle moonlight. But maybe that was simply the effect she had, or maybe the twinge was about Donny, possessor of the X factor, which he shared with Melanie and Adam, Anita and Andonati, and the stars.

Why, in her pensive moment, had she decided to tell me more about Donny than I needed to know? Maybe she thought we would bonus him, or tenure him. That fit her. She tended to keep us all stitched up, and together.

Whether PT's news about Donny's satellite family and Uptown diluted the envy, I couldn't say for sure, but the next time he was in the café, I saw him differently. The street looked different. It was mid-afternoon on an anomalous fall day, more like early spring. A dusting of new snow had fallen overnight and the day was clear and balmy with a melt in progress on the sidewalk. Donny had paired his vacation day with a regular off-day. Now he was back outside in the front, surveying Broadway.

"You're early," I said.

"Can't stay away. You know how it is, *kemosabe.*" His hands were stuffed in the pockets of a bomber jacket, black leather, and he was wearing his jogging shoes as usual, road runner.

"How was vacation?"

"Stayed out of trouble. Watched the Bears game yesterday."

"At Soldier Field?

"No way, freeze my tush off. I'm a TV fan. Did you see that one?"

I was ready to admit I hadn't, which would damage my Chicago cred, but I was saved by a vision. We both saw it. "Is that a hawk?"

It had alighted on the top of the telephone pole across the street between electric lines. The low sun was like a rifle and we had to shield our eyes. Broad-shouldered and heavier than a gull, its rust-colored wings were speckled white, with the colors reversed on its breast. It had the majestic head of a raptor.

"Red-tail," Donny said. "Brother lives all over the city, mainly in the parks. Maybe this guy sees mice in these stores, like in the restaurant last night."

I gave him the wince he was going for. I imagined him kidding his daughter.

"How long do you want to drive?"

He looked surprised. "Full night. I'm charged up."

"No, I mean period. Big picture. You're great at it, but—"

"Oh, you're talking life story, like where are you going to be in five years, parole officer shit. I take it light. Captive gig, not for me. That was my old man. Stuck on the rez, soused out, died on the rez. He like did what he was told, what do they say, model prisoner." He shook his head, sardonic grin.

"Driving's like hunting." He checked me and I nodded because I knew what he meant. "You got to stay open to posse-bility. It's the land of the free, *ke-mo-sabe.*"

I wondered if he had other family back home but didn't ask. We were here, both immigrants, and his family was in Uptown.

"If you ever want to come inside, learn to work the counter . . . we'll need a manager at some point."

His shrug was, what can I say? "Yo, will let you know." But Donny was looking at the hawk, and I imagined no time soon.

A jolting bang beside us, behind Donny's shoulder. Concussion of wood and metal, and a bell—Mohammed's door flying back against the wall of our vestibule.

A fugitive blur, dark cloth coat, stocking cap, clutching a jacket, merchandise. Breaking away from us on the sidewalk.

"Hey!" Mohammed in the door. "Hey!" He clutched a moment between the store and the thief, and in the instant, Donny was past him.

The runner hauled down the sidewalk, clipping a woman with a child in tow. She bundled the boy against the drugstore window as Donny veered around them. The guy had him by half a block. I shook off paralysis and chased after them both.

At the Oakdale corner, the thief broke right. He hit a slick patch and dropped to one knee and hand, scrambled up again, and kept going. Donny closed the distance, cut the corner, and disappeared.

When I reached Oakdale, Donny had him down on the sidewalk. Red and black cap—Bulls. They were rolling, grappling for the jacket. Together, we could pin the guy. Then what?

The punk was kicking and then scrambling on all fours. Donny let him run. He was on his feet, back toward me, inspecting the jacket when I caught up.

"It's ripped," he panted. The silk lining hung open, torn a couple of inches on the side of the pocket. Blood was starting through a scrape on the back of his hand.

"You're crazy, man," I puffed and slapped his shoulder. "Good work."

He rotated the sport coat, gray silk, and brushed off a snow patch.

"Are you okay?" Mohammed chugged up behind me. "Thank you, thank you."

Donny handed over the jacket, showing the lining. "He trashed it."

"*Sharmouta*. Shits on the street, fucking scum, so many. You are hurt."

"It's no big. I'll clean up in the café."

He reminded me that it was open and untended with a couple in a booth. We headed back together with Donny shaking out his hand, and I picked up the pace for the last half-block.

By the time he had washed up and patched with a café Band-Aid, Mohammed was waiting in the café with more thanks and a gift certificate for him to use whenever he pleased, no expiration. Our driver in Consort attire challenged the imagination, but who could call what Donny might do?

Mohammed made a police report, although he said he probably wouldn't file a claim for the jacket because it wouldn't be his first. The two cops took statements from both of us, and Donny echoed my description of the perpetrator, generic punk, no distinguishing features but the Bulls beanie. I was glad to see the officers were not Duchamp and Hecker and glad to see them go.

When all had died down and I was refreshing the slices in the front window, I heard a high-pitched cry, followed by another. They could have been notes on a Fender E-string around the twentieth fret. Or a screech Dale could squeeze out of an electric violin. When I checked the pole, Donny's red-tailed brother was gone.

Chapter 23

In the days after the theft and the rundown, Donny and I were a team: Lanier and George, or the other way around. First we recounted the story of Donny's heroic takedown for Corey, then for Lorenzo. By the time we came to Bruce, we had our act down. I did the setup--you missed the heist, et cetera. Then Donny divulged the details one more time, modestly as Superman. I'm done with it, but the feat shall live on in cafe lore.

Wray would be on the hook for this duty, or at least sharing the hook with me, if tomorrow was not the Monday after Thanksgiving weekend. He had traded his Monday off for last Saturday, so he'll be copying.

Because Arlington is our biz address, John got the invite. Riley-Strauss signed one of their acts to a deal with Isabel Records, a Decca label. Lefty Dizz is a mad dog blues dude Wray and I caught once in Kingston Mines. The party for him is in Marina City, god knows why. To make the scene with Anita--how cool that would have been.

You know there's a reason
For the words that let you go
But goodbye is the hardest word I know.

That's it, the rest is junk. Can't even write
a song about it.
Anita, Pat. I should take Luz Guillen off the
market. Who needs to talk about anything? Dinner
on Sundays with sister's family. Learn a little
salsa and bachata. "Duello" sounds Latin anyway--
the lowlife said so.

I rolled around in the garage, winding down circles, then took an elevator up thirty-six floors. I had made the mistake of menuing one of the two Marina City towers in the early days, but although each building had sixty-some stories of doors, it was too far outside our delivery zone.

I pressed the doorbell but couldn't hear the buzzer over the R&B inside, I guessed Dinah Washington. A bouncer-sized brother cracked the door as far as his foot. He wore an argyle sweater and gold tinted glasses, smooth, like a handler for Ray Charles. I held my invitation high and he opened the door wide then shut it quickly behind me.

In the living room about a dozen guests were trying to make themselves heard over Dinah. Most looked South Side, some North, and Marina City suddenly made sense, between the worlds. In a sinking moment it dawned on me that I was underdressed. I was wearing my one hip shirt, purple silk, but my leather jacket and jeans were nowhere. Most of the brothers had cool threads, à la blues Sunday on Cottage Grove, and the sisters' hems were high. A couple of dashikis stood out, and I had to look twice at a senior cat in alligator loafers who could have been John Lee Hooker. A few were vertical, but the rest spread out on a white leather sectional and chairs. Nothing I could do about the jeans now. A brightly lit dining room was the first stop.

A caterer around my age, serious looking in a white kufi cap and black fitted jacket, manned the table. I nodded and he played statue. There were circular crackers with a salmon-colored spread, barbecued wings, and fried shrimp, Piper-Heidsieck and a keg of Molson's, plastic split glasses and beer mugs. I ordered a mug of draft and forced myself back in to work the room.

At the far end in a wing chair, a window at his back, had to be the guest of honor. He was turned to two brothers at his side, his face half-hidden by a white Panama hat. The svelte sister on his other side I took to be Dizzette number one. A tyke at his feet was playing with a toy guitar. I would introduce myself to his highness and speak the name of Duello, but the higher priority was to do the same with Riley-Strauss. I sidled along the wall and followed a dashiki with electric hair down a hall toward the bedrooms.

Right away I was in deeper forest. The living and dining rooms were open and bright, but the bedrooms were low-lit ambience. In the first, a trio clumped together around a bedside table under a low lamp, a waifish couple partnered in La Mere Vipere and a lanky Bowie-head with a straw in his nostril working a line. A dance beat came from a source unseen, likely a boombox in the bathroom—"Le Freak" by Chic.

I went on to the master bedroom, more crowded and heavier in perfume and cigarette smoke. A pair of disco dudes in poly and patent leather were on their way out as I worked my way in. The rooms could be mapped by their party drugs. A few tablets, white and pink, were available on a glass-top dresser. I picked up the tang of pot smoke for the first time, stronger closer to the master bath.

"Hey man, glad you could make it." A group had cleared in front of me, and I was suddenly standing a few feet from Randy Strauss where he sat on the end of a bed. "This is Shandra and Elise."

Dusky Shandra reminded me of Thalia. Blonde Elise had an out-of-season tan that could have been Cabo but more likely, Vegas.

"This is one of our new acts, Duello. They're a duo, folk." I saw their eyes switch off. "Where's your other half?"

"John had a conflict tonight, a family thing." I was nodding but Randy didn't nod. He wore his hair long and sported a beard like a Bee Gee Gibb, probably to look older, but his blue eyes were boyish, pupils dilated. He was a couple of years older at most, floating on percentages, flanked by admirers. "But we really appreciate—"

"Did you get a chance to meet Lefty?"

"Not yet, but—"

"He's a fucking legend. And this is his first. You'd think Chess would have signed him long ago. I'm glad we could make it happen for him." He was nodding now and I nodded.

"That's great, incredible. Isabel—"

"They're basically Decca in France. Decca is huge in Europe, more than here."

I nodded one large one. I was humble, the eager pupil.

"They're all hard. But hang in. It could happen to you."

"Mark said maybe Flying Fish—"

"Hey hey!" Randy and the two ladies' faces lit up. They were looking at my shoulder, past my shoulder. "My man!"

Then Randy was on his feet and soul shaking, and his free hand was pounding the back of the new dude who glowed in a powder blue western shirt. He took after Cleavon Little.

"Greetings from Austin, my man." He whipped the hand he had been hiding behind his back over Randy's head and deposited a hat, a black Stetson with a silver star in front. Randy nodded to the girls, admiring and gleeful, then doffed it to admire.

"Black, not white? I'm bad."

"You're bad," Cleavon confirmed. "You're bad."

Then they were off on the tour—Houston and Austin and the Continental Club and what it was like to perform on TV. I had no idea who Cleavon was. Soon he was chatting up Shandra but keeping Elise hopeful with eye contact. It was a cozy quartet. I needed an exit line.

"So Randy, is Mark around? I missed him."

His gaze swung around to me, the kid tugging at his pants leg. "He's in the Big Apple."

Should I have known? Did they split? I did the up-nod of understanding, understanding nothing. Randy nodded and his Stetson rim tipped up and down and I was nodding, and thanking. Cleavon uncapped a tiny plastic vial. As the ladies watched, two pink tabs appeared in his palm like candy.

I didn't turn my back but I did sidle. I picked out the dashiki with the hair again across the room, this time with his arm around a sister, gold top, black jeans. They were heading for the door. I took a deep draw as I passed the emanation from the master bath and followed my Virgil out of the bedroom. Back in the brightness I saw Lefty was free, emptying a plastic Champagne glass.

"Hey man, congratulations. My name is Mitch, I'm with Duello. We have Mark and Randy too."

He peered up from under his brim. Clearly, I needed a hat. His eyes looked older than I thought he was, but it was hard to tell. With a receding chin, he resembled a turtle, and all turtles looked fatigued. Maybe his likeness motivated him. Whatever it took—he was the one with the contract. On the wall beside him an Isabel Records poster displayed an array of album cover images with titles in French.

"That's cool," he said and I shook Lefty's right hand. It felt like calf skin. Fat rings.

Dizzette assessed me, working on a wing. She had her hat, a charcoal beret, French-themed or Black Panther or both. Two paper plates sat beside her, one with partially gnawed chicken and shrimp, likely by the junior guitarist at their feet.

"What do you play?" Dizz asked.

"It's acoustic music, folk-influenced but with improv—stretched out. Tim Buckley . . ." I was fishing, trying to trigger a blink, anything. "And there are spoken parts . . ." Dizzette was sizing me up.

"Damn, you gonna be cuttin' in Paris." A brother had materialized, bleach blond, lighter skin, freckles dabbed across his cheekbones. Serious musculature stretched the ribs of his turtleneck. His chokehold could snap my neck. It was hard to envision his role in music, maybe bodyguard. Wide grin, silver tooth. Soul shake.

"Thas wat they say, gay Paree." Lefty had come to life. With no warning, little Dizz began chopping his plastic guitar into the carpet.

"Wow!" I forced a smile. "He'll be another Pete Townshend." Lefty looked puzzled. "Or Hendrix." They were all staring, six eyes. Then Dizzette bent down and stopped the chop. Little Dizz let out a wail.

Three freaking seventy-five. And how long was I there? An hour and a half. Less. The parking attendant surveyed the Mustang—no parking pass, don't know this one. He took his time making change, finally raising the gate. *Suck these funky fumes. Welcome to my world.*

I rolled onto State heading north and hit it. *Hit the road, Jack.* By the light I was backing off. The parking was an investment, like the flyers. The cost of doing business. It was a write-off, Malowitz would be pleased to point out, which would be more of an advantage if Duello had income.

But what did Duello have to do with that crowd? What were Wray and I doing? Corey and I? There was a theme here. But Wray and I were the new kids, and so much of it was only about time. How much? *Overnight success after twenty.* How long for Dizz? Maybe Chicago just buries you.

On Sunday night traffic was light, but LaSalle would be faster. I wanted no obstructions. The Cavern might be empty and haunted, but it meant headspace and wine to unwind. At the next light I turned west.

Had I done any good? I got the face of Duello in front of the man, at least one of them. That was job one. Had I done any harm? I could say my presence had been low-impact, on the scale of a Fender flat pick. I would tell Wray it was fine, it was great. Maybe he'll go next time. Cop your threads at Consort, I'll advise. Don't skip the beret.

The light was turning and I thought about running it, but it was not my night, so I sat facing the red at the empty intersection. A lemon-colored Malibu wagon rolled through heading one-way south on Clark, and the fog of oil smoke it was trailing must have been the reason I watched it, hoping it would be busted. That was how I spotted the other car parked on Clark south of the corner.

The streetlight washed out the color, but the body looked the same. On green, I hung a left and braked long enough to recognize the plate. Eagle feathers hung from the mirror. Donny's Road Runner was less than half a block from O'Banion's. I tried to recall whether he was on the schedule and couldn't think of a reason he wouldn't be. It was going on ten, so Corey could have let him off, but it would be early for a Sunday. We could have a delivery to the club, but it would be a first. Spaces were open toward the far end of the block and I pulled over.

In the misty chill I started back toward the only likely destination. O'Banion's was a punk's paradise, a charcoal boxcar with two blacked-out windows, spectral, a single cone lamp over the door in a halo of fog. I could hang back by the door and try to spot him. I doubted there was a cover charge on Sunday. If he was schmoozing on the job, I was in no mood to nail him, but Corey and I would have a discussion. I would have a beer myself if I could get deep enough into the shadows. And maybe he wasn't even there.

The night was damp and cold enough to bite, and I zipped the jacket higher but only to the spot above the solar plexus where a zipper tooth had been broken for a couple of months. Half a block before O'Banion's, I picked up the low reverb of bass and drums and listened for a vocal. If not for that instinct, seeking a voice, I probably would have missed them, the way we sleep through muffled voices we know but wake to others that could spell a threat. Voices out of context, crooked, origin out of sight in the alley.

One familiar tone, or was it even that? Recognition, or self-deception? We hear what we think we hear. It could have been a word at most, or not a word, guttural. From the obscure enclosure of the alley, too close to pass.

I left the sidewalk for the alley asphalt and flattened against a brick wall. Two dumpsters sat even with the rear of the club. Crouching, I crept toward them below the line of sight. At the cold steel, reek of beer and garbage. Halfway down the alley, gusting steam from a vent like a crack in the inferno.

"You know." A voice ahead in the dark. A mumble, something indistinct. Thrum of bass from an opening door, someone leaving O'Banion's. They could pass the alley, be curious.

"You know that, motherfucker. How you know? Who tell you?"

Voice in a nightmare. Prison yard.

"Nobody. I fucking work there. I know him." The voice was clear in the cold air. Donny's. "The Paki comes in the store—"

"We seen you—is not your turf." Another voice, accent, mud-thick. Slavic? "You know when . . . where . . ." something . . . "the hits in the coat. Lotta hits, man." Russian? "Who tip you, Starcik? Who?" A thud, gut-muffled, grunt then gasp, drowning man.

I angled a view around the side of the dumpster. No alley light, faint moonlight, slicks of packed snow on asphalt. In the middle of the next back wall two had him, one in front, one behind. Donny was bent at the waist, his jacket open, arms hooked from behind by the shorter one—the Bulls cap, scrambling away on Oakdale.

"You want push here, we know." The one in front, the Russian, hulking, black coat, had Donny by fifty pounds.

"You know shit. Is—"

The Russian slapped his face, toying with him.

The cap kneed him from behind, snarled in his ear, "Is shit." Something. "You go back long time, we know. No fucking diff. You here now. We be on your ass, man. You are fucking dead man."

The Russian slapped his face the other way, harder. He rifled Donny's jacket pockets, stripped a wallet and flung it down the alley. Then he pulled a hand-sized wad from inside his jacket, inspected it, held out for the cap to see, and ducked it into his own coat.

"You want to live?" The Russian hulked over him, growled at his hanging head. "Who tol' you?"

Nobody behind me. No curious passersby drawn as I was into this vortex. No sound from O'Banion's.

We could not lose our best driver. That was rationale. But now I was also on the Lee Elementary School playground in summer with Eddie Poole, no teachers, the season of random punks. He had come from nowhere across the lot, drifting closer, eyeing us, shorter but dirty-looking, like he lived outside. Then he cut between us, intercepted my pitch to Eddie, spiked the baseball into the clay. I came back trash-talking. He threw one punch that caught my chin and I was sitting in the dirt. Stunned, I let him walk away and told neither of my parents. I knew what Hank would have said to do. I had been ashamed of that day since I was nine. So it wasn't only a matter of rationale. Besides, Donny and I were immigrants to the city, both of us. I thought of yelling, catching them frozen-faced, letting Donny break free. But I could see how they had him, the punk arm-locking him from behind, the Russian resetting, planting his feet.

Up and around the steel bin. Cold legs stiff as cable. Wet slip under foot but catching the steel corner. Still upright. Drive.

Donny's head hanging, the Russian's back to me, torso rotating, arm drawing back. Drive.

Through him was the one thought, fold arms and drive. Think all the way through him like a fastball through the catcher. Straight through between the shoulder blades. Drive block. He never heard me.

My face flattened into his coat, mildew and smoke. It felt like ramming a padded wall, but the wall did give.

The Russian pitched forward and I rolled over and past him, taking the asphalt on my arm and shoulder. He dropped to his hands and knees but that was all. It had been my one clear shot.

Donny and the cap were staring, stunned. One of Donny's arms was free.

"Run!" I choked out, fighting for breath.

He twisted loose and made one clear stride but the cap lunged at him, tackling around the thighs, and they both went down. Donny beat at him but the cap tucked his head, face buried in Donny's legs. I knew I could kick him free.

The Russian swiveled on his knees. Spotted me, huffing and empty-faced, black-eyed, roused like a bull, a pick in his hump. Rolling on my side, gaining my feet. I broke for Donny and the cap. The Russian came at me but I was fifteen feet from them, twenty at most. A gloss of blood on Donny's mouth. Impact at my shoulder, stiff-arm. On one foot, canting sideways.

Canting, like football. I could do it, I knew in the long slow second. Displacement game, game of off-center. Spin to footing. Get a hand down and break the fall. But the asphalt flew up. Padded only by jacket, shoulder hit, arm compressed ribs, breath gone. I rolled onto knees, gasping, chest not working. Pushing up from knees, bent and coughing. Donny had kicked free, glint of his silver chain.

Head hanging, dark shoes on the periphery, coming like animal shadows, predatory. In the fog-filtered moonlight, in the blink before impact I caught the sheen of knuckles, not brass but stainless steel.

The slug on the jaw, a snapping sound below the ear. A swinging thread of saliva, string of light. Brain jam. Still standing, head lolling back to take him in. Tuck head, hands up. But arms were dead weight. No time.

The other side, cheekbone and eye. Burst of white shattering dots in a dark field. Asphalt stone-hard on the face, gulping breath of piss smell and cold. High above was an eye, and tiny creatures in the alley.

I heard Donny's voice but not words. A kick I tried to block landed heavily in my chest, and a hand, my left, was burning. There was a booming of a heart. A scent of vomit. Omnivorous cold.

Gliding high above, wheeling in the field of a hawk, an eye observed one on his side, diminutive, fetal.

Donny was wailing. Sinking. Shutting down.

What more did he want from me? Humiliation not complete? Lefty Dizz was peering through eyes half-mast, derision in his lips. His expression was saying, why? Why in the spark-flinging inferno of the Chicago night are you in this place?

I could be awake. I could be only slipping from a dream to a lesser dream. Sighting through one eye across the asphalt and a smear of snow, I played dead, only breathing, letting my face freeze one with the alley floor. I needed to know. Counting breaths was a start. I passed three, and five. On ten I raised my head and turned back to the alley. Empty.

I felt my face with my free hand. The right jaw was huge, and numb. My left eye, an inch from the pavement, wasn't working. I rocked, testing for pain, then rolled onto my stomach, unpinning my left arm. I inched up to all fours and began to unfold, pushing on one knee then the other. Lifting the head was not possible. I let it hang down, reclaiming its blood, hands on knees. White spots drifted in and vanished. I swore I wouldn't faint, staying with the breath, drawing in the cold air past the ache in my chest.

Blood to the head brought the pain. The right side of my face throbbed and I tested the jaw. It would open, but not halfway. Testing for teeth, running my tongue. All felt in place, but I tasted iron for the first time and spat blood until it cleared. My left eye was swollen shut and the socket ached. With numb fingertips on cheek and brow, I spread the lids enough to make out a sliver of the alley. A wave of nausea rolled up and I breathed the cold air and stared into the asphalt spattered with spit and blood until it passed. As the brain was resetting, in the space before making sense, it came to me unbidden, battered loose, a place and a happening I had put away.

Three large pizzas in the Gonzo hot box, waiting for the elevator in the marble lobby, chandelier of glass icicles and low black sofa and seats framed in chrome. One way to the pool and another to the spa and whatever was the "Jungle Room."

Hands still on knees, I glanced across the alley at the spots where I had hit the Russian's back and where I had last seen Donny. Between the two were remnants. I dragged toward them dumbly, although I had guessed what they were already, the only tangible evidence of what had incomprehensibly happened. I bent over for throbbing seconds and scraped up the business cards. I left a wrapped condom lying a few feet away. The Russian had pilfered

Donny's wallet, dumped what he didn't want, and flung it. I squinted in the direction through one eye toward the wall and another dumpster but saw nothing more. A charge ran through me and I slapped my hip pocket. Still there. I pulled my wallet and checked the bills, and my license. They didn't care about my few bucks. It had all been about Donny.

The door swung open and Charlie's Angel greeted me— the brunette, Sabrina look-alike in a low black jumpsuit with a gold sash. In the apartment behind her mingled the men and women of the cast, glittery and hip. "Voulez-Vous Coucher Avec Moi Ce Soir." Delivery to the boss's party pad was a trust, and the tip would not disappoint. Sabrina directed me to the glass-top coffee table and I put the boxes down beside the straws and the razor blade.

Shivering, I stuffed the cards into my jacket pocket. The top of my silk shirt had lost a button and I tried to clutch the jacket collar closed. At the end of the alley the mist was lit by a streetlight. I slid my shoes toward it, ready for any nightmare, for the Mustang to be towed or stolen. I could breathe again when it came into view. At the opposite end of the block was a space where Donny's car had been.

I checked my watch. Ten to eleven. I tried to calculate how long I had been unconscious. Twenty minutes? Half an hour? At the car I gave up.

"Fuck! Jesus fuck!" Only dead Clark Street heard me. My right hand had not been damaged, but it took my numb fingers most of a frozen minute to work the keys out of my jeans pocket.

Inside with the door pulled tight, back in the bucket seat, heat was priority one. I turned on the engine and revved it, waiting until the heater could blow warmth. With both eyes shut I counted three breaths then tilted the mirror toward my face.

Opposite sides were swollen and distorted from the two blows. The left jaw bulged where the steel knuck had landed, and my right eye looked as expected, swollen shut and already blue-black to the socket. I checked from all angles. When no perfect view wiped it all away, I tilted the mirror back.

For the first time I focused on my left hand on the wheel. Lacerations glinted on the index and middle fingers and the knuckles were swelling, mid-fingers and hand. I flexed it and squeezed the fingers for breaks, trying to ignore that it could be a worse problem, muscles or tendons, thinking through the chords I wouldn't be able to play and wondering for how long. And there would be days gone from the café, and maybe Donny drove his own car home and would show up as though nothing had happened, or maybe he didn't. That lay in the future, now was about getting home.

My neck felt too stiff to turn. Shaking as I checked the mirror, I pulled out and boosted the heat to high. One left at the light and then another, and I was heading north. No radio, no associations, just focus through my cyclops eye. With the vents trained on my hands, sensation started to return and my fingers began to burn.

I forked onto Lincoln Avenue. On that long diagonal came the last piece of recollection.

Ozzie and the poker-faced look he gave you, flat affect, as though he could buy you and he knew it, buy anybody. Ozzie and the bills from the cash box that he would peel off and pocket. And his North Side 'fro. Sabrina glued to him like her salvation. And the chain I knew I had seen before when Donny wore it at the café counter—the chain around Ozzie's throat that night as he peeled off two tens and slipped them into my hand. The same CTX on his silver neck chain, and the closed loop.

I had all the pieces in my head clearly, with what they were beginning to mean, by the time I pulled over on my block. But as I lifted the door handle with my right hand and rolled out through the pain in my chest, I let them go and focused on washing myself clean, and on refuge.

Halfway up the walk I saw a patch of low light on the ground in front of my window, I guessed from the hall, and tried to remember how I had left it on.

I had just unlocked the door.

She was standing in her black nightgown in the half-light of the hallway sconce.

"God, what . . ." Anita was on me then, inspecting my damage. Those eyes I had tried to extinguish. I turned away, ashamed, trying to hide, but turned back because I had to see her. Her hands were on my shoulders. Her fine shoulders and collarbone, bird of the night.

I clutched her to me, and it was a wonder in all ways, not least that the crown of her head fit under my chin, hiding my ugliness. But Anita would have none of it, and over the next hour she drew the bath and helped me out of my clothes and left me only when I was in the water with ice in a towel to alternate between my jaw and my eye.

When we were in the bed with my head propped on two pillows and a cushion, I tried to explain as much as she needed to know to comprehend my condition, to try to come to terms with the last vision of me she had expected to find. She touched my arm and shoulder as though they could break. I told her I had always wanted her to use her key.

Soon I was slipping beneath the surface, letting go, and the shocks and images of violence, taken and given, were fading, as though possibly the night had never happened. Only one thought was keeping me conscious, haunting me, denying my release, but I refused to ask about him or them. No matter, Anita read me anyway.

"It's over," she said.

Chapter 24

"HOW about some tea, guys?" Anita padded into the living room, hair up, glasses from homework, white shirt and black tights.

"It's my speed now," I explained to Corey. "She says no coffee yet." It hurt to grin.

"Tea would be great," he said.

"We have English breakfast and an herbal," she recalled. "The herbal is—"

"Red Zinger?"

"What a guess," I told him. I had brought it home in the early days before we had overloaded on almost all products we sold. I was probably thinking about company back then, no doubt Melanie.

"English breakfast, please." After the sight of me, and what I had laid on him, no doubt Corey could have used a stronger infusion. I nodded the same. His eyes followed her back through the dining room.

"Sheesh," he said, seated in my desk chair across from me, pillow-propped on the sofa. He was picking up the thread again. "And you think Donny knew there was a drop in the pocket. Why didn't the punk just take that? Why try to rip off the whole jacket?"

"Maybe Mohammed surprised him. Maybe he couldn't get it out in the store, who knows?" My jaw wasn't working right. I swiveled it gingerly. How long would it take to break that habit?

"And Ozzie is the main man . . . because he and Donny have the same necklace?"

"One of them told Donny in the alley—the cap or the Russian, I don't remember which—'you go back, we know'. And how long did Donny drive for Gonzo? He said from the start, all the way back. And Ozzie always with a cash bag or a roll of bills. A cash business, right?"

"So Donny was in all the way, maybe freelancing, going out on his own." He looked at me flatly, wheels turning behind his glasses. No more cross-exam.

"When he didn't come back, I tried his beeper a couple of times. Lorenzo took the last three orders. None were late."

"Good."

"Versatility," he added lamely and gave a thumbs up.

"What are we going to do?" I said.

He pointed to his eye socket. "That'll take a couple of weeks. We can't have you freaking the customers."

"I could get a Nixon mask."

"And you should probably get your ribs X-rayed."

"I thought I'd give it a week." That was a bill I didn't need. Plus, my left hand might cost something, which was a bigger concern.

"I bet we could get Kat back—I'll give a call. And Donny could show."

Wherever he was now. And whoever had his car.

"We should give Bruce and Lorenzo a raise," he continued, not proposed, a given. "Fifty cents an hour."

We could never afford raises, but now we could less afford to lose either of them. I was in no position to object. As always, the solution was raising sales. Maybe I could menu when my hand recovered, although no sane person would hold a high-rise door for me. No doubt menuing would be door-to-door in December in gloves.

"Would you do it again?" Corey's question landed from afar, simple but mind-boggling, the koan of the hour. He looked curious, and delighted. A yes or a no.

"What would you do?" The instant I blurted it at him I realized the laughable stupidity of it. John would not have been in that position in any imaginable scenario, but I had been, wondering how far to go, soon to be punched out in an alley, alum of UNC Chapel Hill, the product of my choices.

He gave me a look that said fundamentally that.

"You didn't grow up here," he said. "People get hammered for a lot less."

I was a newbie, an import. He thought that was unarguable, but the truth was, I had seen more of the city than the North Side kid probably ever would. I let him make his point, though, the sage of all things Chicago. With no rebuttal, I sucked on the Heineken bottle and then he did the same.

I had tried to come up with a way to postpone telling him, but to wait longer would have made no sense when he eventually found out. So the day after talking to Corey I called John and warned him what to expect when I arrived at his apartment. Now the Mossman sat in a stand three feet from his leg and it was hard to ignore the fact that on any other Tuesday night when I had come down to Arlington, we would be practicing. I was the undeniable, beat-up proof of his original argument, café versus music.

"What do we do if Randy and Mark call?" There was an edge in his voice. Since we had no gig for the next two weeks, there was nothing to cancel yet.

"We could probably push it a week or so. It won't take me long to get back." I knew what I was saying, that it was the last thing we would want to do and that my entire mission to genuflect at the throne of Lefty Dizz was to get opportunities, not turn them down.

"What chords can you play?" I didn't appreciate the interrogation, but I owed him that much.

"G. No F's or barre chords, obviously." Or anything else, was the truth of it. I could tell what he was thinking. "It isn't that bad. This is padding." I had wrapped the left hand in gauze to shield the first two fingers and knuckles. Maybe not the best choice. "I'll get a bottleneck slide." I demoed with the Heineken bottle on the neck of an air guitar. "Keith," I cited. "'No Expectations'. It's just swollen, nothing broken."

"How do you know?"

"You know. You can tell." What experience did I have? I lifted the same hand, fingers folded, and pointed to my ringless ring finger, which flared outward from the last knuckle. "High school basketball," I said.

"I never knew you were a hoopster. You have to explain yourself."

"I think it was in PE."

"You're probably double-jointed. Selectively."

We participated in the ritual of beer again and I was feeling the weight lift. Wray reached for the Mossman and I suspected we were past it.

He tuned to drop-D and began wending his way into a piece I hadn't heard. He slipped on the fingerpicks, and his thumb set up a Travis pattern, alternating bass. The lead consisted of four-bar figures, theme and variation, major and minor. I closed my eyes and focused on the bright fingerpicks on the steel strings and the sonorous tone of the Mossman. The bass took on a cadence like the pulse of driving wheels, and I saw flat land and a night train rolling out of Chicago on straight track over a level plain. That Wray could conjure the image of charging steel in darkness brought it all back. I had been compelled to do what I did with Donny, but my duty to the music was higher. John had made his point in his usual way.

The train was still running in my head as I started driving back. I couldn't stop myself from taking a silly route, down Wrightwood toward the lake, checking the sidewalks and lighted windows as though I could catch a glimpse of her. Anita hadn't told me the address, and I wasn't allowed in until she had finished setting up. Even if I picked her out framed in a window, I knew she had school the next day, and the station, and I was a partial wreck, and it made no sense. That didn't stop the longing, maybe even fueled it, inversely proportional to the odds.

In the last couple of blocks before the water, a sense of the place came over me—Anita's street, John behind me on Arlington, Janis's building tucked behind his on Deming, Melanie a few blocks south on Belden. This patch of a ward had come to own parts of me, in the city that still felt partly accidental, a place I had never seriously planned to be. On Lincoln Park West I turned north, then took Diversey, my back to the lake, the café passing a few blocks to my right. I was weightless, an observer tumbling outside my world.

Back home, I knew it made even less sense than cruising Anita's street, but it was just as irresistible. John's doubts had me on edge, amping my fears. I popped open the Favilla case and unwound the gauze from my hand. The cool neck I seldom paid attention to felt too wide and the steel strings resisted pressure. As I had told John with no certainty, I could manage a G chord. The index finger knuckle made a C impossible, and a D brought the middle finger knuckle into play, which was equally painful. I didn't need to try the barre chords but I did anyway. Dead strings and a buzz. I laid the guitar to rest and clenched and stretched the hand. There would be exercises I could do, therapy. I inspected the swelling again to settle myself down. Nothing broken, remember that.

Ten twenty-five. One more chance for a miracle. I called the café and Bruce answered. My partner had departed for home, leaving an employee to close, and I couldn't blame him. Bruce told me Corey had tried the beeper twice, at the beginning and end of the night, and no miracle. Still no Donny.

Between times when Anita could visit, I had little to do but read, let the TV rattle in the background, and try to write lyrics with no accompaniment, with predictable results. I both wanted to know and didn't, so I spent more than a day mulling it over. My overall uselessness was the deciding factor, leaving me with no excuse not to call PT.

Because she knew nothing of the rumble, for my request to make sense, I had to go through it all again. She agreed to be my guide. When I picked her up, she was probably more shocked than she let on, but soon she went into healer mode, prescribing vitamin E and the B complex. I wasn't familiar with Clybourn, so I took Lincoln to Armitage, then it was only six blocks south on Larrabee.

As we neared Donny's building, I checked the street for his car, my last memory of it still too vivid. No Road Runner. The two-story clapboard on the edge of an industrial district sagged with the weight of Chicago winters. Pat led me around the side where a steel pin on a chain was the only lock on a chain-link gate. We climbed the gray back stairs between patches of old snow. On the second landing we could see in through the half-tilted Venetian blinds.

The kitchen was tidy but bare, empty Formica counters, no dishes or utensils visible. Through the door to the living room, we could see only a stuffed chair and an end table and the corner of a sofa. All lay in repose, as though a landlady had prepped the rooms to show to the next month-to-month tenant. Pat recalled that he had a Redbone poster and a Mr. Coffee in the kitchen and a bucket seat by the back door. Gone. Donny had been replaced by emptiness. A raw wind carried the murmur of traffic from Clybourn.

Back in the warmth of the car I fished the card out of my shirt pocket. It was a restaurant card—Monterey Del Sol on Foster, a red lobster and a snapper in the corners. I guessed it could have been their first date. Half of the back was stained a mud color from the alley where I had rescued it, but the name and address Donny had printed in ink were clear: Vicky Portillo, on Dover. PT couldn't confirm the number, only that Donny had told her Vicky and their daughter were in Uptown. Dover ran through it, east of Clark.

Corey and I didn't go right away. We were still half-expecting Donny to saunter in one night, making suckers of us all, magically rewinding everything. After four days as my shiner turned to yellow, I worked in as a driver, wearing makeup supplied by Anita. Kat was back, and with occasional fill-ins by Lorenzo, we made it through until we hired a new driver, a tall, doe-eyed kid named Tony, a freshman at Wilbur Wright. I migrated back inside, but on the pizza table only, facing the back wall. The hand was recovering by degrees with the aid of a used book on sports rehab with a chapter of hand exercises. I practiced F and barre chords on the pizza paddle handle. Simple progressions were coming back, but the barres were a work in progress.

It was the season, and I was in charge of trimming the front window with lights. Corey brought a tree for a back table, and customers were invited to decorate it, which they did with ribbons, spare baubles, and napkin stars, no doubt a fire code violation. Beth was singing regular church gigs, and Corey was paying PT to watch Arlo as needed. It would be his third Christmas, and Santa was planning to bring him a metal car he could sit in and pedal. My present was soon to be more time with Anita, with her winter break starting in a few days.

We waited out the possibility of Donny's return. Three weeks after the alley episode and a week before Christmas, the time had come. Saturday night sales had been good, and we knew it would hurt, but we agreed on three hundred. On Sunday afternoon I picked up Corey and we headed for Uptown.

In the Sheridan Park neighborhood, developers began deconstructing grand hotels into apartments in the forties. Vicky's building on Dover appeared to be one, gray brick and limestone with bay windows, ornate oriels, on the first two floors. We spotted the Portillo apartment number, but instead of trying to explain ourselves through an antique intercom, we skipped the buzzer. After a few minutes of loitering in the lobby, a mother exited with two youngsters, all of them bundled. Corey held the outer door and I caught the inner.

Apartment four-eleven was on the back of the building, farthest from the elevator. A faint sound like carnival music filtered through the door. I buzzed and we both took a step back from the peep hole.

After long moments as we were being inspected, the door opened the length of the chain: a woman of a certain age, strokes of black in her silver hair drawn back, a strong jaw. Since I had proposed the scheme, it was up to me.

"*Señora* Portillo?" The slightest nod, ready to dismiss the salesmen. "We are friends, acquaintances, of Donny George." Her eyes tightened. "He drove for us—made deliveries, for our restaurant." I glanced at Corey. Neither of us could tell if she understood.

"*Para nuestro café,*" Corey tried, "*entrega . . . en auto, si?* Pizza."

The door closed, we heard the chain slide, and it reopened. Behind the *señora* in the living room, a cartoon calliope was circling on the TV. A junior viewer on the floor glanced at us, dark eyes, then back. Cooking smells, roasting and cilantro. Centered in the window and raised on a hassock, a short tree was decorated with tinsel, tiny lights, and ornaments of colored straw.

"We have something of his for Vicky," I said, showing the envelope.

"She is working." Her English was clear, and she held the door firmly with the bearing of a lady who had once resided in the Sheridan Park Hotel before it diminished around her.

"Donny earned it," Corey added, "but we did not have time to pay him. . . . He is gone, yes?"

"*No sé*. We have not seen him." For the first time *señora* Portillo averted her eyes, a fast-moving cloud like a moment of shame. Then she returned to us, a look of resignation and weariness.

"If you could give this to your daughter, please?" I passed the sealed envelope across the same transom Donny had crossed, into the world of Portillo. His daughter was watching us again. Grandmother took it without opening.

"Gracias."

"*Gracias, señora.*" I nodded. The door was closing and I caught the last sight of little dark eyes.

We left the building into steady wind and stray whips of snow. On the walkway to the door a young woman, coat clutched, passed by without looking up. We both glanced back after her, wondering. No way to know. We started the return drive, the lights in the apartment windows anomalous against the darkening afternoon and the grays of Uptown.

"Well, she didn't slam the door in our face." Corey summed up our letdown. We had both hoped to see who Vicky was and delight her by playing Santa. "Cute kid."

"What's your theory? About Donny." Except for my proposal to make the donation, and a few more calls to his beeper, we had barely mentioned him since Corey's visit to the Cavern.

"Black Ensemble Theater," he said, completely non sequitur, reading a marquee. He sat watching apartments click by. "I bet he flew," he picked up. "Maybe back to Minnesota . . . isn't that where he was from? Donny was a bird. He had a lot of red, and some white. Lots of energy, unassigned. He gave me a headache."

I should have known better. Donny and the red bird aura. And Corey thought I was delusional. Donny as the cardinal. But then I flashed on the red-tail.

"He didn't translate," he added matter-of-factly, the Eckist euphemism for passing on. He kept looking out the window, at the sky or the sad faces of the apartment buildings, or beyond them.

                                                    Dec. 19

We don't see it--Corey or John, Melanie or Anita, or any of the rest of us--but we're in a suspension here, dark and deep. Predators rise to take the unwise, or the unwary, or the weak. The Donnys and the Kips--we seldom see them, much less lose them.

The omnivorous city that is like its great lake that is like an ocean takes it all in. It dwarfs and humbles and can absorb anything, as it absorbed Donny. As it could absorb us and reduce us if we're careless in our little time slice, our frangible moment, the city with its crushing depths and layers of time and vastness.

Donny was here among us, now not. Who was he besides our experiences of him now past--his X factor, my envy, the father of Vicky's kid, beep-beep, the would-be entrepreneur purveyor of intoxicants ecstatic and sad? It's as though he both was and was not at once, as though what we knew of him or thought we knew was all of him, our story of Donny, both splendid in our memories and empty as his place on Larrabee.

Thirteen days until the new year. I'm sensing time like an old man, pages turning. If you slow down you start to sink, and time can pick you off. This will be the year to break out, get free! It will be because it has to be.

New Year's, 1979

Chapter 25

"YOU don't mean it. Do you?" Anita was surveying me, eyes wide.

"Of course I do. I told you, it's great. It's you, so of course." I could recognize her in the apartment, at least part of her, and I could see how she might have been shy about showing me because it was straighter than the Cavern and the impromptu digs of most of our crowd, more upright. In the studio, her bed sat in a nook, a built-in frame along the opposite wall. The furnishings were spare but mostly new, not the scrounged or thrift store variety that most of us favored. Bright throw pillows accented an ivory sofa. In front of built-in bookcases, a white Japanese lantern globe hung beside a stuffed chair that could have been a holdover. A ficus in a basket at the end of the windows looked healthy enough to survive the winter. Her paper shades were pulled high, admitting whatever light passed the fourth floor in January. She could have rented a yurt—I was just grateful to have been admitted, finally, to her sanctum.

"Who are these guys?" They were cheeping, the center of attention.

"Guy and gal, please. Abelard and Heloise." As we closed in on their bamboo cage the parakeets fell silent, one perched on a bridge of tiny rope and sticks, the other on a swing. They snapped their heads and we regarded one another.

"Have you had birds before?" I thought out loud, then realized I could have meant her former life on Lincoln Park West, a time I didn't care to revisit.

"When I was a kid. They're easy to take care of, except for this." She meant the flaxen seed on the dark hardwood. "This is what happens when you're gone for a day."

I caught her before she could get a broom. "Hey, thank you."

"I just wanted it to look right first. This is new for me." I kissed her cheek and then we were front-to-front and my hands were happy to be roaming. I was increasingly aware of the location of her bed, but no doubt it would be too much too soon.

"Your hand seems fully recovered." She pinched my stomach and led me to the sofa.

"It's a little stiff but fine. How did it sound last night?"

It was the most nervous I had been about playing any gig—including in front of Anita at Last Blast—and it was only a New Year's Eve affair. We had settled on John's place because it was central to most of us and large enough to accommodate the usual suspects, plus wildcards. Snow started before anybody arrived. Janis was there sans Gary or any of the other Stepps but with two women classmates from her Loyola days. PT brought both Coleman and Spike while Dale was stuck until ten on his restaurant shift. Melanie and Adam arrived fashionably late as John and I were tuning and they gravitated to Anita, which was fine with me. Corey entertained Carlos Calderon and two lovely companions, and Beth looked flushed and high and delightful. Sasha kept us refilled with cheap champagne, navigating among us in her personal emanation, the reason angels are depicted with halos, as Corey would attest.

That we would play was a given. It was our first time since the rumble in the alley. The left hand had regained the ability to squeeze chords without buzzing or flattening notes most of the time, but that had only been in the last week. We opened with a couple of standards from our sets and then took requests, playing whatever we knew that was close. Spike asked for "The Heart of Saturday Night," as though anyone could cover it, so I resuscitated "Thank the Lord for the Night Time," which we did only in the spin-downs at the tail-end of practice. We picked up "Rave On" and stretched it out, raising the key by a full step, which kept the crowd bopping. To finish, Wray switched to the Mossman and did his signature fingerpicking closer, *Highline*, allowing me to lay back and add color.

Before midnight the fireworks started, regardless of the snow. Corey and I toasted our anniversary, a year to the night since we met in the Gonzo emporium. I recalled the gunshots into the sky and Corey reconfirmed, "Morons."

Wray put on the Butterfield Blues Band, then his black-and-white TV with no sound and we watched the replay of Dick Clark counting down in Times Square. We all hugged and kissed, starting with significant others and working outward.

When Butterfield ended, a contingent led by Corey, Wray, and me harangued Beth for a number to launch the new year. In front of John's windows and with occasional flares in the sky behind her, she obliged with a few pin-drop minutes of Copland's "Simple Gifts," her tone as pure and unselfconscious as a blessing. That was a highlight of the night, as was surviving our set for me, but the topper came between the set and midnight.

"You weren't going to tell me until you knew my hand was working, right?" I interrogated Wray inside his back door where he had led me out of the party to give me the news.

"I spaced. Hosting a party is a bitch." His face was hard to read, but knowing John, spacing was more than possible.

"Yeah, right. I've seen the place but what's the deal? You said Mark was hot on it." That was what I asked then.

"John said it's the Body Politic, I got that much," Anita said on the sofa, tucking her leg and black tights under her and giving full attention.

"It's a performing space on Lincoln, no booze, they sell tickets like a theater. It's a 'poetry and music' night. Mark Riley thinks it would be perfect for us, an audience that comes to listen, et cetera, kind of like the MoMing reading—"

"When you didn't talk to me."

"The same." It gave me an excuse to peck her lips. "So it's a cool venue. And we're on the bill with a poet, Robert Bly."

"What? *The*—"

"*The* Robert Bly. Crazy, isn't it? And they want the music after his reading, for whatever reason. It's like Bly is our warm-up act. Crazy." It was sinking in as I was telling her, and the thrill in Anita's eyes made it more real and raised a wave of butterflies.

"It's perfect for you guys. I can't wait. When?" Of course Anita would be there, but behind her I saw the Circle circle filling in. I had thought I wanted an audience like the one at MoMing. Now what would we do with it?

"It's in February, over a month off."

At least we had time to practice, and to ruminate. We needed to make the most of one and the least of the other.

Jan. 16, 1979

In less than two weeks, January slipped the track. The snow started the night of the 12th, a Friday. By the end of the weekend, the city was paralyzed. The tracks froze and the El that never stopped, stopped. On Saturday we pushed Tony out of a snow dune then sent him home, and Corey and I each delivered a couple on the bus. On Sunday

we closed at eight. Deliveries had become impossible.

For the plows to clear the arterials, parked
cars are being towed and dumped in Lincoln Park.
They look like strays that have wandered from
their owners. At least it's stopped now and the
plows are getting through, piling the curbs with
berms that won't be gone for months.

The wind whipped our backs as we hauled our gear to
the Body Politic Theatre. Anita held the door and Sasha had
John's Gibson case. It might have been a month later by the
calendar, but with the blizzard and the café and John's job
where a coworker had missed a week with the flu, we could
work in only two practices.

As instructed, we arrived early, and if not for "Duello" on
the marquee in front, we could have had the wrong night.
The lobby was spare and empty. We called a couple of
hellos, and a guy with wavy locks emerged from a door
behind a counter set with plastic cups and wine glasses.
Projecting calm, either from his personal vibe or being
seriously stoned, he introduced himself as Keith, the
producer for the night, then led us through double doors
into the performing space.

"Lean and mean," Wray said as we began to unpack.

The auditorium was as spartan as the lobby. I guessed it
could seat two hundred on rows of benches with a few pews
in the rear, but most of the seating was backless.

"Acoustics should be killer," I said, and the room did not
disappoint during sound check. We settled behind the
mikes and played, unplugged and plugged, while Keith
tweaked a mixer in the back. Our sound bloomed huge and
clear in the nearly empty space like our tape through the
speakers in Groove Town. As soon as Wray had played eight
bars through the Pignose with no feedback, Keith came
down the aisle grinning, cleared our stools off the stage, and

rolled in a lectern. Buzz and chatter had started outside, and Wray and I followed Sasha and Anita into the lobby.

Bly, red-scarved with wind-whipped hair, had arrived with his retinue. I recognized Andonati and Paul Carroll in a sailor's cap, the Don and the Don's Don. Several early arrivals took glasses from the counter. Melanie and Adam came in the next wave with Janis our angel who had not only hand-printed the venue and date on the bottom of twenty flyers but posted them on poles and bulletin boards across Lincoln Park. Wray and I gave her a hug and admired her rhinestone tiara which she was wearing for the hell of it. Anita took Sasha to introduce her to Andonati, Melanie, and Adam. Corey was absent, covering the counter for Bruce who was taking his vacation day, a perk we had extended from the drivers to employees. PT arrived as the lights were dimming and the doors opened to the auditorium.

Keith pointed Wray and me to two chairs in the front, stage right. The room lights had been lowered by half, but they were bright on the lectern. Our guitar stands and stools had been moved back from the lectern to the edge of the light. We would be sitting in silence through the act everyone had really come to hear, with nothing to do but think. Attendees were filling in from the front. Behind the Circle people, front and center, I recognized the *Another Chicago Magazine* crowd, then Carlos and the *La Raza* group. A bright-eyed company they were, expectant and discerning, paying customers who had braved a cold night to listen. It was the audience we wanted, was it not? My pulse and dry throat were saying otherwise. Beside me John's knee was pistoning, which I didn't need to see. My left hand was tightening, and I worked on stretching it with the right.

Bly and Carroll took the stage together. Carroll towered over his colleague as he rummaged in an oversized leather duffel and transferred books to the lectern. Bly had shed his overcoat and was sporting a red and gold vest. Light played on the fine rims of his glasses. Carroll would handle the introduction.

Except for a few in the back, the audience was seated. A pair of guys had followed Bly and Carroll up the far steps onto the stage and timidly approached the lectern. They wore the uniform of working-class poets, sweatshirts and jeans, and each carried a slim volume. The one in the lead extended his to the master, soliciting an autograph. Bly managed a flattered smile and obliged. After the reading would have been protocol, but the proletarian getup of the two probably made them impossible to dismiss. Carroll was clearly battling annoyance, embarrassed for the domain of poetry citywide.

I glanced back at Anita, seated beside Andonati and exchanging whispers with Sasha on her other side. She had just fluttered a wave.

I caught it on the periphery, in the brighter light. The action was out of mind, dystonic, flat-footing us like the shot of an assassin.

The first autograph seeker, taller and bushy-haired, had finished and stepped aside, back toward me. The other, shorter and broader, had taken his place. The blur that caught my eye was his, the sudden lunging motion in the brightness. In the second before, which I didn't see and which no one saw coming, he must have switched his book for what it concealed beneath. His thrust at Bly from the shoulder, startling as a thrown punch, was the eye-catcher in the light.

The flavor could have been lemon, or banana. A pie heavy with meringue caught Bly full in the face. Gobs flew over his shoulders and tumbled down his vest of red and gold.

All froze. Carroll stared at the meringue blob on his coat as though he had taken a stray bullet. Then he clutched Bly around the shoulders with one arm and threw up a protective hand between victim and assailant. No need. The two conspirators flung their books onto the stage and pivoted toward the audience. Thrusting arms up and flashing victory signs, they shouted, *"Vive la poésie!"* out of sync, like an echo. Then they were off the front of the stage into the center aisle.

Shouts rose in the crowd and some were on their feet. A man on the end of a row clutched at the taller one in the lead who shook him off easily and kept going. From the rear of the auditorium, Keith was striding down the aisle, no smile.

"Poseur! Cochon!" The half dozen already on their feet were shouting, flinging papers, yellow sheets, into the seats around them. "Bly is a fraud! Save poetry!"

Keith had the tall one but only by a handful of his sweatshirt, and he was shoving back. The stocky pie thrower joined in and Keith collapsed into two women on the end of a bench.

The others standing broke out of their rows, slinging their sheets into the air in yellow arcs. They rushed to the rear behind the two leaders who shouldered open the double doors. The last two hecklers had swiped an empty bench, and in the lobby they halted and heaved it behind them. It crashed against the door frame, discouraging pursuit.

Wray and I headed for Sasha and Anita. Nearly everyone was standing in general commotion, some trying to catch a last glimpse of the fugitives, some blank-faced, others half-bemused, testing reality, whether it had been a travesty or part of the show.

"Oh, yes." Andonati was nodding to a couple on his right, Circle associates or assistants. "They're locally infamous." Sasha looked uncharacteristically appalled and John hugged her. Anita was playing it cool, but I could see the upset in her eyes. She handed me one of the yellow flyers. The title, bold and centered: SURREALISME CHICAGO. *Poetry not puppetry, liberty not hypocrisy.* It went on about Bly as poet manqué, a Disney factory buffoon, and more of the same. A motto for all true poets followed: *Pure psychic automatism!* Last was a quote attributed to Andre Breton:

The man who cannot visualize a horse galloping on a tomato is an idiot.

Adam was clarifying to his end of the row. "The Chicago Surrealists. They call themselves a school but they're just pranksters. A school of scoundrels." He appeared pleased with himself.

Keith projected from the front of the stage, trying to be heard off mike. "Apologize . . . interruption . . . gone . . . seated, please." He had produced a towel for Bly and Carroll. Bly's face was mostly clear and he was working on his glasses. Carroll was inundating him, no doubt with apologies. His jaunty cap was gone and he was shaking his head.

"Police have been called, the doors are secure." Keith had retreated to the lectern mike. "Please be seated and we'll get under way. Thank you, thank you."

Most were trusting their benches again, but many still stood, jawing and chuckling, processing their flyers and the bonus they had been treated to for the price of admission. Wray and I returned to the chairs in our far corner. Keith ceded the lectern to Carroll who looked slack-faced and shaken, horrified by what had gone down on his turf.

"Good evening," his voice boomed, "and welcome to Romper Room." The audience broke up, the tension level dropping. There was scattered applause. "The toddlers have had their tantrum and have been put to bed." More applause. "Our guest of honor just observed to me that acknowledgment may come in sundry forms." Bly, his hands crossed on his book, stood unfazed behind him. Carroll went on to apologize without dignifying the insurgents by name. Then he shifted to the poet's bio and a selected litany of praise. When he ended with his name, Bly was met with a standing ovation, a statement of solidarity. He pressed his palms together and bowed humbly.

As the lights tightened and he began his reading, the Circle crowd were attuned, or appeared to be. I was registering nothing, trying to piece together how we could pull off our set in the wake of chaos and following the clear headliner who now had gods and sympathy on his side. Light played finely on his golden rims, and I wondered if the glasses were a conscious choice, the performing pair. He wore the spotlight like a shimmer of ectoplasm.

With my arms folded and left hand out of sight, I was flexing and miming chords. The standing ovation had encouraged more to remain on their feet, mostly around the walls and chatting in the back. There was a new camaraderie and a looser vibe, and a few were swaying to the reading although the rhythms were either subtle or nonexistent. Two ladies roughly a generation apart, the elder in a tie-dyed top, were grooving along the opposite wall close to the stage. Bly couldn't miss them, and no doubt they were his inspiration. After a few short poems he retreated to his duffel and produced a bouzouki, short-necked, with elaborate inlay around the sound hole. It had an outsized sound, a steely punch. He strummed with a pick and set up a chant like an Ojibwa. The room fell in with him, clapping along and echoing any refrains they could mimic. Over most of an hour he alternated chants with readings and by the end, the room was rocking. For us, I tried to imagine how it could be worse.

Following the final ovation, the lights came up and an adoring mob of about half the crowd trailed behind him into the lobby. Carroll and Andonati were among them, but our loyal core stayed put.

Keith rambled into a mike about resuming in a few minutes, and I did hear "Duello," which landed to no effect. As he wheeled away the lectern and repositioned our stools and mikes, Wray and I huddled in the wing and ran through last-minute tuning. I thought of trying a lame loosener about Bly being easier to follow than Springsteen, but John was ashen-faced and a muscle was working in his jaw.

"Ladies and gentlemen," Keith was saying all too soon, bending to a vocal mike and reading from a note, "Body Politic Theatre . . . Riley-Strauss Productions . . . welcome Duello." We were out of the safety of the wing into social applause. Keith passed us smiling, back in his placid persona. Less than half of the bench space was occupied. A number were milling around the back giving off a barroom mumble. As we sat, the lights tightened down and I saw that one of the rear doors was open, a bright rectangle on the lobby where a post-reading reception was in progress with another round of Champagne.

Deep breath, bottom of the ribs like a bellows. I nodded to Wray. A detectable tremble in his fingers on the neck. His head bowed to the sound hole in the Gibson and his notes walked out on the tightwire, one by one. Last breath.

The nerveless men

A silhouette crossing the bright rectangle of the rear door.

Are abiding like sentries

The forms of Anita and Sasha, Melanie and Janis, but not their faces, featureless pearls.

Through nights of near ice and withering days

Slack face in the front row like a walk-in scanning the menu board for burgers. Had I faced off across the counter in my red apron?

Heads full of desert wind that whirs without ceasing

The tie-dye on the side wall whispering to her young partner. A hollow laugh cracking in the back.

For whom time has no meaning
Whom no promise binds

Halfway down the mike stand, a glob of meringue.

In the tacet, jabbering bubbled up in the back by the doors. And then we had started "The Island." The worst was over, remember that. The lines would come. Trust the flow. And I did, numbly cruising. But by the end of the first verse I could sense it, and I knew Wray would have picked it up before me. We were playing inward, not talking, pushing. Back off, leave space, let the music come, we knew all that, but the immediate question was, could we hide it? The muffled chatter in the back and the converse with the bright lobby through the open door had us off our game. We were too loud and too tight, straining to connect. We were in survival mode, cooking in the lights.

Two on the left side were getting up, or three. Leaving or only standing? We were trapped in set one, the wrong set. But the audience was to be the MoMing crowd, coming to listen. And they did, but not to us. Lefty was glowering. Could he be appeased?

We soldiered through the set on automatic. It may have been Adam who tried a shout first. Then a patch of applause began in our group and puckered outward to an aftermath of mumbling.

My shirt was soaked. John had finished the set on the Mossman, and he wasted no time. He switched back to the Gibson, cranked the volume on the Pignose, and ripped off two bars of "Brown-Eyed Girl." A hoot rose from the dark in the back. "Road Away" was our emergency rescue number, upbeat and loud, and it was time for it, past time. John's three-chord theme came first and then my chords descended into his and we were off and hurtling downhill.

When he left his home in San Jose
He was just a boy of nine

Wray joined in on the chorus. A few drifted back in from the lobby, lured by the volume. Suddenly we were good-timey, garage band, bar band. Cooler and looser, stressing less. The applause rose, but it was not a high bar. Next we backed off with "No Second Chances." Then, because Wray had built his intro as an elaborate teaser that chewed up time, finally resolving into the iconic two-finger slides, we finished with "Memphis." The rhythm was weak in first position so I squeezed out a few barre chords in the break, knowing the hand torture was nearly over.

We may have been five minutes short or a little more, but Keith could sue us. We were done. We thanked all for coming as the applause swelled then dwindled. Wray was off the stage before me. The lights came up and Keith was on the sound system from the back booth thanking and pitching the upcoming attractions at the Body Politic.

Our group met us with little flags of applause. Janis was genuinely bright-faced, and all managed smiles but Sasha, who looked annoyed and wary. Melanie was projecting a comforting grin, and even Adam gave a thumbs up at the end of the line. I was focused on Anita's eyes and smile, and they were doing their best.

"Sorry, I'm sweaty," I whispered as I squeezed her.

"I like your sweaty," she whispered back.

In the lobby we received kind words from a couple of departing guests, which was more than enough for a fleeting high, since we could find encouragement in almost anything. The front door swinging open still admitted an inhospitable wind. There was talk of beer at Oxford Pub, and while most of our crowd were up for it, John and I were encumbered with gear and he needed to drive Sasha home. Instead, we thanked and hugged all around and stepped out into the Hawk. Sasha was through the door first with John's Gibson.

"Hey," I told the back of his head, "they didn't throw any pies."

"Victory." He made a V with his free hand, grinning hard in the cold.

"And super 'Road Away'." Half of his attention was on Sasha who was heading down the sidewalk into the wind, her hair whipping back, and he didn't understand me. "I said, good job. Hang in there."

It would have been much finer to be taking Anita to the Cavern, but she had to be at the studio by nine, so I drove her down Wrightwood instead. We rehashed the Bly episode, and she assured me that we had been fine, we had been great, enough times that I was fairly sure it had been as rocky as I feared. Her loving attempts only stoked my ardor, making it harder to drop her at her door, but drop her I did.

After heading north for only a few blocks, I had to tune to a blues station and punch up the volume to stay awake. The heater was blowing and blood was flowing in the limbs, and all nerves were letting go. A shower and a Leinie were within range, the brew first, but I was weighing the notion of a detour to a Jewel market I knew on Broadway. What were the odds? I had a fierce craving for lemon meringue pie.

It was a dumping of March snow, sloppy and gobbed on meters and hydrants. The series of freakish events, of which this felt like one more, had begun with the demise of our cheese grinder a few nights after Body Politic. We had to buy pre-ground at twice the price of blocks for the week it took to get it fixed. Next was Bruce's scramble for an apartment after the kitchen caught fire on the floor above him and burned through the roof. Both Corey's car and mine were pressed into service to get him moved. Tony going down in the March mini-blizzard fit right in.

We were changing shifts at five and the phone was ringing, as usual whenever there was snow. Corey had just found an apron when Tony's call came in. Not only would we need him for the rest of the night, the nineteen-year-old sounded anything but his usual cool. We took both cars and half a dozen large pizza boxes, unfolded.

He had been routing around a manhole cordoned off for work on Newport. Any workers would have been gone by mid-afternoon when the snow started. It was an abnormal stretch of the street with a drainage ditch, and the Pinto sat on the shoulder with the rear in it, the tires in a sludge of mud and snow. We started by jamming flat boxes under the rear wheels. Staying light on the gas, Tony was able to roll a box length forward before spinning again. We doubled the box path in front of the rear tires and Corey crammed two under the front wheels. The snow continued fat and wet as we set up behind the flat back of the Pinto.

Tony eased on the gas and we pushed. As he rolled forward my shoes plowed backward into the muck. In the second before he reached the asphalt, we were two cartoon characters, elongated, groundless, bodies nearly flat out. And then we were down on hands and knees in the slop, coughing out exhaust. A leg at a time we rose to our feet, mud from the knees down. Corey had used the phrase several times in the café, whenever a piece of equipment died or a drain backed up or we found ourselves in another tragically trivial mess: the final absurdity. This time he didn't have to say it. We were laughing idiotically. He was red-faced, stocking cap flocked and wet.

"How're you gonna work like that?" I blubbered.

"I'll swing by my place and change."

"Want me to let Lorenzo know?"

"I'll call him. Hey," he said, "it's us against the world." That was exactly how it felt, one more time. We slapped palms, mud to mud.

I thought about that climbing Wray's back stairs. It applied to us equally, to Duello. But the café and the music were both hanging in. Corey and Wray and I shared the distinction: renegades against the odds, and there was comradeship in that.

It wasn't a practice. John had called the café to let me know our checks had arrived for the Body Politic survival exercise. To save us from having to file as a partnership and pay for a business bank account, Riley-Strauss cut checks in our names. He also said there was something else. I was later than I said I would be.

"You look like hell," he said as I left my shoes on the mat.

"Thanks. Driver insanity. You don't want to know." More like I didn't want to get into it and the two masters debate again. He popped a beer for me and put it on the counter. The radiator ticked and the apartment was warm. Outside the broad bay windows the snow had abated.

"They came a couple of days ago. I thought you could get by without it." He handed over the check and I saw what he meant, two figures after our agents' cut.

"Didn't we get more at No Exit? But hey, we're paying the dues. It's about the future." I took a swig and sat in the practice chair.

"And on that note," he said still standing, "Mark gave a call yesterday." He paused for effect but he didn't need to. He had my full attention. They were dropping us after the fiasco.

"We're booked into Barleycorn's in May." He said it deadpan, statement of fact.

"No shit!" I was up, bumping bottles. John Barleycorn Memorial Pub on Lincoln was like a mirage. "Are we talking prime target here or what? Like huge stepping stone?" We had been over the dream of Barleycorn's a few times. "To the Earl, that is. As in Earl of Old Town, sports fans. Maybe we'll open for Dunbar. Or not." And anybody knew that for our kind of jam, playing the Earl would be a prereq for any label. "It looks like Mark is as good as his word, right? As in Flying Fish."

I was probably over the top, blowing him down. He sat in his usual spot on the practice sofa bed, seeming partially catatonic, probably from work.

"What are you, sniffing too much toner?"

He took a swig and I went back to the chair. Time to cool out, get with John's rhythm.

"And great that it's May," I added. "Two months for practice." I noticed for the first time that where the guitars would have been, the Mossman in its case on the floor and the Gibson in its stand by Wray's leg, there was space and old varnished hardwood. And then I felt a shift, a bump in the earth, a moment off-center and blurred, like an instant of remembering something important I had forgotten to do.

"I'm quitting," he said.

Chapter 26

I didn't ask Wray to repeat because the incomprehensible had tried to settle itself in the cold fright of stages and the spotlight rings and the wheeling circles in the New Trier parking lot at the top of the world and in the space behind the windows on Arlington with a bitter night outside when practice was our solitary lifeboat. The incomprehensible had failed.

"Uh . . ." I said, mugging a dumb look, like I had been asked to name all fools. Wray was looking down through his wireframes, searching the linoleum.

"It's just time," he said, his jaw working as though he could clench it shut and leave it.

"That's freaking nuts. It's just the opposite. That Body Politic farce was a blip, one in a million. And we made it through. Do you think Mark and Randy didn't hear about it and dig it? What's the evidence? They got us Barleycorn's."

"It's not Body Politic. Not that relevant, really."

I didn't need coy. "What?"

"I'm moving to Evanston at the end of the month."

"So?"

"I applied to Northwestern for the fall. I need . . ."

"What?"

"Something solid."

"Fine, it's a summer away. Look what's happening now. A year ago the odds of an agent . . .? Same with Barleycorn's, am I right? We've got the momentum, finally. That's solid. You're on some denial—"

"Denial is you, man." We locked eye-to-eye. "Today is some driver shit. That's today. You'll never be able to do the time. Guys like Dunbar live it—they play all week, it's what they do. We can't compete."

"It's not how they started. They all had day gigs—"

"And most are still doing them. We don't hear about those. There's no didn't-make-it label. They hustle their asses off for years and they don't make it. They get old."

I tried to block the specter of Dizz. John leaned forward and stared into me.

"I make copies for kids who are going way past me." He held up his check. "For this, right? I've paid the dues. Copy boy," he added, frozen smile. "Look in the mirror, man."

He didn't have to say it. *Pizza boy.* I couldn't let it get to me. There were times when I had to handle John with kid gloves, it came with the territory. This was the time of times.

"After Barleycorn's you'll feel totally different. You can go to school and play, no sweat. I did it at Chapel Hill."

He sat back and I sat back. I wanted the dynamited particulate of the room to settle. He took a swig and put the bottle on the floor. This was the time when he would reach for one of the guitars. I could see it. Right now.

"I'll be out of here in May," he said. "Sash wants to go to Europe together. Our flight is booked."

"Sash," I said. It wasn't a contest of wills, it was betrayal. I wasn't debating John anymore. There was a team behind him, coaching him, in his head. I couldn't sit. I was up, tracking a path to nowhere on his floor. I hefted the bottle, a grenade I could heave through the middle window.

"So this has been in the works, even before Body Politic."

"What? No."

"What nothing. You've been playing me."

"We just got the flight—"

"And you got a freaking apartment overnight, right? Look, what difference." I wasn't seeing him clearly anymore. John was a blur to me, to himself. "You're copping out, sucking up to your North Shore crowd, letting them jerk you around. Exactly what you refused to do when we started. Sasha, your parents—they've got you in some fucking ozone space, man. Wake the fuck up!"

I wasn't aware I was moving until I backed into the table, the one with his turntable. In the second it took me to steady the Bang and Olufsen, the table was flat on its feet again. The turntable had been off, but it held an album, hip Windham Hill, William Ackerman. The needle had skipped across the tracks halfway to the label. I started to replace the tone arm on its stand but Wray was on me and grabbed the sublimely engineered, feather-light titanium tube before I could screw anything else up. We both had it tight for a moment, and one twist could rip it out of its socket joint.

"Sorry," I said, releasing.

Red-faced, he didn't look at me, only at the arm settled back on its pedestal and the cartridge and probably the tracks to detect any scratch. I flashed on taking the bottle to his head.

What diff. It was betrayal.

By April, spring had warmed enough to menu outside without gloves. Wray was in his apartment in Evanston, which I imagine he shared with Sasha, although I didn't ask. And neither did I help him move, not that it would have taken much effort since he had the sparest place of any of us. Over a year ago I had helped him angle his box spring up those back stairs.

More I could have done? Impossible. I called him at work the next day and apologized again for the turntable incident, offered to replace the album. It wasn't scratched, he said. I proposed a beer at Oxford, but he claimed he was busy after the move—settling Sasha in, I guessed. He hadn't told our agent, so I could decide what I wanted to do, a perverse courtesy. After a couple of days I was ready to grovel. I tried his old number on Arlington in case he had transferred it, but it was disconnected, which meant I had to give Riley-Strauss mine instead, and my address. There was no new listing in Evanston. His parents in Winnetka were in the book, but the odds of catching him were minimal, and because I was probably regarded as a pernicious influence on Johnny, calling there was more than I could do.

I was on Byron Street west of Sheffield working blocks of houses and two-flats and apartment buildings with banks of mailboxes in the lobbies, most boxes the kind with a slit wide enough to take a menu folded down the middle. A lot of the mailboxes on the houses were metal, mounted beside the doors, with hinged lids. I could slip menus in between envelopes, a crime but an accepted one. It was mid-afternoon and the mail had come, so I could have missed it in the first few boxes I did. The one I noticed had no envelopes, only one piece, and I recognized the logo instantly on a bright white menu from Gonzo Pizza Pie. I checked the sidewalks in both directions. The menu could have been a couple of hours old, or a year. I slipped it into the side of my bag, replaced it with ours.

The next two buildings had mail slots in the doors, the second with a dog that slammed against the inside, barking its head off. The next had another door-side box, and this time I paid attention. A Gonzo was there, with the mail of the day. Byron was thirty-nine hundred north, the top of Gonzo's delivery range, past it as I recalled. Most of their business was from Diversey south. I executed the replacement.

For the rest of the block, my mission morphed from advertising to reclaiming territory. Working the other side of the street, I found more of the same. It was hard not to be impressed, and depressed. It was *coverage*. Ozzie probably hired a crew, guys on work release like Dewayne. Maybe I would run into Donny, or maybe not.

I needed to assess the full extent. I hustled back to the car and headed east, crossing Sheffield. In another couple of blocks I pulled over in front of a monolithic horseshoe building with five entrances. I checked the first lobby. The slots were stuffed with folded white like paper airplanes that had dived halfway into the boxes. I started pulling as fast as I could go and stuffing into the bag. Crossing between the lobbies I checked for any sign of the crew, no longer only curious. If Ozzie found out, he would be displeased. I could spend the rest of the afternoon trying to undo the blocks and it could be time well spent, but I had another level to check.

The bag in the seat beside me was Gonzo white on top as I headed toward the lake, then crossed Pine Grove onto Sheridan Road. At the end of Sheridan, the building I had in mind stood about a dozen floors with views of the lake from the upper half. It wasn't the hardest building for me in a button-down blue Oxford, but I was hoping Ozzie's crew couldn't crack the high-rises. This time a delivery or service type in a khaki uniform shirt held the door for me on his way out. Alone in the elevator I held my breath for the top floors, then let it go and stepped out.

A number of tenants had opened their doors to leave or come home, but on the tops of the other door handles, wedged in the frame: fat, white Gonzo rectangles. I bore down the center of the hall pulling from both sides, no time for replacements, no time for anything but eradication. They were like locusts. I would never get them all.

That Friday could have meant anything or nothing. It was so slow that I let Kat go at nine. On Sunday night both Corey and I were working, giving Bruce a weekend off.

"Think we should train Tony for counter?" I asked mainly to break the silence. I was rinsing a pan and Corey sat by the empty phone.

"Not if it's like this."

It had been more than a night, an entire weekend. Delivery orders once bound for us had to be diverting a dozen blocks south to Gonzo.

"Starting Thursday I'll hit it hard, especially along Lake Shore." Experience had taught us it was the most effective time to menu. We had a week's supply of menus at most. We would both try to duck the next delivery from the printer to buy a few days by mailing the check.

"Maybe we should have a crew," Corey said. "Round up the usual inmates." As if we had the cash flow even for that.

"We could ask Tony." He had day classes, but he might want to do a few hours. We needed him more as a driver for nights. "Or maybe Kat." I trailed off, sensing no enthusiasm. "Think they're trying to drive us out?"

Corey was looking down, massaging his forehead.

"What have you got, a headache?"

He nodded, looking annoyed at himself.

"Go. I'll shut down."

I handled a few walk-ins, but I was able to break down the Taylor and do most of the cleaning in advance. I locked the door an hour early, exchanged a buck for quarters while doing the receipts, and put on "Born to Run." It always reminded me of driving into the West Side, crossing the line into the vastness where the spokes of the El fanned out, beyond the reach of my little community, rules and expectations, in the land of Luz Guillen. And of PT, my heart's physician. And then there was Janis, who crossed her own line to come to the Cavern. All of us were running to each other, into each other, and beyond. There was no propellant like loneliness. None of my mopping reverie meant I didn't treasure Anita, I did, more every day. It was escapism, pure and worthless. "Baby, we were born to run,"

I chorused and swabbed the tile in front of the jukebox. Wray was checked out. We were getting carpet bombed by Gonzo. I was going nowhere, no way.

Circle campus environs were not entirely Soviet. At a metal table on the patio of the student union, I was admiring sunlit maples along a walkway, spunky dwarves recovering from winter. A couple at another table were testing the warmth of the sun. I was disregarding my last visit, my desperate mission in that other year of ignorance and mania.

I could have spent the rest of the day menuing, but that morning I had hit four-twenty Melrose, which was always a good building for us, and a four-plus-one on the same block and I was rationing menus for the run-up to the weekend. Anita and I had talked about John when it first happened, but I hadn't seen her for over a week, only checked in one night by phone after her shift at the station, and even then, she had homework. I hadn't told her about the menuing wars, and I was hoping to unload some of that on her too. I insisted on picking her up after classes and was planning to work in dinner at a Greek place we liked on Webster, subject to the student's availability. I was a few minutes early, staring blankly at the doors of the union, smoked glass.

"Hey, stranger."

"Wow, hey hey." Melanie had sneaked up behind me. I felt a complicated rush. I wasn't expecting an awkward scene with Anita, but I couldn't be sure. She pulled out the other chair.

"Anita's going to be a little late. I ran into her outside Douglass Hall. She needs to meet with one of her profs and he's running behind." She looked fresh and perky, pleased with the coincidence. "I'm the messenger." She was squinting, glare in her eyes. She angled her chair and the sun lit up her hair, reddish aurora. On the phone Anita had mentioned a credit, theology of science or science of theology, a required foundation course she had taken a year ago.

"Thanks, messenger. It's good to see you."

"The last time was Body Politic."

I hadn't told anyone but Anita about John. Part of it was fear that it could get back to Riley-Strauss. Denial was probably the main reason.

"Are you submitting anything these days?"

"Only to the UI rag. This term has been a lot of papers."

"In the summer you have the *TriQuarterly* gig, don't you? That's super." As I said it I recalled she hadn't told me. I heard it from Janis, but I didn't have to explain. We all shared the same grapevine.

"Part-time, but it's something."

Melanie was in her world, but she was here also. I took a breath.

"John pulled out." I heard myself, testing the sound of it. It was true, but not real. Melanie stared, not comprehending. "Out of Duello. Quit the music. I think it was about Body Politic, mainly."

She made a jaw-drop face then reverted, as though pieces were coming together. "And Sasha?"

"I'm impressed." Stunned was closer to it. How women can read women.

"He could change his mind. He's good at that, isn't he?"

She had picked up on that too.

"I don't think so. He's out of the Arlington apartment. They have a place together in Evanston." I had gone that far, no reason to stop. "The agent booked us into Barleycorn's in May."

She lit up, grabbed my hand. "That's great! Everybody will come. When?"

"They booked Duello. I haven't told them yet."

"You could play it yourself. You should. Of course." She was projecting full confidence, but whether she was only pep-talking was hard to tell.

"Our sets wouldn't make sense. I've never played a gig as a single, even back in Tar Pit days." Melanie was among the few people in the world who would know what I was talking about. The memory pricked, and talking about Barleycorn's was starting to turn my stomach. "More to the point," I went on, thinking of changing the subject by exploding it, blowing it up to the philosophical, atomizing it to the realm of the academic, "what's the point? I always used to think that was a pussy question. If you had to ask it, you should just shut up."

She didn't look shocked exactly, maybe only gauging whether I was serious. Was this better or worse? She looked out over the patio. The other couple had vacated their table.

"I'd say the point is evolution," she announced. "That's pretty critical."

"Evolution, you say. That sounds . . . pretty grand."

"You're pushing the envelope. You're all about art."

"Art, right. Glad you think so. We know how much the music-consuming public cares about art. That would be squat. Maybe once."

"People listen to you. I've been in the audience—"

"They don't need the tops of their heads lifted. They want to get jingled and hooked. It's pop till you drop, same old story. It's what drives the biz." I flashed on Cal Jam and the masses littering the desert. "To do anything else you have to be insanely special, and even then . . . it isn't like Jim Dewey's coffeehouse days when every kid with a guitar got recorded."

"But a lot of good people have a niche and a following, right? And some step out. Every step forward takes somebody stepping out first." Not Melanie's most original, but she was trying. "What you and John are doing—it's audacious, exciting. That's why the agent."

"*Were* doing, maybe."

"John could come around. Or maybe you could look for another guitarist. It's a big town and you already have the agent. How many would kill for that? Hey, but I digress. You said what's the point." I saw her check the glass doors and I did also, probably both of us half-expecting Anita. Three high schoolers and two pairs of parents passed by on the walk. Their guide reminded me of Tony, stepping nimbly backwards as he spoke, a UI senior giving a campus tour. Melanie and I were those high schoolers once, before we met.

"When you're playing and it all comes together—when the audience is getting it and you can feel it—isn't that an incredible high? Writing, music, whatever—all art is the same. It lifts life. Suddenly you're a cloud walker. You're not on earth for a so-delightful time. There are metaphors for it, but no substitute. Besides, it's who you are."

What a fabulist she was, as Anita said. Melanie needed us to be more than we were, someone fantastic.

"Maybe it's just who you think I am. But thank you."

She looked content with her argument, but her eyes didn't match her smile. She was scanning me in the extra-perceptive way she had, betraying concern.

"Sorry, I have a late class," she said. "A must-do for my social sci credit. It's the time of year. Everybody's catching up on requirements." She pulled the book out of her bag far enough to show the title, *Topics in Folklore*. "At least there's a lot of Campbell." I recalled the four white volumes in the bookcase on Elizabeth Street, *The Masks of God*.

I thanked her again for saying what she had, wanting to agree but not sure that I could, whether it was a matter of agreement or belief. We hugged and kissed cheeks and off she went. In that moment it felt unnatural not to be going with her and I found myself walking it off, keeping an eye on the glass doors.

By the time Anita stepped through them, I was back on the patio. I was on her in a second and probably surprised her with a tight hug and a full kiss. She had worn her trench coat on the cool morning and now it was open. She was warm from hurrying to meet me and the light scent she wore worked on me. I took her book bag and she asked right away if Melanie had found me, and I assured her that she had.

In the car we talked first about her credit issue and how it resolved. I envisioned her professor ready to acknowledge any lost assignment, enchanted, deconstructed. I felt sorry for profs, to a point, their libidos switched on-off, on-off, ad infinitum. Then I was off, into other territory. I needed to compare their responses. Maybe Anita would let me off the hook. I had already mentioned the booking when I told her about John.

"You know the Barleycorn's gig—"

"In May . . . second week?" She forgot little, maybe nothing.

"I'm not sure what I'm going to do about it."

She was staring at me, between puzzled and annoyed.

"You're going to play it, aren't you?" Her look shifted. "Sorry, I sound like a dago housewife. It's your decision, of course." But then, "But it's what you do, and you do it beautifully. And you have an agent. If you turn it down . . . I'm just sayin', Henry. You don't want to regret because you didn't try." She squeezed the back of my hand and looked out the window. I put on the radio and the free wind whipped our hair and we talked little for the rest of the way.

In her apartment I had intended to ask about school and the station, but factors conspired—the memory of her warm scent and her skirt riding above her knees in the seat beside me and her South Side level-headedness and cheerleading from the heart. We were barely inside her door. I stripped off her coat and Abelard and Heloise set up a racket in their cage, but they failed to derail us. Barleycorn's and Riley-Strauss, pop versus art, and even the background drumbeat of duty to the café had been playing in my head over the long drive, and I buried all of them in Anita.

We skipped the restaurant. Instead we scavenged from her refrig: roma tomatoes and lettuce, Boston and romaine; Ligurian olives from Janis's Chalet; chunks of mostaccioli, her casserole for the week; and cold jug Chablis. She didn't keep red wine because, she said, it gave her headaches and stained her teeth.

We flipped on the black-and-white TV and ate on her sofa and watched *Tales of the Unexpected*. We could both start late the next day, and sleep when it came was blissful.

Sometime in the pit of the night I made my way to her bathroom. In the little cell with the door closed, I was standing naked with only my traitorous thoughts, lacking rational defenses, and it came misting down on me, the cold impossibility of it enveloping, and I was alone on the stage in steely fear.

Chapter 27

Barleycorn's Minus Six

Commitment to date: changed Duello's address and phone from John's to mine, as of two days ago. Before the call I spent the morning prepping for questions from Randy or Mark, but neither picked up. I left a message on their tape and no questions so far.

This says nothing about Barleycorn's. The thought makes me sick. If I sick out, I sick out, that's all.

I traded Corey for next Saturday off and have worked the extra hours already. If I blow off the gig, I could haul with Anita to O'Hare, abscond to Brazil. I did the hours behind the counter. We needed menuing more, but that would have meant time to ruminate, too much time. I said it makes me sick.

Set One:
Reason to Believe (Hardin)
Black Sheep Girl
Blue Day
Bill's Song

In and Out of Her Arms
Peace on the Sea

Set Two:
Ella Speed
What the Blues Is Made Of
Wrong is Right
No Second Chances
Gotta Go
Stay a Little Longer
You Would Know

B. Minus Four
What was your brilliant delusion--
both emptiness and an inferno decaying like
the sun?

The left hand, the barre hand, the Russian
thug hand, cramped in practice today. Count on
nothing. Monkey with a trick hand. Clown with two
mikes.

I had to check Barleycorn's ad in the Reader
before I crammed it in the drawer. Duello is
there all right, and the Saturday after, who but
Jim Post, the Moses of Chicago folk. What am I
doing? This gig is suicide. I'll call R-S. Four
days should give them time to sub. NO MONKEY
CLOWN!

NO
FREAKING
WAY

B. Minus Two
Janis has been the captain of the cheerlead-
ers, no surprise. I don't know where she came up
with the crew she must have had, but the lamp

posts and phone poles across Lincoln Park have
been hit with Duello flyers. Again, she hand-
printed the venue and date at the bottom of each
one, under the photo of Wray and me on the
mountain of pulp. A sad part of me wonders if
he'll show.

    Set One:
    Long River/I'm Not Sayin' (Lightfoot)
    Blue Day
    Bill's Song
    Black Sheep Girl
    Could Never Believe
    In and Out of Her Arms

    Set Two:
    Ella Speed
    No Second Chances
    It's About Time
    You Would Know
    Stay a Little Longer
    Gotta Go
    Peace on the Sea

One more day. Not where I need to be. Thinking
makes me sick.

"Hey, you." I heard the greeting seconds after pulling the
door to John Barleycorn Memorial Pub. PT was floating like
a lifesaver in the front of the room. There were hugs for
Anita and me which we returned with our free arms, our
others dedicated to lugging my guitars. The bar was busy
and loud, and most of the tables were taken, all with
strangers. She pep-talked me with no mention of John,
which meant she already knew. Everybody knew.

"They're next door," she said. "I'll be along in a few."

The wide door to the music room opened past the end of the bar, but first came a part I dreaded as much as playing. Anita hung with me as we had planned, toting the Favilla case. I told the bartender, who bore a resemblance to Bonnie Raitt, that I needed to check in with the manager. In a minute a bearded bear type introduced himself as Lou. He was a double too but hard to place, maybe Dave Van Ronk.

"You're Duello? I thought—"

"My other partner came down with strep throat. Timing couldn't be worse. But it's fine, you can just introduce Duello. I kick it off." Lou had a choice, us or nothing. Anita smiled and may have batted her lashes, but she didn't need to. Nor did she have to claim to be my stand-in partner. Lou was smiling back.

"You can set up on stage and move the mikes wherever you want. We'll go in about fifteen. Get you some beers?" He put it to Anita who declined. I took a mug of draft. My mid-afternoon joint was a dim memory.

As we rounded the corner I felt the familiar first hit—the fearsome wave of the crowd of strangers. Wray had always absorbed half of it. The room was deep but intimate, low lighting and beer bouquet. Wooden booths lined the far wall of exposed brick, and round black-top café tables were arranged tightly on the floor. Not every seat was taken, but it was close. Four silver mike stands gleamed ominously on the stage. Our group was front and center. Melanie spotted us first and waved.

"Eh, the man of the hour." Corey was on his feet, shaking my hand in his overly formal mode. We had agreed Lorenzo could handle the counter for a couple of hours, and we were starting to break in Tony. Beside him Bruce popped up too, and on his other side Beth was smiling, projecting vibes. Corey seized the opportunity to squeeze Anita.

I was surprised he had brought Bruce, but the entire turnout was a surprise. Smiles and greetings came from a cluster of half a dozen tables and I worked my way through them, shaking hands and thanking. Janis was looking splendid in a burgundy velvet dress with her two girlfriends from New Year's.

"I can blame you for most of this, can't I?" I pecked her cheek.

"Why, whatever do you mean?" She was all shock.

I imagined others had worked the grapevine too, including Melanie. Besides Adam, I saw more familiar Circles, although not Andonati. The other poetry factions were represented, including Jerry Lala and Lurlene, which was scary. Carlos's *La Raza* crew filled two tables, one in front where Sasha probably would have been. I quashed the thought. Corey had saved Anita a spot and I had worked my way around the tables. The time had come.

"Well," I said and gave her a squeeze.

"Love you," she whispered.

I took a deep swig from the mug and part of another, and then the guitar cases were dead weights, one in each hand. From the steps at the end, the stage looked as long as a runway. The Favilla went in a stand, and I switched off two of the mikes and pointed them away at a Fender amp, stage left. John's mikes.

I slipped the Martin's strap over my shoulder and faced the back of the stage. It would be in tune—tapping the harmonics was only a ritual. I had decided on steel fingerpicks for the first number because the fingering was easy and I wanted the full tone of the twelve-string padding my voice, covering any wavers. Slipping them on, I fumbled one but caught it against my leg. I needed to turn around.

I searched the room for Lou. He was chatting up Bonnie Raitt or snorting himself into bliss. The heads were out there, plenty of them. My tribe was watching me, nursing smiles, but most of the rest were talking, oblivious to the stage. How long before I introduced myself? Hi, I'm Duello? Jesus. Do something.

To smooth my voice if it was going to quaver, I started fingering the intro. I could close the fifteen feet to the mikes, easing into the background like the ambience music that should have been playing.

"Ladies and gentlemen," the voice shocked, seized the room. The spirit of Lou was in command. "Good evening and welcome to Saturday night at John Barleycorn's in the heart of Lincoln Avenue. Please put your hands together for . . . Duello."

Faces snapped to the front and the light changed. The polished rosewood top of the Martin and the stainless steel mikes gleamed, and darkness fell everywhere outside my little patch of stage. I stepped into the conventional applause, sliding the intro on the neck, ascending, descending. D, G-D bass, Dmaj7, G-D bass. The guitar mike picked it up, full and brassy, and the fade-in was right. That mike was working—I had assumed, not checked. And the vocal? Only one way to know.

"Good evening." I forced it out and a wave of relief rolled back as my voice filled the room. "Thanks for coming" was going to be next, followed by a spontaneous explanation for why Duello was now one guy taking a grandiose moniker like Prince, as though anyone cared, but my breath caught. A crash like unbreakable mugs in a steel sink sounded from the bar, followed by a spew of laughter. Get in, get it over. Dmaj7, G-D bass.

I'm not saying that I love you

Don't push. Keep it light. Light for Lightfoot. Lay the vocal in. Let the Martin carry it.

My eyes were adjusting and the faces began to fill in. I met Anita's eyes like a beacon to pull for, and the faces in front of me looked fresh and encouraging. Behind them, in and out of view, were the horrors to ignore: the blank-faced horror, the horror of the beef-headed man, the horror of the floating heads turning back to their chats before I interrupted. Keep it light.

Straight ahead at the back of the room I could make out a dark credenza, and on top of it, a silver samovar, a showpiece. I could play to the samovar as to the multitudes, the fringe of the crowd on the far hill. I could elude the horrors by playing over their heads, and so I alternated focus between the samovar and the neck of the twelve-string.

I'm not saying I'll be true but I'll try

Dmaj7, G-D bass, D. Let it ring. The long beat of silence, then private laughter in a booth. Then the applause that restarted the heart.

I was attuned as a bat, hypersensitive to the nuances of response, a hint of a vibe, anything beyond the standard gratuity. It was over in two thank-yous. Someone, probably Janis, clapped hard and seconds too long, taking up the slack. I had needed an easy opener but it was too simple, a ho-hum. I could have lost them already. Now there was no escaping—I would have to explain.

"Thank you. And thanks for coming out tonight. You may have been expecting someone else up here . . . I mean another someone . . ." At first all I could make out in the darkened room were shadowy figures, two or three on the side wall edging toward the stage. By the time I recognized them, PT, the last in line, was splitting off to a table, guiding a young boy to a chair. I wasn't ready to take in what was happening. Dale and Coleman, lugging instrument cases and drums, stepped into the half-light on the stage steps, awaiting permission to come aboard.

"So please welcome some friends of mine to Duello." Random applause came back, fetched as it was, uncertain.

"Sorry we're late," Dale said, grinning, nodding, depositing his fiddle case, and unzipping a guitar bag at the same time. "Coleman had to pick up his kid."

"Out freaking rageous," I told them both. "Too much." Out of words, I pressed palms together.

Coleman was grinning. With his congas he had brought a marching snare, and he set it up on a stand. I had expected Dale's guitar to be a bass, but he strapped on a Stratocaster.

"You haven't heard this one," I said. "Come in whenever."

"Check this." Dale had plugged into the Fender amp and with volume near zero, sent three familiar notes out on a tightwire. "Set one?"

"We jammed with your tape, man," Coleman explained.

I was recalling Dunbar and his sing-along, our bar band singles in the Body Politic. Dale picked up on my misgivings. "It's killer," he said.

"Hey, it's your funeral too," I said. "Ready when you are."

I switched to the flat pick. Dale raised the volume and punched out one triplet and then the next. Dale stood ready at the congas. Stoked by their confidence, I turned back to the mikes and the room.

Feel it. Wait for the spot.

The nerveless men
Are abiding like sentries

The eyes were fixed on the stage, the ones I could make out, most with the what-in-hell look, so familiar, so right.

Through nights of near ice
And withering days

My eyes met PT's at the side table with Coleman's little boy who they had smuggled in or made a case for somehow. I wondered when she had played instigator. It could have been any time since I had told Anita or Melanie, or maybe she had heard it from John himself. I could see her clearly, leaking the news to Dale and Coleman that Duello was down to one.

The only voice left in the room was mine. The chatter had dwindled to held breath. Dale's triplets, asynchronous like Wray's, sounded over the room, the room in suspension.

For whom time has no meaning

Whom no promise binds

Sustain the tacet. Another beat. Flat pick signature, down-up, down-up, filled the mike.

No bridge off the island, men here let it fall

Sea birds on the pilings till they hear the ocean call

Coleman's conga came in at my side, a rhythm and a pulse like a human pulse, like a hand on my shoulder. Dale's lead felt its way in, answering my vocal, twining around it. He was taking off from Wray's, but it was clearly his own, riding the Fender's twang tone.

The set flowed, holding together, a medley of numbers linked each to each, as John and I had conceived it. That Coleman and Dale had learned by playing with the tape was a new high, a validation like the ethereal broadcast at New Trier. I was picking out faces from the boosting front tables back to the samovar. We seemed to be holding the room. The charge of playing a full set for the first time was powering us along, and we were starting to trust enough to riff, but not too much.

As we led into the closer, I took the first verse of "Peace on the Sea" alone. Coleman switched to the snare and set up a stately, ghostly pace with a brush and one stick. Dale stayed with his fiddle on the verses but kept the Fender strapped on, punched the volume, and tore into a break, tormenting the Strat. It glimmered like mainline adrenaline, and I was sure everyone felt it. On the last verse, Coleman double-timed on the snare and Dale joined me on the vocal mike for the final chorus. The room was cut loose and rising, suspended in the pure seconds that anybody plays for. We struck the last chord and let it carry and hung on the silence. Always too long but longer this time. Did they hate it? We had done all we could do.

Our tables started it, the applause and hollers, and then there was a burst from the tables behind them and the booths on the side.

I was thanking, and then, "Coleman Lewis," and the applause bumped, and "Dale Manion," and it swelled louder and there were hoots from our tables and others. "Duello. Thank you!" So high I was barely processing, I thought I said the standard words about a short break and being right back. Our group was on their feet and whooping, and we descended the stage steps into the last of it. At PT's table Coleman's little boy had the final claps.

Anita's face said it, all eyes and smile, and I clenched her first. Melanie stood, palms together, as though a prayer had been answered. Janis was beaming. PT had made it to the front and we huddled and hugged. Coleman hoisted his little boy, who surveyed the boisterous, childish adults. Bruce was on his feet nodding his approval, and Beth wore a proud smile like a vocal coach after a student's less-than-tragic recital. Corey had vanished, but he reappeared with three frosted mugs.

"For the band," he proclaimed and set them down before us, grinning, delighted. I hoisted mine.

"To the stupefying angels of mercy who saved my butt. I am your slave forever."

"Let it be so." Dale grinned, bouncing, barely containing himself.

"Amen, brother," Coleman joined in and Coleman junior echoed, "Amen!"

In the presence of our acquired family, we three clacked our mugs and toasted our victory, and my swig of brew tasted like elation, cold and pure.

"I had to pay Ori." I was through the door at five, and Corey was waiting for me on his perch by the phone. I circled behind him and flipped open the checkbook, knowing already what we had owed for the menus, the new batch and the batch before that. "Two-fifty," Corey confirmed, as though I couldn't read his tight figures on the stub. I was more focused on our grand remaining balance of two-eighty-four, sixty-seven.

What was I going to do, flog him for not breaking out the back fast enough to duck the bill? The case could be made that a balance under three hundred signaled a survival emergency, and survival depended on perspective. I looked to my plastic trophy on top of the pop cooler for guidance. It was about eight inches tall, including pedestal. The guitar player could have been a balladeer, Woody or Pete, but his pompadour made a strong case for Elvis. Both Corey and Bruce presented it to me a couple of days after Barleycorn's. Corey had picked it up at a game and novelty shop on Irving Park, and Bruce was responsible for the Magic Marker inscription on the base: Gig Master.

That stellar night was ten nights ago, and it could have been a former lifetime. For the second set we were buzzed and confident. We dropped back to a few numbers I had planned for the first set, followed by Hardin's "Southern Butterfly" in three-four and a jam that wound around in no way we could ever re-create to "Love Is a Rose." We capped the set with a Stewart house rocker, "Wolves in the Kitchen." We were taking bows and ready to pack up when we had our first, and possibly last, occasion to honor the nonstop ovation, driven by our tables, with an encore. Because Dale and I could try to imitate horns on the Fender and harmonica and Coleman could drive the snare with two sticks and we could all pretend to be Wilson Pickett, we went with "In the Midnight Hour." When we left we had waves and words of praise from strangers. That was the pinnacle. Fifteen minutes.

"Did Warhol say 'world-famous for fifteen minutes', or Lennon?"

"Probably neither," Corey opined. "Lennon was 'more popular than Jesus'. He lives in the Dakota now. Beth sang and I panhandled in front of it once. Even back then it drew groupies because *Rosemary's Baby* was shot there. We had just moved in together. I was living in Hell's Kitchen." No doubt, I thought, and it cheered me up for no reason I could describe.

"How many last night?" Lorenzo had closed but Corey would have counted the tickets.

"Nine." Even for a Tuesday, nine deliveries was a dismal showing, and worse, it was one more in a series. Gonzo was bleeding us. The weather had turned and we hoped foot traffic would make up for part of the deliveries, but the gross was in the phone orders. Judging from the complete prep, I could see the afternoon had been slow. I closed the checkbook and stowed it.

"The new case?"

"In the back." Corey nodded to the storage room. I pictured tuning with Wray by the mop bucket. I needed to make sure the box was on a pallet; no moisture near the menus.

"I want to wait until Friday—it's only one case. I could do a confiscation run tomorrow. Any ideas where they've been hitting?"

"Not since Tony reported Belden and Webster. That was a week ago. I told Kat to keep an eye out. Hey," he added, "don't get caught."

He knew I knew what he meant. We had no proof of anything related to Donny, but we were disinclined to have Ozzie find out I was trashing their menus. Corey was taking off his apron and I was putting mine on, red badge of bondage. But it was all about perspective, and in my mind I was casting back a lifetime.

Gotta wake up the child

There's wolves in the kitchen

The phone rang next to Corey and he took it.

"For you." My first thought was Anita. "It's Janis," he added.

"Mitch, I'm with Melanie . . ." Short of breath, voice trembling. "She took something . . . I can't wake her up."

Chapter 28

I popped the latch on the wooden back gate and took the stairs two at a time to Melanie's apartment over the garage. Janis had left the door ajar.

"Where are you?" I was halfway across the living room where I had been almost two years before. Wray and I had played that night and it was my first memory of Dale. Living apart from Melanie wasn't real then and could have meant anything, a month or two. I came to hate the memory of the place, and now it was back, making no sense. Janis was deeper in the apartment, bedroom or bath—water running, light in the bathroom.

They were twin humps kneeling on the vinyl tile, rear ends toward me, Melanie's head over the side of the tub. Water was rushing from the spigot and splattering. Melanie's hair was plastered down, and her pullover was soaked to her cutoffs.

"I threw water on her in bed," Janis said over the rush. "I couldn't wake her—"

"911?"

"Before I called you." Janis's long hair was pinned back, and her brown top with the Chalet monogram was soaked. She had a hand on Melanie's shoulder, keeping her head down. She had been trying to get her to throw up in the tub, with some success.

"Christ, what did she take?"

"There's a Valium bottle by the bed, top off, one left in it."

Melanie sputtered and puked a bit. Kneeling beside them, I slopped water in her face, mouth slack, eyes dropped shut.

"She could choke," I said. "Did you walk her in here or have to drag her?"

"Pretty much . . ."

I was trying to see her breathe. I killed the water.

"Let's get her walking." I hefted under her arms and she came up easily. She was too short for me to wrap her arm over my shoulders, but it worked on Janis's side. I gripped her upper arm and the top of her shorts, and together we drag-walked her into the bedroom. One moment her eyelids would open half-mast, and then we would lose her.

"Hey," I shouted and tapped her cheek, "hey, let's walk. You're doing fine." We patrolled around her bed with the soaked pillow, on her nightstand the deep kitchen pan Janis had used to douse her.

"Feel funny," she mumbled suddenly, her first words. "Feet funny, not working."

"Feet funny, right. That's great, you're funny. Keep walking."

Janis appeared to be flagging.

"Want to rest a minute? We can keep her sitting up." We had parked on the side of the bed when we heard heavy tread and then two hard knocks and the doorbell.

"Medic, 911 medic." A male voice carried through the apartment.

"Back here," I called. There was a thud of gear in the living room.

"We're emergency medical techs. We're here to assist. Can you tell us what happened?" The black man in the lead, compact and quick, posed the question, clear and dispassionate as a cop reading us Miranda. He dropped his bag on the floor then checked Melanie's eyes and took her pulse at her throat, blue gloves. His name tag said James. His partner Julia, stocky and no-nonsense looking, asked other questions, some of which we couldn't answer. We gave her the Valium bottle but we had no idea how many Melanie had taken. Janis found her purse in the closet.

"Diazepam, ten," Julia told James.

"Let's lay her flat." He unzipped the bag.

Julia excused us and took over, angling Melanie supine on the bed. She was out again. James returned, syringe in hand.

"Flumey," he informed his partner. He saw me staring. "Flumazenil," he translated, equally meaningless but appreciated. He poked her shoulder, prompting no reaction, and injected deliberately, over seconds.

"Give it a minute," he said. We stood suspended, hanging on Melanie's state of consciousness. Her pillow was wet, and her sheet. I could see water seeping through her floorboards then welling under her and Melanie was buoyed, floating like the painting of Ophelia in the brook. There was an explanation. She had had an allergic reaction. I was jamming on other possibilities. Whatever the reason, she was not with us. I fought the urge to slap her awake. Her chest continued to rise and fall, but barely. James took another paper pack of flumazenil from his bag but was waiting to open it.

Then it could have been only a minute but I had no way to know. A hypnotist snapped his fingers. Melanie's eyes opened and she was searching us wordlessly, as though we were dream creatures. Julia sat beside her on the bed.

"Melanie, we're paramedics. Your friends called us because you took something and passed out. Was it Valium, hon?" Melanie scrunched her face. "That's okay, you're fine now. Follow my finger." Julia's index finger traveled out and back and Melanie's eyes tracked it. "Good."

"Feeling funny," she slurred.

"You're doing fine. We're just going to take you in so somebody can be with you while you sleep. Do you have a preferred hospital?" Julia checked Melanie and then us, a formality. "We'll go to St. Joseph's—it's closest. Your friend will bring your purse with your ID." James brought the stretcher from the living room. "We're going to be strapping you down now. We don't want you going nowhere."

In a few minutes they were outside and down the stairs and Melanie, strapped to her stretcher, disappeared inside the ambulance. I knew the hospital, parallel to the café on Lake Shore, and Janis and I followed. It was our first chance to talk, and I didn't have to ask.

"Adam called me at the store," she said. "He's gone, as in out of Chicago. Grinnell, in Iowa. He was offered an assistant professorship in the English department. I don't know the details because I'm getting all this through him, but it had to have been going on for weeks at least. Melanie knew nothing about it. He said he didn't want to upset her at the end of the term, but I bet he had his sights set and just wormed his way out.

"Anyway, they had a big fight. Serial phone calls. She accused him of screwing this diva of the creative writing group, which of course he denies. They had both met her at a reading at the Iowa Workshop. I totally believe it."

I tried to picture Melanie on the receiving end. He knew at Barleycorn's but she didn't.

"So they were having the phone fights—working on it, he called it—and at one point she was 'getting illogical', spinning out about killing herself, then she hung up. He said he waited an hour for her to cool down and then called back several times but she didn't pick up. He didn't have Anita's number, but he knew where I worked so he asked could I go over—there was a spare key under a cinderblock behind the stairs." She fished in her smock pocket and produced a note. "He left his number, his new number. I should probably call him back sometime."

"How are you doing?"

"Pissed at both of them. He's a heartbreaker, that boy."

The power he had over them still surprised me, their young Shelley. Against the Melanie I knew, I flashed back to her at Last Blast, searching the little crowd for him when he had slipped away, the Melanie she was with him. There were multiple Melanies, and the same for the rest of us. It only took others to tease them out.

At the hospital we waited in a hall across from a plate glass window, our reflections wan and rung out. We looked older, and we were. A social worker questioned us and inventoried Melanie's things. I was given the option to phone her parents, which I did. The sound of her mother's voice again in the family house triggered a strobe of memories— wiffle ball in her backyard and weighty discussions of writing and music with her at the long dining table and praising brother Davey's flawless recitations of *Monty Python and the Holy Grail*. Her mom and dad were ready to come north immediately, but the social worker took over the call, assuring them that Melanie was stable, she was under care, and visitors weren't permitted on the floor until morning. Soon we were excused too. Our response to Melanie's act had taken hours, but when it was over, I could only recall snapshots. By the time I dropped Janis at her building, it was nearly nine and dark. I swung back to the café, and Corey could finally go home.

When visiting hours began at ten, I was back in the halls of St. Joseph's.

"You're looking rosy," I said and she was, relatively, head elevated and hair combed, but her eyes were different, perturbed.

"Back from the dead. Through no fault of mine, right?"

"And Valium, for chrissake. Know how many it would take?" I pecked her on the forehead, shampoo smell. A half-size spiral notebook was open on her tray table, handwriting on a few lines. A curtain bisected the room, but I couldn't see her roommate on the other side.

"Really dumb," she continued. "Sorry. And thanks doesn't do it, but thank you for coming and for being you. I want to thank Janis too. This hit both of you out of nowhere. I feel so stupid."

"Janis had to start at the Chalet at ten. I told Anita but nobody else. Corey thinks Janis needed an emergency ride to her parents' place last night. They both want to come by, Anita after her class around two, and Janis gets off at four. Of course, you may be sprung by then. They'll call first."

"Mom said you phoned last night. Thank you for that too. They'll be coming in soon." She started to tear up and I took her hand.

"He's way cool maybe, but—"

"You're right, not worth it."

"None of us. We only want one thing, and that's TBD." She half-laughed and the tears started and I waited them out. She had tissue beside her under the sheet.

"Sorry, it was *so silly*." She balled the Kleenex in her fist.

"No, just promise—"

"Of course no—no, I wouldn't."

We both needed a dose of normalcy.

"Anything you want from the outside world?"

"I have class tomorrow but I'll miss that one. I told the folks I'd stay in HQ for a few days." It was the kids' name for the house in Hyde Park. "We'll swing by my place on the way."

"Have they said anything about when you can go?"

"They had me talk to a social worker this morning during rounds, a shrink type. I'm guessing it depends on whether I passed."

"As long as it's before dinner . . . Salisbury steak . . . instant spuds . . ."

"Peas."

A TV began to cackle and clap behind the curtain, *The Price Is Right*. I wondered if I could trust Melanie. It was new territory for me. I needed a question that would trigger the perfect response, one that would spell assurance. Or I needed to see her eyes match my memory.

I had achieved neither in the few minutes before the Barrs arrived. Her mother was unstintingly gracious, thanking me for calling and being there, and her dad shook my hand, but apprehension of parents was in their eyes. We exchanged places and I drew the chair I hadn't used up to the bedside. I thought of kissing the patient before leaving, on the forehead again or the cheek, but my time was up.

Her mom extended the invitation to come by the house anytime, as though nearly two years had not intervened. They assured me I was welcome and I believed them because it wasn't a social moment, all of us undefended, reminded of the pricelessness of connection. But it was an impossible moment too, of not knowing how much they knew of Melanie and me and no way to explain everything that had changed. If we had reversed fortunes in matters of the heart, the high made low, I found no satisfaction in it. But if I had been found wanting in magic in her former life, at least in this one I had been there. I waved my goodbye and Melanie blew a kiss.

She had troubled the waters, her aftershocks coming in waves, on levels. I cut over the few blocks from the hospital to the café to bring change for Bruce to open, but I parked and sat with no radio, waiting for the rolling to flatten out. If it could happen to Melanie, spirited and charmed, favored of the gods of the academy and to whom blessings flowed, it could happen to any of us. Life could happen, the one that came no joke, complete with icy slips and connections missed and dropouts.

I was expecting the hotline to ring and it did, a little after two. Anita told me that when she called the hospital after class, Melanie had been discharged in the care of her parents.

I led off with the twelve-string rhythm and vocal only as long as they needed, which was less than a full play-through. Then we changed to percussion first. Coleman set up the lead-in, a rolling three-four on congas. Dale came next on fuzz-tone base, a rumbling semi and fat tires on wet blacktop.

High people on the road tonight
Summer burnin', turnin' the wheel

The composition leaned on Buckley and the Dead with plenty of room to stretch out and riff.

July lay like a river
For the highway heroes
And the angels of steel

We were jamming in the dining room of the Cavern, and outside the broad windows the afternoon had been gathering. Even with the fan on, we were sweating. I had one window open a foot but not both because we were high on our new power and I was mindful of our volume because the neighborhood would be coming home from work.

Dale had found the amp, a twelve-inch Mesa Boogie that could rock a warehouse, and we all went in on it. I donated a used microphone, since I was the lead singer, although Dale was becoming more of a vocal presence. I also invested in DeArmond pickups for the guitars. They lost shades of color electrified, especially the Martin, but the volume expanded our repertoire and options. I found my gear in a *Reader* classified, which turned out to lead to a music store, Sajewski's on Milwaukee and Ashland. The prices must have been Polish.

"Tight!" Dale crowed when we reached the end, and although it wasn't, it was something fresh. We gulped from our cans of Foster's Lager, long since gone flat.

"I could hear the tabla," Coleman, sweaty and enthused, shared with Dale.

"Instead of the congas?"

"With. I'll bring them next time."

"Bravo." Anita gave three claps. She was leaning in the doorway, drawn from the far end of the apartment by our new sound or in hopes that practice was over, or both. Her hair was up and she wore an olive army surplus T and cutoffs, with an anklet chain I had given her.

"Thank ya, thank ya very much," Dale was doing his Elvis. Anita tended to inspire performance. It would take them a while to get used to seeing her.

"What are we thinking," Dale directed at me, "one, maybe two more practices and we cut the demo? I could give Curtis a heads-up."

"Two is probably right," I said. "But let's do one a week, keep it fresh." I was thinking about the café, where sales needed to be and where they were.

"We've got it now." Dale was shaking his head, shedding the bass. "We could do whatever takes we need and let Curtis work his magic. Don't sweat the bucks, he's not going to rake me. You bring the agent, I bring Curtis." His proposal made perfect sense for any wannabee band with day jobs. "He's on a whole other level from when you and John were there. Seamless dubs, feeds. I heard two singles he did for Poison Squirrel. They burn." He shook his head admiringly.

"It's coming together real good," Coleman added.

"Okay, talk to Curtis about ten days out."

I had heard nothing from Riley-Strauss since Barleycorn's. When my check arrived, I had split it between Dale and Coleman. John's was still in the drawer. Mark and Randy knew nothing about Duello becoming three because it wasn't yet. When I told them, I wanted to have the new demo in hand, and it needed to showcase our range, acoustic and electric, and be pro, undeniable. Anita was leaning on the door frame and I joined her.

"As soon as we have three, maybe four gigs, we should think about going full-time." Dale was zipping his bag, still jazzed. "I'm saying because we should like, start saving now. It's the only way, live the music. Get a cheap house outside the city, studio in the basement."

I was hearing echoes of living the music, none of which made any sense.

"DeKalb," Coleman added.

"Right," Dale said, "your uncle?"

"Cousin. He's got a house out there, big old farmhouse, two-story, three-bedroom, porch all around. It's like two-fifty a month, man."

Why was Coleman pitching me? He was a driver for Monkey Wards. He could only dream about quitting. And for me, music full time would mean the café on auto, as always. The only echo that made sense was Corey's: it's all about sales. Anita slipped away to the kitchen, and in a moment I heard the back screen door close.

"Maybe someday not crazy," I said, "and maybe not that far off. Let's focus on the Earl now, and if Flying Fish happens—"

"It's demo time," Coleman said, and we could all agree to that in principle.

"Gotta beat this rain," Dale said, and we settled on the next practice date and they lugged their gear out the front door. I found Anita in the back with a cigarette. It was in the upper eighties and the air was heavy.

"You thirsty?" I had sweated out the beer already. She half-shook her head, took a draw, and blew it out like Silvana Magnano, like Monica Vitti. We were in a recess behind the apartment, a sad sort of amenity, basically a concrete trench. She was resting her forearms on the top like the railing of an ocean liner.

"You're thinking something," I said. She glanced at me then back, demurring. "I'm not going anywhere if that's what you're wondering. Neither are they, it's all smoke. Trippy-land."

The rain started spotting the two-car patch of asphalt behind the building. Then it came in gossamers, and in a minute the blacktop was slick. She remained staunchly enigmatic, annoying. One more draw and she flipped her cigarette like a pro, over the asphalt and into the alley where it died in the water. I had said or done . . . what? Not enough for her graduation? Should I have blown off the day and gone to Circle? The rain was coming down in nickel-sized pocks, and the air smelled new. We were starting to get splattered and moved back under the overhang. With no cigarette, she folded her arms, looking locked up.

"What's this all about?" I had a feeling that what I was going to say next would be a bad idea. I had had it before. That didn't mean I could stop it. "Are you the moody Italian princess now?"

She gave me a quick slap, not much of one but a wakeup.

"Jeez!"

I wasn't seeing a smile exactly but wicked little curls at the corners of her mouth. Then she was past me, pulling the screen door. I caught it before it closed and followed her in.

She was already in the bathroom adjusting her hair in the mirror, or pretending to. There were dark moist spots on her olive T. The amygdala did the calculation. Whatever penalty slaps were coming, they would be worth it.

I planted myself against her backside and enfolded her from behind. I got more of a bump than a struggle.

"Ha-hah," she responded in the mirror, "I thought you wanted me for my mind."

There was distant marauding thunder. How much might have been left-over high from the practice or the release of summer rain on the streets or the stealth of heat lightning working in from the plains or my volatile Catholic signorina's tease, I couldn't tell. Or it could just have been the way the princess of a Little Italy flipped her cigarette.

I pulled the bottom of her T-shirt over her head. She was a brief, brilliant snapshot in the mirror and then I turned her around and we were front-to-front. She started to object, but her eyes betrayed her and I covered her mouth with mine. I popped the steel button on her cutoffs and dropped the zipper. The whack I gave her rear end was payback, understood. Her breathing was heavy.

The vanity top of white tile was broad and I cleared it and boosted her up. We had lots of gentle times, but neither of us needed this to be one. We were breathing each other's breath. Her leg went over my shoulder, the gold anklet. Soon sweat was slick on us and the mirror fogged.

At some point we migrated to the bed, rain-cooled air spilling over us from the half-open window. Afterward she rolled to her side, head propped on hand, and studied me, her face soft.

"You're young, Henry," she said. "And that's beautiful."

Surely she meant it, but I couldn't shake the feeling that it wasn't all she meant. Whether she was taking off from the new Duello with my youthful bandmates or the adolescent fantasy of quitting work to play for a living, she was calling out a distance between us, one I never wanted.

June 26, 1979
In the long blue spell of evening
South wind blowing a dream of a Chicago night
On the neon nightlight river
Broadway buses burning, turning out of sight

Anita is asleep and I'm in the dining room by the light of the screen. I needed to get the lyrics down on this night that feels like paradise. It's only a start, no chorus yet, no hook. But it's not the only thing keeping me awake. Should I propose to Anita? Not the first time I've asked myself. How better to close whatever distance she's feeling? What more could I want?

But we haven't even lived together, as in merging our things, as in every day. And it's soon for her, no doubt too soon. Worse, I would follow an attorney. Add to that, she has a "field." She's a Master of Comms, and applying. She'll be a professional woman at a station in the Loop. So it's back to the distance, how to close it. My senior partner is a married man and dad. I could get his hit. How many married men do I know?

Corey inspected me as though a bug of mortality was crawling across my face.

"I take that as a no." I didn't think asking about Anita was worthy of ridicule. *Married rhymes with buried*, Wray liked to say, but he could easily be proposing to Sasha that minute in a hostelry on the Rhine. From across the table in his red apron Corey went on staring, and then a tumbler seemed to fall into place behind the stare.

"Funny question," he said. "The epitome of irony, comic type. Contrary to expectation, your authority on holy matrimony has been dumped. So, wrong time to ask, and wrong guy." He made a move to slide out of the booth.

"Hey," I said, and I was the one staring this time.

"Beth's gone. She took Arlo. To her parents' place in Champaign. She was with Arlo in a park and got accosted, not hurt but robbed, a few bucks and her credit card.

Trash-talked. It was three punks, teenagers, Latin Kings or Royals. Arlo was okay." I recalled the Royals graffiti on walls in Logan Square.

"She hated Chicago," he said, and I knew it well. Beth's taking off hit his dream with a hard light—rusty, unrealistic.

"Do you want to haul out there? I could cover."

"Not now, I think she's too hot. Maybe sometime." He was looking away. "I don't know if she's coming back."

"Of course she is. She's freaked—who wouldn't be? She just needs a break."

"Before she left she was talking about elementary school out there."

"He's not even four, right? That's way off."

"Don't know. I had nothing to tell her, no argument. What would it be here, private school? The Latin School, big bucks. And school's only part of it.

"I didn't want . . . it's about Arlo, you know, not her. She's a precious person, really."

They had history, it was all over his face. More than I had ever had.

"Hey, we'll get there. Just keep building the sales. Execute the plan." I knew who I sounded like. "Freaking Carbondale or bust."

"Her folks are down on the city too. Agrarians. Ha!"

"I could cover."

"I'll let you know." He rubbed his forehead.

I got none of the exegesis I was expecting: the marriage contract versus the questing heart, kids or no, the warm socks joys of the hearth, the married and buried. Or was this my answer, my expert witness silenced by inevitable failure? How the world ends. How life, regardless of our self-tortures and half-made plans, goes on its own way so that it only seems to play tricks.

He migrated to the drawer beside the phone. "We got mail," he said and plopped two envelopes on the counter. From where I sat I caught a glimpse of the blue return address on one, the sight of which always flipped my stomach.

He had already opened it. I pulled out the contents like an automaton. Quarterly state sales tax form, the same as always, the same as those to come. One of two things certain.

The envelope was addressed to both of us as owners; the other, unopened, to me from NC National, the holder of our loan. I skipped the intro and skimmed to the substance. Rate increase, another half a point, our new payment amount. Dancing on the page was the face of Malowitz of the golden cigar knife, our guru, his take that rates would remain stable.

"Check the book," Corey said and migrated toward the front window, leaving me to absorb what he already knew. I flipped open the checkbook and saw the balance. The bills for utilities and rent were in the drawer, due in two weeks. Gonzo had depleted our reserves. We had talked about the next move as long as we had been treading water and I had been able to hold off. Corey had come back and was only standing, watching me, no need to ask the obvious.

"Time to call," I said, my insides dropping, loaded with what it would mean. Anita, the music, all but the café sucked away at warp speed. In front of the store on a beautiful day in June, foot traffic was picking up. In his red apron, massaging his forehead, Sisyphus went to open the door.

Chapter 29

IN the living room of the Cavern sitting next to the hotline, I stared at the note I kept in my wallet but rarely consulted, the one with Valerie's phone number. It was eleven on Sunday in Lynchburg, a likely time for Sis and Chuck to be home on the cheapest day for long distance. But as I dialed I was hoping they would be out making a summer family scene and I could leave a message and get a call back at a time when I wasn't tying my insides in knots over it.

After two rings Val picked up. Her tone said I had caught her in the middle of something, but for little brother calling out of nowhere, her voice softened. She had been folding laundry. A toddler's voice bubbled up in the background. I didn't remember Betsy's age, but three, like Arlo's, was a lucky guess. Picturing Betsy in the living room brought back the rest of the house: brick, two stories and a basement, square in all ways, solid and airy, scruffy patch of lawn in front bordered with oaks.

Val and Chuck were busy but fine, I was fine. She even asked about the music. All was fine. And nothing was. I took a deep breath, blew it out away from the receiver.

"I hate to ask you this."

"Oh god. What?" We were back in high school mode. I had dinged the bumper on the garage door frame and I needed her not to tell Hank, or a similar plea. We had been there, same notes, same tone.

"We have a situation in the café . . . a cash crunch. We got hit with a surprise bill—a bump, but the timing was the worst. We just need to float for a few weeks." Eyes closed, I focused on the silence, and the fuzz on the line between time zones. "Biz is good, basically really good. We can pay you back with interest, market rate plus. Like having a super CD . . . super short-term. You could put your money to work, have it back in two, three months max." Betsy sounded off, a short musical sentence, noodling. Silence.

"It was your choice, Mitch—the café, right? To use your school fund for it. Is that gone?"

"No way, it's all there. We have a loan against it. So think, even if the worst happened—and it's not going to—we could sell the business and pay you off first, and then the loan that's already secured by the fund. No way could you lose." I wanted to believe she was taking it in.

"How much?" Just asking was bad, and the idea of being on the hook for what I was about to propose raised a swell of nausea. But Corey and I had wrangled to a number, and I stuck with the plan.

"Ten K right now would take it to a whole new level. We'd be this close to going on auto—turning it over to employees. That's always been the goal. We could pay you back like I said or you could see after three months about leaving it in. By the time you'd be looking at say, private school for Betsy, it could be a cash machine. No guarantees, but we know what happens, right? This is how families do it. It just takes a little faith. We'd handle all the front-line day-to-day. You'd be the silent partner."

"Ten thousand dollars?" Incredulous. "You know how many mortgage payments that is? How many cars?" I had bought the Mustang with one red door and another in the back seat in Durham for six hundred, but I didn't bring that up. "What do you have to have or you drop dead?"

"Just to get over this hump . . . five. But that would be status quo, not growth for any of us." Corey had advised me to use *step factor growth*, but I couldn't make myself say it.

Chuck was out. They would talk and get back to me by the next day. After that we both tried to resurrect the conversation, but our usual wisecracking banter no longer fit. I left the café number as well and tried to end the call as humbly as I could with thanks for considering.

As humiliating as it had been, I was left with the feeling I had put the case too lightly and fantasized about calling back, leveling with her about the mess we had made for ourselves. A remnant of pride stopped me. Plus, it was late. If they refused and we imploded, it would be that much less to repay.

The call came to the café around eight. I was behind the counter alone, so to be safe I waited another hour before calling Corey, although the Sunday night rush never materialized. Sebastian was the only customer, in a booth in front.

"We got five," I said.

"Okay, well . . ." Clearly, he had been dreaming higher. "Back from the dead! Good work. If we had gone in asking for five . . ."

"Yep."

"We can cover the bills in the drawer and have two-thirds left. We'll talk about it. What's it like in there?"

"Dead. I'm going to let Chris go." He was new, in his thirties with UPS experience. We both knew we would probably lose him. Kat would finish the night. "What are you up to?" Meaning how was he doing in the empty apartment. He mumbled a few words about working on *Flash*. I thought about being with Anita—how Corey's scene and mine had reversed, like mine and Melanie's. "Hey, call up Thalia. We have a ticket for her somewhere, maybe two. Or come in here and mop. I'll save it for you."

"See you tomorrow."

"Right."

"Slow night?" Sebastian asked on his way out, George Harrison with a backpack. He and Claire had stepped up to a room in a house, and he had even paid for his slice of the night.

"Deliveries are off," I said. He was close enough to the restaurant business to get the picture. I wondered how much he had heard of the call with Corey.

"It's always a battle, right? People think it's way rad to have your own café. Be your own boss."

"Dare to be great." Nothing better than venting with a kindred spirit. "They have no freaking idea."

"Hang in, brother," he said, upraised fist to a peace sign. Then he was out into the warm night.

With the door open, the jukebox would probably pull in a stray or two. I fished for a quarter and scanned our list. I needed something different, a funk-cutter, maybe Van the Man, "Moondance" or "Domino." All the titles and artists, all with labels. The Band-Aid loan was in the mail, reprieve from big sister, like getting probation for DUI. With that ignominy in the cause of survival behind me, the music had to be next.

"A souvenir," Dale stated. "Priceless artifact. You can't have it, but you can touch it." He put the half-album, cracked down the middle, on the table between us. Enough of the label was intact to make out the title and the artist. *Love to Love You Baby*, Donna Summer. The tracks were stamped with dust from shoe treads.

"Hold out for the Bee Gees," PT advised. "He has a forty-five with two cracks, but it's in one piece. The skips are bitchin'." She took a sip from her pint glass of amber, her eyes blue mischief over the rim.

"Did you scrounge these off the men's room floor?" I asked.

"No way. The field."

Disco Demolition Night at Comiskey Park was topping the local news. The White Sox promo event had gone epically sideways.

"It was outrageous. Records were all over the field, mostly from the explosion, but people were flipping them out of the stands all game like Frisbees. The place was jammed, SRO."

"What was the deal, if you brought a record—"

"Ninety-eight cents admission if you brought a disco record to blow up."

"KC and the Sunshine Band." PT nodded at him and he mimed gagging on two fingers.

"It was a Steve Dahl gig, you know the shock jock, KLUP. The place went ape-shit after the explosion, out of the stands and onto the field. Cops were everywhere, like in riot gear. Days of rage, déjà vu. Total train wreck," he said admiringly.

"Who won the game?"

"Tigers."

"Figures."

"It was a doubleheader. The second game was postponed, rain check, like anybody cared."

It was mid-July around sunset and early in the week. The Oxford Pub was mostly empty with enough chatter and low music to take the edge off. No disco.

"So, death to disco." It was a safe toast. We clicked our glasses.

"If there is a god," Dale said. "But there's always enough crap right behind it. Like Kiss and Bowie, stadium acts, they're like franchises. Corporate schlock, Moog and loops, all production. I don't know, you know? And now rap is a thing. Have you heard 'Kim Tim the Third'?" I confessed I hadn't. "It's like music is getting blown up. Reamed out."

"That's a lot of demolition," I said. "What's a body to do?" I was being flip, but his melodrama was asking for it.

"Bowie is an androgyne," Pat put in. "He reproduces by parthenogenesis, like wasps and geckos."

"Screw that," Dale quipped.

"It isn't well known," she added. "In the future we'll have all sexes. But about the music . . . there are a lot of scenes, and audiences that aren't the average American—"

"The average American is mudfish bait," Dale opined.

"Can I quote you? I want to hear PT."

"Your scene is different," she went on. "You could get lucky." I had heard it from her before but maybe Dale hadn't because he perked up.

"Coleman's stoked," he said. "Thursday practice is at the Cavern, right?" I had asked to meet for a reason and Dale was fishing for it. Corey and I had met after the loan and the conclusions were inevitable. We reassigned Tony to deliveries only. After the weekend we planned to trim Bruce's hours, with a prayer that we wouldn't lose him. If Duello cut a new demo, to what purpose? If Riley-Strauss signed us for gigs, how could I play them? After half a beer, I could come up with no elegant way to get into it.

"I need to talk to you about that. Deliveries are off in the café. I'm going to have to pull more hours. Not sure for how long, but maybe a month or two. So we need to push the demo out." Dale's face dropped.

"Oh man, we need to haul, not push out. Is this like immediate? Let's at least cut the demo while we're hot. It'll be in the sound. If we pull back and then try to get it together again after months . . ."

I knew what he feared. I also knew that on the Thursday evening we had booked for practice, I was now booked for deliveries, and menuing during the day.

"What I'm saying is, I can't commit to a string of gigs right now. That's the kind of momentum we need, right? It would be bad news to get them and then have to bail. Worst would be to jerk Mark and Randy around." If Mark and

Randy even remembered who Duello was. Or if they would remember after another month or two.

Dale sat back, receding. The café—the parasite Corey and I had given birth to—was sucking him away. PT was looking let down too, maybe for Dale, maybe for all. She had been the matchmaker, bringing the three of us together. I kept repeating that the setback was temporary until I was tired of hearing it. When we split up, I implored Dale to convey the same to Coleman—a delay of a few weeks only.

When Corey and I met after my call to Valerie, it was the first time I had seen him in over a week with Beth and Arlo gone. He had a few days' growth, and his face looked pudgy and paler. Normally, he would have been babbling about *Flash*, but he didn't bring it up and neither did I. The café was what Corey had left. I would have less time for Anita, but we still had each other. Whether it was a dream or a pipedream, the café had come down to make or break. We were rolling back time to the early days. Maybe John Wray had been right all along.

The Thursday of the canceled practice came and went. Soon I chose to dig myself in deeper. Corey and Beth had talked, but he still hadn't been to her parents' place to see her and Arlo. His desultory drag from Logan Square to the café and back was hard to think about. Beyond that, his mood was a dark cloud over Bruce and the drivers, and customers had to pick up on it. When I proposed the idea, the last point tipped the argument. He would take three days off at the beginning of the week, the slowest nights, to go to Champaign and I would cover. By Wednesday night I was feeling zomboid, less from work than from boredom. I reminded myself we both worked every night when we opened, which was both a pep talk and a depressive. With half the shift to go and Tony doing homework at the back table, Sebastian and Claire breezed in, hippie and pixie, our midsummer sprites.

"Thanks for waking me up. The usual?" I had two kinds of slices for him, and the crêpe griddle was still on for her.

"Yes, sir. And this is settle-up night." He produced two tens and flattened them on the counter.

"Really?"

"We are outward bound, man." They were waiting for me to guess.

"New Zealand," Claire added, eyes a-twinkle.

"Really."

"We have this friend, he's started a winery . . . it's on the South Island, in Nelson Tasman. We'll be working it with him. Partners, like you two." Good luck with that, god help you.

"What kind—"

"Varieties?" Claire jumped in. "Chardonnay and Pinot Noir, both from mature root stock. You can't make wine overnight, but—it will take a couple of years. And the winery is organic, totally."

"Paul wants a bakery-café thing while the winery is getting going, so, yeah! Which reminds me, we have a little present for you . . . right after dinner."

They took off for their table. By the time they were done, Tony was back on the road with a delivery to Aldine. Sebastian approached the counter and Claire was grinning behind him.

"We're going to need your mixer," he announced, "and the whole wheat flour you use for your crêpes. And the honey. A cup of your mozzarella. I've got caraway and dill seed."

Going on nine, the prospect of messing up the Hobart mixer, which we did four times a week to make dough, did not thrill me. I must have been obvious.

"Ten minutes max. Cleanup is on us."

"Hey, take it away. I only work here." I pulled the bin of whole wheat flour.

The two chefs measured the ingredients into the stainless steel bowl. They added water and the mixer whipped until the dough was pliant.

"Feel this." Sebastian handed me a plug. "This is the texture you want. Not too much gluten." He rolled the ball cleanly onto the table, and Claire began washing the bowl. He cleaved off a chunk and weighed it. "About right for a slice pie? Go ahead and roll it out—you won't be able to stretch it on your knuckles. Don't top it yet."

He retrieved an olive oil tin we displayed close to the front window and sniffed the contents. A quarter-sized dollop went into the center of the dough circle and he spread it to the edge with his fingertips.

"You coat with the olive oil, all around. It's critical—a few cents more but it gives it a rich taste, outrageous. It can be virgin or extra virgin but fresh, not this old."

"A few cents," I said, thinking of the cheese and the honey and the spices. Keep the cost of sales under a third.

"You charge more. They'll always pay—it's the primo experience that everybody wants. Mwaaa." He smooched his fingertips like Chef Boyardee. If Corey were there he would echo the wisdom, being consistently in favor of the maximum expense. "Okay, you can put whatever on it now, maybe half veg, half plain cheese the first time so you can taste the crust." He cut the rest of the master doughball into three and we sealed them in plastic wrap.

"I could write down the recipe." He doodled with an air pen and I gave him one of Corey's ledger sheets from the drawer. He took the stool by the phone and used the pen. I topped the whole wheat crust, half-and-half, dropped the oven door, and slid it in.

"Your creation?"

"Somebody from Daybreak Farm." I knew he meant his commune days.

"Natalia from Warsaw, taught him everything he knows," Claire sing-songed, replacing the stainless bowl in the mixer. It was clearly a topic with history. "Not everything," she added and poked him. "Let's go, guy."

Sebastian presented me with the green sheet and the secret recipe inscribed on half a dozen rows. "We owed you, man," he said, "both of you." He wished us good luck with the recipe and we thanked each other and hugged. I made them promise to come by whenever they were back in the States, wondering if it would ever happen, and if it did, if Corey and I would still be there, two more guys who never made it out of Chicago. We parted on the sidewalk in front of the café and I watched them go down the block together, surprised that I was clearing my eyes.

Back inside the smell was delicious, like edible air. I gave the slice pie a few more minutes then dropped the oven door and the aroma rolled out—Polish rye met with tomato and olive oil, garlic and oregano. I would try an experiment.

Instead of the usual eight wedges, I cut the slice pie into two-by-two squares. Four went onto paper plates on the counter. The door was still open, and soon drifters were drawn to the free samples. Over the next hour I used two of Sebastian's remaining three doughballs for orders placed on the spot.

It was Corey's return night from Champaign, nearly ten-thirty. I was betting he would still be awake, and after four rings, he picked up. We addressed his trip in two sentences. He clearly didn't want to get into more of it then, and I wanted to come to the point. He would be opening the next day.

"I'll meet you in here at eleven-thirty," I said. "There's something you need to see."

Chapter 30

COREY had unlocked the door by the time I arrived. Before explaining anything, even the green sheet, I went to the drawer and thumbed through our black book of numbers.

"Ori. It's Mitch at New American. Have you started our run yet?" We had placed the order days ago based on our new infusion of capital: five boxes of menus. I was happy to hear a vague excuse. "No, no problem. Look, I need you to hold on that. Two, three days max." That would give us enough time to decide.

"I need to keep a copy of these numbers," I told Corey, who was looking understandably clueless. "Sebastian and Claire were in last night." I unfolded the green sheet. He pushed up his glasses and read. I told him about the experiment and pulled the tub of wrapped doughballs from the cooler, the remaining darker wheat one among the whites. He hefted it, unwrapped part, and sniffed.

"Results," he said, "have to be confirmed."

I agreed and started rolling out the slice pie. He watched through the spreading of the olive oil, then we finished the prep together and opened at noon. I let him pull the pizza to savor the aroma. Again I sliced half into squares and put out the samples on the counter. Soon foot traffic was diverting through the door and the night before was starting to repeat.

"I'm going to make a batch," I said. He studied me, not ready to approve. We had trained employees to run the mixer during prep time only, never with guests in the store. "I think we'll need it."

We were almost out of whole wheat flour, and we had only the caraway and dill that Sebastian had brought. The four pies from my modest doughball were gone before five.

I hung around to watch but also to hear Corey say it. As the last of the four went out the door with a customer, he had new lights in his eyes. My partner was reviving from his comatose state.

"Let's call Janis," he said.

I did, to kick off the steps to get the whole wheat crust on the menu. We would meet to talk design, she would turn around a concept, and we would meet again for approval. The redesign would go to the printer and we would plead with Ori for priority, which no doubt would entail half payment in advance.

In the meantime Corey drew on all his ingenuity to create a coupon. With stick-on letters and symbols, he fashioned a two-by-four rectangle with dollar signs in the corners and two centered lines:

Try Our New Whole Wheat Crust
$1 Off First Order

He filled a sheet with paste-ups then copied the sheet onto green paper. We stapled a coupon to each delivery box and bag. The day after we debuted his creation, he showed up in the store on fire with another idea. I had arrived at four-thirty, and we each rolled out a whole wheat. By five he was leaving on his delivery run with two twelve-inches in a hotbox.

"Corey hit them both—Terkel and Ebert—back-to-back in one trip. He knew he could do it, no doubt at all. He tracked down Ebert at the Billy Goat, just walked up to the bar and presented the box. You can see him bowing, right? Studs had ordered from us before, a couple of times. Corey found one of the tickets with his address. He's in a grand old brownstone above Montrose on the lake. Corey rang the bell and *voilà*. Who else do we know who could do that?"

Anita laughed and her nose crinkled, making a perfect, gloriously hot August day in Lincoln Park more perfect. I could see her eyes through her shades.

"Of course, the idea is to get some kind of mention, on air or in print. Maybe. Who knows."

She was wearing a bright white tunic, and with her tanned throat and chest and dark glasses and Italian hair up, delightful sprigs pulled down by her ears, she could have been at a café table in St. Tropez. I hadn't seen her in close to a week and would have preferred the privacy of her apartment to a table in the park, even a rare unoccupied one in the shade, but she said she had been working overtime at the studio and was dying for fresh air. It was mid-afternoon, a couple of hours before I had to report for duty. We were splitting a bag of cold green grapes.

"Janis added the whole wheat prices to the menu and did a great 'delicious new pizza crust' blurb in a starburst by Weevil's head. Corey dropped off the art boards at the printer today. The new photo masters will be a couple hundred more, but . . ." Anita was half-smiling but noncommittal, maybe only indulging me. "What do you think?"

"I think it's great news. I love to hear you enthusiastic again."

It could have been *enthusiastic*, the way she said it, the formality of it, like an observation, or it could have been nothing. She was looking down into her hands, turning a grape in her fingertips. A pigeon was watching from a patch of brown grass. She took a perceptible breath.

"I have to tell you something." She was a girl beginning confession, searching for the words. She looked up.

"I have a job offer from a station, WETA. It's in Washington."

We were together at the table in the park in the same summer, wrapped in the same shimmering light, but where were we?

"D.C.?" I said dumbly. She was quiet. I searched her face, her obscured eyes, for any sign of reality.

"It's PBS headquarters. I'm going to take it." The young girl was gone, a phase, a phantom. Anita's tone was resolute, mature. Years between us that had collapsed to nothing reasserted themselves, reforming like stone guardians of things as they are. I couldn't go with her, I thought but could not admit, unable to consider the fact that she hadn't asked. She had ripped the green skin.

"How long . . . you never—"

"The offer came yesterday. I couldn't sleep last night."

I was dropping in a shaft.

"I know this is—"

"You never even told me you interviewed."

"At the station, a couple of weeks ago."

"You decided not to tell me."

"No, I really didn't think . . ."

Incredibly, people were still strolling in the park, passive, complicit. This was why she had wanted to meet here, buffered by a company of strangers, shielded from having to handle me alone. Her glasses came off and her eyes tightened against the glare.

"You could come with me," she said finally.

"Of course I can't. How can you just . . ." I tried to throttle back. "Anita, I love you, don't you know that? I want us to be married. I haven't asked you because of the café. I want it to be totally solid. It's been rocky at first, of course, but that's going to change now, I know it." Her eyes were brimming. "I want us to be like them when we're that age." We both saw the white-haired couple going slowly, hand-in-hand, on the walk by the lake.

She wiped her eyes, tracked cheeks, smeared mascara. I was glad to see her tears. I gave her my handkerchief and used it myself after her. She took deep breaths then watched me closely, maybe assessing my honesty, maybe hesitating.

"And what about your music?" she said.

"What about it? It's nothing between us—"

"It's your calling," she said, her eyes firming. "You have to want it above everything else. Everything. You have to give all if you want it."

"That's about you."

She shook her head and went on. "You have to *become* it, and it, you. Or else you'll be their age and looking back, knowing you didn't have the courage at that one time that could have made the difference. And that would be the worst, for you, me, people like Melanie and Corey and Janis, all of us."

I was spinning, refusing to acknowledge in any way but numbly her words of conviction and how, from Catholic school girl to policeman's daughter to attorney's wife, she had earned them.

"When?" I said, conceding nothing, only keeping her engaged, buying time to think. I could retrieve pieces of an argument. They would come to me soon because they were obvious and true.

"I fly out next week, Wednesday. I come back for stuff the following weekend." Itinerary and connections, things she would take or leave, details, nonsensical.

"What? Look, we have to be able to talk. Not here, this is crazy." She knew where. Her place was a block from the park.

"Not good right now."

"Not good? What are we, going to send postcards?"

"Just not right now."

A shiver ran through me in our patch of shade that had been fortuitous and welcoming. At the edge of the park cars rolled, silent as hearses, windows and chrome flaring the sun.

I was dropping, no net. I covered her hands with mine, hanging on, knowing how mine must feel to her, cold, bloodless. I could do nothing in a park. Focusing on our hands, heaped as though they had collapsed around some prayer, I started over.

Downshifting, I argued quietly but nonstop, promising anything to get to her apartment. No touching her, no more about marriage. It wasn't only *her* future. There were pieces we needed to talk through. Options. She owed us at least that.

She conceded, a discussion only. In her apartment I filibustered. She kept me at arm's length physically and tried to emotionally, but talk and tears rolled out of both of us. I was aware of four-thirty closing in with the specter of the café. At a point we were drained but far from finished. Anita had tried to remain adamant, but she was looking ragged and wounded and nearly as tired of hurting as I was. We promised to talk the next day. She could call on her lunch break. It was paltry, but I felt nothing but grateful. I could go slow, tiny steps, whatever it took.

That night in the café Kat was driving, and I was glad because the odds of getting into anything about our personal lives was nearer to zero with her than with Tony. It wasn't my first robotic shift behind the counter, but it was the most oblivious. I made slice pies and rang sales off the street. I must have taken phone orders and made them because of the times Kat was gone. In the dead spots I prepped ahead and cleaned, anything to block panic and try to focus. I needed wits to come up with alternatives. There were five days before Wednesday, plenty of time to turn her around.

Catch her leaving the studio. But I would be in a loop, back to stalking her at Circle after our fight. Better, camp outside her door. She was in a pushover building—I had menued it before without her letting me in. It may have been in the early days when she was shy about allowing me to see her place. I was leaning on the butcher block table facing the back wall under the bright light, seeing her hallway again and her door. The back of my hand was wet, and I blinked and dried it off.

There was time. I needed arguments, clear and persuasive, to get back into her apartment, or into the car and to the Cavern or to any place alone with her. There was no reason to leave. Everything was here in her hometown. Not just me, her mother and sister. Her connections, everyone she knew. Plenty of stations to work for. Everything but her dream.

Chapter 31

I remembered when Anita had left the blouse. It was the last Friday in June, the night of the White Sox game. She had come from work and changed into her Sox T-shirt. The white cotton on my face was cool from the closet. I could still detect a trace of her, the perfume of her warm day. I rehung it at the end of the bar and slid my shirt against it. I was unsure whether to take it back to her. That was only yesterday.

The memory came to me in a speechless moment in the living room, and it felt like a betrayal although I couldn't say exactly of whom. But I knew then I would be keeping the blouse, after I learned how it had all gone down.

My bell rang a little before ten. I had closed the night before and hadn't had coffee or shaved. Awake for less than half an hour, I was already keyed up, focused on picking up Anita after work. The perky chime came out of nowhere. If Jehovah's Witnesses, I would wait them out. Through the bedroom blinds I checked the fisheye mirror mounted on the fence to take in the basement apartment. The sight was more than I was ready for. I switched on the box fan in the living room and unlocked the door.

"You're a vision," was all I could think to say, over-whelmed by the daylight and the presence of both Melanie

and Janis on my doorstep. "Come on in. To what do I . . ."
They were hiply but professionally dressed, Melanie in a
light blue shift and heel sandals and Janis in a splashy
caftan top and tights. "Can I get you some coffee? I have
donuts."

They declined and I angled the fan. They sat on the sofa
and I brought a practice chair from the dining room. Corey
and I had worked through the menu with Janis a week
earlier, but I hadn't seen Melanie since the hospital. She
was looking tanned and bright-eyed and like Melanie again.
They wore kindly smiles that didn't put me at ease.

"How do you like your place?" I started, aiming mainly at
Melanie. Janis had told me during the menu revision that
they were splitting a three-bedroom flat on Sedgwick below
Armitage. After a couple of weeks at home, Melanie had
sublet her place on Belden.

"Love it," she said nodding, keeping the smile, and I
expected her to go on but she didn't.

"The Ravenswood stops at Armitage—it should be a
quick shot to Circle."

"Anita . . ." Janis cut in, clearly as tense as I was,
unable to avoid the point any longer. "She wanted us to tell
you. We just took her to O'Hare." I flashed on the parental-
looking car I had seen on the street behind them. Melanie's
parents.

"No way, this is Tuesday. Her flight is Wednesday."

"She spent last night at our place," Melanie said quietly,
open-faced, in caring mode, her explanation explaining
nothing. I was going to pick Anita up; we would spend the
night together. I would take her to the airport. In the talks
we had had since the park, gut-wrenching and tearful, two
on the phone and one on the way to her bus in the morning
after I intercepted her in her lobby, nothing I could say
could change her mind. But we had agreed we would call
each other and I would fly out to visit her soon. Then, when
the café was on its feet and running with employees the way

Corey and I had always planned, I would join her. "She didn't want to hurt you anymore."

Coming from Melanie, that coda was rich. What was I supposed to do, thank them? Were they expecting me to decompose?

"I'll pick her up next week, all right?" I was confirming, not asking. She would be back to ship things on that Saturday, and I was echoing what we had decided.

"She's asked some people to send her things." Janis this time. I wondered who that would be. Someone with a key. Present company, and maybe her ex. Someone not me.

"Well," I said, "it's great to have friends." Conspiratorial ones. I was stunned, locked up, unable to react in front of them for all the reasons. Stunned was better. She wouldn't ship the birds. Her ex could drive them—birds, boxes, plant, sofa. One U-Haul. D.C. had to be a great town for attorneys. They could start over, two yuppies working hard, playing hard, putting down roots.

We sat and they checked me, eyes crawling over me. They were watching the iceman, waiting for me to change state. Expecting me to vaporize. I could have been slumping, having bitten the power line. Numb. Familiar state. If the dumb silence with the dull rush of the fan was oppressive, I didn't make it. Janis glanced at Melanie then checked her watch.

"I want to pop over to the drugstore on the corner," she said. "I'll be right back. I have half an hour."

"I'm dropping Janis at her agency on Dearborn," Melanie put in. She was explaining again, trying to steer us back to a world where explanations could make sense.

"It's half-time right now, but it gives me a chance to work on my own stuff, like for you guys." She was on her feet, picking up on Melanie, striking a cheerful note. "I cut the Chalet back to two days."

"Congrats," I said, nodding along, imitating myself. I was starting to wonder how much of their visit was choreographed.

"Back in a few," she said, and then I was alone with Melanie on my sofa, she looking centered and wise like Myrna Loy. We had more in common now than when we were together. We had both lost others, and each other. Her expression said, come in here with me. As though I could. Instead I asked about *TriQuarterly*. The summer editorship had ended, but she had been hired at Circle as a TA for a grad course in the fall.

"It could be worse," she said.

"Good for connections." All my women, making connections.

"I've also been waitressing at the Spot. I'll have to quit before any students see me." The Spot in Evanston. Students, like John Wray. She smiled easily, maybe trying to let me know she was the same girl. There was nothing seductive in the way she was sitting, but I felt the old pull. She was trying. I should be able to reciprocate in some way, but silence had come over me, heavy as deep water. How could I be in this place again? It was like a recurring nightmare, like an inside joke that fate had ordered Melanie and me to share.

"You're doing shitty, I'm sure." She was off the sofa and beside me, touching my shoulder, tears in her eyes. I was on my feet and we clenched. She felt compact against me, and steadying, and I was hanging on. We kissed cheeks. We had diverged from each other and gone out too far, that was all, but now we were back in safe harbor. But no. We stood, arms around each other, and rocked. She looked up at me, eyes moist.

"I could come back," she said. We were pressed together and the desire was back, undeniably. But the rest was confusion. The scent of Anita's blouse. We hung there like an unresolved chord.

"Thank you." I kissed her forehead. "But I'm not much good right now."

We held tight and my thoughts tumbled back over our territory, times impassioned but removed now, meetings of magnetism with accident, including the fact that if not for Melanie, I would never have known Anita.

We hung on, not saying more than we had, which was fine with me, getting sticky despite the fan in the late morning that had turned hot. In a few minutes, Janis was back at the screen door. Then, at the end of the walk they turned and blew kisses, caring, chilling, and they were on their way in Melanie's parents' Cutlass. Gone. All were gone.

I was in the kitchen then, starting the coffee, but a vacuum was draining blood from the brain. I retreated to the bed and sat, head hung over. White dots floated in from the margins, burned out.

I needed to remember, she would send her number and then we would talk. I would fly out for a day or two and soon, or in not so long, I would follow her. I slid my shirt over on the rod. The slim white torso of the blouse had fit her. Her delicate shoulders took the shape of the hanger. Her neckline. I picked up the trace of her scent and drew it in like a fix.

How could she have done that? I saw her on the plane, she who had worn the blouse, graced the bed. What if? Lightheaded again, I sat and tested the worst case. If Anita was truly gone, was I alone in the world? My tribe was here, and we were alone but together. And I had Val, to whom I was now bound by birth and debt. The end of my loan life was coming up fast, a few weeks at most. I would need to persuade them to stay in. If we tried to repay them, we would dig ourselves back into the hole. Corey and I were in the same boat in every way. What did we have to survive in the wilderness? Boxes of the new menus and nothing but time. What's it all about? It's about making the freaking phone ring.

```
                                        Sept.  3
```
    Labor Day again. We decided on no repeat of
Last Blast. Too much has changed. I told Corey
about Anita and he appreciated the irony that our
lives were now so alike, our women not with us
but, we hoped, not gone.
    Last night we closed an hour early and got
half-ripped at Julia's. I had never seen Corey
drunk. I assume he made it home in one piece, the
place neither of us wanted to go. We'll have
plenty of opportunity to stay away. We've enjoyed
a bump in orders but not nearly enough. While
under the influence he agreed to join me in
menuing soon.

Melanie and Janis had said Anita's phone number
would come by mail. A couple of nights ago my phone rang
late, but it was a hangup. It would have been an hour later
for her. I decided to call Melanie. Of the two of them, she
would be more likely to have any number.

That was before I spotted an envelope in the box between a bill and an ad. I was on my way out to menu, and
the day before had been back-to-back, so I hadn't checked
my mail.

Her handwriting on the card envelope, postmarked three
days earlier. Paper smell, no perfume. I used a kitchen knife
to keep from tearing it. On the front of the card, flowers in a
vase by an artist who was familiar but who would require
focus to recall, and mine was on her script. Dear Mitch.
Sorry she had taken so long to send. Getting the phone
installed had taken forever—she had been in line. It would
be lovely to talk, followed by her number, alone on the line.
Love, Anita. Love, it said, Anita.

```
                                        Sept.  7
```
    Cloud nine! Heaven on earth!

Fighting the compulsion to call. The time has
to be right. She's probably working. Corey has
the counter tonight. My seven, her eight could be
perfect. Going to menu now, keeping it simple.
Plenty of time to think it through.

"Hey, you!"

"Hey!" She sounded happy but smaller, far away.

"It's great to hear your voice. I just got your card today—"

"Just today . . ."

"I think it probably came yesterday but I couldn't get
mail all day, so—but how are you out there in capital city?"

She had taken a weekly rental room but found an
apartment on the third day. That was why the phone had
taken a while, which was good to hear. Apartment hunting
had been a scramble, cutthroat compared to Chicago. Her
studio was on the border of Arlington where she said the
PBS studio was.

"It's the first floor of a three-flat, kind of quaint, more
like run-down. I needed to get *some* place. I may not stay
forever—it's month-to-month. How are *you*?"

"Well," I said, sticking to the script I had rehearsed to
soft-pedal it, "I miss you."

"I miss you too, Henry." She sounded sweet but I was
listening for more. I took a breath.

"So . . . I thought we were going to be together on your
last night."

"Did Melanie—"

"Oh yeah, Melanie and Janis did their job. They said you
didn't want to hurt me. But we agreed." I didn't like it but I
had to get it out.

"I couldn't, okay? It was about me as much as you."

I wanted to believe. "I get it. But it wasn't goodbye, right?
Just for a while. And you said you were coming back for
your stuff."

She fell silent. Was I berating her? What was she supposed to say? She had already said it. I wanted to take it back.

"It's mostly in storage here now."

Get perspective. Not a total loss. Things in storage are there for the future. Hearing her go on was a relief. We were past the blaming and I wasn't going back.

"I can help you get it. I've been looking at a weekend to come out, or maybe during the week when the café is slower . . . but I guess you're already working?"

"I am."

"Okay, if weekends would be better, I'll swing it. I could trade Corey for a trip to Champaign. Beth is there with his kid, if you remember."

"I do." She sounded tiny, birdlike. Keep focused. Talk her back.

"Well, how's the studio? Are you working on any shows yet?"

She reported on her duties and a couple of the people, but I couldn't have passed a test. I was tuned to her tone and rhythm, trying to pick up any true notes, revealing ones. Mostly I was hoping to hear regret.

"So I'm thinking about the end of the month, that weekend." I floated it and listened. There was a silent beat that I was trying to deny. I knew before I proposed it, neither the time nor the money was realistic at the moment and might not be by then, and maybe she was picking up on that.

"Let's think about that weekend," she said. "I just can't promise."

"What?"

"What I might have to do."

"Hey, what is it?"

"I'm trying to do a million things. It's a new life for me, you know?" She sounded pushed.

"Sorry, of course. I get it. I just miss you. I miss us."

"I miss you, Henry," she said again. Then we were saying more but the words slipped away. I sensed the end coming and tried to forget everything else and focus on the last three chords, end on an up-note, and commit to talk again in a week.

I sat beside the hotline facing the bookcase, chair, lamp, and wall, seeing none of them, only the ghosts of her and us in the room. There was no blowup, no severance, I needed to remember that. She was still there at the end of the line, our lifeline. All of that stood against the emptiness that was welling up, the lack like a presence, a nemesis.

I was on my feet, shaking it off, into the bedroom. Whatever she might have to do, a million things. What I might need to do, take the initiative and book a flight. Arlington, she had said, somewhere on the edge of Arlington. Her envelope was still there on the dresser, and I took in the front at a glance. Flipped it over. Not on the back either. Of course not, I would have seen it. No return address.

I menued every day of the next week, both low blocks and high-rises, and worked the counter for half the nights. That I had the lopsided share of work for a while didn't matter. I craved the distraction over the hours and days to the next call with Anita. I was also bolstering my case for trading time at the end of the month.

I was still finding Gonzo menus and treating them like litter, but we were gaining an edge. Corey joined me, which increased our coverage for a day and a half, but while working a two-flat, he fell coming down the front steps. He survived but admitted feeling dizzy, so I sent him home and closed that night. Instead of Corey I enlisted Tony to help with menuing a couple of floating days—his choice—between Thursday and Sunday. He stayed in the flats only, nothing in the towers. We didn't need to lose half of our delivery team either hassled by cops or arrested, and I needed no disasters before Friday evening.

"Hi, it's me. It's about eight your time." I listened to the unresponsive terminus of our lifeline in the borderlands of Arlington, Virginia. "I close tomorrow but I'll try you again on Sunday." The answering machine must have been part of her new lifestyle. "Love you," I added and hung up.

How much was an answering machine? I would be working most of Saturday, and if she called the Cavern I would miss her. Messages on tape could be our new mode. Notes in a bottle.

Saturday brought two notable events. An envelope from the bank was waiting with its usual shot of panic when I arrived. Corey had opened it.

"Another bump," he announced. "Half a point." Interest rates were rising nonstop. In the war against inflation, any business with a variable rate loan was caught in the crossfire. I was tempted to ask if Malowitz could tell us whether this was the worst time in a century to start a leveraged business. Corey's glasses were taped at the nosepiece, a casualty of his fall, and he looked too beaten and pitiful to taunt.

Then, before he took off, Kat called from the road. Her car was dead in a gas line. Corey noted her location and said he would catch her on the way home. His response to the shortages was to carry a spare can of gas in his trunk which, although insane in theory, now made him look like a genius.

"It's in *Barron's*," he said. "Sixty percent of stations are closed nationwide. Carter thinks we're going to bring Iran to heel. It took Alexander to whip the Persians."

"Hi. Are you around?" A thousand one, a thousand two. "I hope you got my message on Friday." A thousand one, a thousand two. "I guess I missed you again. You could call me at either number, here or the café. Okay?" I left the café number again, in case whatever note she might have made once was in her storage locker.

I didn't wait another week. Wednesday was long enough, after nine her time. I had no way to be sure, but the odds of her working had to be slim. After two rings, no pickup. After four. The answering machine was gone, or off, or her line was unplugged. After five rings I stopped counting and only focused on the tones, identically uninflected, identically spaced, like a tympanum in a requiem, pounding recognition into me. Pounding sense. Lifeline unplugged.

Dresser or kitchen? I considered the meager stash in the back of my dresser drawer, and the effort to roll a joint, and opted for the jug of red in the kitchen instead. Big bites, slugging them down. I put on a fallback from the Melanie split-up days, album cover beaten up and frayed on the edge, but I knew where it was in the stack—the Stones, *Got Live If You Want It*, howling it out in Albert Hall.

Under my thumb there's a girl

Was it time for rage? Wrenching grief well known to the gut? More fitting by far than paralysis, uncertainty, suspension.

After both sides of *Got Live*, I pulled out *Blonde on Blonde*. I forced myself to wait a full two hours. TV on, no sound. I couldn't resist WTTW, but besides being PBS, it had nothing to do with her station. Clicked the dial past it. Sox over the A's, five to two. *Dukes of Hazzard.*

You go your way and I'll go mine

Getting too wasted? I could still talk, and cordially. If she could. If she could have the decency to be where I, ripped with Inglenook Burgundy, heart beating its stoned butterfly wings, might hope and expect her to be. At two past eleven on her coast, seated on the floor, jug beside me and back against the sofa, I lifted the handset of the hotline and dialed.

Ma Bell gave me her impression of a ring. After the first two, I echoed back. That went on.

"Nice talking," I said after seven then rested the handset in the cradle. I poured a refill. Maybe three glasses left in the jug. It should be enough for one night. After that? Be here freaking now. We know what the future is good for. Or maybe possibly not.

As a newbie, maybe she had to take the graveyard shift. Or her machine was broken, or both. She had to move because her quaint building turned out to be a rat trap of junkies and her phone was in transit. She had admitted to herself that D.C. was a misstep and was on her way back, but she couldn't bring herself to tell me yet. All were possibilities. More than possible.

Sept. 29

We come and we go. This big-ass city takes some like Donny--city of vanishing. A few, very few, make it out. Thread the needle to freedom. Like Adam, like Anita. And we never know who will be who. Pinball physics.

This was going to be our weekend. Rather, my weekend to take time I couldn't spare and spend savings I didn't have to chase my dream who didn't want to be caught. Over the last two weeks I made three or four calls. Two dozen rings. Our times together are rising like ghosts and I'm flaming them out.

Melanie said once when we were stoned and waxing profound that the only purpose of loving is to make its holy imprint--empty a space in us that becomes the capacity to love. We treasure and praise it, but if it's only a hole in our unhealed selves, then anyone could fill it.

There's something terrible in that. Whatever the
story is, of all of us, it cloaks its purpose. It
is not a composition, not a tidy plot with no
loose ends and a denouement. Not one born to win
or built for the ages. Tears have no meaning.

Chapter 32

Make a friend, you lose a friend
He's gone forever
People change places, times are unsure
Is there anything that we made together
Anything that time will endure?

Received a call from Mark--a stunner not only because my two calls to Riley-Strauss since Barleycorn's had gone unreturned, but because it was their first time calling my number. They had an out-of-town gig in Lake Forest--bizarre location but good money--but not until Dec. Not to worry, they would be backfilling, we could expect others before then. They had been busy expanding, setting up a New York office--it will be great for you guys, etc. Of course, I accepted for the three of us, although Mark and Randy hadn't heard the new Duello, and the demo is as far off as it was a month ago. Anything about the Earl? They're working on it. I almost had to laugh.

Another Chicago fall. Runt maples that had soaked up enough of summer to add an inch or two were starting to flame, prepping to spill their leaves again. Afternoons were all honeyed light and sharp shadows, a season as stuffed with poignancy as a Chinese landscape. I needed none of it.

I cared about nothing. I wanted no feelings, no thoughts. I was menuing and driving and counter. My acts and I were inseparable. The café was refuge and work was sedation. Sales were showing improvement but not enough to get free. The best news came on menuing rounds. The only Gonzo menus I was finding were crammed into tin door-side boxes with other random flyers or abandoned in the mail rooms. In the menuing wars, we were finally winning.

The worst came out of nowhere. I was closing or driving most of the week, so my waking hours shifted later. Rising before ten became the exception. By eleven-thirty on a Thursday, I had finished breakfast and was considering getting back to two songs I had started but lacked the will to move along. From the kitchen table I could see the Favilla case in the corner of the dining room. The phone rang.

Anita was back, clearer than memory, not the phone but Anita herself. I broke for the living room and lunged for the hotline on the second ring.

"Mitch?"

"Yes, hi, sorry, a little out of breath." I knew how I sounded, hyper, maybe juiced. Valerie sounded the same as always.

"You all right?"

"Me? Sure. I was just practicing."

"Is this a bad time? Is your group—"

"No, it's fine, they can wait. We were ready to break anyway." The lie was natural, simplest and best. I needed focus for what had to be coming.

"We were wondering, how's the café?"

"Fine, actually. Great. Sales are up." Not a total lie. "You guys were lifesavers, getting us over that hump."

"Chuck is concerned. He wants to go private, transition to contracting, and that means a new truck. And he needs to have more of a cushion." She wasn't necessarily implying how foolhardy I had been, but I knew she was thinking it. Chuck the electrician may have a certificate, not a diploma, but he was smarter in some ways than her head-in-the-clouds brother. A service business, next to no inventory.

"Funny, Corey and I were just talking. We thought you might want to hang in now that we're rolling." Dead air. "But let us get back together on that—"

"As I said, Chuck wants to get moving. His boss is a new guy this year, a real SOB. Chuck's best bud quit last week."

Now the story had context, and urgency. Maybe it was a fiction, a token of more creativity than I had given Valerie credit for, my sister trying to backpedal out of a commitment, naïvely made against her better judgment, that was troubling the waters at home.

"Let me talk to Corey. The first half shouldn't be a problem at all. I'd say a week, maybe two. With the interest we agreed on," I added to seal the deal, with no idea where even the principal would come from.

I called the meeting at Sammy's because it was the kind you needed coffee for, and morning inspiration, and I wanted to be far away from the café, the agenda item. As luck would have it, the waitress told us Sammy was in Miami, which could mean he was retired, buying margaritas for senoritas. He could easily be on auto; the tables were mostly full, as always. Or he could be opening a Tastee-Freez in Lauderdale. Whatever the occasion, I was glad Sammy was gone. I wanted no interruptions.

"I got the call from Valerie," I began. Corey had dragged in a few minutes after me looking barely awake. He sat back in the booth, fueling on coffee, eyebrows raised. As I related the conversation, I had the feeling he was indulging me while I stated the obvious. He wasted no time.

"I've been working on this, doing some research." He slid his mug out of the way and unfolded a newspaper, flattened it on the table, and rotated it for me to see. *The Wall Street Journal.* "I know you don't follow the markets, but I suppose you've heard, gold has had a huge ride. It will be a sad joke in the future—'I missed gold in 79'. Ha! Anyway, so has silver." He pointed to a graph in a piece titled "Metals Power Through Technical Stops." Two of three lines were arcing upward. "Precious metals react to inflation, uncertainty. Basically they move inversely to stocks. Now check copper." It was the third line, serrated but generally flat. "It hasn't happened yet. It's in a trading range, only fifteen percent higher than last year's close. I've been watching the trend. It's up over the last week, not much but it's starting to move. Volume has been up the last three sessions."

"So we hoard pennies? Sell pans?"

"It's a commodities play, totally obvious. We put fifteen hundred on copper, we could triple it in two weeks. Pay off the loan completely. It happens on the Board of Trade all the time."

"And train wrecks happen too, right? Isn't commodities like casinos? The house wins, the brokers win, the rest get shafted."

"Because most traders are ignorant," he explained. "They don't understand fundamentals."

"There are more fundamental fundamentals."

"What, than fear and greed? They drive the markets."

"We've got enough of both. Why not blackjack instead?"

"No risk, no reward."

"You're obsessed with originality. Hell, take the risk out of it. Push crank. Buddy can supply from Miami. Load up a Taylor, double barrel."

Corey slumped back, lampooned, drained of inspiration. "What's your idea? We have a buffer of what?"

"Maybe six hundred if we defer Great Lakes another week."

"Sammy would know a loan shark. We could kick it down the road." He was staring idly over tables, hearing himself talk. "Worse in the long run."

"Day of reckoning." I dropped it in, profundity in search of a grin. We had reached that point—not the final absurdity, but close enough.

"Sell organs." Corey got with the vibe. "There was a piece in the Sunday *Trib* about that," he added, deadpan.

"You can do fine with one kidney," I agreed.

"One lung."

"How much for two nuts?"

"Depends on whose."

"I already gave."

He tried to stifle a guffaw, drooling coffee. Mercifully, breakfast came.

It was a Friday, my day to open, which meant Corey could go back home for six hours. I deployed Tony with a couple of hundred menus to work Halsted to Sheffield. Over the day Valerie and Chuck edged out Anita in obsessive thoughts. Repay the first half in a week or two, no problem. With interest. I was ready for the loan shark. Who needed Sammy? This was Chicago; it had to be crawling with them. Probably even Ozzie, or his brother in Tinley Park. How low could we go?

Over the ride home I couldn't shake the ruminations. In vino would be solace. I was inside the door for fifteen minutes and had put on John McLaughlin and the Mahavishnu Orchestra for the brain-wiping volume when I thought I heard the phone. I lifted the needle and the confirmation came sharply: another ring. Valerie again? What could I tell her? Yes, we had talked or no, we hadn't, and either way, I had nothing for her. Ring three. But what if Anita? It was Friday evening, maybe she was lonely too.

"Hello?" The background was familiar, but subconsciously—the burr of a cooler, the door sliding shut—before I heard his voice.

"Can you get back in here? Shit." I heard a thud like a pop can hitting the floor. Corey sounded ready to crack. "The phone's ringing off the hook. It was Studs."

When I arrived Corey had stacked four boxes on the counter, and Tony was checking the tickets. Two booths were taken. Bruce was working furiously at the back table. Corey had induced him.

"Time and a half," he explained. "Lucky to get him. You take the Clifton—the rest are all north. I'll have two more for you in a minute." He reserved the Clifton box for me. I held the door and Tony was gone with his three.

The phone went off and I took it—fortunately, a pickup. Unfortunately, a whole wheat crust. I saw only a few wheat doughballs in the cooler with the whites. Bruce hadn't been trained on the new product, which meant Corey and I would both be occupied, one making the order and the other working the mixer. The galley looked like a battleground with pans in the sink and empty prep pots, two in the front window and one on the floor.

"Studs' show was on Tuesday," Corey began, taking the ticket and a doughball to the front table. "He plugged the whole wheat crust on air—totally loves it. The *Reader* covered the show because Pavarotti was on, and they got into a whole trip about pizza and the best Chicago pizza. Studs mentioned Giordano's, and us. The issue hit the streets yesterday. A sales rep was in already, right before you." That explained the *Reader* business card and the new copy of the paper by the phone. "We should talk about a blow-in."

I folded two boxes in the front window and pulled the pies before they burned. Then, with our golden recipe from the drawer, I started on the mixer. In a minute Corey had my three deliveries stacked on the counter and added a side order bag.

"The Hobart's loaded," I said. "Watch the consistency."

"Hey," he panted, pushing his glasses up by the taped nosepiece, "it's all happening."

"Hey," I said, backing out of the door with hands full, nodding in the general direction of his head, "now you can get new frames. Please."

Indeed it was all happening, and over the next week we caught ourselves staring at each other and laughing like skydivers who had landed on their feet. The Terkel show, the *Reader* article, and the menuing combined to boost deliveries, and our coupons were getting repeats. Corey learned the next time Studs was taping, and we both drove a delivery down to the studio for the star and the staff. We tipped Kat, our resident photo freak, to shoot us with the icon himself. It was Corey's idea. When her color print is matted and mounted, it will hang in the entryway opposite the counter. Corey schemed how to do the same with Ebert.

The football season was upon us, which always made the phone ring on the weekends. Before opening on a Friday, we trained Bruce and Tony on the art of the whole wheat crust. Our golden recipe went from the green sheet to a laminated card chained to the frame under the phone counter.

Soon Corey was laying out his case for a blow-in. For investing the last of our loan surplus, we would get an automated insertion of a menu into every *Reader* distributed on the North Side. Ordinarily my cost aversion would pop up to protect us, but it had been overcome by euphoria from making large deposits.

A few days before the publication date, we made our biggest move. We couldn't match his salary at Lou Mitchell's, but our flexibility and general vibe allowed us to hire Dale away. My control of the schedule let us close the loop on the music and start planning practices for Lake

Forest in December. Bringing on Dale and restoring Bruce
to his regular schedule allowed Tony to go back on the road.
We hired another part-time driver, Louis from Taiwan, who
was studying violin at Roosevelt. He lived on Pine Grove,
close enough to call for emergency fill-ins, and he and Dale
could talk fiddle.

We made our moves none too soon. When the blow-in
issue hit the streets, Corey had the right to gloat, but no
time. None of us did. The phone exploded. It was all hands
on deck and all tables and counters in use throughout the
weekend.

Three weeks after our talk, I was able to call Val: a check
for the first half of the loan was in the mail, expect the rest
in mid-November. It was a huge weight off. The next day we
started Louis's Vietnamese girlfriend Linh ten hours a week
behind the counter. We could see from the start that Louis
had been right—she was smart and quick and capable of
more.

```
                                        Oct. 26
    Corey and I are alternating nights off for the
first time in weeks. Neither of us is admitting
it yet to avoid jinxing, but we can feel it--a
corner has been turned. Probably best, our orders
are generating repeaters, a Corey "fundamental."
```

Last night Melanie and Janis hosted at their place, a
pre-Halloween fête. It was also a celebration of a break-
through for Janis, a show of her Little Boxes at the
Waggoner Gallery in the week before Christmas. Melanie
presented as a cat, which was her true former incarnation,
and Janis made a tempting sultan with a cockaded turban
and beard. I was River Rat Gonzalez, which meant I could
pull out a flowered shirt and straw hat that dated back to
High Point. It was the first time I had seen the whole sick
crew, as Pynchon would have them, since Barleycorn's,

which seemed like another century. Dale was closing, so Duello was off the hook for entertaining. Instead Janis had persuaded a couple of the Stepps, including Jeff from Last Blast, to do a scene from a piece by Mamet called *Lakeboat*, which they planned to premier in the new year.

The musical theme was Motown, which meant everybody dancing, no holdouts. I danced with several women, including Melanie, whose main suitor for the evening appeared to be a *TriQuarterly* type with a Zorro mask and cape. She had her own reason to celebrate, a contract to finish a script for a film short, a safety video starring a Wonder Woman character who tells kids to wear their life jackets and stay off motorcycles. While it wasn't exactly fare for wide screens, it could easily be a kids spot for PBS stations. Anita may have supplied the connection. Melanie belittled it as schmaltz, but I told her it was fantastic. I could see she was jazzed, and why not?

Corey arrived after his shift ended at nine, and he took Melanie's news as proof that the time was spot-on for superheroes like Flash. He was entertained by Maya in a time warp from Janis's third floor. I was happy for him.

For me, Anita's vacant space was there taunting, challenging me to make it smaller. PT, in fairy layers of chiffon, appeared to be trailing two young hopefuls. Fortunately, generously, she joined me for a while in the pantry which had a closing door. For the old times, old days. Everybody needs to forget. Halloween again. I have an awful memory. It remembers everything.

At Melanie's I told Coleman about the Lake Forest gig, but we three hadn't met to decide on practice dates; plus, we needed to restart the prep for the new demo. For our meeting we chose a Tuesday at four in the café, a slow time between shifts. Dale would close, so he only had to arrive an hour early.

"They kick you out then they don't let you go." Coleman slid into the booth catching his breath, a few minutes late.

"How does that work?" I said.

"New punch-out protocol. Now the man's cut our hours, he's got a whole new card, new routine, BS. Takes too long to get out of there."

The door dinged and a guy entered, stocking cap and zipped jacket, glancing around. Corey turned from his prep and covered him.

"How many hours now?" Dale asked.

"Thirty-two," Coleman went on. "All about the gas, through the roof. Monkey is leaving stuff in the warehouse until it's bought. It's like, the next thing, know what I'm sayin'?"

The guy and Corey exchanged a few words and the guy passed him an envelope. Then he was gone, no order.

"Hey, more time to practice," Dale said, bringing us to the point. I wondered what Corey was reading, but it was my cue.

"The first half of the week would be better. We can move more people around then."

Corey was looking up at me from the end of the counter. Dale proposed Tuesdays, this time or an hour later. Coleman started running through his work schedule. I held up a finger, time out.

Corey was wearing a twisted grin of incredulity, eyebrows up, as though he was watching Jimmy Carter on banjo. As though Bo Derek was hip-hopping on a table. As though he was witnessing the final absurdity. He held up the letter for me and I was coming.

He delivered it like a punchline: "It's from Ozzie."

Chapter 33

"HEY, hey." Corey greeted me at his door on the second floor. He was wearing a flannel shirt and the same glasses, although he had retaped the nosepiece. "Victory!" he crowed and we high-fived, and he led the way to the bright kitchen.

The night before he was off to an Eck meeting, and I had to wrap up with Coleman and Dale before the phone started to ring. We had no way to deal with the letter, so we decided on the next morning in the privacy of his place on Troy. I wanted to feel the paper again like proof that we hadn't shared a hallucination or I hadn't dreamt it over the night of half-waking when I could invent anything. He had it displayed unfolded on the kitchen table like the Magna Carta.

He rounded the counter with a coffee mug in each hand, eyes bright. "What do you think?"

The print was assertive but refined, with a calligraphic touch, like a vestige of graphics designer in Ozzie's past.

Guys,

So you made the big time. Congrats. Just remember where you got your start. Ha-hah.

Seriously, Joe and I want to buy you out. Think in the 40s. Serious offer, no BS. Let's talk.

He followed his name with two phone numbers. We both recognized Gonzo's. The second must have been his personal, in the condo of black leather and chrome with the line of coke on the glass-top table.

I knew what I thought from the first time I saw it in the café. I had circled back to it between the swells of elation, and nothing as I replayed it over the night or on the drive to Logan Square had changed my mind. Ozzie with his dull-eyed poker face taking the measure of everyone in range, scanning for weaknesses, was a shark. He cleaned out the less-evolved. In no way would he clean out the café, by ingestion. We had taken his best shot and we were still standing, and thriving. We had won. It was clear and obvious, or it should have been.

Corey was waiting, no doubt knowing me well enough to assume what I would say, but I took a sip instead. Standing in the light of his kitchen was undermining what I thought I knew in the gut, incontrovertible, with no conscious interference. I hadn't been in the apartment since his demo of the TRS-80, and when Beth left, my picture of the place where Corey had been living was more or less the same. But I had sensed the difference from the time we shared the last laugh at the door and I followed him in. To that point I had been less than discriminating about what would be our biggest decision.

He was watching, no doubt wondering what I was doing, as I went to the end of the kitchen and crossed the transom. There was a new chill. Through the windows the November sky was leaden, and the living room and office beyond were dimmed, drained of color. Books and *Barron's* and a stack of the *Sun-Times* had collected where Arlo's toys had been. Beth's upright was still in the living room, fallboard closed, no doubt dusty to the touch. The trapped air smelled of newsprint. We were victorious, I reminded myself, but the life I remembered in the apartment had been emptied out.

"The downside," I said, turning back, "is that Ozzie is a slime. He was Donny's connection, I know it." But I had gone out far enough, and what had been simple and clear was now clouded with concerns of a higher order. "On the other side, think about it. No more loans over our heads, right?" I heard myself talking, testing the thought. "No more health inspectors on the take. No more busted cheese machine and register and who knows what's next, fill in the blank. I could buy a lot of time for the music, maybe finally get it moving, and if not, at least find out. Maybe you could put a down payment on a place outside of here, just like you told Beth when we started. We're on a roll now, but who knows for how long, or what could happen if a driver hits some kid. Or who knows where we'll be a year from now—if it's still behind the counter and we're looking back." I was hearing echoes of Anita and they silenced me.

He made a sound in his head like he heard me and let a moment pass. "That's not what I thought you'd say." He looked out the window over the patch of backyard. The limbs of the maples had already turned to whips. "If he isn't blowing smoke and we net twenty-five after the loan, half each wouldn't go that far. And it would all be capital gain." He rubbed his forehead, estimating tax. "Maybe we could talk him up. Or maybe a partnership?" We both winced. Suddenly he turned back, facing me squarely. He looked bemused, shifting gears, or planes.

"I got confused," he said. "'Ball of Confusion', you remember that song? I lost the thread, about what we're doing, its nature." I was detecting a whiff of Eckism from the night before.

"Tony's mudster, right?" he continued. We had joked about it often enough that it was code, like the final absurdity. Pushing the rear of the Pinto out of the ditch of mud and slush, slipping and going out flat, prostrating to the gods of be-your-own-boss. And what Corey said after, about us against the world. "Hey," he finished, "now we've got the world on the run."

Then he went off again on watching Mohammed's shop and checking in with him for any signs of failure or hints that he might not renew his lease. That would be easiest, to expand into his space. Looking for another location was an option too, the overall goal being a full-service restaurant, keeping the delivery, adding an oven with racks for an in-house bakery that featured cheese bread based on the whole wheat recipe. I beheld him, wherever he was coming from.

"New American Café is a dream," he rolled on, "as in *aspiration*. We're still dreaming, not free of it yet. We haven't threaded the needle." It felt unnerving. I couldn't recall using that phrase with him, but I must have. "When we're free, we'll know it." I had the clear arguments, he had foggy fantasies, dream babble. But he was humbling me, rendering me sheepish for playing the right notes while he was wailing on another level. "What is the café anyway, but potential?"

By the time I left, I had been around the block. If not exactly proud, I was at least willing to admit my first instinct had been right. But Corey was giving up his sure thing. Ten or twelve thousand wouldn't qualify for a dream house, but it could give them a restart and let him deliver on his promise. We had our integrity but it came at a cost, higher for him. Maybe he was only deferring. Maybe he had it right, and we could be world-beaters for long enough that neither of us could deny we were done. It might not take that long.

Nov. 4

Louis delivered our envelope in response. Joe was in but not Ozzie, as usual. Thanks for the vote of confidence, but we're hanging in for now. Best wishes.

It's hard to stop wondering what the money could have meant. Half a year at least free and clear for the music. Maybe Anita, a couple of months ago. But as my upwardly mobile princess insisted by word and deed, it had to be one thing for me. Wray said it too, for that matter. But at the end of 10K, what if Duello were going nowhere? I'm trying to believe Corey has it all in view, and barring any expansion or move whatever, we can ride the café out of here.

We three circled back. It will be two practices a week with focus on the demo. Dale could finally give Curtis the ten-day heads-up.

"Have some change." I opened the bank bag below the counter.

"Thank you, sir." Dale took a roll of each and started cracking them open on the register. He would be closing, but he had regained his old bounce. It was the Wednesday after our reunion practice, and we were both riding high. The new Duello had gotten our groove back, not as tight as we could and would be, but with the same spark. I was in to work the counter and back up Kat if need be. With luck I would check out at nine but who knew. It was getting dark by five, and the weather was wet and steely enough to make the phone ring. Corey was on the phone, and I ducked around him to stow the bag in the bottom of the cabinet. His prep was done, the sign of a moderate midweek day. My self-assigned task was in the back.

Whenever I opened the door and switched on the light and the storage room pounced at me, I saw the mop bucket first. Wray was there beside it on Last Blast, tuning in the perfect acoustic space. It could be expanded into a studio, walls lined with #10 cans of tomato sauce. That's what we could do with Mohammed's space, as soon as he went out of business.

I was less concerned with the cans on the shelves than with the floor. Our rising fortunes meant we needed another cooler for meat and cheese. The only place it could go was within range of the outlet, which meant in the corner under the shelves, on the floor that was covered with pallets.

I started to pull out the boxes of Styro cups, paper plates, and paper towels, and the boxes of Pepsi and Mountain Dew that we had to over-order to make our minimum. Rearranging it all would be a Rubik's cube. I spotted the outlet: of course, behind a column of pop, not the boxes of Styro. I should test it before reworking the world.

I was confident we would be ready for Curtis. After practice Coleman had brought it up sheepishly, I guessed to avoid bruising my feelings. We should cut set one in half for the demo and add two more singles. I imagined he and Dale had talked it over. It required a reset, but I trusted their instinct. The long medley sets were Duello one, the fiery-eyed, give-no-quarter invention of John and Mitch, naïve as they come. Duello two was all about range. We had punch enough for bigger clubs, and we could always drop back to acoustic and intimate. The demo needed to showcase that. Flexible are us. Randy and Mark were in the music biz, and so were we. If PT and Melanie were right, there might even be room for both Duellos.

I dragged out the pop and stood up, lightheaded, looking for the hanging work light that I knew was stowed in there to test the outlet. Then I heard it. Like Wray by the mop bucket, I saw Donny again by the front door. The sound brought him back, the high piercing cry of the hawk, scissoring the sky.

"Mitch." Dale's voice just outside. It could have been the second time he called, the first not quite audible. No hawk. Was it Dale I had heard sliding a booth or a table? The door popped open on the other side of the boxes, a Dale I hadn't seen, child's face of fear. "It's Corey," he coughed out. "He's acting all weird."

Box jamming the door open. Dale in the lead, Corey a dining room away at the end of the counter, back turned.

Door dinging, a woman in a winter coat stepping in. Dropping her hood back, looking up at the menu board. Corey motionless, the phone too far from his head. Woman scanning the board, Corey making no move to greet her.

He's tilting, half the room away. Dale is strides closer.

Corey separating from the counter. Standing? Rap of the dropped phone. Lurching as though hit from behind, as though shot, pulling away from the counter. Then down, impact on the tile floor, whack of chrome stool legs on vinyl.

Woman blank-faced at the counter, empty-eyed, caught in a scene. Recoiling, backing, stopped by the door frame.

"Shit, man." Dale is kneeling beside him, hand on his shoulder. He is on his side, glasses twisted.

I roll him onto his back. His chest is rigid, hard to the touch. Eyes rolled back.

"You all right?" Words without meaning, words in a void. "You're all right. All right." I work his glasses off and his eyes roll down. A tremor runs through him, a juddering. Corey is staring at me or past me, speechless.

I grab the hanging phone, clamber up. The woman at the door is wedged in the corner. We lock eyes. I hit the phone cradle to get a dial tone.

Chapter 34

SHAKING off the cold, waiting for the elevator, I recognized the steps behind me before she said a word.

"How did I miss you?" I must have been only a few strides in front. Melanie and I hugged, and the cold lay on her coat and beret and on her cheek. I missed her, I knew, because I had been barreling through the raw day, head down, intent on the hospital lobby. She shivered but composed a smile.

"Janis had to go by her agency first," she said before I could ask. "She was planning to grab a taxi, so she should be here soon."

The touch of her coat and cheek was like evidence, inconclusive but credible: I was in St. Joseph's again, not in a recurring dream. With Melanie again, and I conflated the trips—both patients strapped onto stretchers, and the whipping lights. But the EMTs on Wednesday night were not the same as Melanie's, and I rode in the front of Corey's ambulance then checked him in. And made the call to Beth in Champaign, her mother answering, suspicious at first. Melanie had to be remembering her transport too.

"We have to stop meeting like this." The old groaner, but something, and she grinned.

"You said he had the seizure Wednesday night, and they operated yesterday. That's incredibly fast."

"Trying to prevent paralysis. They said it was an aggressive tumor." I could see how that landed. "The surgeon was available, *the* guy, they said. Corey was lucky." I heard myself, automatic, banal, trying to reshape it in a comprehensible way. The elevator door slid open and a doctor and nurse exited past us. We were alone riding up.

"You said Beth is here? And their little boy?"

"Right, her parents drove them in yesterday. Mom and Dad are with Arlo in the place on Troy." The four of them in a parents' car on the highway at the same time Corey was under the knife. Under the implements used to open the cranium and do what was needed, all of it. It was the earliest possible visiting time. We would see him in minutes.

We stepped out onto the floor, too familiar. It had been last spring, Janis calling from Melanie's place on Belden. Five months, or six. We were checking the room numbers. Most of the rooms were open, doors propped, patients half-hidden behind curtains. In one, a bald survivor, rawboned in his pale green gown, a bulbous white patch on his temple, stared back at us as we passed. I nearly collided with a nurse. The minor shock reset the senses, uncovered smells I had been repressing, the distinctive blend of alcohol and antiseptics, the artificial green tang of cleaners, the oppressive undercurrent of cafeteria food. Cold hands, heart firing.

I never thought, like some high school inspirational, that anything was possible because there was little reason to believe it wasn't. Now, as after Melanie's overdose, this place exposed our limits, signaling that somehow we were mortal. I glanced at her. Lips tight, as wired as I was.

"This must be it." I stated the obvious to free a breath, to break the silent cord of numbers we had been counting down. We couldn't see Corey's bed from the open door and took a step inside. No way to be ready.

He lay in a double-sized room, required for the jungle of equipment around him. He was flattened, an accident victim, accident of fate, immobilized and tubed, on a bed with steel guard rails. His head and shoulders had been raised to drain him. Unconscious, slack-faced, and wrapped in white to the ears, his skull looked even larger. An oxygen tube bisected his face like a median line in a sketch. Beside the bed a green line inchwormed across a monitor, the one lifeline. But bodies were machines of resilience. They came back. They walked out. Whatever was coming, remember.

Beth was in a chair beside the bed. Melanie crossed to her and hugged her and I followed. It was the first time I had seen her since New Year's Eve at John's. Her eyes were red and her face was weighted with fear. She had spoken with the neurosurgeon the night before and he called the surgery successful. Corey was stable and had youth on his side, and we reminded Beth how positive that was. He would be mostly sedated for the first couple of days. The doctor would come to the room on rounds sometime later in the morning or in the early afternoon, the nurse could not tell her exactly when.

Melanie asked about Arlo and Beth's parents, and as they talked the rest of the room began to come into focus. Light wires, tendril-like, trailed from the bottom of Corey's bandage to another monitor beside the IV rack and pump. EEG, I thought, but I didn't know. I was medically ignorant. I had had the good fortune to be. On the bedside stand with rollers: a box of blue gloves, a plastic tumbler, Beth's purse. The curtains were open a third of the way for a dose of natural light, dirty cotton ball sky. Voices came from the hall, one I knew.

I left the two of them together. In the hall Janis was talking with a nurse positioned in the path to Corey's room. Dale, Coleman, and PT drew up behind them. They were focused on the nurse. Then Janis saw me.

"Mitch, they won't allow—"

"I have to tell your friends, Mr. McGowan cannot have more than his wife and two visitors in the room at a time." The nurse, slight but resolute, had the advantage by an authoritative number of years.

"I completely understand," I said. "But perhaps only at the door . . ." A burly-looking orderly was ambling by, a distracting reminder of someone I couldn't place. "Or just to say a word to his wife?" She made eye contact with the orderly and he slowed. "They wouldn't be more than a few minutes . . ."

An alarm sounded in a room down the hall, an insistent beeping that would disturb any patient with an open door. No one else was covering. Her jaw tightened.

"Not more than a few minutes. Please—it's hospital policy." She padded away quickly, and the beeping was off by the time we entered Corey's room. Janis went to Beth and Melanie, and I thanked the others. As I thought, Coleman admitted it was a work day. I had told Melanie and Janis and word had spread from there. I was wondering if John Wray might appear, knowing at the same time the grapevine probably didn't reach that far.

We were all adjusting to Corey's presence in our own ways. We traded a few words with Beth, speculating about recovery time, spinning unrealistically positive, since none of us had any way of knowing yet. Like a toddler with a toy, Corey kept drawing us back, the center of attention.

Our small talk was faltering when Bruce appeared in the doorway, awkwardly bearing a jade plant in a plastic pot. I ushered him in before the nurse could spot him. He situated the pot on the open third of window ledge, and Beth thanked him from across the room.

The others had formed a half-ring around the bed, and Bruce and I joined them. On the end Beth was holding Janis's hand. I realized they were all holding hands, and I took Melanie's in my left and Bruce's in my right.

Soon the faint tick of the round wall clock was the only sound. We were filling the silence with thoughts for our fallen comrade, wrapped and wired. I visualized him popping his eyes open and searching for his glasses. Some of us could have been praying. Beth's eyes were closed. I closed mine and tried to find the frequency, the exact wavelength where Corey and I could riff off each other's thoughts.

Laughter passed in the hall, two nurses on their break. Beeping from a distant room. I opened my eyes and saw us standing, a circle around him. A squeaking wheelchair, or a cart rolling on the tile. I closed them again and tried to stay with the circle, connected by both hands, the circle unbroken. Following the taps of the clock, incremental, each closer to the zone, I was nearly there, in the fine band where we had opened with a busted door closer, greased the palms of the grifters, lusted after the Thalias, delivered on the bus in the blizzard, ducked invoices, scattered thousands of menus, outlasted the locusts, kept the door open.

From the first tentative notes I heard, I was thinking of Beth, knowing at the same time it was by association only— she would not have started it, she couldn't have. It was a soft voice, wavering but determined.

'Tis the gift to be simple, 'tis the gift to be free

Janis was singing solo, our Lady Madonna. Melanie joined beside me, and then we all joined, humming along or remembering what we could of the lyrics, a few lines only, one verse.

'Twill be in the valley of love and delight

Through it once, we let a moment round it off, and then we began again, this time recalling more of the words.

'Tis the gift to come down where we ought to be

Corey was wrapped in the vibration, the low tones of our chorus pianissimo. Unplaced tones, they arose from our throats and hearts.

The third time around, all of us singing the words lowly. Beth holding Corey's hand under the sheet, her face glistening. And finally, letting the round pass into the valley, into silence, filling it with our hopes, silent words, and visions.

"I'm sorry." From where she had been standing in the doorway, the nurse entered in her noiseless white shoes. She had clearly been giving us time. As the ringleader, I responded with a nod intended to acknowledge that we were over our time and rules were rules. She headed for the bedside and the monitors. We said or nodded our goodbyes to Beth and filed out into the hall. I would be returning to talk with the surgeon.

At the nurse's station a couple had been waiting their turn. He, bearded and lanky, could have been a math professor, a hippie in his past life. She, petite and prim, held a simple bouquet at her waist like a bridesmaid. Eckists, I guessed, or friends of Beth or them both. They nodded on their way in.

Dale and Bruce would open the café. Coleman returned to his route. Janis and Melanie and I discussed staggering our visiting times. I would take the early shift, between ten and eleven. Then Janis went on but Melanie hung back.

"I thought it would be a shock, but . . ." Her eyes tightened and she looked away. I saw her letting herself feel it for the first time. "Do you really think he'll—"

"Of course. I have no doubt he'll make it. He has too much to do." Beth and Arlo, *Flash*, the café, which I couldn't contemplate. "It will take time for sure, but the doc said he got it all and he's young and strong otherwise, and . . . I'll let you know what I find out."

"Do, please." She searched me, unconvinced. Melanie needed more, we both did, a sense like belief, or at least reassurance, quaint notions in the corridor and rooms of moment-to-moment, mutable truth. We were what, energy or particles, waves or form?

"Hey," I said, "what are any of us but potential?" The elevator was opening again, and I waved as she stepped in.

To give the visiting couple time, I started down the hall, no longer paying attention to the rooms. I was seeing only one. The hall turned right at the end, and a man was coming toward me as I rounded the corner, probably Corey's age, in a jacket and tie, bound for the Loop or returning from it, stone-faced. He was pushing his mother in a wheelchair, neck frozen in a biblical contortion by stroke, expressionless. We the visitors were killing time as it killed us. Different times, or all the same?

In a visitors' lounge at the end, a likely grandmother sat between toddlers, trying to entertain them with coloring books. The boy was complaining. In the room as warm as an incubator, I sank into a chair in the opposite corner and started to flip through a *Field and Stream*. Wild turkey in Kansas. Smallmouth in the Blue Ridge. The photos slid by, tugging at memories of High Point—a dock on Oak Hollow Lake and high brown grass. Soon I was nodding. Anita, where were you now with your god and your prayers, like mine once, for your parents' immortality and then their everlasting life, and for good grades and winning races and whatever chances for love? The clock tapping in the round black frame brought me back. Tapping, repeating. Five to eleven. Repeating a question, nascent, malformed: how could this be happening?

I hadn't checked the time when I left Corey's room, but I couldn't wait any longer and started back slowly. Time to kill. Everything Beth and I would ask the surgeon would come down to time. How long will he stay? How long for recovery?

A few doors from his room I heard a rumbling behind me. At the end of the corridor an orderly was coming, pushing a metal cart on the tile. Rolling down on me, he could have been late, or he had just given notice and was on his last run and didn't care and in the next second he could dive on top and glide. Then I recognized him, the same orderly—thick shoulders and chest—who had backed up the nurse. I flashed on Dewayne in Gonzo, the king of the one-handed push-up, but no. The cart of empty trays and the remains of breakfast came thundering, and I caught the look on his face as he passed. He was saving himself, rolling out of what he could not fathom, fixed on a window where there was no window and beyond, a flat ocean of a lake and a borderland of tall grass, where outward was all that mattered. Down the hall he displaced a nurse, and at the end he disappeared into the service elevator.

I realized I was leaning against the wall, catching breath. When I was steady, I took the last steps and peered around the door into Corey's room. Beth was alone with him, as she had been before we all came and left. She looked up as he lay in a world outside us, and I went in to wait.

Chapter 35

I needed to settle down. That must have been why I went to the dining room, the practice room in the Cavern, not because I was thinking clearly but out of habit, because habits ground us and take us home.

I knelt beside the Martin case, lay it on its back, and popped the four latches. Maybe because I hadn't played in weeks, I was struck by the beauty of the instrument in its case—the light spruce table bisected by the leather strap against the velveteen lining of royal blue. But I was paid to play, not look. The Lake Forest gig was still on, and we needed to reschedule the demo, get back on track. I needed to touch it, lift it out by the neck, but I couldn't yet. The issue with playing, as Wray liked to say, was that you can't push the river. I was still wired, and far away.

I flipped on the light in the kitchen, unscrewed the cap on the Inglenook jug, and poured a bistro glass, the medium one, hefty and indestructible. I needed to wash away the taste of the meeting, and the images. I left the dining room lights off, took a chair at the table, and downed the first half.

An hour earlier I had been in Malowitz's office, across from Ozzie and his attorney, executing closing documents. Malowitz tried to score points with his opponent, an ice queen with frosted hair in a square-shoulder blazer, a whiff of dominatrix, very much a friend of Ozzie. He soon gave up. Ozzie wore a new neck chain, gold and bolder than his Ecstasy model. He expressed his unctuous sympathies. He and Joe planned to overhaul the physical plant, installing new ovens and a cooler. They would close for a couple of weeks to extend the kitchen. The ovens required modifying the ventilation, which meant Queenie would be back, no surprise to Ozzie, I knew. Payola would flow. Let the city take its own. Bruce and Dale would stay on to manage; that was my one non-negotiable.

Outside the broad back windows, low sun angled through clouds onto the brick backsides of the apartment buildings, muted with soot, and the gray back stairs and the one stripped maple. The last day of November.

It had been ten days since the funeral. Most of our group attended but not all. Coleman couldn't lose more work hours. The café was closed, but Bruce could only apologize, which was okay. I knew the hospital visit had unnerved him. Corey's sister and brother-in-law from Pennsylvania had met his mother in Ithaca and flown in from Syracuse. There were friends I didn't know and at least a dozen Eckists. The math professor from the hospital told me that in Eckist terms, Corey had "translated." I told him I understood. The term I had heard Corey use a couple of times especially suited him. Arlo was there this time, with Beth and her parents. Corey's urn traveled back to Troy Street with them.

I imagined seeing him in a couple of days and wondered where he would be. I didn't recall a mantel. His office seemed fitting, but I guessed that room had been repurposed. I had volunteered to pack it up but hadn't heard from Beth. I would see him when I met with her; she didn't yet know why.

The check for Corey's half of the sale, after his half of the bank loan, would come to her from the closing. After my half of the loan, I would reserve Val's from my share. The rest would go to Beth, and if she tried to refuse the check, I had made a promise to Corey and we had an agreement, somewhere along the way. Maybe he just hadn't told her. Financially, my fortunes would soon be little changed from the day we opened, nearly two years earlier. But little else would be the same.

Like the café, our terrain would continue to morph. Despite Ozzie's best-laid plans, even New American Café could become a laundry one day, or Mohammed might expand.

At some inconceivable point in the future, we too will be looking back from other lives. Adam and Anita already on their way. Dale, a manager for Mitchell's. Coleman running a short-haul fleet out of DeKalb. PT, a shaman in Santa Fe. John Wray, the computer programmer Corey knew he should be. Janis in her own West Coast agency. And Melanie, a PhD in a college town with splendid maples, a vita lengthy with publications, and a partner of means with dual Masters degrees. As for me, I plead the Fifth.

Or our outcomes could be—would likely be—more prosaic. From whatever unknowable points in the future, we'll turn back on the days when we collided and entangled for a while. It was the way memory worked. The way, in the hospital, I half-expected to see John Wray, as though he would come walking in out of an old song. And Donny and Adam. And Anita. And Corey in his top hat rising uncorrupted to launch into a chorus of "Ming the Merciless." Our aspirations were matched by our capacity for delusion, but what we did together had a shabby glory nonetheless. We would continue to lose one another, to recede and be recalled. The memory machines were in all of us now, replicated, locked in the holds of our cells.

We may see how it both was and was not. How we clutched at our days together as though they were brimming full, at the same time that they were emptying. Days gone into emptiness which we would trade for nothing. A power in the memories will make them glow stronger, something noble, like Melanie's theory of art lifting life. Days gone but recalled, shimmering silver—our inventions, figments, like stories we told to ourselves.

The radiator rattled then clanged. We were on the hinge of winter in Chicago, neither one season nor the other. For a while my eyes burned. Then I emptied the glass and lifted the twelve-string out of its case by the rosewood neck, familiar and cool. I strummed it once and the practice room came alive with tone. Through the rear windows the sun had declined below the rooftops, but I didn't need it. I still had enough light to tune.

Richard Sanford came of age in the sixties in a small town in the deep South suspended in time and haunted with stories. He is the author of the previous novels *The Soul Snatchers, Ring of Stars, Long Time Gone, Roadkill,* and *The Calling.* Today he makes his home in the Pacific Northwest.

26813930R00241